THE
OLD COMO GANG
LONG GONE

by

LEO T. and MICHAEL J. McCALL

Art and Photographs by Mary Sweeney

This Book is a work of fiction. Names, characters, places and incidents are the product of the author's imagination. Any resemblance to actual events or locales or persons living or dead is entirely coincidental.

Copyright 2001 by Leo McCall
For information regarding this title, please contact

   Leo McCall
   515 South Lexington Parkway #106
   St. Paul, MN 55116
   (651) 699-8458

All rights reserved including the right of reproduction in whole or in part in any form.

Manufactured in the United States of America

ISBN 0-9652038-2-4

Copyright pending

PREFACE

Set in the rough and tumble Como neighborhood in the year 1927, *The Old Como Gang Long Gone* is a promising narrative about a charming young boy named Harry McCool who does not disappoint. A year bursting at the seams with important events, 1927 proves to be a colorful base off of which the story feeds. As the second youngest of six, and son of a recently widowed mother, Harry must contribute to the incessant need to put food on the table, and he does this by carrying papers for the Pioneer Press. During these hard times, religion serves as both comfort and a distraction. Harry contributes to his church by performing altar boy duties, and it is during this time that Harry conjectures outrageously amusing anecdotes about the Catholic Church.

For Harry, 1927 is not a year when he, or his comrades, have difficulty finding precarious situations. He and his Boy Scout Troop, number 92, end up synthesizing mischief on more than one occasion. This year is one of transition, wild adventures, and personal growth for Harry.

No season uneventful, no stone of boyhood experience left unturned, *The Old Como Gang Long Gone* is a humorous look at how tumultuous youth can be. This is a well-sculpted novel that all, young and old, can enjoy and relate to.

Written over a period of a decade, this story is the result of many arduous hours spent at the typewriter, soul-searching, and a very liberal use of poetic license, by the well-known and respected author Leo McCall. His co-author and son, Michael, drew on his vast experience in composing long, informational summaries of the days of yore, and added his touch of spices and seasonings to the work.

Brian McCall
Grandson to Leo T. McCall
Nephew to Michael McCall

TABLE OF CONTENTS

    Prologue vii
1. A Loose Tongue 1
2. The Funeral 11
3. Obedience, Poverty, and Chastity 25
4. The Great Como Park Dog Race 39
5. Winter Carnival Fun 61
6. California Here I Come 83
7. Holy Week at St. Andrews 105
8. Troop 92 Sets Fire to Presbyterian Church 119
9. Lindy Lands 139
10. Ball Game on Barrett Street 155
11. Troop 92 Goes Overnight on St. Croix River 171
12. Lindy Comes Home 193
13. Stars and Stripes Forever 201
14. Halloween on Barrett Street 221
15. Christmas on Barrett Street 239

    Epilogue 255
    Acknowledgements 257

PROLOGUE

ST. ANDREW'S CHURCH
Etched in the cornerstone
the year 1927

In the mid 1920s the city of St. Paul, Minnesota had a modest population of 200000. The terminus of the "war to end all wars", however, brought great promise for the future, and the city was in its greatest historical growth spurt. By the early 1930s, St. Paul was to add another 100000 people swelling the population to over 300000. This rise in population was due, in no small part, to the wave of European immigrants coming to Minnesota. Within the St. Paul City limits there were and still are several lakes. One of these lakes, called Lake Como, is located in the northwest corner of the city proper, and is surrounded by pleasant trees, walking lanes and friendly city streets. Nearby is located a golf course, zoo, conservatory, and cemetery. Such were the limits of Harry McCool's universe in 1927. His "gang" was most certainly not a gang in the sense of a group of organized criminals. No, the "Como Gang" was simply the characters, young and old, but mostly young that populated the Como neighborhood, and gave variety and meaning to Harry's formative years.

Harry McCool was born the fifth child of James and Martha McCool. He had two older brothers, two older sisters, and one younger sister. The McCools lived in a modest two-story bungalow on Barrett Street near Lake Como. The home had a basement that scared the life out of Harry every time his mother made him fetch canned preserves from the dirt floor storage area. You entered the home a scant 12 feet from Barrett Street through an outdoor porch that was used exclusively in the summer. Passing through the front door you encountered a small entry with a coat closet, a 15 by 15 foot living room, a 10 by 15-foot dining room, and finally a 10 by 10 foot kitchen. The second floor had one bathroom with a tub, and two bedrooms, each a modest 12 by 15 feet in size. Next to the stairway was the one live source of entertainment in Harry's home, a piano. All told, the entire home had just over 1000 square feet of living space. The back yard had a ramshackle garage that barely held one car, and an expansive lawn that Martha used to grow tomatoes and rhubarb.

St. Paul was, and still is, dominated by Roman Catholic parishes. People refer to someone as Verne Jones from St Luke's parish, or Terry Johnson from St. Mark's parish, or Mary Lethert from St. Leo's parish. The Catholic Church is so important in St. Paul that all major life decisions require counsel from the parish priest, and all major life events are centered on one of the Catholic Sacraments. In the middle of this small universe, a youngster lived day-to-day with the most influential figures in his or her life, namely the Roman Catholic nuns. These all-powerful figures indoctrinated the youth of St. Paul in the essentials of the faith, focusing primarily on the Catechism and Bible. Everything that a catholic boy or girl needed to know about the world inside and outside the faith came filtered through the eyes, ears, and mouths of the nuns. This parochialism made St. Paul a very little "big" city.

Enter with me now into Harry's world during the year 1927, when walking, bicycles and canary-colored electric trolleys were the main sources of transportation, when summer entertainment could be found listening to outdoor music coming from the live orchestra sitting in the Como Pavilion, when winter entertainment came from the radio, and when televisions wouldn't be ubiquitous in the American homes for another 30 years. Let Harry tell you what life was like for a Catholic boy growing up in St. Paul, Minnesota during the most angst-ridden year of his young life.

1

A LOOSE TONGUE

*The McCool home on
Barrett Street*

No alarm needed to ring to wake up Harry. At 5 A.M. he slid his 5 foot 1 inch 95 pound frame out of bed not even disturbing his two older brothers sleeping in the same room. In the dark he put on and laced his hooked shoes (on cold winter nights he slept with his socks on). He shivered past the room where his mother and his three sisters slept. Then he tiptoed down the steps past his father's body laying in the coffin near his favorite easy chair in the living room. He went into the kitchen where he found a dime left on the counter by his mother next to the sink. Harry rubbed his eyes before checking the coin. Heads up meant his mother wanted white bread from the bakery, tails up meant she wanted wheat bread. A dime signaled fresh bread, a nickel signaled day-old bread. Harry found a dime left heads up. He pocketed the coin, then descended into the basement through the cellar door.

In the basement he shook down the dead ashes through the grate and shoveled more coal on the dying fire. Then he pulled on his overshoes, struggled into his woolen overcoat, and covered his face with his mother's knitted scarf. He leaned down and buckled the metals straps on his overshoes, a maneuver that he never would perform in front of his friends: too drippy. On the early morning paper route, though, there would be no chance of encountering anyone, so the added precaution to keep his feet warm was an astute choice. On the way up the steps from the basement he took his paper route bags off the hook, ducked his head under the straps, and put on a pair of gloves. He unlocked the back door, held his breath, and stepped outside.

He gasped as the wind grabbed the door and swung it wide open. With a quick lunge, he caught the door before it banged against the house and woke his mother. A sideways glance at the thermometer told him the temperature—22 below. His footsteps crackled in the frozen snow. Harry tolerated the cold but hated the wind. A quick look around told him that the wind had blown all night long, creating three and four foot undulating moguls from the new snowfall. And the wind still whistled. Despite the wind and cold, Harry liked these winter mornings. There was an eerie silence promoted by the muffling affect of snow that made him feel like he was the only person on an alien, white, planet.

From the rear door, Harry walked around the side of his home to Barrett Street. The milkman's truck had just passed leaving a trail of deep ruts through the snow in the middle of the street. Harry trudged south, head down, step over step toward Front Avenue, using the truck's maiden path to save precious energy for keeping warm. Upon reaching Front, he was relieved to discover that the Twin Cities Trolley Lines had already been plowed by the vehicle that Harry affectionately called the "cow catcher" for its front end. He turned east onto Front Avenue and never looked up as he plowed his way past the cemetery on the right. Later in the morning his mother, family, friends and relatives would come to the cemetery following the hearse to bury his father, James McCool. He thought that after the funeral he wouldn't feel right about snow skiing over the tombstones.

At the six cornered intersection of Front Avenue, Dale Street and Como Boulevard, Harry found his allotment of newspapers bundled with twine. He wasted no time loading his bags with the 180 St. Paul Pioneer Press newspapers, and headed off along Como to begin his deliveries. As he walked, he quickly folded each newspaper as his older brother Joseph had taught him one year earlier when Harry took over the route. The technique was simple but effective: fold each newspaper from the open end to the bound end, tucking the final fold inside the newspaper forming a tight knot. Then, with hardly a break in motion, Harry would hurl the folded newspaper onto the front steps of a customer. As he tossed the first paper, Harry thought of his big brothers Peter and Joseph, wondering what they might be thinking about their future without a father. Harry would lean on them more than ever now that their father was dead.

Harry put his mind in limbo for the next two hours while delivering one hundred and seventy nine newspapers. His route was a crazy crossed pattern that covered customer homes on Como, Simon, Grotto, Jameson, Orchard, and Avon Streets. There was no excitement that hour in the morning. At least not until he reached old lady Moses' house on Avon. As usual, old lady Moses had left her dog, a chow, out all night. The chow never did take kindly to Harry and leapt at him, fangs first. Harry automatically stuffed old lady Moses' morning news down its throat. "Chew on that you mutt," muttered Harry to the dog. Old lady Moses caught Harry one morning stuffing the paper down the dog's throat and made him stick his tongue to her frozen, outdoor, iron rail. It took a kettle of hot water to loosen Harry's tongue from the rail. Harry's sister Alice claimed that was the reason Harry had a *loose tongue* from that time on.

Harry finished his route just before 7 AM ending at the Swenson's bakery on the corner of Orchard and Como Place. He entered the cozy front room of the shop to greet Annika, the baker's daughter. It was well over 75 degrees in the room thanks to the huge ovens in the back. Harry pulled the dime out of his pocket and flashed it to Annika. She asked "Heads or Tails, Harry?"

Harry answered "Heads."

Annika responded "Let me get you a fresh loaf of white bread, dad just finished a batch".

While Annika was getting the loaf of bread, Harry recalled her dad describing his path via trains and the Inman shipping line from Sweden to St. Paul. Annika's father, Knut, and mother, Elke, had come to America separately just after the beginning of the 20th century. They came, like a million of their countrymen, to escape the agricultural hardships of their homeland, and to live in "The Promise Land". They followed the well-traveled path from Gothenburg, Sweden to England, to New York, to Chicago. From letters received back home before they departed, they had learned that there was a well established Swedish community around Lake Phalen in St. Paul, so they each had continued on train the extra 400 miles from Chicago to this area. Regarding his Swedish heritage, Knut would often times say, "Ya know Harry, there are a million first or second generation Swedish people in America, so we really aren't a minority. In fact, a lot of people call Minnesota the 'Swedish State'. On the other hand, you Harry, being Danish, are a member of a real minority." Knut would always end this discourse with a big belly laugh.

Harry always wondered what was so funny about being Danish, and would remind Knut that he was half Danish, ⅜ Irish and ⅛ Scottish. This never seemed to register with Knut. The Swede only remembered the Danish origin. Harry figured there must be some ancient animosity between the Danes and Swedes that made Knut single out his Danish heritage, but never pursued the history. Harry actually thought very little of his European heritage, but instead only thought of himself as an American. In his neighborhood, though, there was no escaping his European origins.

Knut and Elke met in 1904, fell in love, and married in 1906. Within five years they had 3 children, with Annika being the second. Knut started working for the railroad owned by James J. Hill in 1902, while Elke became a maid in the Turley home on Como Place. Knut told Harry how he hated Hill's famous quote "Give me snuff, whiskey and Swedes, and I will build a railroad to hell". The thought of lining Hill's pockets with his hard labor made Knut determined to escape the railroad and start his own business. Knut also decided that in order to better blend in with the rest of the population, he and his family would have to learn English.

Knut's decision to blend meant leaving the familiarity of the "Little Sweden" that had blossomed around Lake Phalen, and moving his family to the more integrated community around Lake Como. Knut's decision to start his own business meant that he and Elke had to save every penny possible. Another reason for their fiscal sacrifice was to give their children better prospects for the future via the post high school education opportunities that abounded in Minnesota. Knut and Elke realized their dream in 1920, just after the Great War ended, when they bought a home on Orchard, which they immediately fitted for a bakery. The mood of the country after the war was unbounded optimism, and with the hard work of Knut, Elke, and the children, the Swenson's bakery flourished in the 1920s. Knut did all the baking; Annika's older brother took care of the deliveries, while she and her mom handled the customers. Annika always took the early shift so she could go to the University of Minnesota Nursing School during the afternoon, thus fulfilling part of her father's dream. Annika's matriculation at the University of Minnesota was one of their proudest moments. The one thing that Knut refused to abandon from Little Sweden was religion. He returned every weekend for services at the First Covenant Church on Arcade and Maryland.

Harry's reminiscing was interrupted as Annika returned with a loaf of white bread and slipped it into the bread cutter. Harry always shuddered and looked aside whenever Annika put her hands oh so close to the oscillating blades as she pushed the bread through the magnificent machine. He felt certain that one day the cutter would claim one of Annika's fingers. Good luck prevailed, though, and out the back came the fresh loaf of white bread sliced without any bloodied fingers. Annika carefully wrapped it in wax paper, tucking the ends in to preserve the freshness. She then bagged the bread and handed it Harry saying "Sorry about your dad, Harry. I always enjoyed his morning jokes when he stopped by on the way to the railroad."

Harry winced as he was reminded of his dead father, and wondered why his dad joked with Annika, but seldom at home. He answered in a somber voice "Thanks Annika. The funeral is at St. Andrews, and he is going to be buried at Calvary Cemetery." Harry immediately stuffed the bread into one of his paper route bags, braced for the return outside, pushed open the door, and headed home.

When Harry got back home, the milk bottles on the back porch were frozen. Two inches of cream pushed the caps up like a Popsicle. Clothes hung out the night before "to air" had become stiff as a board. Harry brought in the milk and set the bread and milk on the kitchen table. Harry then set the 180th newspaper (which he would read cover to cover later that day) on the kitchen table, and threw his paper sacks down the basement steps. His frosted scarf stuck to his lips until he jerked it off . . . and he sailed that down the steps too. "Ma," he yelled upstairs, "I'm going to serve." With that, he grabbed his brother Joseph's dry scarf and plunged out again heading for the church.

Harry had made no move to look in at his father lying in the casket in the living room. Despite having two older brothers that he looked up to and loved, the sudden loss of his number one male role model scared Harry deeply. If God can take my father at only 48 years of age, when might he come for me? Even worse, whom can I go to for advice now that my dad is dead? The only way he knew to combat these fears was to keep moving. For now, that meant towards church and the comfort of Mass.

Harry walked the short half-mile to St. Andrews Catholic Church in 7 minutes. Cold biting wind made a person move very quickly indeed. He pulled the old oaken door open and stepped inside. The church was dark. Only the vigil light flickered on the altar. Harry didn't mind the dark; at least the church was warm. He never stumbled a step as he walked the cathedral distance to the altar railing—grabbing a pew every few steps. He could find his way on this familiar route with his eyes closed. Once to the railing, he genuflected and felt his way into the sacristy.

In the convent next door to the church, the nuns were getting up. The night before they had laid out the proper color vestments for the Mass of the day, in today's case, green. Right next to the priestly vestments they laid out their favorite server's, namely Harry's, surplice and cassock. Before Father Patton arrived, Harry had lit two altar candles and set the wine and water on a table by the altar. He then switched on two front ceiling beams—enough light for the two old women that always attended early mass. On a cold morning the good old Father could whip through the mass in 18 minutes. As usual, Father Patton entered the sacristy and immediately cuffed Harry behind the ears.

"You should be a priest, Harry. You like to get up in the morning."

"Yes, Father."

Father Patton boomed on, "And I'll tell you why you should become a priest . . . because it's the future of America. You know Bertrand Russell? You know what he says? He says that within 100 years the United States will be Catholic! That's right, the Roman Catholic Church will dominate America. And it will do so by sheer force of numbers. Now Bertrand Russell doesn't like us. And to him this is a grave matter and will have its effects on the whole civilized world because more and more America will tend to rule the world. If our growth continues as it is blossoming now, there will be no such thing as Protestantism in this country, and eventually fewer religions other than Catholicism in the world. And you know what else he says?"

"No, Father."

"He says that 90 percent of the marriages between Catholics and Protestants within the first year or so have resulted in the Protestants becoming Catholic. Isn't that wonderful?"

"Yes, Father."

'What will your mother do with all you kids, now that her husband is dead? Send a girl off to the convent?"

"I don't know, Father."

"My suggestion is to send the middle girl to the convent and you to the seminary. Two of you will get a fine education and enough to eat."

Harry replied "Yes, Father," as he thought to himself . . . but I don't want my favorite sister Sheila to go away, and I certainly don't want to go away to a seminary and leave the comfort of my own home.

"Where's the other server?" continued Father.

"I don't know, Father."

Mass usually required two servers, but Father Patton had full confidence that Harry could manage alone, and he hated to start Mass a minute after the prescribed 7:30 AM. One of the advantages of being the lone server at an expedited Mass was that Harry would be kept busy doing double duty, no time to let his mind wander and get bored. Harry remembered Sister Bernice's admonition 'An idle mind is the devil's workshop, so always keep yourself busy'. As Harry thought about the good sister's advice, his reverie was interrupted by Father Patton saying "Harry, ring the bell, let's get this Mass started."

"Yes, Father."

Father Patton and Harry entered the church. Father Patton bowed and Harry genuflected as they reached the area directly in front of the tabernacle. Father Patton walked up two steps to the altar, kissed the Missal, opened the great book, and began in Latin, *"In nomine Patris, et Filii, et Spiritus Sancti."* He joined his hands before his breast as he continued, *"Introibo ad altare Dei."*

Harry responded in Latin, *"Ad Deum qui laetificat juventutem meam."*

Father blazed through the rest of the introductory prayers and epistle in Latin. Harry kept his head bowed as he recited the Latin responses that he so diligently learned to become a Server. He would never forget the long hours of practice to memorize these prayers before his first recitation in front of Sister Bernice. He liked the Mass in Latin even though he didn't understand it. The deep roaring voice of the priest's Latin gave a mystery to the ceremony. A few more minutes and Father polished off the gospel and creed. Next came Harry's first physical duty, namely the presentation of the water and wine for the gifts. Father carefully, oh so carefully, tempted a drop of water to fall into the chalice. He then poured all of the wine into the chalice. Several more muffled prayers led to the Consecration of the Body and Blood of Christ. Harry deftly picked up the ringer and timed the bells to the raising of the host and chalice by Father Patton.

Within minutes, the "Our Father" was recited, bread broken, and Communion prayer said with Harry timing the bell ringing to Father's genuflections. Father took his host, a big gulp of the wine, and then turned to give Harry and the little old ladies their communion hosts. Harry scrambled to get the gold plated Communion Plate that he needed to hold so delicately under the ladies' throats as they received the **"Body of Christ"**. Harry was always a little nervous that he might let the Body of Christ touch the floor if they let the host fall out of their quivering lips. A matter of permanent damnation he was sure. With a quick turn back to the altar, Father Patton replaced the chalice and locked the tabernacle. Within seconds he gave the last Blessing and ended the mass at 7:48, 18 minutes to the tee.

The only English ever spoken by Father Patton on the altar (outside of marriages, funerals and baptisms) was a weekly request for money . . . and this only on Sunday when there were more to hear. He would never think of giving an eloquent sermon to an audience of two.

Back in the sacristy after Mass, Father quickly took off his vestments, put on his overcoat, and left. Harry smothered the candles, switched off all of the lights and felt his way to the wine cabinet. After two quick swigs of wine, he left too, dreading the return home not to mention the return to church at 10:00 o'clock for his father's funeral ceremony.

2

THE FUNERAL

The main problem with burying a body in January in Minnesota is the frozen ground. In small towns, the procedure is to store the bodies until spring when gravediggers could dig through the thawed ground. In larger cities like St. Paul, gravediggers burned coal on the ground and then used picks to dig six feet down into a warmed earth. Martha expected no problems with her husband's burial at the large Calgary Catholic Cemetery just down the block from the McCool home. Calgary had a good supply of coal, and two full time gravediggers. Imagine how surprised she was when the cemetery supervisor, a newspaper customer of Harry's named Jack Prinor, called the night before the funeral to tell her that the only two gravediggers were sick! Martha didn't panic at this news, though. She immediately called the Ancient Order of Hibernians (AOH).

The **Ancient Order of Hibernians** was founded in 1565 (or 1641 depending upon the historical source) to defend Gaelic values and to protect the church and clergy in Ireland. Of course in the 16th and 17th centuries there was a lot of religious protection needed, in particular against the Virgin Queen Elizabeth of England. The AOH followed the hordes of Irish immigrants that came to America in the 19th and 20th centuries, where the charter changed from protecting the church and clergy to smoothing the path for Irish immigrants into America and preserving the Irish cultural heritage in America. These Irish immigrant hordes included three of Harry's paternal great grandparents who came to America between 1850 and 1860, just after the time of the great potato famine in Ireland. Happy to have survived the disaster, these hardy ancestors of Harry felt that America offered much better future prospects than their poor depleted Ireland. Following a series of train, boat, steamer and ox cart trips, two of Harry's great grandparents found their way to Mankato, Minnesota where they brought Harry's paternal grandfather, John Paul McCool.

John Paul McCool was a stone mason who built bridges, culverts, and roads. In 1872, John met and married his wife, **Mary Bridgette Riley**, a pure daughter of the Irish with parents born in Cloonraine Balleneine, country of Mayo, Ireland. Over the next 20 years, John Paul and Mary Bridgette gave birth to 10 children, including their third son, James Edward McCool, Harry's father, on May 19,1879. By the mid 1880s, John Paul was a civic leader in Mankato. In 1885-1886 John served as alderman for Mankato and was commissioner of streets. With the encouragement of his Irish wife and Irish mother, a lass nee Mary Kingsley, he became a charter member of the local Catholic Church, named St. John's, and secretary for the AOH lodge. As a charter member of the church, he helped lay the foundation for the original edifice. As secretary for the lodge, he served for over 30 years.

James Edward McCool, Harry's father, grew up a Catholic Irish boy in Mankato. When James came of age in 1900, he immediately followed in his father's footsteps and became a lifetime member of the AOH. With his father's encouragement to "go west young man", he headed for Wyoming where he met Harry's mother, **Martha Marie Jensen**. After Harry's parents married in 1905, they moved to St. Paul where James started to work for the Northern Pacific railroad, and participated in AOH activities on a regular basis. It was no surprise, then, when Martha called the AOH the night before the funeral and the men immediately offered to dig the grave themselves. Martha never cried, even when she lost her first baby at childbirth. But when the AOH chapter president told her about the AOH men digging the grave, she smiled ever so mildly. This was a veritable torrent of emotion for Martha.

The funeral started at the home of James and Martha. James was laid out in a pine casket in the living room. It had been a long, agonizing six weeks since he had contracted pneumonia. Here, in this little two-story house, James and Martha lived with all six children. It was crowded for sleeping quarters, but would be less so with the death of the father James. The eleven-month-old daughter, Mary Helen, would now move to an upstairs bedroom. She had been in the dining room downstairs because there was no room upstairs in either of the two bedrooms. Harry and his brother Joseph slept in a double bed in what they called the back bedroom. Along side them, with the one window in the bedroom at his feet, was the oldest boy, Peter. Now in the front bedroom would be Martha, the oldest daughter Alice, the middle daughter Sheila, and the baby Mary Helen.

Relatives from Wyoming and Utah, coming for the funeral, found sleeping quarters in Mankato, 80 miles away. Mankato was also the home of James' mother and father . . . too old to come to the funeral because of the cold weather. On the night before the funeral, Martha kept a vigil light burning by the side of the casket. This morning all the children took turns in reciting the Rosary . . . each a decade at a time. Harry finished his decade and then his mother, Martha, stepped between him and the casket. She stood there without a tear in her eyes. Suddenly, she took her dead husband's left hand. She held it high above the casket for Harry to see.

"Look at the twisted little finger!" she said. Harry tried to turn away, but she grabbed him by the shoulder and made him look as she continued: "He got that crooked finger from a switch change in the railroad tracks. Remember he worked under the Western Avenue Bridge for 22 years."

Why is mom making me look at dad, Harry thought. Doesn't she know how much it scares me to look at him? Harry managed to writhe away from looking at his dad as he asked, "How did it happen?"

"He caught it in one of the switches that jammed. He pulled it out just before a train came down the track."

"Why is it still twisted?"

"Your father didn't think it serious enough to see a doctor . . . so the finger stayed just as you see it."

Harry finally pulled away from his mother. He didn't want to see or talk about the twisted finger anymore, let alone be in such close proximity to his father's corpse. It wasn't as if the body smelled bad. In fact, the many carnations and roses around the coffin made his living room smell the best he could remember. No, it was the waxen look on his father's face that Harry knew would haunt him forever if he gazed too long.

Martha continued "He always called me a stubborn Dane. Maybe he got some stubbornness from me."

Harry had seen the twisted finger before . . . down at Como Lake when his father had taught him how to skip rocks over the water. He always wondered about the finger but didn't ask. His dad was not a conversationalist. Martha put the hand down gently and turned away from the casket. Harry rattled off the last decades of the rosary. When Harry finished, his sister, Alice, took his place. As Alice started the third decade of the Sorrowful Mysteries . . . The Crowning with Thorns . . . she jerked around, pointed at the wall, and said: 'That doesn't belong there."

Above the casket on the wall hung a crucifix and a photo of Will Rogers. Will Rogers was a favorite of James, so Martha thought it appropriate to hang above her husband resting in the coffin. Alice turned back towards the casket, reached over the body, and took down the picture of Rogers. "This is not the time nor the place for that to hang, mom. Dad's death doesn't seem in the least bit funny to me" she scolded her mother.

Martha said nothing.

The casket filled half the room. Heat from the coal-burning furnace came up through a grille in the middle of the living room floor. All the children huddled over the grille as it poured heat into the room, waiting their turn to say the Rosary. Alice completed her decade. Next came Peter. Martha took him by the arm, whiffed his breath, and said, "Peter, have you been smoking again?"

"You smell smoke from the furnace, Ma. You know I quit last month after that beating I got from Pa."

"I hope you have stopped . . . It will stunt your growth if you keep it up. You better not be drinking any rotten liquor with your buddies either," she added. What Martha didn't mention was that she was far more frightened that Peter would die from tainted moonshine, than she was worried about his smoking. Prohibition had spawned far too many illegal stills, many of which produced poisoned liquor. There had even been recent reports of deaths from bad hooch. She hoped that Peter was only smoking on the sly, and that he was smart enough to avoid bootlegged liquor.

Peter, at 18 years of age and six feet tall, was already the tallest person in the family, and it seemed much too late for Martha to influence his growth or social habits. Nevertheless, Martha's admonitions about his smoking and drinking showed that she had already taken control of her children, even before her husband was buried. Up to this time, James had ruled over the boys with an iron hand. Martha felt obligated to assume his parental role with the boys, and there was no time like the present to start. As a matter of fact, Martha was just beginning the transfer of affection and attention from her husband James to her three sons. Unfortunately for her boys, this change in Martha was to become even more powerful than the typical mother-son relationship that seems so prevalent in middle class America. Peter meekly returned to mumbling his decade.

Off the grille next came Sheila . . . red hair from her father's side of the family. She piously held the Rosary in between the thumb and forefinger of each hand. Her dark neckerchief pulled down over her ears and her ankle long dress made her look like a nun. Just as she finished her decade, the Cemetery superintendent knocked on the rear door. "Please put the children's overshoes and overcoats on as we can now start for the church."

With a gentle pull, he took Sheila away from the casket and shut the lid for the last time. "Martha", said the cemetery man, "You and the girls please get in the car in front of the hearse."

Martha wrapped the baby, Mary Helen, in a wool blanket and

then she put on her own dark coat. Meanwhile Alice put on her overcoat and at the same time said to Sheila: "Be sure that Putzer (their German dog) is in the basement, and don't forget to lock the door."

With that last remark Alice tugged on her overshoes, pushed open the front door, and plowed through the snow to the fancy Packard car parked just in front of the hearse. The snow, which had fallen all night, came up to the knees of Martha, Alice and Sheila. Martha thought how much James looked forward to the day he could afford a Packard himself. "Ask the man who owns one" James would often say after reading an ad in The St. Paul Pioneer Press. How ironic that his wife would finally take her first ride in a Packard as he took his last ride on earth in a hearse.

Room in this Single Six Packard Sedan held the driver, Martha, the baby Mary Helen, Alice and Sheila. With no car heater, there were also winter blankets and winter clothing to take the rest of the space and to keep the riders warm for the short ride to the church. The night before, Martha cautioned Peter to park his Model T Ford in the street, should they need it for the funeral. And they did need it for the three boys to follow behind the hearse and the car Martha and the girls were stuffed in.

The Packard and hearse started down the street . . . no problem with the snow. But not so with the Model T. After Peter cranked the engine to start the car (electronic ignitions wouldn't be available for quite a few more years), he jumped in and yelled, "Let's go." Unfortunately, with the car parked outside overnight, the unexpected snowstorm had semi buried the car. The snow came to the top of the fenders and the first turn of the wheels resulted in no forward movement. The car was immediately stuck and the more gas Peter gave the motor, the higher the engine screamed, but no forward movement was managed as the wheels simply dug deeper and deeper.

Getting a car stuck in a snowdrift is a common occurrence in Minnesota, but with adequate manpower the solution is always the same: muscle it out of the drift. "Joe, Harry, get out and push!" pleaded Peter. Even though Joe and Harry immediately complied, they weren't strong enough to move the Model T, and the car just stayed in the same spot. Luckily, the Six pallbearers from the Ancient Order of Hibernians were just ahead and they came back to help push and pull the car out of the snow. With six new helpers, however, came six new opinions as to how to get the car out of the snowdrift.

"Gas it" . . . "Push it backwards" . . . "Slide it to the side" . . . "Get some shovels" . . . "Stand on the fenders" . . . "Lift it out".

After several minutes of bickering, Harry, the thinker in the family, came to the rescue: "Rock it," he cried. The men looked at each other, laughed, but then rocked the Model T as suggested. Back and forth, back and forth, and out it came. But not for long was it to stay free to move. As Peter stepped on the gas, the Model T caught up to the Packard carrying his mother and sisters. To avoid hitting the Packard, he swerved to the side of the road, roared into a snow bank, and really got stuck. One quick look confirmed that this predicament would take more than a simple rock.

"Mass at ten, we'll never make it" said a panicky Peter.

"We better crowd into the funeral car carrying Ma," volunteered Harry.

And this they did. The additional weight on the funeral car got this car stuck at once—right in the middle of the road. Once again the AOH men were called in for help.

"Do you think a little prayer to St. Anthony will help us get out of the snow?" asked Sheila.

Harry said, "Sheila, you pray to St. Anthony when something is lost, not when you are stuck."

Alice added 'There is no Saint for being stuck in the snow that I know of."

Martha weighed in with "I think more pushing by the Hibernian men will help more than any Saint we can pray to."

Sure enough, with one last heave ho by the Hibernian men . . . out came the Packard. For the third time, the Hibernians got back into the pallbearer car. Peter, Joseph and Harry jumped on the running board as the driver—the funeral director's son—wove the car down the street to the next obstacle . . . the Northern Pacific railroad tracks.

"Speed 'er up over the tracks," cried Peter, "you don't want to get the tires stuck between the tracks. We may need more than just the Hibernians to rescue us then."

"I can't go any faster in this snow," returned the driver.

"Look out for trains," said Martha ever so softly.

As the funeral cars approached the tracks, fortune was on their side. The high stick sign had not signaled the coming of any trains. Neither car had to slow a bit and risk getting stuck. Sheila made a quick sign of the cross and the cars plowed over the tracks. When Como Avenue was reached, the trio of boys got off the running board and squeezed into the car. At long last the funeral cars came to a thankful stop in front of the church.

The Ancient Order of Hibernians got out of their car, changed roles from car pushers to pallbearers, and carried the casket up the slippery steps. With great care they rose, one step at a time, to the church door. At the top step stood Father Patton. Next to him waited two servers—Clarence Zacardi and George Scanlon. Each boy had requested the honor of serving at the funeral Mass of his friend Harry's father. The nun in charge of servers, Sister Bernice, didn't take too kindly to the idea of Clarence and George doing the honor. She had always tried to match servers by height, but in this case Zacardi was five feet one inch and Scanlon was six feet two inches. Zacardi had coal, Italian black hair that waved and waved all over his head. The movie idol of the time, Rudolph Valentino, would have looked better in Zacardi's hair than his own had Clarence not plastered it all over his head. Scanlon, the nun's favorite besides Harry, had hair properly combed. Since Sister Bernice wanted to ease the McCool's trauma at the death of the father, she relaxed her rule and let Clarence and George serve the funeral.

Clarence held the censer while George added incense that he lit with a candle. Father Patton took the censer from Clarence. As he circled the casket, he swung the censer from the attached chain in lazy figure eight's releasing incense. As he walked, he said: "May this incense lead James into the after life". After one complete circuit of the casket, he returned the censer to Clarence, then lead the pallbearers and family into the church.

Just when everybody was seated in the pews, the little 10-month-old baby Mary Helen began to cry. Sheila took her away from her mother and hurried to the vestibule of the church. Once there she walked the baby back and forth until only a whimper could be heard. By the time Father Patton started the Mass all was quiet. Sheila silently returned to the pew with her baby sister now fast asleep.

On such a cold and windy morning, Martha expected no neighbors to attend. But some did. Mrs. Rush, one of Martha's backyard neighbors sat right behind the family. She could be heard whispering to her daughter, "Thank God—poor Martha won't have to have any more children to feed."

"Won't she get all his life insurance?" asked Mrs. Rush's daughter, Rose.

"Be quiet," said Mrs. Rush. "They will hear you." And young Harry did hear them.

A few other neighbors came to church—some that weren't even Catholic like Andy and Esther Johnson with their two children, Buddy and Donald. Gilbert Black, a Lutheran, knelt in the last pew in church. He wasn't used to kneeling but squirmed the best he could never knowing when to stand up, when to sit down, or when to kneel. His mother, a good Lutheran by birth, made Gilbert attend the funeral. She didn't want to be caught in a Catholic Church, but she sure wanted to know what went on inside. The funeral seemed like the perfect opportunity to get the "lay of the land". She still couldn't go, but her son was a perfect substitute. As a result, she sent Gilbert with instructions to report back on all he saw and heard. Gilbert had a note pad in his hand to write everything down. Gilbert leaned over to the woman on his left and asked, "Is this the coldest pew in the whole church?"

"They're all cold," whispered the Presbyterian lady, next door neighbor to Martha and James. "Our church is much warmer than this one." This woman had two girls, Maggie and Margaret. Maggie was a terrific Charleston dancer and one of Gilbert's favorites at Saturday night dances in Como Hall just across the street from the cemetery. Gilbert was glad that Maggie's mother came alone, he didn't want to explain to Maggie his presence in a Catholic Church.

Martha's sister-in-law, Sarah, also came to the funeral. She brought her husband, John, and their two daughters, Eleanor and Elaine. John was a railroad man like his brother James but he was higher up in the railroad—an engineer, as compared to James who was a mere switchman. Sarah, the sister-in-law knew of only two smart and beautiful girls in the world and both of them were hers. Elaine was the smart one and Eleanor was the beautiful one. Both came with winter coats up to their necks but dressed beneath them they looked like store models for Easter Sunday—which was still three months away.

In from Mankato came Noddy and Nellie. They came on the Chicago Northwestern Train that started in Omaha and stopped for passengers occasionally in Mankato and St. Peter. Noddy was Harry's favorite uncle because he always brought with him candy, baseballs and bats. But this time he brought no candy, no balls and no bats. Noddy and Nellie lived in Mankato right down the hill from the "Our Lady of Good Counsel" convent—the training grounds for nuns to be. "I just know that Martha will send Sheila to Our Lady of Good Counsel", said Nellie to Noddy.

Noddy replied, "She sure won't have enough money to feed all six."

Father Patton said an introductory prayer in Latin, and walked over to the casket. The two servers added more incense to the censer. Father took the censer away from them and circled the casket after telling the servers to wait in chairs on the altar while he rocked the censer over the casket saying "May this incense take James' soul upward to the clouds where he will spend eternity in heaven." Father continued with, "You may think that this is not a happy occasion, but it is", and with that the good Father started the Mass. For the first time since her husband's death, Martha began to sob. She was so quiet about it though, that even her family didn't hear the subdued cries. Father Patton handed the incense back to Clarence.

The prayers were announced in Latin until the Mass came to the Nicene Creed, at which time Father walked over to the pulpit and said: "Sister Bernice tells me that Sheila is the best reader she has in the school, and suggested that she read the Creed in English." Without a moment of hesitation, Sheila got up from her seat in the pew and climbed the few steps to the pulpit. Father handed her the Missal and she started to read the Creed.

"I Believe in God, the Father almighty, maker of heaven and earth. I believe in Jesus Christ, the only Son of the Father, eternally begotten of the Father, God from God, Light from Light, true God from true God, begotten not made, one in being with the Father. Through him all things were made, for us men and for our salvation he came down from Heaven. By the power of the Holy Spirit he was born of the Virgin Mary and became man. For our sake he was crucified under Pontius Pilate. He suffered, died and was buried. On the third day he arose again in fulfillment of the Scriptures. He ascended into heaven and is seated at the right hand of the Father. He will come again in glory to judge the living and the dead and his kingdom will have no end."

Just as Sheila finished the last sentence, a dog started walking up the aisle. It was Putzer, of course. Sheila stepped down off the pulpit and grabbed Putzer by the collar. He didn't stop wagging his tail even though she dragged him down the aisle to the vestibule. "Go home, Putzer!" she yelled for all in the church to hear. Then she slammed the church door, and started back for the pulpit.

Meanwhile, Father said, "A dog is a girl's best friend."

Alice whispered to her mother, "I told Sheila to lock the basement door before we left for church."

Martha just shook her head. "I hope he goes right home in this cold weather. He follows Sheila everywhere."

Sheila overheard her mom's remark on her way up the center aisle, and responded "I told him to go straight home and stay there. I know he will obey." With that last out loud whisper to her mother, Sheila returned to the pulpit and continued where she left off in the Creed.

"We believe in the Holy Ghost, the Lord, the giver of life . . . who proceeds from the Father and the Son. With the Father and the Son he is worshipped and glorified. He has spoken though the Prophets. We believe in one holy Catholic and apostolic church. We acknowledge one baptism for the forgiveness of sins and we look for the resurrection of the dead and the life of the world to come. Amen."

Sheila closed the prayer book and left the Pulpit to go and sit with her family. Father Patton then moved to the Pulpit for his remarks. "This is a good time to tell of James and what he did for the church and his family. He gave us Martha who was born in Denmark and was brought up by a Lutheran for her first 16 years. James made a convert of her before they married. Martha, as you know, came to Green River, Wyoming from Denmark. Most of Martha's sisters and brothers left Green River and drifted to Utah where even up until today, they are Mormons. But James saved her from the Mormons for us and heaven."

"James and Martha together have had all their children that you see before us today brought up Catholic. All but the baby, that you heard crying earlier, have received Communion and the Sacrament of Confirmation. Each and every child goes to our school for $1.00 a month. For this amount will be charged by me now that James can no longer support the family like he would have wanted to. As you know, Martha, your husband received the Last Sacrament, one-hour before he passed away. You and I, Martha, witnessed this beautiful death."

Father Patton then continued his theme with "My Mother told me as a child that death is expected of us all. She had prepared a 'Lay Away Set' not only for us, but also for all of the neighbors who came to her for religious needs. This 'Set' had candlesticks and holy water. She said the only way to go was with holy water and candles. Unfortunately we had no time for this 'Lay Away Set' at St. John's Hospital where James died. Death is the great Christian climax of life. In all our prayers we ask the good Lord for a happy death. James had a good life and a good death. He will be remembered by all of us for the way he prepared his children as Christians to meet death, a necessary end that will come when it will come. We must make sure we face it with faith and hope of an eternity with Christ in Heaven. Live a good life and you will meet a good end. For myself, I look forward to meeting Christ and most of all St. Patrick. He is someone I intend to meet when I get there. Of course I am not anxious to go just yet, I still have many Baptisms, Marriages and Funerals to celebrate." With this final prediction, Father Patton turned back to the altar and continued with the Mass.

Father Patton especially enjoyed funeral days when he could wax eloquent to an audience and say the Mass with a great deal of flourish. Forget the 18-minute special, a funeral Mass was never said in less than one hour, and it always included a personalized sermon. Don't forget that he would need to prepare another Consecrated Body and Blood of Christ, mandating another big swig of wine at Communion time. Father's only regret was that he couldn't sing a funeral Mass. Too out of synch with crying relatives and the spirit of the event, you know.

Meanwhile, Gilbert's report for his Lutheran Mother on what took place had just this one note, "I see a great similarity between Catholics and Lutherans . . . especially when Sheila recited the Creed . . . it's the same thing you have been teaching me for years." The rest of the time Gilbert focused on the rituals of a funeral.

As the clock reached 11:00 AM, Father said the last blessing, sprinkled some holy water over the casket, and motioned the pallbearers to escort the casket out of the church. As they pushed the casket down the center aisle, Father Patton paused at the family pew a moment and said: "Martha, I don't want you to go to the cemetery with the little baby . . . it's too cold. I will go myself with the pallbearers and make a short prayer there." Martha looked past Father at the altar for several meaningful seconds, and then headed for the rear exit to the church with her daughters. Harry noticed the stare and wondered what his mother was thinking. He knew the chances were nil that she would share her inner thoughts with any of her children. Meanwhile Father Patton went into the sacristy with the two servers.

As Martha and her family got up to leave, Martha's neighbor, Mrs. Toot, took her by the sleeve and said for all to hear in her broken English: "I am bringing over at noon my Hungarian goulash. There is enough for your family and all your relatives. I want to tell you something now before I forget. When Andy (her husband) was in the life he told me that if he died before I died, I should forget him right away. Don't dwell too long, think only of yourself and Robert (her only son) . . . and your next meal, he said."

Harry took one last look back at his father's coffin, and then darted out the rear door of the church but didn't head home. Instead he returned to the church by the side door and entered the sacristy. Having served many a funeral ceremony, Harry was fully aware of the custom wherein the servers got anywhere from a nickel to a quarter for their participation. As Father Patton was changing his vestments for the cemetery, Harry whispered to Clarence and George "I am sorry, guys, but we don't have enough money to tip you for the funeral service".

George answered "No problem, Harry, we are just proud to be here and help in any way we can". Clarence nodded his agreement, and Harry hurried to catch up with his older brothers.

The loss of Harry's father on this cold January day in 1927 was to be but the first of many times that Harry was to part with a family member or friend over the course of his years growing up in the Lake Como area. As he hustled through the snow, he wondered who would be the next "to go". Father Patton's words about even a child having to expect death made Harry resolve to be a better Catholic lest his time come before he was ready. Certainly the Catholic Church had the answers for this terrible predicament that he and his family faced without their father, he thought. If only it didn't scare him so to think about the future, then maybe he could survive today.

3

OBEDIENCE, POVERTY, AND CHASTITY

The McCool family and relatives arrived at 1023 Barrett Street shortly after 11 AM. Putzer, on the other hand, was home before the funeral ended. When he got home he knew where to go . . . ***the Doghouse***! On cold winter months, Sheila's mother, Martha, wanted Sheila to "keep the beast in the basement", near the furnace and the heat. But it mattered not to Sheila—not the below zero temperature, not the fierce wind that blew, not how deep the snow covered the Dog house . . . she always kept Putzer in the Dog House. Whether it was spring, summer, fall, or winter she kept Putzer in the doghouse. And most certainly if he misbehaved—like barking in church and wagging his tail as he walked up the aisle of the church in the middle of a funeral Mass—he would be relegated to the Dog House. No mercy would be forthcoming from Sheila because of bad weather.

Putzer knew he was in trouble just the way Sheila dragged him by the tail out of the church. The northwest wind, in just over an hour since they had left for church, had blown the loose packed snow and covered the door to his house. But he had to get into shelter before Sheila got back, so with forepaws in quick action, he cleared the entrance and ducked into his home. An old rag rug made from one of Peter's discarded neckties lay waiting for him to cuddle up in. This is where Sheila found him when she got back from the funeral mass. "You can come out of there now," Sheila said. Putzer immediately responded and leapt out. "I will get your sled out of the garage and we'll run around the block a few times to warm up." Putzer barked his approval.

From the back door of the house, Martha shouted: "Sheila, come in right now and bring the dog with you." Putzer heard her. In four hops and one lunge he went right through the back door and past Martha. He slid to a stop in front of the stove. Martha smiled, "He can smell that Hungarian goulash of Mrs. Toot's." Putzer was the family garbage collector. He collected leftovers from the dining room table—slipped to him most of the time by Sheila. Martha obliged Putzer's forlorn look with a scrap of food. Putzer grabbed the scrap and headed for the heat.

The Tin Lizzie (i.e., Model T) was in the yard after the three boys got it back off the street, with the help from several neighbors, and into their driveway. "I see Putzer is back okay," said Harry. Putzer was now on the grille in the living room. His stone cold bones needed warming up, and no better way than chewing some food over the heat coming up from the furnace in the basement.

The telephone rang. Peter answered it. It was for Sheila. "Sister Bernadine wants to talk to Sheila," said Peter.

"You know what she wants, don't you?" Harry asked Sheila.

"She is after me to be a nun again." was Sheila's quick reply.

"What do you mean again?" This came from a very interested Martha.

Sheila ignored her mother's question, took the phone from Peter and said "Hello? Yes Sister, it was a very sad funeral but Father Patton spoke kindly of our father." Sheila continued, "I can't see you until Friday after our company is gone."

Martha said "Is that Sister after you about being a nun?"

"Yes, mother."

"You will need my permission you know."

"Yes, mother, I know that."

"That nun has no right to call Sheila . . . today of all days," interjected Alice.

"Tell Sister you are too busy getting Putzer ready for the race at Lake Como this Saturday." advised Harry.

Peter corrected, "I don't think her decision to become a nun has anything to do with the race on Saturday, Harry." Sheila gave her brothers a forlorn look, and then put the receiver down over the hook.

"Peter, how soon can you bring the gramophone up from the basement?" Martha asked. "I want some music for our guests."

"Right now," was Peter's quick reply, and down the steps he went followed by Joseph.

In the late 1920s, there were three popular forms of entertainment in the home, namely a gramophone, a radio, and a piano. Some products even combined the gramophone and radio. Harry always laughed when he thought about the commercials for these products that ran regularly in the St. Paul newspapers. For the **Victrola and Radiola** gramophone, the catch phrase was "Everything on the Air, Everything on Records". For the **Atwater Kent Radio** the ad ran "One dial—one hand, You sweep the air with One dial as a searchlight sweeps the sky, Why not listen to Programs instead of Arguments." Harry often wondered how many gullible people believed that a radio could solve their domestic problems.

Peter and Joseph carried the Academy cabinet gramophone carefully up from the basement, and set it where the casket had been. "Alice, I want you to play the records while we are having the Hungarian goulash", said Martha. Martha's favorite record of the time was *Listen to the Mocking Bird* as sung by Alma Gluck—bird voices by Charles Kellogg. Martha would tease Putzer by showing him the Victrola record picture of a dog looking into a table top gramophone megaphone. And when Alma sang *Listen to the Mocking Bird*, Putzer howled.

"What records?" asked Alice.

"James' two favorites," replied Martha.

"You mean *Adeste Fideles* and *A Little Bit of Heaven* by John McCormack?" asked an incredulous Alice, who couldn't believe her mother could listen to this while eating Hungarian goulash and mourning her husband's death.

"I like *Adeste Fideles* and your father liked *A Little Bit of Heaven*," Martha corrected.

The early Gramophones needed energy to play music. Its primary source was derived from potential energy produced from winding up a spring loaded inside the unit. Joseph wound up the Gramophone. Alice put on *Adeste Fideles* first, thinking a religious song more appropriate just after the funeral. Mrs. Toots began to dish out her food. Being Hungarian she didn't care what they played.

As the family started to take their usual places at the dinner table, a problem surfaced, namely James' place at the head of the table. Should someone take his seat, or should the seat be left vacant in memory of the dead husband and father? Martha provided the answer: "Peter, you are the male head of the family now. You sit in your father's chair." With this simple assertion, Martha made it known that she would not shy away from the difficult task of steering a fatherless family through the turbulent future they all expected, but dared not talk about.

The family quickly sat and started to devour Mrs. Toot's Hungarian goulash and the meatballs left by their Swedish neighbor Esther Johnson. Mrs. Toot didn't sit down with the family, but felt that providing the meal gave her the green light to talk. She began with her favorite subject "Martha, my husband Andy loved America. Even though he only lived here 5 years before dying, it wasn't because of your country. He always blamed the Hapsburgs for starting that silly war and driving us into ruin. When they took away our land and gave it to the Czechs, Andy said we had to leave." The Hungarians lost 72% of their territory and 64% of their population as a result of the Treaty of Trianon June 4th, 1920 to be exact.

With everyone eating, no one interrupted, so Mrs. Toot continued her monologue "Andy said America is the place to go. He couldn't stand to see the Czechs, Serbs, and Rumanians take away our Hungary, our livestock, and our beautiful valleys and hills. He said pack up and don't look back or come back no matter what. I'm not so sure he took his own advice, though. I think he died prematurely because the crushing of our homeland broke his heart. After he died I did want to go back home, but I trusted

Andy. I think now the time has come for you to trust your husband James and stay here in our neighborhood."

Martha had no intention of leaving the home on Barrett Street, so she wondered what had motivated Mrs. Toot's advice? After a seconds thought, however, she recalled that she never understood Mrs. Toot no matter what the subject, so she silently nodded assent in her direction.

The Toots weren't the only Hungarians to leave their homeland after World War I and come to St. Paul. In fact, there were so many Hungarians in Harry's neighborhood, that they called the area 'Hungk Valley'. Harry's mother worried that these 'foreigners' would corrupt her children, so she always asked Harry's new friends their nationality when first introduced. Harry had no difficulty recognizing the Hungarians since they looked darker than the northern Europeans, hung together in clannish groups, and sometimes lapsed into their native language when angry.

While Mrs. Toot finished her monologue, everyone's meal finished, but not before the two records had played at least 10 times. Martha brought out her contribution to the meal: Danish pudding. The boys devoured the desert in record time. Just as she finished her food, Sheila put on her coat and overshoes. Putzer, quite warm by this time, stood wagging his tail—waiting by the back door.

"Where to now, Sheila?" asked Martha.

"One trip on the sled around Lake Como" replied Sheila.

"In this cold?" objected Martha.

"Mom, the temperature has climbed to zero already . . . and Putzer needs the training for Saturday's race for the title . . . "

"Some title," said Peter, "Queen of the Mushers".

"Peter," asked Sheila, "Won't you run on ahead for Putzer to follow you around the lake?"

"What's he going to do during the race? I can't have all the other dogs following me?"

Harry broke in, "Don't worry about the other dogs following you . . . you'll be following them."

"Peter, you're right," said Sheila. "You better stay home today. I have to teach Putzer to run alone . . . not to just follow the other dogs like he did last year. We don't stand a chance if Putzer won't lead."

"Good idea Sheila," replied a relieved Peter. No true Minnesota native went out in the cold without a solid reason, and helping a dog and a girl win a race in the winter was no reason at all for Peter.

"All of you are more interested in the dog race than how I am to get to my piano lessons" interrupted Alice. Sheila and the three boys ignored her comment.

Martha realized that Alice was surfacing an important topic and said, "I don't know if we can afford you taking piano lessons anymore, Alice. Let me think about it. I need to talk to Father Patton and see if St. Andrew's parochial school is really going to cost us only $1, or if he was showing off at the funeral mass. You know that a Catholic Education is a must for this family's future."

"In that case," said Peter, "There goes my trombone lessons. Dad always thought I could some day play in the Paul Whiteman band."

Harry never heard a decent note come out of Peter's trombone. All Peter ever did was spit and sputter during his "practice" sessions. This seemed a perfect opportunity to kid his big brother, so he said "How much do you think you can sell that brass spittoon for, Peter?"

"Stop bickering . . . all of you . . . " this came from an angry Martha. "Go ahead Sheila. I want you to win the race Saturday."

The dog track around the lake measured 1.8 miles. It started at the Pavilion and headed south along Como Boulevard, the beginning of a large, ellipsoidal route around the lake. On the right side, as the mushers pulled their precious human cargo, came the "rich" houses of St. Andrew's parish elite. It was considered Chic to have a "Lake View" from your front window. Then, as the mushers turned east, they quickly reached the south end of the lake at *Union Park* . . . this could be Putzer's first problem. It was crucial that Putzer stayed on the course by turning northeast at the park. One sharp turn by Putzer to the south would send Sheila and the dog sled back home to 1023 Barrett Street.

At the south end of the lake, three 3-story houses took up

more than a block. The middle house belonged to Dr. (Hand me the Knife) Carlson . . . the family doctor who women afflicted with bad appendix' or gall bladder trouble went to consult. Once Putzer and Sheila reached this end of the lake, they were halfway home to the finish line. The second problem for Putzer came if the other dogs fell by the wayside and Putzer was alone in the lead. Sheila often said, "Putzer is no leader. If he gets out in front, he'll just keep looking back for the rest of the hounds."

Alice, the family skeptic decided to return the conversation to the race, and said "What makes you think Putzer will be in front?"

"I don't know if he will be in front," Sheila jumped on this critic.

"When he gets to Maryland Avenue, Sheila," said Joseph, "Look for me and I'll run ahead of him. "

"You can't do that," said Sheila. "The race officials will yell FOUL."

Maryland Street dead-ended into the lake and the racetrack. "No official will be that far from the finish line . . . it's over a mile away," volunteered Harry. He felt particularly qualified to comment since he frequently ran around the lake for exercise, and knew the precise distance from point-to-point.

"If he slows down, I'll pick up the sled and run myself," and Sheila meant this final tone to end the conversation. Putting on her coat, Sheila went out with Putzer for one more practice run around the Lake Como racetrack.

Aunt Rose took exception to all this talk about the dog racing. "My God," she said. "You are talking about a dog race and right now they are burying your father at Calvary." She had come to the Barrett house late for the funeral but early for the food. She was the housekeeper for the Pastor at the oldest church in the State of Minnesota located in Mendota—a beautiful New England looking church—spire and all. Being late for the funeral didn't stop her from her usual two cents worth of conversation . . . and lip. What was most annoying about her lip, though, was that she was correct in her assessment. The family was trying to forget about the death of their breadwinner as soon as possible, and they didn't like being told as much.

"The Pastor thought it was too cold for us to go to the cemetery and that is why we are here." answered Martha, as always defending her children.

Aunt Rose decided to try a new line of thought: "Martha, do you still want me to play the piano?"

"Of course," said Martha.

Rose was about to play when Alice asked her, "Do you still play the only song you know—the Black Widow Waltz?"

"It is not the Black Widow Waltz—it is the *Black Hawk Waltz*", corrected Rose. She appeared to be insulted. "I only play that because it is the only one I have ever mastered."

Alice advised, "I don't think this is the time for the Black Widow Waltz, do you Rose?"

"Well, Alice, you have been taking all those fancy lessons at the St. Joseph Music School, what can you play?" asked Rose, "and it is Black Hawk, not Black Widow, Waltz."

"I can play Chopin's Piano Concerto by heart".

"Which one?" demanded Rose?

"I didn't know there was more than one," replied Alice.

The phone rang. Martha answered before anyone could get to it. "She isn't here now. She has taken the dog to the park."

"Is that the nun again?" Alice asked gingerly.

"Yes, be quiet. I can't hear what she is saying," said Martha. Then Martha responded to her caller with "We don't know yet how we will manage."

Alice couldn't help but getting involved. "You know she is after Sheila to be a nun again."

"How do you know there is anything wrong in being a nun?" was Rose's reentry into the foray. Since she had been living like a nun ever since her husband had run off and left her with a young four-year old boy, she felt particularly qualified to offer an opinion on the subject.

"Keep out of this Rose," cautioned Martha. She knew Rose would speak her mind even when it didn't concern her. With a hurt look on her face, Rose walked to the piano and began playing the *Black Hawk Waltz*.

Just then Peter came down from the upstairs all dressed in his new Western Union uniform. Rose stopped playing the piano and with a laugh cried, "Where in the world did you get that uniform and why are you wearing it?"

"I start delivering telegrams tomorrow", said Peter. "I thought I would try on the uniform to make sure it fits." And with that, he clicked his heels.

"You need a bike for that, don't you?" asked Rose.

"I have a bike."

"How could you afford one?"

"Dad got it for me on my birthday."

"Why?"

"Because I gave up smoking," proudly replied Peter.

Martha interrupted Rose's flow of questions with "He's going to make money delivering Western Union Telegrams."

But Rose broke through again with . . . "Ride a bike in the snow and cold?"

"Why not?" bravely retorted Peter.

"I have to carry papers in the same weather Peter will have for delivering telegrams, so what's the big deal?" interjected Harry.

"It's easier to walk through a snow drift than ride a bike through one," answered Rose. She just wouldn't give up.

"Well, I have to leave now and deliver the afternoon papers, please continue the debate without me" said Harry. And off he went to the basement to dress for the deliveries.

You may wonder why Harry had to deliver newspapers a second time the day of his father's funeral. In 1927, the St. Paul public's primary form of information was the newspaper. Television wouldn't be popular in the home for another 20 years (even though it was first publicly demonstrated in 1927), and even the radio wouldn't be expected to impart information of substance until FDR began his fireside chats in the next decade. As a result, daily newspapers were THE source of information. You just had to look at the one page ad for the papers that ran every Sunday:

YOU GET THE NEWS RIGHT DOWN TO THE MINUTE
WITHOUT A BREADTH'S DELAY
FROM THE 12 HOUR NEWSPAPERS

ST PAUL PIONEER PRESS
ST PAUL DISPATCH

NO EXAGGGERATIONS
NO GUESS WORK
NO SECOND-HAND INFORMATION
NO PARTISANSHIP

Every morning you could hear young paperboys in downtown St. Paul carrying an armful of papers calling out teasers like "Extra, Extra, Hot off the Press . . . Read all about it . . . City Council votes to raise property taxes". A paper from one of these street vendors cost 2 cents each. To inform the public at home, there were young boys like Harry McCool who covered a prescribed route in their neighborhoods delivering papers door to door. Home delivered newspapers cost only 1 cent each. Depending upon how compelling the headline of the day, a businessman might grab a paper from a downtown hawker, or await delivery of the evening newspaper.

On Sundays, the newspapers were combined into a veritable masterpiece. There were special sections on Real Estate, the Home, and Travel, to name a few. In addition, The Sunday paper usually ran a current novel from a popular author in installments. Readers would not only receive the latest news, but they would also be culturally enlightened.

So as to meet the demand for more timely access to news that broke around the clock, St. Paul produced two newspapers every day, namely the St. Paul Pioneer Press for morning delivery, and the St. Paul Dispatch for evening delivery. As you can now see, Harry had a most important job: deliver the news. Just then he returned from the basement. With no further ado, he threw a scarf over his mouth and slammed the door before the wind did, on the way to delivering the Dispatch.

With Harry gone, Rose decided to return to the convent discussion. She prodded Martha with, "Don't you realize, Martha, that you would have one less mouth to feed with Sheila in a convent?"

"Rose, what I do with my children is my business. You are in no position to help me, are you?" Marsha couldn't help but ask old busy body this question. What annoyed her, though, wasn't so much that Rose interrupted, but that Rose was probably correct. Martha was quite frightened about how she would manage the family without James's income and didn't appreciate Rose airing the crux of her problem.

"Martha, that is no way to talk to me. You know I don't have any money." And these remarks came from a new conciliatory Rose.

Martha's stubborn Danish came to the front now. "If I want your advice on how to bring up my children, I'll ask for it. Don't tell me what Sheila should or shouldn't do. If she wants to be a nun, that is fine with me." Martha turned away from Rose, and began to clear the table of dishes, conversation over.

Just then the superintendent of cemeteries knocked on the door. Peter answered it. "Tell your mother the burial is over," the superintendent shouted into the house.

"Is that it?" said Peter.

"Yes," replied the superintendent . . . and with that he left for his car in front of the house. As the Packard's tires spun in the snow, the roar of the engine took the car and the superintendent into the middle of the road and safely away.

Rose let out a sigh and said "Well, Martha, I am leaving. I have to get Father Timothy's dinner. And besides, there is nothing more I can do here." (Besides playing the piano, she had done nothing). Even though she had her coat on, she wasn't through with the nun discussion. Rose kept after Martha. "Do you know the vows Sheila will have to take to be a nun?"

"How would you know?" interrupted Alice.

"Father Timothy talks to me while I am feeding him. He is very informed about the life of the nuns" answered Rose.

"How would a pastor know?" asked Martha.

Alice clarified with "He is supposed to know, mom, that's why. Those nuns tell all their sins in the confessional, and then all their personal issues out of the confessional. Harry is out delivering papers now, Rose, but he knows even more than you do about nuns because he serves for them at Mass all the time. "

"What do you mean he serves for them?" asked Rose.

"The nuns are responsible for assigning altar boys as servers for mass. They tell Harry when it is his turn to serve mass, that is what I mean," angrily returned Alice.

"What does that have to do with knowing about a nun's life? Have they told him about the vows a nun must take?" wondered Rose.

"Why would they tell him that?" responded Alice.

"Well, I can tell you, they take the vows of **Obedience, Poverty, and Chastity**", Rose volunteered sassily.

"I'll tell you the one vow she will have no trouble with and that is *poverty*," interjected Martha. "Sheila is an absolute miser when it comes to spending money on anything."

Just then in came Harry after finishing his afternoon paper route. "Rose still here?" he asked with a quick glance around the living room. Rose was not his favorite aunt. One time he considered her like a Pekinese dog: small, fat and always yapping, biting, and nipping at your feet.

"Yes I am still here," Rose answered as she came into the living room from the kitchen. "But I'll be leaving soon . . . I am not through telling your mother what vows a nun must take. Poverty means they can never own anything and obedience means to do whatever their nun superior tells them do to."

"Are you through now?" asked Martha.

"And don't forget chastity?" added Alice. Rose looked at Alice with a leer and slammed the door as she left.

"How will she get back home?" asked Martha. "Can't the boys give her a ride?"

"She would rather take the streetcar," replied Alice.

"The streetcar doesn't go to Mendota," offered Harry.

"How did she get here?" asked Alice.

"Her son drove her here," said Martha.

"Where is he now?"

"Back home." replied Martha. The concern about Rose ended. If her son was going to strand her at Martha's home, why should they feel responsible?

Soon thereafter Sheila came home from the warm up run around the lake. Her scarf was iced and she was cold in every bone. Putzer went to the basement door looking for a quick trip to the furnace. "How did the practice run go around the lake?" asked Harry.

"He still won't take off and lead," said Sheila, in a way disgusted.

"You know what that means," said Harry.

"It means he won't win, he'll always be behind the lead dog," sighed Sheila. "And that will be the German Shepherd who won last year's race."

"How can we teach him to lead?" asked Harry. "It seems like your only choice is to get someone to lead him around the lake. Any volunteers?"

"Not me," emphasized Peter.

"Let's ask Rose. Get her to come back in," continued Peter. "If she runs as fast as she walks, lets have her lead. Putzer can't miss if he stays with her."

"That is not funny," scolded Martha. "She means well." Despite her own differences with Rose, Martha wanted her children to behave with respect towards adults. She knew that Christian charity was an essential component of a good Catholic's character, and she meant to have all her children develop good character. It was one thing for her to argue with Rose to her face, but she didn't want her children using Rose as a punching bag in her absence.

"What do they do to make rabbits run?" said Peter, realizing that discussing Rose was now off limits.

"They shoot at them with a shot gun." said the always loquacious, if sometimes misinformed, Harry.

"Maybe Sheila can tell us what she plans," said Martha who decided to bring an end to this whole conversation.

Just when Martha and the children thought that Rose had gone home . . . she came back knocking at the door. "Let me in. A street car won't be by for another 20 minutes." And for the next 10 minutes, she told Martha again all about being a nun:

"Remember my mother Molly, Martha? She wanted me to be a nun when I was just 14 years old. It even went so far that the nuns from the Mankato convent came to take me. You are just a convert, Martha," A true fact. "I'll tell you what it means. It means you must take the vows of *Obedience, Poverty and, Chastity*. They told me that I could never have a bank account. I could never have anything I could call my own. I could not own a car and I would live in a convent the rest of my life. And you know what obedience meant? I would have to do whatever my sister superior told me to do. She could send me as far away from home as Washington, 1,000 miles from here on Barrett Street. That's what obedience will mean to Sheila. And you know what Chastity means? . . . You can never kiss a boy! Even if you wanted to. I refused to go, especially since I liked Bernard our neighbor on the next 40 acres who I knew was the best dancer in the whole county. Remember all this Martha." Rose finished her monologue and buckled up her coat for the second time and left.

As she left, she said, "Tell Bobby (her son) to pick me up at 7:00 P.M. at the end of the 7th Street streetcar line when he calls."

On Rose's final departure, Harry sighed a great relief. Rose was one relative that Harry never minded leaving. The family spent the next couple of hours avoiding any more discussions about the convent or the death of their father. The Catholic funeral and reception for James McCool this cold day in January of 1927 formed a powerful image in Harry's mind. For years to come, he considered the McCool's stoic behavior at the funeral of their father the proper demeanor at the death of a loved one.

4

THE GREAT COMO PARK DOG RACE

Como Park Pavilion

Putzer

Como Lake was just a hop, skip and a jump from Martha's house on Barrett Street. Go out the front door, turn left, and hop for one hundred yards. Next skip over the Northern Pacific railroad tracks. Finally one "jump" of fifty yards and you reached Como Lake.

Before Martha and James moved to Barrett, they lived near Rice Street on Galtier. But in 1914 a real estate salesman told them for an up-and-coming couple, the place to get to was Como Park or as near to it as possible. The salesman went on and on about the Como Park area, and left brochures that read:

COMO LAKE

The Department of Natural Resources reports excellent bass fishing and walleyes on Como Lake. Only bass and walleye over 16 inches long are permitted to be removed and only electric trolling motors are allowed on City lakes.

COMO LAKE SIDE PAVILION

Concerts and plays are offered regularly throughout the summer at the Como Lake Side Pavilion. Featured also—full service restaurant, banquet room and paddleboard rentals.

COMO CONSERVATORY

A variety of seasonal flowers are offered throughout the year in the Como Conservatory.
This facility is available for wedding sites, should there be a need for one.

COMO BAND BOX

A walkway connects the Lakeside Pavilion to a floating bandbox. It is here that local bands perform outstanding concerts, in the summer of course.

COMO LAKE SHORE DRIVE

Miles of paths surround the Lake.
In the summer there are bicycle races and baby-buggy contests

> *. . . And for the young, pavement dances.*
> *In the winter, there are dog races.*
>
> ### YET TO COME—*COMO ZOO*
>
> *There will soon be a zoo with large cats, like Siberian tigers, African lions, snow leopards and cougars. The zoo will also house Hoofed stock barn bison, mountain goats, African crowned cranes, Aquatic animals, polar bears, penguins, diving birds, seals and sea lions. There will be a Monkey island, amusement rides, wolf woods, gorillas and orangutans in their outdoor displays plus a real Japanese Garden!*

After he finished reading the brochure, the real estate salesman told about skating on Lake Como and dog races in the snow in the winter. The McCools were hooked, and a master plan was formed: save every penny to buy a home in Como Park. James gave Martha a red bound ledger, which she used to record every single expenditure made for the family. For two years, James and Martha pinched every penny. Finally, in February of 1916, their chance came. James had been watching the development of the Como Park area and he noticed a foreclosure sign on the lot at 1023 Barrett Street. After some quick analysis, James learned that the lot owner, a Mr. Elmer Jorgonson, needed a quick sale to escape some overpowering debt. James approached Elmer, and within one month he had the lot and the two-story bungalow for the sum of $1000 plus the assumption of back taxes from 1913 and a $1000 mortgage. Here in the middle of winter in 1927 was where SHEILA McCOOL was to seek the crown "Queen of the Mushers"!

The racetrack around the lake was cemented in Sheila's mind. The competition was also firmly fixed in Sheila's mind. She knew that Daddy Long Leg's dog, a German Shepherd named KARL, with MARIA mushing, would be out in front like a year ago. It would take a miracle to pass her. If, by some minor miracle, PUTZER did pass her, he would stop for her to go ahead again. This big German Shepherd carried a light sled, and with MARIA only weighing 90 pounds, the dog could "run like the wind", according to Harry.

On the eve of the race, Harry and Joseph got going on a plan to make SHEILA the winner. Harry started the conversation with "We have to do something about Sheila's chances tomorrow."

"Like what?" Joe asked.

"It will be up to you, Joe, to make sure that Putzer gets off to a good start" returned Harry.

"It's your idea Harry. Why is it up to me?"

"I can't be at the starting gate and the halfway point too," explained Harry.

"Why are you going to be at the halfway point when the race starts?" asked Joe.

"Genevieve wants me to watch the race from her house."

"You mean the doctor's daughter?"

This reply was irritating to Harry because Joe knew who she was, and that she lived in the last house on the boulevard, on the paper route. "You know, the girl in my class who lives at the half way mark of the race down on the south end of the lake."

This worried Joe. He cautioned Harry "That could be a mistake. Don't let Putzer see you. If he does, he will run over to you and forget all about the rest of the race for the *Queen of the Mushers*".

"I'll make sure he doesn't see me." This reply from Harry didn't take too well with Joe. He knew Harry would be bragging about *his* dog, PUTZER—especially if Putzer was running first at the time.

"I'll make sure SHEILA gets off and running at the start" guaranteed Joe. "So don't you hurt their chances down at the half way marker with one mile still to go."

Harry ignored the slight and continued with his plan: "If Daddy Long Leg's dog, KARL is ahead at the half way marker, I am sure PUTZER won't be far behind. "

"What can we do then?" asked Joe.

"The only way I know," said Harry, "is to get KARL into a fight with some other dog."

In a hopeless voice Joe said "But all the other dogs will be one quarter mile behind."

"The only chance then," smiled Harry, "is to bring an outside dog in that doesn't like KARL."

"How can we do that?"

"I know of the perfect dog for the task, but unfortunately it belongs to Genevieve, which is why I have to be at her home." Harry really wasn't all that anxious to spend time at Genevieve's home, but was willing to make the sacrifice for his sister.

"How do you know that?" asked Joe.

"Last summer Genevieve asked me to go on her bicycle with her for a ride around Como Lake. She brought her dog BARCLEY to run along side the bike. We went by Daddy Long Leg's house and last year's winner, KARL, was out in the yard. BARCLEY and KARL got into a horrible fight. It took Daddy Long Legs, Genevieve and me five minutes to break them apart. Really Joe, it was a five minute job."

"Are you saying?" asked Joe, "That if KARL is in the lead at the halfway mark, you will bring Genevieve's dog BARCLEY to fight KARL?"

"Now you understand my strategy, Joe."

"What does SHEILA think of that?"

"I haven't told SHEILA," confessed Harry.

"Do you think that is fair?" asked Joe.

"I don't know if that is fair. It isn't like a horse race which is most certainly unfair since according to Peter you can fix the jockey," said Harry. Peter, being 6 years older than Harry, was Harry's prime source of worldly wisdom in matters of the 'street'. Harry continued with "But I really want Sheila to win, so I came up with this plan."

When Harry made this comment about horse racing, Joe couldn't help asking, "What do you know about horse races being fixed?"

"I only know what I read in the papers that I deliver each morning and night, and, of course, what Peter says."

After this smart remark by Harry, Joe shook his head in bewilderment over his younger brother's logic and said: "I intend to be in two places, I'll be at the starting gate to make sure SHEILA and PUTZER get off and running. After the start of the race, I will go back east of the Pavilion across the skating rink and be at the spot one half mile short of the finish line."

"Why do you need to be in two places if I am going to man the halfway point at Genevieve's home? How are you going to be of help near the end of the race?" asked Harry.

"If SHEILA and PUTZER are still in the race, I will make sure they get to the finish line by running ahead of them so PUTZER can follow someone right to the end." And this statement by Joe ran on the great supposition that PUTZER would follow him instead of looking for the other dogs.

Harry didn't like this stratagem at all. "You can't run ahead of PUTZER to the finish line. You know Daddy Long Legs will be watching the end like he always does, with his binoculars. If he sees you do that he will have the officials disqualify PUTZER and SHEILA."

Joe said: "Do you mean he will be in that upside down ice cream cone shaped house on top of his porch?"

Harry replied: "That is where he is every year. It is not called an ice cream cone shaped house. Mom made me look it up last year in the dictionary, and it is called a 'cupola'. He sits with his binoculars at one of the three windows on the bottom of this cupola to watch the race."

"What can he see from there?" asked Joe.

"He can see the start of the race, the dogs running right on past the Bridal Bridge, past the 'Lady of the Lake' in her winter boarded covers, and then on down to where the dogs go right by his house. But once by his house, he loses track of the dogs because of the many turns in the road. He won't pick up much of a view until the first turn for the finish—just at the bridge that goes over the Lagoon. "

"Why is he spying on the girl's dog race anyway?" asked Joe.

"Because he has his daughter running again, and she will be atop KARL just like last year when they won. In fact, his German Shepherd, KARL, has won the race three year's in a row," and this was said by Harry with deep sorrow in his voice.

"You mean if anything looks illegal he will cry 'FOUL' if little MARIA on KARL loses the race?" Joe asked in disbelief.

Harry said, "This is the last year he will have a daughter young enough to qualify for the race. As a result, he is very anxious that his dog KARL wins."

"How many dogs besides PUTZER will be running?"

"It's a crowded field. There will be seven all together," said Harry. "And the reason I know is that SHEILA found out the field yesterday from Andy Johnson."

"Our neighbor starts the race?" asked Joe slightly surprised.

"You know he always does that," returned Harry.

"He won't be starting it off with the shotgun that he uses on New Year's Eve, will he?"

"They won't allow that. It will be his usual—get ready, get set, GO" corrected Harry.

With that last go, Martha came into the room and said, "It's time to go to bed, especially for you Harry. Five o'clock in the morning is just seven hours away. You need your rest to deliver the morning paper." No argument from either Harry or Joe, and off they went to bed.

On the next morning, the temperature had risen to 25 degrees above zero. This was a very good temperature for the seven dogs and their seven sled riders. On the race day morning, Harry took PUTZER with him on his paper route to get the dog acclimated to the temperature of the day. Martha met Harry on his return. She angrily said, "Don't you think you should have rested PUTZER before he runs in today's race for *Queen of the Mushers*?"

Harry said, "I just got him warmed up."

"Worn out is more like what you have done" returned Martha.

Harry always felt uncomfortable when his mother criticized him, especially when he felt that his actions were justified. As a result, he explained, "PUTZER started to howl when I left without him. And you know how long Alice would have stood that. I thought it better to take him and keep her from storming down from the upstairs at 5:00 A.M. and getting everybody out of bed."

"Well, she does get upset," agreed Martha. "I guess that was very thoughtful of you Harry, sorry."

Harry was taken aback momentarily by his mom's apology. She rarely shared her feelings, and even more rarely admitted mistakes. Nevertheless he recovered to say, "Apology accepted, Mom."

"Eat your cream of wheat and when you are through with breakfast, go down and throw more coal on the fire." Harry felt relieved at this comment. Giving orders was more like his mother!

SHEILA walked into the kitchen—She had on tennis shoes all ready for the big race. "What in the world are you doing with tennis shoes on at below freezing?" said Martha in a scolding tone of voice.

"I might have to run most of the race if PUTZER somehow gets in the lead," answered SHEILA. She knew that this question was coming, and had prepared a ready reply. "I couldn't possibly keep up if I was wearing overshoes. Besides, the course is packed down, and I don't really need the boots."

"If we get the lead," continued SHEILA, "he'll wait for the other dogs to catch up to him. Remember PUTZER is a follower. If that happens, I'll have to pick up the sled and coax Putzer to run the rest of the way around the lake. That's why I am wearing the tennis shoes."

"So you think PUTZER will be leading?" asked Harry.

"I said **IF** he gets out in front at the start, he'll just wait for the rest of the pack so he can have someone to follow."

"Why?" asked Harry, even though he knew the answer.

"He just won't lead—he is a follower—just like you Harry. You follow Joe everywhere he goes. That is right, isn't it Joe?" asked Sheila.

"That's right, Sheila," replied Joe, "Harry is my protégé. I intend on teaching him everything I know," as he winked at Harry.

"Would that include how to get into the *trouble* that seems to be your middle name?" asked Sheila.

"I don't call it trouble, I call it exploring the world," answered Joe with a laugh.

Harry objected to the follower remark, so he interjected "Listen Sheila, the only time I ever followed Joe is when he showed me the paper route." Harry had inherited his paper route from his older brother Joe, who had inherited it from their oldest brother Peter. Harry really did follow his older brother, but didn't want everyone implying that he was an easily influenced lackey.

Martha couldn't take much more of this bickering and said:

"SHEILA, eat your breakfast. You'll need a big one for that run around the lake."

"Please, Mother, heat up my Orphan Annie's Ovaltine" cajoled Sheila. Like most of the youngsters of the day, Sheila was seduced by the high sugar content of this 'Breakfast Drink', and thought that because it was hot and tasted great, it must be good for her.

"Put in a cup for PUTZER, Mother. He is the one doing the work pulling the sled with SHEILA on it" advised Harry.

Peter now came into the kitchen. He had on his new Western Union uniform. Peter said to Joe, "I hope you didn't drink my raw milk again today like you did yesterday."

Harry said to Joe: "You know what will happen to you by drinking that raw milk, don't you? "

"I'll get Tuberculosis. right?" came back Joe.

"Stop that nonsense about tuberculosis. What is the difference if Peter doesn't like his milk pasteurized, let him drink it raw." This response from Martha was somewhat out of character, since she was usually overly protective of her children, and might be expected to question the danger of drinking raw milk. No one in the family ever asked Peter why he liked the milk raw.

All his relatives, farmers and everyone, from Mankato couldn't drink milk no matter how it came. Peter was heard to say to his neighbor friend, Maggie Horn, in a moment of braggadocio, "I have never met a farm girl yet who could drink any kind of milk, raw or pasteurized. "

Maggie had responded jealously with "How many farm girls do you know living right here in the middle of St. Paul?" Peter never could answer that smart question from Maggie, so he had let the subject die.

Just as SHEILA finished her breakfast, Alice's step could be heard coming down the stairs. She stormed into the room. And with her entrance, all became silent. Alice, being the oldest child, commanded a level of fear and respect from her younger siblings. She lashed out with "I heard PUTZER howling at 5:00 this morning. Where is he now?" Alice didn't bother to say good morning or hello even to her mother.

"He's resting for the big race . . . right now he is in the basement by the furnace." replied Harry, never too afraid to speak his mind.

"Alice, I see you have been down in the Golden Rule basement bargain room again," Martha changed the conversation.

"This hand made silk dress came from the Philippines", replied Alice. And with that answer she changed her tune from angry to happy. She spun around, smile on her face, expecting all to enjoy her wardrobe.

"It must have cost a small fortune?" inquired Peter.

"If you call $1.49 a fortune."

"To me that is a fortune. That is about what I make a day delivering telegrams," replied Peter.

To add more fire on the fire, Alice bragged. "These Princess slippers cost 79 cents. I don't wear anything but the best."

"Mom, we aren't going to end up the poorhouse because dad died, are we?" asked Harry. Just that morning there had been an article in the newspaper about the Ramsey County Poor Farm. It was located altogether too close to home for Harry's comfort in Maplewood. He never wanted to end up having other people feel sorry for him, and having to live in the poorhouse was a certain ticket to just this type of shame.

"No, Harry. I think we have more than enough income to manage without your father" answered Martha. "Remember, your sister only spends her own money. She doesn't take anything away from household essentials."

This didn't stop Harry from continuing the grilling of Alice. "You do get things from all over the world don't you Alice? Tell us where your gloves came from. I saw them on the dining room table last night and they had a Puerto Rican label on them," remarked Harry.

"Keep you hands off my clothes and mind your own business Harry," was the quick reply from Alice.

"Well, did they come from Puerto Rico?" persisted Harry.

Martha set the record straight. "She finds those bargains in the Golden Rule bargain basement. Alice, eat your breakfast. We have to clean up the kitchen before we get PUTZER ready for the race."

"What race?"

"The big Como Park Dog Race is today," SHEILA said with

hurt feelings that Alice didn't remember about her big race of the day.

"Is the whole family going down to see her off?" asked Alice.

"Evidently everybody but you, Alice," said Martha.

"Mother, don't you think you should stay home away from the cold?" Alice asked.

Martha returned with, "I am just going down to the edge of the Lake. I have made arrangements to watch the race with Mother Superior."

"She's up to getting SHEILA into the convent, isn't she?" asked a concerned Alice. If Sheila left for the convent, someone would have to pick up the slack and do all the chores that Sheila performed. More work around the house didn't appeal in the least to Alice. Well, thought, Alice, if Sheila goes off to the convent, I had better light a fire under Clayton Moore at the bakery. Maybe I can even get him to propose marriage to me this summer at the Pavilion?

"I suppose that is why she wants me to watch the race with her," responded Martha.

"What have you decided to do with SHEILA about joining the convent?" asked Alice.

"I think a lot of it has to do with SHEILA. You know she always talks about being a nun," replied Martha.

"She is not old enough to decide. You know she has to get your approval," cautioned Alice.

"The only thing she will miss here is the dog, PUTZER." And this came from worldly Peter.

"From the looks of some of those heavy set nuns, she won't ever go hungry," interjected Harry. He couldn't help saying this because his teacher in school was—as far as he could tell from what was underneath the gaberdine she had on—as big as a St. Bernard dog.

"That is not a nice thing to say, Harry," said his mother.

"Sorry, ma," humbly returned Harry.

"I wonder how SHEILA will get along with the vows she will have to take—like Obedience, Poverty, and Chastity?" asked Alice.

"When did you learn about the vows?" asked Peter.

"I've learned about the vows from SHEILA—one night she told me." Alice explained.

Joe interrupted the flow with "It's a good thing Alice isn't in line for the monastery. The way she needs clothes she couldn't pass poverty."

"That is enough conversation about vows and SHEILA—right now we better get ready for the big race," said Martha. With that last comment by Martha, the family scattered. Alice went back to bed, Peter went to the Western Union office, Joe headed for the starting gate by the Como Pavilion, and Harry headed for Genevieve's home. Martha got ready to go down to the Lake and meet the Mother Superior, and SHEILA headed for the Lake with PUTZER.

As Sheila started for the lake, Andy Johnson, their next door neighbor and the Commissioner of Parks and Playgrounds, offered Sheila a ride in his Essex. To save energy, she took the offer. She climbed in the front seat, and put Putzer and the sled in the back seat. Andy owned a tire shop near downtown and his specialty was retreading old tires for reuse. One year he lost his job as Commissioner and the next year his campaign slogan was "You retired me and now I want you to let me *retire* you while you *rehire* me." Evidently the populace liked his self-effacing humor, and besides buying a ton of tires, they reelected him.

Andy printed a complete program for the girl's dog race with his name at the bottom after the list of participants. "SHEILA' asked Andy. "Do you want to see who is in the race with you today?"

SHEILA came back with "I know who I have to beat. You told me yesterday Mr. Johnson."

Andy wanted to show off his handy work, so he ignored Sheila's comment and continued with "There are seven dogs altogether. Here, take a look at my program." And with that remark, Andy handed her the program:

ENTRIES FOR THE GREAT COMO PARK GIRL'S DOG RACE ARE LISTED WITH THE BREED OF THE DOG . . . THE GIRL RIDER'S NAME AND THE DOG OWNER.

The Old Como Gang Long Gone

DOG #1   PUTZER   Mongrel from the Dog Pound
                RIDER   SHEILA McCOOL
                OWNER   SHEILA AND HARRY McCOOL

DOG #2   KARL   German Shepherd—Police Dog
                RIDER   MARIA SCHMIDT
                OWNER   DADDY LONG LEGS SCHMIDT

DOG #3   NINA   Irish Setter
                RIDER   SOPHIA ZACARDI
                OWNER   CLARENCE ZACARDI

DOG #4   ALICE   Native Siberian Samoyed—Primarily a sled dog
                RIDER   AMANDA SCANLON
                OWNER   GEORGE SCANLON

DOG #5   SNIFFEY   Blood Hound
                RIDER   ROSIE RASH
                OWNER   MRS. RAY RASH

DOG #6   OLE   Great Dane—Primarily a watch dog—not a runner
                RIDER   ERNIE JENSEN
                OWNER   ERNIE JENSEN

DOG #7   RUBY   A rare 2 foot Airdale
                RIDER   RALPH TRAIN
                OWNER   GILBERT (aka CHOO CHOO) TRAIN

DOGS ENTERED AND IN THE WINGS IN CASE OF NO SHOWS:

POINTER   PARTRIDGE HUNTER HOLDS BODY RIGID ON SPYING GAME. DISQUALIFIED LAST YEAR BECAUSE AT THE SOUND OF THE STARTING GUN THE DOG NEVER LEFT THE STARTING GATE BUT STOOD POINTING AT ANDY JOHNSON.

MIKE   SHETLAND SHEEP DOG—ANDY RULED OUT OF PRIME LINEUP THIS YEAR FOR FEAR DOG NOT BIG ENOUGH TO RUN WITH THE LARGER HOUNDS—1.8 MILE TRACK TOO LONG FOR THIS SHEEPHERDER.

GEORGE   GREYHOUND—TOO FAST FOR OTHER

	DOGS—RAN THE DISTANCE IN RECORD TIME LAST YEAR WITHOUT HIS RIDER WHO SLIPPED OFF THE SLED AT THE STARTING GATE. DISQUALIFIED FOR NOT FINISHING WITH RIDER ON BOARD SLED.
FRED	BOSTON TERRIER BRED PRIMARILY FOR PIT FIGHTING—NOT DOG SLED RACING. DISQUALIFIED BECAUSE AS ANDY SAID, "I JUST DON'T LIKE HIS LOOKS."

The owners of the alternative dogs POINTER, MIKE, GREYHOUND GEORGE AND FRED, the Boston Terrier, will bring their dogs just in case one of the seven chosen doesn't show up. SHEILA handed the Program back to Andy. "Pretty impressive, Mr. Johnson, you really did a lot of research on the entrants. Thanks for letting me see the program."

"You are entirely welcome," replied Andy. He continued with "Did your brothers sharpen up those runners on your sled?"

"Yes, Peter did his usual sharpening job. The runners are as smooth as silk."

"Smooth as silk, eh?"

"He gave me his usual big brother advice. Even though he has never been in a dog race himself."

"What advice was that?" asked Andy.

"Stay warm."

When they arrived at the Lake, Joe came up to the car to help SHEILA take her dog and sled to the line. "Let's keep PUTZER away from the rest of the dogs. I don't want any fights before the race even begins." And this from Joe who usually wasn't partial at all for SHEILA.

Como Park spectators were agog at this great event of the day. On this Saturday, the second to the last Saturday in the month of January—nothing else took place. Joe took SHEILA's sled by the hand, and led her to the front of the Pavilion by the Band Box where the race would begin as soon as Andy Johnson got all the seven dogs in line. Interestingly enough, all seven of the original entries had shown up.

Many sporting events took place during the month of January in and around the Lake, but the only event this Saturday was the dog race. Extending out into the lake from the main Pavilion was the BANDBOX. This summer bandstand was connected to the main Pavilion by a wooden walkway. It was here in this BANDBOX that the local police band gave concerts "in the good old summer time". Summer time in St. Paul came in June, July and August. Not just the 4th of July as told to visitors (or expected visitors) from the South or East by local braggers who liked to boast about the saintly city's arctic weather.

The BOX stood on wooden legs sunk deep into the Lake's bottom very near the shoreline where the water depth was shallow. The theory was that any tipsy band member falling off the runway couldn't drown in just four feet of water. This theory was tested one year when the first violinist missed a few notes during *AMERICA THE BEAUTIFUL*, and fell into the lake. All that happened to the poor violinist was that he got stuck in the mud. The concept proved sound.

Very few spectators who came to watch the dog race stood even near the BANDBOX nor on the second level of the Pavilion. Even though the day was mild for late January, many crowded into the warming house down in the ground level of the Pavilion. True Minnesotans know to stay near any heat source whenever possible in the winter. This forethought in a cold climate helps contribute to the high longevity rate of the people in the state.

The Como Park Pavilion was not a Greek classical structure, but then no kid from the old Como Gang would have known the difference. The 14-pillar building did what it had to do. Namely, keep half-frozen St. Paulites warm if they could find space in the always-crowded warming house. Down in the warming house, one could keep from freezing temperatures and escape the cold, cold north winds.

On this day for the great race, the hardy spectators (those outside) stood three deep along the first 100 yards of the snow and ice covered racetrack, totaling at least three hundred people. Among the hardy teeth clacking group stood 11 sisters from the St. Andrews parish nunnery. Among this group stood their cheerleader, Sister Bernadine. She knew the weather and was dressed in total black with a white scarf over her neck. Heaven only knew what she wore under this array of nunnery garb. When SHEILA would race past these nuns she would certainly hear Sister Bernadine's bell ringing voice traveling like a sharp gunshot under water. And this would be heard through her single pleated garment held in place by a forehead band. Meanwhile Martha was standing with the Mother Superior at the south end turn in the road. Here the two would decide SHEILA's fate after the race.

"The Mother Superior is no piece of cake," claimed Peter who once was caught smoking in the boy's bathroom by Yeno, the baseball coach. Yeno told the nun everything that went wrong everywhere in the school, including Peter's smoking incident. Peter was far more worried about facing Mother Superior than having to listen to coach Yeno's admonitions. One day Peter heard Yeno say about the Mother Superior "The management in Mankato made her a superior because she couldn't get along with the rest of the nuns." Fortunately this bit of wisdom from Yeno never did make it back to Mother Superior.

The clock now struck 10:00 A.M. Andy Johnson blew the whistle for all the riders, dogs and sleds to get ready for the start of the race. Everyone was in his or her place. Harry was with Genevieve at the mile mark on the southeast end of the Lake—Joe was at the starting point. After the dogs were gone, Joe would head for the north side of the lake where there was just a quarter of a mile to go to the finish. Martha was with Mother Superior at the first turn that headed along the backstretch, a mile and a quarter to go.

Daddy Long Legs Schmidt, in an unusual twist, was at the Dr. Rudolph Schiffman spray fountain just 100 yards down from the starting line. He wanted to make sure that this daughter, MARIA, on the favorite, KARL, the German Shepherd police dog, wouldn't head for home but continue on around the Lake.

Joe gave his last minute advice to SHEILA, "Stay on the left side of the street path—It's the shortest way around the lake." Thanks to unknown friends on the racing committee, SHEILA drew the number 1 lane and would start on the inside track nearest the lake. KARL drew number 7 and in between came all the rest of the entrants.

The brother of Greyhound George's owner called Andy Johnson, the official starter, aside before the race. "George didn't arrive last night from Florida so you can take him off as a maybe fill-in. The owner, Al Michael, my brother, doesn't want him up here in the north. Last year's entry caught pneumonia and died on the train back to Florida. You know how fragile these greyhounds are."

Andy couldn't help but notice that the other three fill-ins showed up, namely POINTER the PARTRIDGE HUNTER, MIKE the Shetland sheep dog, and Fred, the Boston Terrier. Andy said, "Remember that to win you must leave the starting line on top of your sled, travel the entire course around the lake, and be on top of your sled when you cross the finish line."

"All is in readiness," so announced Andy Johnson's wife, Esther. She was an English teacher at Washington High School three miles down the road from the Como track.

Andy acknowledged his wife's statement with a nod of his head. He scanned the dogs, the riders, and the crowd, lifted his pistol and yelled, "Get ready—Get set—GO . . . GO." With the last GO, Andy shot off the 4th of July firecracker pistol he had borrowed from his son, Donald.

The Number 4 dog ALICE, the native Siberian Samoyed, got off first and led the others through the Bridal gate. The bridal gate was where young couples exchanged marriage vows in June—that is if they weren't Catholic, in which case they exchanged their vows in nearby St. Andrews Church. In the winter this same gate was covered with snow and icicles and could easily be mistaken for an igloo. KARL, Dog No. 2, was on his tail as they headed for the LADY OF THE LAKE. In the summer, this LADY OF THE LAKE was a fountain, an elegant and costly spray edifice. However, in the winter, this semi-clad lady was covered with a wooden triangular enclosure to protect it from the elements.

Daddy Long Legs was aghast that KARL wasn't leading. He stood screaming at KARL. He wanted KARL the front runner, not second. But here at the beginning of the race was this imported

Samoyed sled dog running first in a race that traditionally belonged to KARL. Meanwhile back at the starting line PUTZER watched as the rest of the dogs took off. Joe hit SHEILA on the back of the head and shouted, "Pick up the sled and start running yourself!"

SHEILA did as Joe told her to do. This prompted PUTZER to take off. As PUTZER whistled past Sheila, she fell onto the sled. By this time SHEILA was ahead only of SNIFFEY who was smelling the air for what direction he should be going. OLE, the Great Dane, went as far as the Bridal gate and stood there and wouldn't let RUBY, the two foot Airedale, pass through it. NINA with Sophia and PUTZER with Sheila aboard were immediately backed up behind the confrontation.

The owner of RUBY, Nick Choo Choo Train, decided to take the matter into his own hands. He ran up to the gate and took OLE by the neck, which wasn't a smart thing to do. When one takes a Great Dane dog by the neck you better make sure you can throw him to the ground. The opposite happened. OLE shook Choo Choo off and tossed him into a nearby snow bank.

While performing this maneuver, however, OLE had left his post at the bridal gate. This opened the course for the rest of the dogs. NINA, the Irish Setter, headed for the Lady of the Lake followed by PUTZER and SHEILA. Choo Choo Train and Ernie Jensen, the owner of OLE, stood arguing while their dogs fought in the snow. Since RUBY and OLE couldn't get back on track, they dropped out of the race. Meanwhile SNIFFEY had whiffed a passing bread truck and headed off in pursuit of the best odor available. This left ALICE, KARL, NINA, and PUTZER to fight for the prize.

As PUTZER passed the nuns from St. Andrews, Sister Bernadine cried out as loud as she could, "Mush you malamutes!" The first grade nun, Helena, wanted to know if *malamute* was a swear word. Sister Bernadine assured her that it wasn't and yelled out in an even a louder voice than before "MUSH YOU MALAMUTES!"

Now the race was truly getting started. ALICE had reached the houses of the elite of Como, the rich families of the men who worked for the Empire Builder, James J. Hill. In January, these houses had a boulevard laden with leafless elms and snow covered oak trees. Named by the frogtown boys (from the French neighborhood south of Calvary Cemetery) as the first pit stop, it didn't slow down ALICE or KARL. Next (75 yards behind) came NINA with SOPHIA followed by PUTZER and SHEILA.

With the first one-half mile of the track completed, the dogs turned east and headed for Harry and Genevieve. Right at the turning point stood Martha and Mother Superior. At the start of the race they had been discussing SHEILA's future as a nun in Mankato. Mother Superior opened the discussion, "What are you going to be doing with all of the children now that James has passed away?"

Martha began with a rundown of the family. "Peter works for the Western Union. Harry and Joseph will continue to carry papers. Alice has just got a degree in accounting and will work beginning this summer for a wholesale bakery. SHEILA will be at home with me and my baby, Mary Helen. "

"Do you have any money from the death of James?"

"We are going to get $2,000 in life insurance," answered Martha.

"How long will that last?"

"The welfare lady tells me that I will be well taken care of if I just give them the $2,000. It will last until the baby reaches 18."

What Martha left out of her story was the difficult time she had deciding how to use the life insurance money. On the one hand, she was loath to part with any money, let alone the sum of $2000. On the other hand, even though she had many years of experience accounting for every penny spent on household needs and saving wherever possible, she didn't really have any idea how much money would be needed to carry her for the next 17 years until Mary Helen came of age. The thought of just handing the $2000 over to an outside entity that would oversee finances seemed very comforting. In fact, she felt a deep calm having the money in someone else's hands, much as if her husband was still there providing the income and security. In the end, this thought of security won out, and she resolved to give the $2000 life insurance to the welfare lady.

Martha was awakened from her reverie by Mother Superior's

next question: "Nothing much there to take care of education for SHEILA, is there?" Mother Superior showed more concern about SHEILA than anyone else.

"SHEILA often talks about being a nun." With this answer, Martha opened the door for the Mother's next offer.

"We can give SHEILA a finishing high school education in Mankato at Good Council."

"It is all right with me if SHEILA is willing to go."

"You just send her over to me on Monday and we'll take it from there," offered the Mother Superior. So here on this wintry day at Como Park, SHEILA's future was pretty well taken care of. And just as this offer from the Mother Superior was made, the front runner in the dog race, KARL and MARIA came racing by followed by ALICE and AMANDA. Daddy Long Legs' admonishment had worked, and KARL had gained the lead.

They had almost reached the half way mark and were fast approaching Harry and Genevieve at the front of the Doctor's house. Harry spotted them and cried "It's KARL and another dog!"

"I don't see PUTZER in sight," cried Genevieve, sounding alarmed. But it didn't matter just then if PUTZER was nearby for what happened next to ALICE and KARL made "Queen of the Mushers" history.

Daddy Long Legs, in his training KARL, had never really stopped him from chasing streetcars. Unfortunately for little MARIA, the Dale/Maryland streetcar line that started and stopped at Maryland and Como was just leaving as the lead dogs and riders arrived. KARL spotted and heard the streetcar, and leapt over the snow bank protecting the track and headed after the streetcar with ALICE right behind him. Harry didn't even have to let loose Barcley to divert KARL.

Right then the race belonged to PUTZER and NINA. They were just coming up to the Doctor's house as KARL and ALICE disappeared, last seen running East on Maryland, headed for Dale Street. PUTZER and NINA whistled past Harry and Genevieve. Harry let out a whoop "Go PUTZER". Fortunately, PUTZER was more interested in NINA and didn't hear Harry. He kept running around the East Side of the lake all the way till the final turn for home.

While all this excitement was happening with the dogs and riders, Joe had run over to the quarter mile finishing line, exactly opposite the Pavilion. Here he waited for SHEILA and PUTZER to encourage them on to the finish. Much to his surprise, the only two dogs in sight were PUTZER and NINA. To deepen the plot, Clarence Zacardi, the owner of NINA was already standing at the quarter milepost.

"Here comes NINA," cried Clarence.

"That's PUTZER right behind her," shouted Joe.

The Irish Setter, NINA, ran right up to Clarence and jumped happily into his arms. NINA really liked Clarence but of course, this Irish Setter didn't know the difference between an Italian and an Irishman. Joe once said, "Doesn't it seem funny that an Irish Setter likes an Italian kid? I guess the dog doesn't know any better."

PUTZER spotted Joe and ran to him.

"SHEILA," an alarmed Joe roared. "Pick up the sled and start running. You have only a quarter mile to go."

"You pick it up," came back a tired SHEILA.

Joe never hesitated. He picked up the sled and started off. Clarence did the same. So the race became a run off between Joe and Clarence. The dogs followed. SHEILA and SOPHIA now ran behind the foursome.

Clarence at 5 feet one and 100 pounds was no match for Joe at 5 feet nine and 130 pounds. Clarence was brought up on pasta, and Joe was brought up on Cream of Wheat and Wheaties. When Joe reached the bridge over the lagoon he was 100 yards ahead of NINA and Clarence. But he knew he couldn't finish the race like that so he waited for SHEILA, handed the sled to her, and said, "You better run the rest of the way.

"But I have to finish the race riding the sled. What will I do?"

"Whisper to PUTZER at the 25 yard marker that Andy Johnson is waiting for him."

"Is that all right to do?"

"Why not? You want to win don't you?"

So now SHEILA was carrying the sled and it was a good thing she had on her tennis shoes because SOPHIA was coming just ten yards behind. While Joe and SHEILA were talking, Clarence almost caught up to them. Just when it seemed like NINA would retake the lead, fate intervened. Good old next door neighbor, Andy Johnson, saw PUTZER and screamed, "Come on PUTZER!"

PUTZER liked Andy and ran for him. At the last ten yards SHEILA dropped on the sled and crossed the finish line, the— WINNER!

Cameramen from the newspaper snapped SHEILA and PUTZER's picture. The next day it made headlines in the Sports Page. This was the last bit of notoriety she would ever know. The big news at the Good Council in Mankato was whispered "Sheila McCool, Queen of the Mushers" was about to become a nun. On the following Monday, she left for the Convent and Mankato. She knew full well that the Convent didn't allow dogs and that once a nun she would see her family again only on the death of her mother or father. In SHEILA's case, it would be the death of her mother, 43 years later.

The Great Como Park Dog Race was to be the last time Harry would consort with his older sister Sheila. In two short days, she would be the second member of his immediate family to leave Barrett Street forever.

The whole funeral, dog race, finance, and nunnery ordeal created a flood of turmoil within Harry. On the one hand he mourned the loss of his sister and pal. On the other hand, he was relieved that the pressure to have him enter the seminary had subsided with Sheila's departure. Most of all, though, he felt **guilt**. Guilt because his sister went and he stayed. Guilt because he was relieved not to have to go into the seminary. Guilt because it was the strongest emotion he learned from the Catholic nuns, and it seemed to cover all situations. There was no escaping this emotion as his conscience reminded him that his was an imperfect life that would forever require trips to the confessional.

5

WINTER CARNIVAL FUN

The two older McCool boys and Gil Bratner climbing the canopy of the Ryan Hotel on Robert Street for a better view of Carnival parade.

The notorious Vulcan Crew of the Winter Carnival.

Harry not only had a large nuclear family, with three sisters and two brothers, but he also had a very extensive set of cousins. His father had six brothers and three sisters, while his mother had three brothers and five sisters. Harry could barely keep track of all his aunts and uncles, let alone count the number of first cousins he had. There were two first cousins, however, that Harry did keep track of, namely Amy and Roberta Jensen. Harry was always fascinated with these two sisters because they lived in Redondo Beach, California, the land of Hollywood. To find out how their parents ended up in California, we need to return to the late 1800s in Denmark.

The basic tale of European Immigration into the United States is widely attributed to a set of factors including population pressure, economic and agricultural hardship, and widespread political and religious dissent. Some countries, like Sweden and Denmark, were practically without war for the entire century contributing to rapid population increase. Ironically enough, whereas the discovery of a vaccination for smallpox was widely proclaimed as a wonderful advance for mankind, the resulting population increase because of reduced infant mortality was not so widely appreciated. Another ironic factor that spurred emigration from Europe was the improved literacy rate being realized throughout Europe in the 19th century. With more people able to read the optimistic letters sent home to Europe from the American Pioneers, more demand was created to leave home and enjoy the "Land of Plenty". Harry's maternal grandfather was one such emigrant.

Ole Jensen and **Sorline Gregersen** were Martha's parents. Ole and Sorline were born in 1863 in **Vitten, Aarhus, Denmark** and Gronbeck, Viborg, Denmark, respectively. They married in 1885 and settled in Ole's hometown for the next 15 years. Economic conditions were very tough, however, and by 1900 the Jensens had given birth to three girls and three boys putting considerable pressure on Ole to provide for a fairly large family. **Martha**, Harry's mother, was the oldest, **born in 1886**. In 1900, Ole started reading letters from a friend who had gone to Wyoming to find work. He wrote that the opportunities were plentiful. Ole needed no further convincing and he sailed from Denmark to England, then from

Southhampton, England to America arriving at the ever-popular entry point of Ellis Island, New York in March of 1900.

Ole spent as little time as possible in the cesspool of new immigrants that teemed everywhere in New York and caught the first train available for Wyoming. For the next 13 months Ole worked daytime in the coalmines, with occasional nighttime stints working on the railroad. Every penny was pinched until he could afford to bring his wife and children over the 'pond'. Ole discovered that the cheapest route for his family was through Canada, so Sorline and the children disembarked in Montreal, Canada May of 1901, and then took the train to Wyoming. Ole and Sorline made Wyoming their home, and never moved again.

Whenever Harry's grandparents visited St. Paul, and it wasn't too often, Harry always made his grandmother tell how she came in through customs. The story goes that Sorline, knowing practically no English, was quite worried when the custom official made her open her clothes trunk. She was convinced that he would find something objectionable and make her return to Denmark. As Sorline opened the trunk, the official was greeted with the overpowering odor of Limburger Cheese, a favorite of Ole's. The official took one whiff, closed the trunk, and waved Sorline and the kids through. Ole was doubly thankful for the cheese.

The Jensens added three more daughters in Wyoming. One of the sons, however, hated the winters and didn't particularly care for the summers either. When he came of age in 1910, he headed for California and the land of sunshine. Within seven years he had a bride and two lovely daughters.

Despite having two brothers and three sisters, Harry's only siblings close in age were Joe and Sheila. With Sheila gone, that left only Joe. The void created by Sheila's absence gave Harry the idea to have his mother invite these two first cousins from California to come to St. Paul for the annual Winter Carnival. Neither cousin had ever seen snow. No better time, thought Harry, to break them in than during the St. Paul Winter Carnival, always held the last week in January. The two female cousins, Amy, thirteen years old, and Roberta, ten, would need a very good argument to convince them to leave the fair winter weather of California for the coldest week of the year in Minnesota.

To get them excited about Minnesota, and to provide them an excuse for getting off school, Harry sent them information on the history of the St. Paul Winter Carnival. He pointed out that this trip could be considered an assignment about one of the most unusual festivals in the United States. IT ALL STARTED WHEN (in 1886) a New York newspaper correspondent described St. Paul as "another Siberia, unfit for habitation in winter." Civic leaders set out to prove him wrong, and the St. Paul Winter Carnival was born in the following story:

THE WINTER CARNIVAL LEGEND

Boreas, King of the Winds, and his four siblings, Princes of the Four Winds, traveled to the winter paradise known as Minnesota and made historical Saint Paul and its seven hills the capitol and winter playground of the realm of Boreas. With the Queen of the Snows, Boreas created a Winter Carnival with joyful celebration, music, dancing, feasting and frolic. The King and Queen, along with Winds and Princesses, reigned over the festivities.

On the final night of celebration, however, trouble came. Vulcanus Rex, King of fire, and his Crew stormed Boreas' magnificent castle and confronted the King's Guards who made ready for battle. Upon good counsel of the Queen and in the interest of peace and goodwill, Boreas decided not to fight, but to leave Minnesota to Vulcanus and his Crew. He bade farewell to the people of his winter capital, and returned to Olympus. Vulcanus Rex restored the warmth of springtime to the seven hills of St. Paul, and reigned until the annual return of Boreas and his Winter Carnival each January.

After this Legend for the girls to read, Harry continued his invitation with a listing of interesting Carnival events:

"First I will take you to the Opening Day Parade!" Thousands of marchers and dozens of floats will go by as we watch from my favorite spot, over the canopy at the entrance of our historic

RYAN HOTEL. After the parade we will go out and do something in the winter Wonderland of St. Paul. Here are just a few things you will be doing for the first time in your life (and for the time of your life):

   a. You will play Baseball in the snow.
   b. You will curl with a 42 pound rock and sweep the ice with a broom.
   c. You will fish in a hole in the ice.
   d. You will get a ride in a hot air balloon.
   e. You will ride a toboggan down a slide at 35 miles an hour.
   f. Men dressed like the Devil himself will be after you for kisses.
   g. You will ride a sled pulled by real reindeer!
   h. You will take a guided tour through the largest ice palace in the world.
   i. You will see the Coronation of a Queen, escorted by handsome King's guards.

I have purposely omitted window-shopping. But if you are like typical girls and crave shopping I might get my older sister Alice to take you on a trip to Minneapolis, the home of great department stores. Don't expect me to join you, though, I detest shopping and Minneapolis.

Harry concluded his invitation with instructions for the girls to "get your mother and father's permission and tell your teachers at school that you are going on an educational trip—a once in a lifetime experience it will be. My brothers, Joseph and Peter, and I will meet you at the train depot".

Since Roberta and Amy knew nothing of the rigors of a Minnesota winter, and plenty about the drudgery of school, they thrilled at the invitation. But their parents . . . dad from Wyoming and mother from Minnesota . . . knew this trip would not only be no picnic, it would entail getting winter clothes for girls who had never been in cold weather in their young lives. Despite the details, they reasoned that the girls should experience for themselves, first hand, the rigors of a Minnesota winter. Who knows, they thought, maybe they will like it, and it will give us a chance to spend some time alone. Their winter clothes could be sent to the Salvation Army upon their return to California for charity's use. As P.S. in his invitation, Harry wrote, "Big Winter Carnival Parade opens festivities on January 30. You should arrive by Friday the 29th of January."

Harry received a return postcard from Roberta and Amy's parents with the message . . . "Precious girls dressed for snow and ice will arrive on the 29th. Schools says O.K. and so do we."

There was no place to put the girls when they arrived at Barrett Street. But Martha, Harry's always-industrious mother, worked it out. "You know, Harry, that these two little girls have never been anywhere so cold in their lives." So on the night before the girls arrived, Martha, borrowed some blankets from her next door neighbors, the Johnsons, and borrowed an air mattress from the Boy Scout leader, Yeno. With the blankets and mattress, she made two beds on the living room floor. She wisely put them down next to the grate in the living room floor where the girls would benefit from the furnace heat. This meager grate was responsible for heating the whole frigid house, but the closer a person came to the grate, the warmer.

The girls arrived at the St. Paul train depot, as scheduled, on the 29th of January. Harry, as promised, picked them up with his brothers and whisked them to their home on Barrett Street. The girls introduced themselves to Martha politely on arrival. Harry did the honors of telling them apart. "Mother, the older one is Amy. Notice the ponytail and the real blonde hair. The younger of the two is Roberta, and she has kind of blonde hair with the fringe over her forehead."

Roberta corrected Harry's remark. "These are called bangs," she said, pointing to her forehead.

Harry nodded, then continued "She tells me that she has the new 'IT' girl's look like Clara Bow."

Roberta jumped back in "Our next door neighbor in California says I have sparkling eyes just like Clara Bow."

Amy interjected with "I think she looks more like Zazu Pitts."

Martha realized the unflattering nature of this remark and said, "That's not nice Amy."

Peter came in from the outside and said, "How do you southern girls like it here in the far north?"

Amy declared, "We consider ourselves from the west, not the south, and I can't wait until I jump in a snow drift."

Harry reassumed charge by saying, "You won't have to wait long. Follow me." Harry led the two girls, with his brothers trailing, to the back door. He opened it and pointed to the porch . . . . "Just run and jump. Amy, you're older, you go first," urged Harry.

"Where do I jump?", Amy asked.

"Just run off the back porch . . . there is no railing . . . and fly into space."

Harry held the door open and Amy sailed by him and leapt into what she immediately found to be three feet of snow. Roberta, a little more conservative than Amy, hesitated. Joseph and Peter threw her headfirst into the three foot snow pile. She came out bragging, "That's fun. Let's do it again. "

And the two girls jumped again and again into the snow. Roberta started to shiver after the tenth time, so Martha came to the rescue. "That is enough boys. Let them back into the house before they freeze to death."

Amy didn't want to go back in the house. Peter had to carry her back in, and this thrilled Amy as much as jumping into the snow. Peter then turned his attention to Roberta and said, "O.K. Dimples, you're next." He picked her up and deposited her on the kitchen floor.

"Don't you call me Dimples," howled Roberta, because she didn't like that nickname, although it fit her very well.

Martha decided that after the arduous train trip, coupled with changing two time zones, the girls needed rest and food. She gave them a light dinner, and then told the two girls to get ready for bed. "You'll find the bathroom upstairs, the first room to the right."

Amy and Roberta were thus introduced to the what the Boys called "THE COLD ROOM." The Cold Room, located on the northwest corner of the second floor, caught the northwest wind through one window. The closest heat was the grate in the middle of the first floor. With the feeble convection of heat from the first to the second floor, the temperature never rose above 50 degrees the whole month of January in this room. The bathroom did, however, have indoor plumbing to service a pull chain toilet, a bathtub but no shower, and a sink. The girls didn't realize how lucky they were since the indoor toilet relieved them of having to use an outhouse in the winter, a common 'inconvenience' in Harry's neighborhood.

Amy and Roberta entered the cold room, took a quick look around at the amenities, then put on their summer pajamas in record time. On their exit from the room, Martha instructed them: "Girls, come back downstairs where you will sleep next to the grate on an air mattress under the blankets already laid out for you." The girls quickly obeyed this inviting command and fell asleep from exhaustion in record time.

At three o'clock in the morning, Amy was awakened by a noise in the basement. She stirred Roberta who now lay on the grate for warmth. "Roberta, wake up! Someone is in the basement."

"I don't hear anyone," replied a groggy Roberta.

"Listen to the noise, it's coming right up through that grate you are on." Amy jumped up in terror. "Roberta, can't you hear that noise?"

"Yes, Amy, I can hear it now. Run upstairs and tell Martha."

Just then the kitchen light came on. Harry stood in the doorway to the dining room. Amy asked him, "What is that noise in the basement, do you have a burglar?"

"Don't be so melodramatic Amy, I was just shoveling coal on the fire," replied Harry.

"At three o'clock in the in the morning?" Roberta asked as she stood up, still over the grate.

"You must have left your watch on California time. We are two hours ahead of California time here in Minnesota. It's 5 am, not 3 am," answered Harry.

"What in the world are you doing up?" continued Roberta.

"I carry papers. Do you want to go along?" This question was for either cousin. The girls looked at each other and wondered if Harry was kidding. Since neither sister had any intention whatsoever of going outside in the cold and dark, no answer was forthcoming. Just then the dog, Putzer, stormed into the room and leapt at Roberta sending her off the grate and unto the cold, cold floor, like a cake of ice.

"Don't be afraid," smiled Harry. "He likes you. When I return from delivering my papers we will discuss going to the BIG PARADE this afternoon." With that promise, Harry and Putzer departed.

Assured that no one was robbing the place, the girls tried to go back to sleep. But it wasn't easy. One and one half-hour later, Martha came downstairs to start breakfast preparations. At 7:00 A.M., two hours after the false burglar alarm, Harry returned. He came into room with the announcement; "RUDY VALLEE will lead the St. Paul Winter Carnival Parade today. But before the Big Parade we have to get over to the toboggan slide. I hope you girls can get ready by 9:00."

Roberta and Amy realized that no more sleep was possible, so they rolled out of the blankets. Amy was the first to respond with, "What is a toboggan?"

Roberta said, "You don't know what a toboggan is?"

Harry interrupted this harmless squabble by saying: "I know you two have to report back to your teachers in California what has been taking place here in the winter capital of the world. In expectation of your query, here is a definition of a toboggan right out of the Webster's Dictionary—"Tobogganing is the sport of sliding down a snow covered slope on artificial ice covered chutes using a runner less sled called a toboggan. The toboggan is light in weight and will support a heavy load. It is usually built of thin straight grained boards of hickory or birch fastened together by light crosspieces. The front is bent up and back to form the "hood" and is braced by rope leather thongs."

"Take that to your teachers when you get back . . . 'cause that is what we are now going to sail down Como Hill on . . . "

Roberta, the practical one, asked, "How fast does a toboggan go when it reaches maximum speed?"

"I have read," said Harry, "that if the starting point is 600 feet high and the length of the run a mile, you can go 60 mph or a mile a minute."

"Is the Como Park toboggan run that long?" asked Roberta, hoping the answer was no.

"No, not quite," Harry assured her. "We would have to go to St. Moritz in Switzerland to find a place high enough to go 60 miles an hour."

"What about Como Park, how high and long is the toboggan run?" persisted Roberta.

"All I can tell you about Como Park is that Putzer, without a head start, can run down to the bottom of the hill faster than our toboggan will take us. And Putzer is no racing dog, although he did win the *Queen of the Mushers* race two weeks ago at Como Lake" proudly added Harry.

"Is Putzer going to come along for the toboggan ride?" asked Amy.

"No," answered Harry. "I don't like to take him on the streetcar. The conductor gives me and my pals enough lip already. Taking my dog on the car with the other passengers would only make the conductor more irritable."

Just then Martha came out from the kitchen and entered the conversation with: "Come girls and get your oatmeal."

Roberta grimaced at the word oatmeal. Martha saw this and said, "Maybe you would like Cream of Wheat better?" This time Amy faked a smile. Martha saw this too and said "How about some cold Shredded Wheat with milk and sugar, a piece of toast with jelly, and some hot Ovaltine?" Since everyone across America knew the phrase "From Breakfast to Bed, eat Shredded Wheat", they both smiled.

"We were afraid you were next going to offer us 'Granola' and only our father can eat that junk food," said Amy.

Harry interrupted this dietary discussion with "We are having company with us on our toboggan run."

"WHY?" asked Martha.

"We had to invite George Scanlon because he is bringing the toboggan."

"Anyone else?" Martha persisted.

"Yes, because we need to have five on the toboggan, I asked

Clarence Zacardi. Anything less than five and the toboggan doesn't get going fast enough to make the ride fun."

"Won't your brothers, Peter and Joseph go along?"

"Peter needs to spend his morning on the Western Union job and Joseph has home work."

"So Clarence is lucky number five?" asked Martha.

"Clarence Zacardi asked to come along because being Italian he likes girls . . . unlike most of the boys I know who can't stand them at ages 13 and 10."

Martha asked "YOU HAVEN'T TOLD Amy and Roberta about these boys, have you?" Martha always kept a watchful eye on her sons' playmates and friends. Even though George and Clarence were quite young and well behaved (good little Catholic altar boys and all), she knew about their pranks with the streetcars and the cemetery graves. If things got worst, Martha intended to be fully prepared to protect her son Harry from George and Clarence. For now she figured that the less Amy and Roberta knew about Harry's friends, the better.

"Not a word, Mother."

"Don't go too fast in the toboggan. You'll scare the daylights out of those young girls. "

"The toboggan," said Harry with a wry smile, "will go only as fast as the hill will take us."

Just as Harry, Amy, and Roberta were getting ready to leave for the toboggan hill, the telephone rang. Martha answered it, then turned to the group and said. "Call Maggie Horn, Harry, her boss wants her on the phone."

Harry stepped to the back door, swung it wide open, and yelled "MAGGIE, MAGGIE!"

Martha turned to the girls to explain, "We need the phone for Harry's paper route. The Horns don't have a phone but use ours." The girls, coming from the land of plenty, thought that sharing a phone was quite backward, but kind of cute.

The Horn house (what there was of it) was just behind Martha's. It was one story with two rooms. In less than ten seconds Maggie was at the back door. Maggie quickly met Harry's cousins from California, Amy and Roberta. "Why they are just as cute as Harry said they would be" offered Maggie. Maggie walked right over to the grate, and Harry handed her the telephone with an irritated shrug just like he had done a thousand times before.

Amy and Roberta watched silently as the drama unfolded. Maggie brushed past them as she took the phone and stood on the grate to keep warm. Everyone could overhear Maggie on the phone say "I am five feet two and I weigh 102 pounds. Tell me, why do you ask?" All waited while Maggie got the answer. She turned to Martha and said, "My boss wants me to be the bouncing girl in the Winter Carnival Parade."

Martha responded, "With the parade this afternoon, he certainly waited until the last minute to ask you."

Maggie explained "The girl whose place I will be taking had an accident yesterday and she can't make it today. "

Harry asked, "What happened to the last girl?"

"My boss said she broke her arm when she got caught in a telephone wire on a practice toss."

"What in the world was she doing up that high?" asked a puzzled Harry.

"She is the bouncing girl for the Athletic Club. You've seen them before, Harry, in the Big Parade. About ten men hold a tarp made of canvas and they get a girl to sit in the middle of it and on the count of three they throw her high up in the air and catch her, of course, on the way down." While Maggie was explaining, the two California girls listened in disbelief.

"And you are going to replace that girl?" asked Martha.

"Yes, my Boss tells me I am just the right size," added Maggie with a smile of pride.

"What if they miss you?" asked Roberta.

"She'll be the right size for a small coffin," answered Amy.

"Don't be silly, they won't let me hit the ground. Pardon me, I must go and tell Mother," said Maggie, suddenly very full of enthusiasm. And with that she left the house on the run.

"Does she come here very often?" asked Amy.

"Only when she is on the phone," Harry said. "Well button up girls. It's time for us to head for the Como Hills."

In the summer the Como Hills were the location of a public

golf course. In the winter the hills of the back nine were snow covered and steep. The phone rang. Amy jumped for it like she was back home. Amy answered, "McCool residence", listened to the reply, then handed the phone to Harry who was standing behind her. "It's for you Harry."

Harry took the receiver, listened for a moment, then said "You'll meet us at the Front streetcar stop?" Harry put down the phone, turned to the girls and said "My friend, Clarence, is still washing his hair and will take the Como-Harriet streetcar from near his house and meet us at the streetcar station at Front and Barrett."

Roberta inquired, "He has to wash his hair before going out in this weather?"

"He said he wants to look his best for my California cousins," explained Harry.

"Roberta, what's wrong with washing your hair in this weather?" asked Amy.

Roberta returned with: "It is too cold, that's why."

"How do you know how cold it is outside? You haven't got off the grate all morning."

Roberta returned with, "I can't help it, I'm used to warmer weather."

Harry said, "Well you better get used to the cold weather because we are all going to the Winter Carnival outdoor affairs before you can go back home. Get ready now and put on those mittens and overshoes because it is to toboggan we go. Hurry up, we'll have to catch Zacardi on the street car as it goes by on Barrett Street."

Roberta asked: "What's a street car?"

"It's a small train that runs on a track down our main streets. The one we want to catch is the Como Harriet line."

Roberta had never used anything like a streetcar before, so she asked "Can't we go in Peter's car?"

Harry hurriedly said, "Peter only takes the car out of the garage for very special occasions, like picking up two cousins with luggage at the train station. Bundle up . . . its warmed up to 15 degrees, but you still need a scarf for our run down the Como Hills."

After the girls were all bundled up they left for the streetcar. A short walk south on Barrett Street brought them to Front Avenue. Within minutes the streetcar arrived. Sure enough, as they got on the back of the streetcar, there was Clarence Zacardi standing on the only place on the car where you could smoke cigarettes. Harry introduced Amy and Roberta to him and he smiled showing his beautiful white teeth, but just coughing a little from the cigarette he just stamped out with his foot.

The streetcar started up with a jerk, as usual. Roberta, the most inquisitive of the two cousins, noticed a rope hanging out the backside. She reached for it simultaneously asking Harry: "What is this rope for?" Before Harry could stop her, she pulled the rope into the car.

Harry, in the commotion, clarified too late "Roberta, you've just pulled the trolley off the line."

And that is exactly what she had done. The lights in the car went off and the streetcar stopped. The conductor came yelling out to see who did the prank, a common trick of the members of the Como Gang. He spotted a face he knew so well, Clarence Zacardi. "Well kid, up to your old tricks again, I see."

"I didn't do it this time," pleaded Clarence.

Harry . . . true Boy Scout . . . stepped in between the conductor and Clarence. "I apologize for my cousin, Roberta from California, sir. She did it by accident."

Just then the Motor man arrived. He spotted Clarence who was standing behind Harry, and said to the conductor. "Same old kid, eh Billy?"

"No, not this time. This boy said his cousin from California did it," replied Billy the conductor.

"Why did you do this, little girl?" asked the Motor man.

"I thought it was a loose rope just hanging out there," replied Roberta. "My mother always says to pick up loose ends."

The motor man noticed how tan the two girls looked and said: "You didn't get that tan here in St. Paul in January, did you? Are you sure that this boy (pointing at Zacardi) didn't show you how it was done? He is a member of that Como gang who are pulling the trolley off the track all the time." No one responded, so the motorman got the trolley back on track and reentered the streetcar. He told Harry and his group: "I want you all inside the car. Nobody is to stand out back and I mean NOBODY, especially cousins from California."

They all went inside and sat down. Amy said to Harry: "You better keep an eye on Roberta."

"Not to worry. I just told Zacardi to keep her in line."

"If Zacardi can keep her in line, then have him give the secret formula to my mother and father—they will welcome the advice" pined Amy.

It was just a short ride from Barrett and Front to the streetcar stop at the station on Horton and Lexington. As they jumped off the streetcar, Harry said to Zacardi and Roberta. "Follow Amy and me through the back route to the golf course. Don't get lost on the way through the snow. Zacardi. Take good care of my sweet little cousin, Roberta."

"No problem, Harry. She is in good hands."

"Do you think Roberta is sweet?" asked Amy of Harry.

"Just as sweet as you Amy."

"Thank you."

"You're welcome."

After this friendly exchange of words Harry and Amy took off for the Como Hills with Zacardi and Roberta trailing about 20 yards behind. It started to snow and the wind started to blow. Zacardi told Roberta, "Follow me, I know a short cut that goes right by the Pavilion. We'll shorten the route to the golf course by avoiding the conservatory hill."

"Anything to shorten my time outside is okay with me" answered Roberta. Zacardi then deviated from the path in the snow being formed by Harry and Amy's footsteps. Minutes later Zacardi and Roberta heard a loud sound like the roar of a lion. "What's that?" cried Roberta.

"No cause for worry. It's just a bear in the zoo."

"I thought bears hibernated in the winter," said Roberta from knowledge she had picked up in the 4th grade.

"They don't hibernate in the Como Zoo. We have them in cages" explained Zacardi.

"Can they get out?"

"They haven't yet," consoled a brave Zacardi.

"Where are Amy and Harry, I don't see them ahead of us anymore."

"Remember my shortcut? They've taken a different route to the golf course. Our route goes by the Pavilion. We'll see it in a couple of minutes, and reunite with Harry and your sister right after that." Despite this assurance, Zacardi was getting a little worried since he couldn't see the Pavilion yet because of the heavy snowfall.

"I want my sister to know where I am right now. Her job is to see that I am O.K," cried Roberta. And now she started to cry. Never having been in a snowstorm, she became frightened. Another load roar of an unknown animal didn't help either.

"There is the Pavilion now," shouted Clarence. "See the big white building with the tall pillars?"

"I'm cold, can we go inside there?" said Roberta through her tears.

"We can't stop now, Harry and Amy will wonder where we are."

The snow and the wind didn't help vision. "Are you sure you know what you are doing?" asked Roberta. They trudged past the big building, and Clarence spotted the golf course hill.

"We go up this winding road and at the top will be Harry and Amy, you can take my word for it," promised Clarence.

"You and your short cuts," smiled Roberta for the first time since they had started on Zacardi short cut. The good news pleased her.

"What's that noise you are making, Roberta?" asked Clarence.

"If you want to know, it's my teeth chattering."

"Keep swinging your arms back and forth . . . then you'll keep warm" offered Clarence as he demonstrated the motion.

Amy spotted Roberta and Clarence before Harry did. She yelled: "Here they come, Harry."

"Where, I don't see them?" asked Harry.

"At the bottom of the hill. That's Roberta waving her arms" answered Amy.

"Zacardi didn't take care of her like I told him to. That short cut was a good ten minutes longer. He just wanted to tell her how he was a singing star in the summertime at the Pavement Dances. That's what he was up to."

Just then George Scanlon came up pulling his big 8-foot toboggan behind him. Harry turned to him when he heard his shoes crackle in the cold and said "Welcome George, you came at the right time. Say hello to Amy."

George gave Amy his nod of approval with a big "Hello".

Never bashful, Amy said, "Hi, you are cuter than the rest of your friends. My sister Roberta is just coming up the hill with that Zacardi guy. You look just like my boyfriend from Redondo Beach."

"Where is Redondo Beach?" asked George, always open to learning more geography. Meanwhile George pulled down his World War I pilot's head gear and tightened his mother made wool scarf around his neck just like he had seen Richard Arlen do in the movie "Wings".

"His teacher thinks he is an angel because he is so well-behaved in school," interjected Harry.

George bragged, "My twin sisters think I look a lot like Richard Arlen—you know he is from St. Paul just like me," boasted George as he pulled his shoulders back for emphasis.

Roberta and Zacardi now arrived. To Roberta, Harry inquired, "How did you like the short cut?"

"It was terrible. To keep my mind off the cold Clarence kept singing *Home on the Range*."

"Why *Home on the Range*?" asked George.

"He said that Minnesota must seem like the *Range* to a girl from California," answered Roberta.

"Did he tell you about his singing in the choir?" asked George.

"Yes, but he also said he sounds much better now that his voice has changed as to when he was a tenor in the school choir," answered Roberta.

"Don't you remember, George, I won the singing contest last summer at the Pavement dances when they wanted a singer to join the band?" clarified Clarence.

"Oh, you mean Amateur night?"

"Let's get the toboggan going. Amy and Roberta are shivering here in the cold," said Harry, who was always business minded.

"Line us up in the toboggan Harry," urged George.

"Who should our leader be?" asked Amy.

"It's my toboggan, I will guide us," chattered George.

"I want to lead," insisted Clarence.

Roberta interrupted, "You had trouble finding an 8 column Pavilion. I don't have very much confidence that you can lead us to the bottom of the hill."

"He will be all right, as long as there are no trees on the way," responded Harry.

"There are no trees between the top and the bottom," claimed Clarence.

"If there are, Clarence will find them," said George. "I'll lead. And like I said before, since it's my toboggan, I decide who leads." That settled the leader position.

Through the wind and the snow, Harry read the take off order: "George, you guide us up front, behind you in this order, Roberta, Clarence, Amy and then, dragging a loose foot for the brakes, me."

"Boy am I lucky," smiled Clarence. "It's my honor to be between the sweetest girls this side of the Mississippi."

George couldn't help but to say, "Like a Devil between two roses."

Amy and Roberta both caught their breath as Harry pushed them off the steepest hill in Como Park. George pulled down his sunglasses, tightened his mama's made wool scarf and yelled, "Scara mouche". This expression he had picked up from reading the novel by Rafael Sabatini.

The toboggan never came near a tree on the trip down the hill, but it did run into the frozen pond at the end of the run. Harry tried to slow the toboggan by dragging his feet. No help. A snow pile at the end of the pond stopped the party of screaming five.

"That wasn't too bad," said Roberta. "It should be a good warm up for our roller coaster ride in New York this summer. My dad is going to take us in early July." Roberta was referring to a brand new roller coaster that was going to be built on Coney Island called The Cyclone. This roller coaster was going to feature an 85-foot plunge, and incredible 60-degree angles. "Now what do we do?" she asked.

First, though, Harry wanted to clarify some history. "Roberta, did you know that the first roller coasters were developed from the early sled rides in the Russian Mountains?"

"Harry, are you making this up?" asked Amy.

"No, it is the truth. The Russians built ice slides in their towns in the Urals, some as high 70 feet in the air. The track was ice and the sleds were ice, with straw stuffed in chiseled hollows to served as seats. You can see what an improvement the modern day toboggan is over these early sleds, now, can't you? Without the ice toboggan, there would be no roller coasters." Harry smiled; he sometimes even surprised himself with the facts that he recalled from reading the daily newspapers.

George, always game for another run down the hill, said "Now we go up and come down again."

Roberta protested, "You mean we have to climb all the way back up that hill again?"

"It's all for the thrill of the ride," cried Clarence.

"I still think that a roller coaster goes faster than that toboggan of yours," said Amy.

Just then a loud siren sounded from atop the hill. "Where's the fire?" a now excited Roberta asked.

"Let's hurry up the hill and see it," cried a curious Clarence. And the boys ran up the hill with the two girls right behind them.

"Even in California they run for fires," claimed a knowledgeable Harry to George. Roberta and Amy ran past the boys in a flash, and reached the top of the hill first. They were used to running in sand while playing volleyball and surprised the boys who thought their athletic training would easily prevail in the dash up the hill. They quickly discovered that running to first base on a flat ball field was a far cry from running up a steep hill laden with snow.

Roberta cried in alarm, "Here come the fireman right for us!"

"You know who that is, don't you, Harry," George said.

"They'll scare the daylights out of those girls," Harry answered, realizing that the crew was composed of an altogether different type of fireman than any fireman that the California girls had ever seen. Sure enough it was the Winter Carnival Vulcan crew in their red devil outfits. They stopped the siren and the whole crew rushed at Roberta and Amy just as they reached the top of the hill.

Amy screamed in delight as one of the men grabbed her and smooched her cheeks with black soot. He was just about to let her go when she took a hold of him and smooched him to his surprise, as the girl is expected to scream for help in this situation. The contrary happened to the Vulcan who tried to smooch Roberta. She slapped him in the face and knocked his hat off. "Leave me alone you big turkey," she cried for all in the area to her. The Vulcan stood there aghast.

"You are suppose to like being smooched," he protested.

Harry and George recognized the voice of Yeno, their Boy Scout leader. "YENO!" yelled George.

"YENO!" also yelled Harry in unison.

"Is that your good deed for the day?" Clarence put his two cents in on the discovery. Yeno said nothing. He just turned around, put his head down and walked to the Vulcan fire wagon like a dog with his tail between his legs.

"No more runs down the hill" advised George.

"What's the hurry George?" asked Harry.

"My mother wants to go to the big Parade and she needs me to go along with her."

Roberta asked, "Do you need the toboggan to watch the parade?"

Harry didn't like his cousin's remark. "Don't be sassy Roberta. Say thank you to George for the ride of a lifetime."

"Thank you George."

"You're welcome." After the thank you, George took his toboggan and headed for home.

"O. K. girls, it's time we left for the Big Carnival Parade, too" said Harry.

Clarence said, "That's just like George to strut over here for one toboggan ride, and then go home. You know he lives on the hill overlooking the park. He think he owns the Park just because his father is so rich."

Harry intervened, "He doesn't think he owns the Park, Clarence. Just because you live 10 yards away from the cemetery doesn't mean you own the cemetery."

Amy said, "I want to see the Big Carnival Parade. Let's get going." Taking Amy's advice, Harry with Clarence guided the girls back to the Como Harriet streetcar and took them back to 1023 Barrett Street.

When the group arrived at Harry's home, Amy and Roberta tore off their scarves and coats, and rushed for the grate on the living room floor. A short tussle ensued, but they managed to share the flow of heat. Martha asked, "Do you mind the cold, girls?"

"I'll tell you one thing," replied Amy, "It's no Redondo Beach."

"I'll bet you can't ride a toboggan in the sands of Redondo Beach?" answered Harry, defending good old Como Park.

"It doesn't beat a roller coaster ride like we are going to get this summer in New York," said Roberta adding more fuel to the competitive fire started by Amy.

"We have roller coasters here in Minnesota nearby us in Excelsior Park," bragged Harry.

"Is it open in the winter?" asked Amy. "I sure would like to see how exciting it is in this cold."

"Our parks don't open in the middle of winter for a summer sport," said Martha.

"You are taking all the room on the grate, Roberta," said Amy. "Move over because I am just as cold as you are."

"Nobody is as cold as I am," returned Roberta. "That is unless you are a polar bear." With that little exchange Amy and Roberta stood together on the warmest place on the face of the earth as far as they were concerned. Alice came into the room just as Martha hushed the girls.

"Good Morning California. How do you like the land of sky blue water?"

"What sky blue water?" the brazen Roberta asked.

Amy added, "It must be under the snow."

"Stay another three months and you'll see plenty of it," encouraged Alice.

"Maybe you can get the girls to help you find the treasure this year," said Martha.

"What is the clue in today's newspaper, Harry?"

"What treasure?" Amy wanted to know.

Harry explained, "Every year during Carnival time, my newspaper has a Treasure Hunt. Clues as to the hidden treasure are given each day until the Treasure is found."

Roberta inquired, "What's the Treasure, a chest of gold?"

"No, just a Medallion."

"What good is the Medallion?"

"If you have a Carnival button and find the Medallion it's worth $50.00 in real money, not just gold," said Harry.

"Where is it hidden?" asked Amy.

"You can bet it'll be in the snow in St. Paul somewhere. And you won't be alone looking for it," said Alice—who could be looking for it herself.

"I'll help you find it," offered Roberta.

"It's not quite that easy," said Harry.

"We will look for the Treasure after the Parade—when we have more clues," said Alice bringing to an end the discussion on the Treasure Hunt.

6

CALIFORNIA HERE I COME

Amy

Roberta

On this cold wintry Saturday in January, FUN got started in St. Paul. Winter Carnival backers defied the wind, the cold and the snow ... or at least they said they did. And just like a Barnum and Bailey circus, the Carnival started with a BIG PARADE. No elephants in snowshoes were needed—just thousands of Minnesota pioneers with an occasional float in color.

Harry, Alice, Amy and Roberta took the streetcar on Front Avenue east, the opposite direction from Como Park, and headed downtown. Harry led the group to his favorite viewing spot ... the canopy just over the Robert Street side of the Ryan Hotel.

The Ryan hotel was built in 1885, financed by Dennis Ryan who made his fortune in mining gold and silver in Utah. Even James J. Hill, the Empire builder, chipped in $25,000 for the construction of the hotel. And so went this seven story Victorian extravaganza. Gothic touches occupied the bottom of a huge open light court in the center of the hotel. The two story high lobby was one of the great rooms in St. Paul's history. Ornate marble columns held everything up. The hotel's other public spaces included a barroom (where John L. Sullivan, legend has it, cracked the solid mahogany bar with an angry smash of his fist). During its long life, the hotel hosted its share of celebrities, among them President Grover Cleveland. The hotel lasted some 75 years before it was demolished in the 1960s.

Here, on the roof of the canopy of the Ryan Hotel, Harry had the two girls climb to his favorite vantage point for full view of the BIG PARADE. As usual, Harry's sister, Alice, grabbed the choice spot. This was an old climb for Harry. Harry and his brothers and the old Como Gang members had made this their Carnival headquarters over the years. Fortunately, none of them ever slipped and fell down to be impaled on the iron grillwork, which formed a fence under the roof of the canopy.

Harry warned Amy and Roberta, "Pay no attention to the sheriff if he tells us to get down from our perch. His name is Kermit Hedman, and he is standing over there across the street. He's too heavy to climb this high in his cowboy boots." Just then, the South St. Paul cowboys went by in their impressive garb riding their quarter horses ... shooting their guns off like you see in the old Tom Mix movies. After them came over 100 (110 to be exact) parade units mixed in among a vast array of uniquely designed floats.

"Isn't this wonderful girls?" cried an excited Harry.

The only answer came from Roberta. "I think my ears and toes are freezing."

"Pull your scarf down over your ears," advised Harry.

"How will that help warm up my toes?"

Amy told her, "Move around and you'll get warm."

Alice screamed, "Here comes Rudy Vallee."

"What is that he has over his mouth?" inquired Roberta.

"That is a megaphone," Alice said as if Roberta didn't know a megaphone when she saw one.

"What is that for?" naively asked Roberta.

With his usual encyclopedia-like mind Harry told her, "A megaphone is a cone shaped device for magnifying or directing the voice when addressing a large audience out of doors."

"Thank you. But that man is singing or it sounds like he is singing. Doesn't it?"

Alice butted in with "He is singing his favorite song . . . the one that we hear him sing on the radio, *MY TIME IS YOUR TIME.*"

Amy . . . no student of the Rudy Vallee show, offered, "Does he always sing through his nose like that?"

"For a thousand dollars a week I would sing through my nose," said Harry.

Alice (whose matinee idol was Rudy Vallee) jumped in with "Harry, you are just as sarcastic as the rest of the family."

"I am more interested in seeing Deanna Durbin in the movies than I am in listening like you do to Rudy Vallee on the radio all the time," returned Harry.

"Harry, do you go to the movies?" Changing the subject was Roberta.

"Yes, of course I do," responded Harry. "We have some great theaters downtown St. Paul and Minneapolis. My favorite is the Orpheum because the balcony swoops out almost to the movie screen."

"Roberta loves all the Hollywood movie stars, but her favorite is

Greta Garbo. I, on the other hand, liked Rudolph Valentino," said Amy. "I wish he hadn't died last year before I could meet him."

"I do like Greta Garbo, but mom and dad won't let me go to her movie **Flesh and the Devil**," piped back Roberta. "They say it is too racy for a little girl. I can't wait until I am old enough to do what I want. When I grow up I am going to be a dancer in Hollywood whether they like it or not. I just know that I can dance better than any actress I've ever seen."

"If she came to live here in Minnesota she would be better off to skate like my cousin Mary, then to dance like a ballerina" advised Harry.

All attention was suddenly turned back to the big Parade as the St. Paul Athletic Club's girl hurling unit came by. "Isn't that Maggie Horn there in the air?" shouted Alice.

"That's Maggie all right," agreed Harry.

"Is that your neighbor who comes in and hogs the heater grate?" asked Roberta.

"That's our neighbor all right," said Harry.

"She also hogs our phone besides our grate," said Alice.

Roberta started to jump up and down . . . swinging her arms to keep warm. "When is the parade over?" stuttered Roberta.

"It lasts for 2 hours," and this bad news for Roberta came from Harry.

Roberta in a tearful plea asked Harry, "Can I get down from here and go in the lobby where it is warm?"

"And miss the rest of the parade?" asked Alice in disbelief.

"I can't help it. I'm cold and I want Amy to go in the hotel with me."

Amy objected, "I want to see the rest of the parade."

Chivalrous Harry, the perfect host said, "I'll take you inside, Roberta." Harry wouldn't dare admit that he was cold too. A person does have their limits, and two paper deliveries, plus one trip to the park, followed by a parade was definitely Harry's limit.

"Thanks Harry. I'll tell Roberta later just what she missed. That is when we all get back on the grate," said Amy

With great relief, Roberta spotted Sheriff Hedman and yelled out "Sheriff . . . I need your help . . . Please take me down."

The Sheriff quickly came over. Roberta leapt into this waiting hands and arms. Harry dropped himself nimbly down the ten feet. Sheriff Hedman growled . . . "What about that other girl, up there. She better get down here too."

"Good luck in getting her to do what you say," cautioned Harry.

"She better get down or I'll come and get her," warned the Sheriff. With that threat Amy leapt the ten-foot drop into the Sheriff's arms, knocking him down into a snow bank. The Sheriff's deputies came running to his rescue. But they were too late to help him up. He had already struggled to his feet, too embarrassed to laugh and too humble to admit he was losing his role as protector of Ramsey County in cases he had never before encountered. He changed the subject. "Where did you get that tan, little girl?"

Amy, while brushing the snow off her coat, said "Roberta, my sister there (pointing to a laughing Roberta), is from California and so am I."

"What in the world are you doing here in Minnesota in the middle of winter?" laughed the Sheriff.

"My cousin over there, wanted us to see the Winter Carnival," explained Amy pointing at Harry.

"Is there anything we should see that is inside? Out of the cold?" pleaded Roberta.

"You just go inside the Ryan Hotel . . . warm up and have good old Harry take you to see curling," slyly answered the Sheriff. The group went inside the hotel to warm up. One half hour later and just a little bit warmer, Harry took the two girls on the Selby Lake streetcar to the St. Paul Curling Club.

"If we're lucky," said Harry, "We can catch your Aunt Madeline in the Winter Carnival Curling contest."

"What's curling?" asked a curious Amy.

"It's bowling a rock on ice" explained Harry.

Harry began to worry about how many activities he would be able to show Amy and Roberta if Roberta continued to complain about the cold weather. He already eliminated the ice skating races, all outdoors at Como, and had eliminated the Hot Air

Balloon rides over the Scenic St. Croix River Valley. It was out of the question to stand on cold, cold White Bear Lake and watch the colorful balloons heat up, up and away. The Torchlight Parade was also a scratch. At night there would be no way he could get Roberta to climb up on the Ryan canopy again. BUT he had to take her on the Treasure Hunt for all that money hidden out there somewhere in St. Paul.

Returning to the present, Harry told Amy as much as he knew about the Curling Rock, "It's a 42 pound round rock with a handle on it."

"How cold is it in there if the sport is done on ice?" asked the ever temperature aware girl, Roberta.

"It will be pleasantly brisk compared to being outdoors" replied Harry.

As they entered the Curling Club, Roberta noticed that the spectators all had the collar of their coats snug around their necks. "Where is my Aunt Madeline?" asked Amy.

"There she is," yelled Harry, "See her out there on the ice with a broom in her hand?"

"That is just like my mother . . . always with A BROOM IN HER HAND," said Amy.

"Here she comes," said Harry. "Let her explain the game to you."

"Hi! You two must be Amy and Roberta" smiled Madeline. "Cold enough for you?"

"I don't want to talk about the Minnesota weather. You don't have weather—just cold" said Roberta with firmness.

Amy explained, "Roberta thinks that there are just two seasons, namely summer and cool summer. She still doesn't believe that anyone can live in a place that has snow and ice."

Madeline empathized, "Today is terribly cold. You must admit, though, that it is warmer in here than outside . . . but let's not talk about it. Let me show you all about the exciting sport of curling."

Harry spotted his neighbor, Andy Johnson out on the ice and asked Madeline, "Isn't that Andy Johnson our next door neighbor out there with those funny shoes on?"

"Yes, that's him, our Skip." Andy came over to meet the two California girls.

"Andy, please tell Harry's cousins all about Curling," coaxed Madeline. "You know more about it than anybody I know."

"That is true," blushed Andy. "And your names?"

"I am Roberta, the younger, of course," said Roberta.

"I am Amy, the older and smarter, of course," replied Amy.

Andy began, "Curling is a team sport . . . four to a team. The best curler is the Skip, and on my team that is ME."

"What position does my Aunt Madeline play?" asked Amy . . . always interested in new sports (heredity from her father she says).

"Madeline is third in order. After me she is the next best curler." returned Andy.

"Madeline, you are on line now," called Andy. "Get your rock ready . . . clean the stone." With that Madeline left the little group and rejoined the curling players on the rink.

"What in the world is a rock? Is that the heavy handled thing Madeline has in her hand?" asked Amy.

"That is a curling stone," corrected Andy. "Our stones at the Club were made in Asia Craig Island on the Scottish coast."

Madeline called back to Andy, "Get down here on the rink for your directions on my throw."

Andy said to Amy and Roberta, "Here take my card," handing them a 3 x 5 card. The girls thought it rather odd that Mr. Johnson needed a card explaining his favorite sport, but they looked it over and read:

Curling is played on a level sheet of ice marked with a 12-foot circle at either end. The four players comprising a team play four stones each, alternating with the opposing team. The "lead" or first curler must be most accurate for his shot the entire strategy of the "end" designed. The second must guard the lead's stones, pushing ahead or bumping out the opponent's stones. The "third" curler often must break up a combination of opposing rocks to permit a clear shot at the circle for the fourth man. The "skip" (Andy), or fourth man, who until he plays directs his team from the opposite end of the sheet behind the target circle, often is the key player determining winning points for his team.

While Amy read the card Andy went down on the ice for the main shot. Roberta, meanwhile, shivered as usual. "The sheriff said it would be warmer here than outside watching the parade. It's colder if you ask me."

Amy responded, "Go get a broom and sweep like those curlers out on the ice. They must keep warm that way."

"Did you read what it says on the other side of that 3 x 5 card?" asked Harry.

Alice turned the card over and continued to read it to Roberta: "Two curlers glide along side every delivered stone at the *skip's* signal, vigorously plying their brooms in front of it. No two curlers agree upon the value of sweeping, BUT tests verify that it adds 12 to 15 feet to the stone's distance."

"I really don't care that much about what is going on out there," impatiently said Roberta.

At that moment a commotion broke out on the ice. "She burned a rock, I tell you," yelled Andy who rushed to the middle of the rink.

Madeline agreed, "I saw it too."

"They burned the rock?" Amy said in disbelief.

Andy went and removed the opponent's suspect rock off to the side, out of play.

"Don't burn your hands on the rock," Amy called.

Andy didn't hear her at all. He was busy giving instructions (with his broom) to Madeline's teammates as she delivered. She couldn't hear him from way down on the end but he was yelling to Madeline. "Go port SIDE!" Roberta meanwhile had found the heat source in the Club and was standing near it . . . so she missed Andy's yell. Madeline with a clean stone went into her delivery. It was smooth. Her free natural swing and relaxed follow through sent the Rock on its way.

Meanwhile Amy had struck up a conversation with what later she learned to be Andy's wife, Esther. "Look," cried Esther, "She made a Double."

What's a double?" asked Amy.

"She removed two enemies' stones from the circle" answered Esther, "a very good thing indeed".

Roberta came back just a little bit warmer, "Isn't this over yet?"

"Are you cold or bored?" smiled Amy.

"Both" came Roberta's short reply.

Esther inquired, "Don't they curl in California?"

"I wouldn't do it if they did. It's more exciting to watch a funeral go by."

"That is not very nice thing to say," scolded Esther. "Your sister seems to like it."

"Everything pleases my sister," added Roberta. "She even thinks boys are nice."

As Roberta was finishing this remark, Andy waved his broom in victory. For the lack of noise made in the Curling Hall, no one would ever know who won. Curlers just don't get excited . . . win or lose emotions are always completely subdued. Esther pointed out that her husband, Andy was reliving his last toss where his rock settled in the very center of the ring. The most jubilant of all the spectators, however, was Roberta who yelled, "If it's over, let's go home."

Harry broke in on Roberta's plea, "Do you think we are too cold up here in Minnesota for you?"

"I really", replied Roberta, "have only one ambition at this time."

"And that is?" asked Harry.

"I want to be back on Barrett Street over the grate."

So Harry and the two girls took a couple of streetcar rides back to Barrett Street. The streetcars transferred from Selby-Dale to Como-Harriet. This meant that Roberta would be out in the cold again, waiting for the streetcars to come. Harry got to know the fine difference between the girls . . . Roberta could never get warm . . . Any would look forward to any new experience joyfully. To Amy, the end of the rainbow would always be gold.

Amy was getting peeved with Roberta. She said to her on the streetcar going to Barrett Street: "Roberta, you must act more friendly. You keep complaining about the weather. Live with it. Harry can do nothing about it and he keeps trying to show us a good time. Your behavior is ruining his day."

"How can you be having a good time when you shiver and quiver all the time?" pleaded Roberta.

"I think you are faking it when you keep chattering your teeth all the time," said Amy. "I have goose bumps on my skin but I don't complain about it," added Amy.

"Wait till you see what this cold is going to do to your skin" Roberta warned.

This by-play between the girls continued until they arrived at Barrett Street. Roberta made a direct path from the front door to the grate. She dropped her winter clothes (scarf, overcoat, and sweater) for the second time that day on the way to the grate. A few minutes on the grate, and her California smile came back, and no longer did she chatter her teeth.

"Finally," said Roberta, "some heat, just like home."

"Can I have some space on that grate?" asked Amy.

"Let her get warm too, Roberta," sternly advised Harry.

He had started to admire the spark in Amy to take the cold the way she was taking it. . . . For Harry mused that she too must feel the King Boreas North Wind. "What's for tomorrow," inquired Amy, always ready for a new adventure.

"If the Treasure hasn't been found, we'll be out looking for our fortune."

"Treasure?"

"Yes, Roberta . . . your cold adventure has just begun."

"Harry," pleaded Roberta, "You mean we have to go out in the cold again?"

"If you want to make easy money you do," explained Harry.

Amy jumped in with, "How much can we make?"

"If you find the Medallion, we can all split at least fifty dollars."

"Let's get started," said Amy, always ready for a new adventure.

"Here's the plan," said Harry. "Tomorrow morning when I bring in the morning paper we'll work on the new clue . . . providing no one has yet found the Medallion."

Just as Amy was warming up the phone rang. Harry answered it. "Yes they both are here right now. Which one would you care to talk to first? Amy, Roberta, your mother is on the phone. Which of you two wants to talk to her first?" asked Harry.

Amy got to the phone first. "Yes, Mother we are still alive. It is cold. But Harry has taken us to where all the action is. First he took us on a toboggan run near Como Hills. He brought along for the fun a cute little boy named Clarence, and an Irish lad named George who owned the toboggan. We only went down the hill once. George had to take his toboggan home because his mother wanted George to take her to the big Parade."

While she was talking, commotion started over the grate. The next door neighbor, Maggie Horn, came in and was pushing Roberta off the grate.

Maggie said to Roberta, "Don't hog the heat little girl. Did you see me get thrown in the air by the Athletic Club members?"

"Too bad they caught you," sassed Roberta.

"Mother says it is 65 and the sun is shining" interrupted Amy.

Who's on the phone, Harry?" Maggie sounded like the phone belonged to her.

"It's Amy and Roberta's mother all the way from California."

"Ask her if the sun is shining in L.A.?" said Maggie as she walked off the grate over to Amy on the phone.

"Be quiet," cried Amy. "I can't hear my mother talking on the other end." A hush came over the top of the grate. Amy continued to talk to her mother, "The Carnival Parade was wonderful. A girl next door here was a part of the Parade. She was thrown way up in the air by some men who held a big canvas sheet. After she made somersaults in the air, they caught her. Then we took in a game called 'curling' that wasn't much to watch, but it did resemble California shuffleboard. The whole game was quiet and dull. Not one contestant jumped or hollered when I think they made a point. But some did raise a broom and smile occasionally."

"The most fun of all the time was on the top of the hill while we were tobogganing on Como's hills. About ten men in red Santa Claus outfits jumped off a fire engine and ran and tried to kiss Roberta and me. Roberta hit one of them, but just in fun I kissed one of them back and he was pleasantly surprised."

Harry interrupted Amy by saying: "Give Roberta the phone—let her tell your mother about all the fun she is having." With that statement done, he took the phone away from Amy and handed it to Roberta. Roberta reluctantly stepped off the grate and took the phone.

"Mama, I want to come back to California. I can't get warm here."

"You shouldn't have let her talk, Harry. She'll just complain," warned Amy.

Roberta continued to tell her mother all . . . "It's so cold in here that there is only one place to get warm: the grate. There are no heaters in the rooms upstairs . . . . In fact, the bathroom is frigid. You can't even take a bath without turning blue. I've taken only one bath since we arrived and I don't think Amy has had a bath at all. Nobody who lives here seems to mind the cold, or so they say. Harry can't stand heights or else he would have taken us on a Hot Air Balloon trip over this arctic zone. Amy tells me I could be mistaken for an ice sculpture that people carve out of big chunks taken from this frozen sky blue water. I can't wait to get back on the warm sands of Redondo Beach."

"Is that Father talking in the background? What is he saying? Don't go Treasure Hunting unless you know exactly where the Medallion is hidden? Goodbye Mother . . . see you soon . . . it can't be soon enough".

Roberta then hung up the receiver and turned to Harry. "My daddy says you must have to know exactly where the Medallion is hidden before you take either Amy or me on a Treasure Hunt. He says that one time his cousin was taken on the hunt when he was just five years old. Uncle Einard left him in the car while he went through 5-foot deep snow to pick up the Medallion. He didn't find the treasure but my dad, a mere tot, nearly froze to death. My dad's cousin never forgot that time sitting in the cold car."

Harry nodded and said, "I agree with your father. We need more clues for the exact location. Tomorrow morning's paper will give us the right clue. Believe me. Roberta I want you along when we find the loot."

"Why me?" asked Roberta.

"You'll find this trip all worth while if we find that Medallion" said Harry. Harry opened the back door for Maggie Horn to leave. She left quietly, not like her at all. He turned to the cousins and said "O.K. girls, get ready for the big searching party tomorrow."

It was just a few hours later that the whole family went to bed . . . . The two girls, as usual, were snug in their blankets on the grate.

No mention was made of a need for a bath after hearing Roberta's comments about the upstairs' bathroom . . . with the Northwest wind howling through the window.

Harry was the last to "HIT THE SACK". He reviewed all the Treasure Hunt Clues in an effort to pinpoint just where the thing was hidden. He went down to Clarence's house where they called in their friend, George, whose Father was a Parks and Playgrounds Commissioner. All three, Harry, Clarence and George huddled together in the basement of Clarence's house. George came prepared to solve all the clues. He began the meeting. "You can't tell your cousins that my father helped us find the Medallion, right?" George pleaded.

Harry asked, "Forget about who takes the credit. The important point is that we find it so put your best brains on this search."

George pulled out the latest paper and began to give his father's ideas where the Treasure was hidden. "The first clue is obvious for it plainly states . . . *The Medallion is hidden in St. Paul.* The next clue is easy 'circling roads that bend and wind'—again obvious—Como Park-right here in our backyard." George hesitated.

Clarence urged him on "Go on George . . . you're on a roll."

"You take the next one, Harry. Listen: *some distance from the hiding place high up in the air are stacks that pour forth smoke.*"

"Koppers Coke!" cried Harry with glee.

George bolted in with; "I told you my father said Como."

Clarence downplayed the excitement with, "Como Park is one big place and the Medallion is one small thing. It could be under a monument at the Calvary Cemetery."

George laughed," Under a monument?"

Clarence came back with, "Once they hid it in a mailbox on Robert Street and you know the penalty for tampering with a government mail box?"

"Why would I know that?"

"Let's get on with the next clue, George?" interrupted Harry.

George read the next clue, *"Signal lights may be near the treasure site."*

"That is right by the police station on Horton and Lexington," cried Harry.

George wanted to get back to the problem at hand, namely the Treasure. *"The treasure is away from private property—near tall trees and scenic beauty* . . . you know right down from the streetcar stop at the police station is the ball field . . . the scenic beauty is from the home runs I hit there."

"George, you brag too much," smiled Clarence. "Just get us to the Treasure site."

"I'll need a few more clues. I know it is Como for sure for one clue says a place where police work a lot and it also mentions Leotards . . . and you know Leo is for Lion in the zoo . . . even though we don't have lions."

Clarence's mother called from her bedroom, "Can we go tomorrow and get the money?"

Clarence called back, "Not yet mother. But we are getting close."

Harry was worried, "Does your mother expect us to split the catch with her too?"

Clarence soothed him, "No, but she sure wants us to find it after all this work."

George interrupted with the next cinch lead, "My dad said it is Como for sure because the 9th clue mentions music and lakes, a golf course and pools and ice capades. And my dad as commissioner of parks and playground says that Como is the only park with band stands for music, a golf course and pools."

"He should know," agreed Harry. "Is the pool in front of the Conservatory the pool he is talking about?"

"That's the one all right."

"Does your dad want some of the loot when we find it?" asked a worried Clarence.

COMO-HARRIET STREET CAR . . .
Original run down Front Street to Chatsworth
and then by the original St. Andrew's school and church.

"Not any more than your mother is concerned about getting," came back George.

Harry thought this bickering premature; "We haven't found the loot yet—so there's little sense fighting over the distribution of it."

"I'll bet you promised those cousins of yours from California some pay off for coming all this way, haven't you Harry?" threatened good old George.

"They are not too hot about going out in the cold at all—let alone looking for the treasure in three feet of snow," returned Harry. "I'm hoping to find the treasure to cheer up my frozen cousin Roberta."

Back to the business at hand, George reeled off a real winner of a clue, Listen he read, *"North from the place where the secret is buried many pictures are taken of couples just married."*

Harry jumped in with, "That's the Como Park Conservatory."

Clarence ran to get his coat, "Let's move."

"It's one o'clock in the morning. You can't get a streetcar until four," warned George.

"Just where are you going to look . . . inside the Conservatory?" Harry realistically cautioned.

"It's usually buried deep in snow, my dad tells me," said George.

"I'll get my mother. She had cousins married in that conservatory," offered Clarence.

"We need more exacting clues. I'm not looking until we know exactly where it is hidden. And don't get up your mother, I think she went to bed. You know how excitable she gets," cautioned Harry to Clarence.

Clarence resented Harry's remarks about his mother. "How do you know my mother gets overly excited?"

"Every time I come to collect for the paper, she screams at your father to get him to come across with the money."

"That's my father's fault and not hers."

"Let's stop for tonight," said George . . . "We can't go any more tonight—tomorrow's clues will tell all. So Harry, when you get home from delivering the papers call us and off we'll go."

"A call won't be necessary," directed Harry, now back in charge. "Just meet me and my cousins at the Horton and Lexington streetcar stop by the police station and I'll know by then just where to pick up the Medallion."

"Can we trust him, George?" the doubting Clarence asked.

"He's a Boy Scout, isn't he?" snapped back George.

"So is my older brother, but he sure finds a way to my piggy bank when he needs money" moaned Clarence.

"I promise I won't get the jump on you even though I should know by 6 A.M. just where to go" said Harry. He actually expected to have the puzzle solved five minutes after he picked up the newspapers at 5:10.

"OK," agreed honest George. "It's all settled. We meet at the streetcar stop at the police station at 9 A.M."

"I still don't like the arrangements, but I'll be there at 9 A.M.!" snarled Clarence.

Just to kid him Harry said, "And don't bring your mother." With that last remark Harry and George went home and to bed.

There wasn't much out of the ordinary going on in the world that eventful day the Treasure was found. Harry came in with the paper at exactly 7:00 A.M. The only party up was Roberta. "What was the temperature in Los Angeles yesterday?"

Harry couldn't believe it; "Don't you want to know the next clue? The temperature is 6 below zero here and 74 above in Los Angeles."

"My father and mother wouldn't want me nor Amy out in this weather," defiantly replied Roberta.

"Let's have Amy speak for herself," said Harry.

Amy heard all this commotion. "Roberta, we leave in a few days. We have to help Harry and his friends find the loot."

"I would rather go to a movie . . . Ben Hur is playing downtown . . . we haven't see that," cried a suddenly excited Roberta. "I am sure that mom and dad wouldn't mind us seeing a religious film, and Harry raved about that Orpheum Theater yesterday."

Harry came up with a solution for Roberta and her phobia about cold. "Forget the movies, you must get plenty of them in California. There will be a lot of people looking for the Medallion, some with nice hot fires. You can keep warm near them while Amy, Clarence, George and I dig up the Treasure."

"That way you'll have all the fun!" said Roberta switching gears.

"I am just thinking of your warmth, Roberta. The Treasure Hunt is just part of all the things still to do . . . like speed skating, hockey games, figure skating, and, of course, the end when you will see the spectacular fireworks."

"Is that all outside?"

"That is the whole idea of the Carnival. Get outside in the winter time for fun."

"My idea of fun is laying in the hot California sun in the sand—not frolicking in the snow." and this statement by Roberta was most emphatic.

"Let get going to see George and Clarence. We don't want them to get the treasure before we get it," cautioned Harry. Amy was all set . . . boots, coat, gloves and scarf. It didn't take long before all three were on their way to destiny.

When they reached their rendezvous, George was there with

Clarence and their mothers. This was no surprise to Harry. Both mothers were dressed like right out of the Yukon. The only difference, no self-respecting women from the Yukon would be caught carrying a rake. "Why the rake?" asked Roberta after introductions.

Clarence's mother—no bigger than a small size snow drift replied, "We need it to dig for the gold."

George's mother (a tad bit bigger, in the range of a Mrs. Paul Bunyon) said, "We are ready to rake in the money my little girl."

"Let's get going," chimed in Harry. "Follow me."

Roberta didn't like George's mother's reference to her being a little girl, and said so: "I am not your little girl."

"You're so cute I wish you were," and this remark took Roberta by surprise.

They all followed Harry who led them to the home plate at the baseball field. He was convinced that the loot was under the snow. Just as Harry had predicted, there were three women already there with a fire going to keep warm—evidently they had been there for a very long time in a futile search for the Medallion.

"What are we doing here?" asked George.

"The clue this morning reads, *recreational facilities in number abound*, then it mentions a structure."

"What structure?" asked Clarence.

"The structure is the backstop," came back Harry quickly.

"And remember they always pace off for the treasure, usually 100 paces. Clarence, you pace off 100 steps East, George, you do 100 West, Mrs. Zacardi and Mrs. Scanlon, pace off 100 North, and I and my cousins will go 100 South. O.K?"

"Who has the compass?" asked Mrs. Scanlon.

"Your son . . . our best boy scout has it, right George?" queried Harry.

George guided everybody to their proper direction, pointing his finger north, east, south, then west. The English teacher, Mrs. Scanlon, couldn't help herself from walking over to the three women by the fire and quoting Macbeth: "When shall we three meet again, in thunder, lightning or in rain?"

The reply came from obviously another English teacher in the group of three who said, "When the hurly burly's done. When the

Medallion lost or won." Then the three all laughed like they knew where the Medallion was hidden.

As Harry, Amy and Roberta started their journey, Roberta stopped by the three women to get herself warmed-up. She couldn't understand why they all looked so happy. "How can you all smile in this cold weather?"

"We have our reasons," replied the lady that had provided the Shakespearean quote.

"We sure do," yelled the other two in unison.

They mumbled something to each other, which Roberta couldn't hear. Just then a squad car came up beyond the backstop and a policeman got out of the car and came over to the women. Harry came back to find Roberta talking to the three women by the fire. He said: "Come on, Roberta—Amy and I are out for the loot. We're waiting for you to help us find it."

"Do I have to leave this nice fire?"

Amy came to help Harry get Roberta to join in on the search. "Come on Roberta. Harry knows just where it is."

"You better find it Harry, cause my father said not to go out in the cold unless you knew just exactly where the Medallion is hidden" stated Roberta.

"We'll never pick it up, Roberta, if you can't get moving," said Harry, now very irritated with her.

Three feet of snow, wind blowing and 5 above zero was no fun. In two minutes, Roberta's teeth started to chatter, her toes turned cold, and she told Harry "I can't go on like this, I hope somebody finds this thing soon."

Amy hurried on ahead and Harry ran to catch her, leaving Roberta behind. Amy loved this weather (completely unlike her sister). At one hundred paces she began digging through the snow . . . with Harry's help . . . but the result was NO Medallion.

Meanwhile Roberta's scarf blew off in the wind exposing her ears to the frigid cold, cold winds. In a few minutes her ears frosted and hurt. She cried (actually screamed) for Harry and Amy. They came running back to find her standing in the snow like an ice sculpture. "I want to go home Harry. This is not for me" pleaded Roberta.

Amy looked at her sister's ears and saw that they were turning white. Just then they heard the police squad car siren coming up to the three women by the fire. All three hurried back to hear the policeman say to the women: "Which one of you has the Medallion?"

"Evelyn has it. Show it to him, Evelyn.

"Why did you call us?" asked the officer.

"We want your protection. This Medallion is worth fifty dollars and we don't want any of these crazy searchers to take it away from us," said the biggest woman of the three.

The police man then said, "Get in the back seat of the squad car."

Evelyn said, "Will you take us down to the newspaper office?"

Just then Roberta came up to the officer and cried, "My ears are falling off my head sir, can you help?"

The officer went to pick up some snow to put on her ears and Harry jumped in and said, "You don't put snow over frozen ears. My Boy Scout manual says to warm your ears with a scarf or with your hands."

The officer asked Harry, "Do you know this girl?"

"Yes sir, she's my cousin from California."

"I want to go home." sobbed Roberta.

The three lucky women with the Treasure were becoming impatient with the trouble this Californian was having with her frozen ears. They plowed into the back seat of the squad car and Evelyn cried, "Let's get going officer!"

The officer went to his car and called over the phone: "Send a car down to pick up a little girl with frozen ears." He then turned to Roberta and said, "Don't worry, little girl. The police station is just around the corner and a squad car will be here in less than 90 seconds". Then he jumped into the car and, with siren whistling, drove away. As this was happening, George, his mother, Clarence, and his mother were returning from a very unsuccessful trek through the snow. They were not happy! Before the women got into the squad car, Harry asked them where they found the Medallion. They told him 'at home plate' right where they had their fire roaring.

Harry was now concerned about Roberta's ears. He knew from his Boy Scout training that the grayish-yellow patch on Robert's ears was a sure sign of frostbite. It was most important to get her inside a warm building and he put his hands over her ears to help keep them warm.

"I want to go home Harry, and I don't mean Barrett Street, I mean California," whined Roberta.

Within 90 seconds another squad car arrived. Roberta, Amy, and Harry jumped into the back seat, gave Harry's home address, and were dropped off within 5 minutes. It was quite a surprise to Harry's mother, Martha, when a police car brought the threesome home to Barrett Street. Harry immediately assured her that no one was in trouble, and she sighed in relief.

Two days later, after a long phone call with her mother and father, Roberta and Amy were sent home. As they left 1023 Barrett Street, Roberta could be heard singing:

CALIFORNIA HERE I COME

Harry's cousins never returned to Minnesota.

7

HOLY WEEK AT ST. ANDREWS

After the departure of Harry's cousins at the end of the St. Paul Winter Carnival, February and March of 1927, with their terrible cold, wind, and snow, dragged on for the McCools. Just when Harry wanted to scream for mercy from the powers that controlled the weather, the end of Lent, with **Holy Week**, arrived. No matter the weather, this week was the highlight of the religious year for Harry, and he always looked forward to his Mass serving assignments. Throughout the calendar year, with the exception of an occasional Wedding or Funeral, Harry's duties at Mass were quite monotonous. Holy Week, however, was an altogether different experience. If Sister Bernice gave him a plumb ceremony to serve, like Maundy Thursday, Good Friday, or Holy Saturday, he got to learn a whole new repertoire. It was with great anticipation, then, that Harry looked over the assignments in the hallway outside of Sister Bernice's classroom the Friday before Palm Sunday. A quick glance told him, much to his delight, that he had struck 'gold', getting Holy Saturday along with George Scanlon and Clarence Zacardi.

Holy Saturday was the longest and most complicated ceremony for an altar boy in the Roman Catholic year. There was nothing ordinary or routine about this service. In fact, the priest wasn't actually allowed to say regular Mass between Holy Thursday and Easter Sunday since the entire congregation was mourning the death of their Savior. Instead, there was an elaborate 90-minute vigil ceremony that began at 10:30 PM Saturday ending with the start of Midnight Mass Easter Sunday. Harry, along with his buddies George and Clarence, was going to have to spend several hours with Sister Bernice running through the ceremony and individual duties. There were candles to be lit, incense to pour, Latin responses to learn, crucifixes to carry, and holy water to sprinkle. In addition, whereas a typical Mass relegated the boys to the limited confines of the altar and tabernacle, Holy Saturday required a veritable field trip around the church. Harry would listen most diligently to Sister Bernice at the practice sessions next week as she walked the boys through the entire ceremony. He fully intended to perform his duties flawlessly.

After checking Sister Bernice's board for his Holy Week assignment, Harry headed over to church to serve Mass for Father Patton. As he entered the sacristy, Father Patton greeted him with, "Good Morning, Harry. Have you given any more thought to becoming a priest?"

Harry seemed to be lost in thought, and instead of answering the question, asked one of his own, "Father, did Archbishop Ireland invent Lent?"

Father could hardly contain his laugh, as he answered, "No, where in the world did you get that idea?"

Harry responded, "Well, I've been thinking. Winters in Minnesota are long and miserable. The months of February and March are particularly awful. Seems like a person ought to get credit for all their suffering during winter, so why not give the time a special name and grant some bonus points to get a person out of purgatory earlier? Sure enough, in comes Lent, just at the right time. Throw in a few days of fasting and abstinence, and there you have your solution! It only seems natural that it would have taken a Minnesota cleric who had first hand experience in the cold Minnesota winters to institute this clever plan. I concluded that it must have been one of our great clergymen like Archbishop Ireland." Harry flashed a broad smile as he concluded his theory.

Father laughed some more and started talking as he began preparing for Mass as follows, "Very ingenious, Harry, but not quite correct. It seems like you need a crash course in the origins of Lent. Let me give you the facts . . . Lent, as you know, is the forty days from Ash Wednesday until Easter Sunday. While some of Lent may fall in February and March, it does not exactly coincide with these two months. The word Lent is derived from the Olde English word **Lencten** which actually refers to spring not winter. So you can see how your logic regarding winter is a little flawed . . . Lent almost certainly began shortly after our Lord died. The original Apostles were heartbroken and lost. They thought, quite naturally, that they should immediately institute a period of prayer and mourning to fix forever in the hearts of all of Jesus' followers the significance of his life and mission. The days just before his crucifixion seemed a perfect choice."

Harry interrupted with, "Father, why are their forty days in Lent?"

Father Patton resumed, "Forty days is a traditional number in the Bible. Remember Moses stayed on the Mountain for forty days, Elijah traveled forty days before he reached the cave where he had his vision, Nineveh was given forty days to repent, and, most importantly, Jesus spent forty days in the wilderness praying and fasting before embarking on his ministry. The Apostles, therefore, chose the most natural number of days for Lent based on Biblical events of significance. Finally, whereas Archbishop John Ireland is one of the more influential American Catholics of the last century, you can see, since he was born more than 1800 years after the start of this liturgical season, that he didn't invent Lent." Father Patton concluded his history lesson just as he finished putting on the last purple vestment for Mass. He made a sign of the cross and turned to Harry to say, "That's all the time we have for a history lesson now, Harry, let's get this Mass started." With that last comment, Harry and Father Patton set into motion the early morning Mass at St. Andrew's Church.

That evening Martha served fish, the traditional meal in the McCool home for Fridays in Lent when meat was prohibited. Harry hated fish, and just pushed the meager meal around his plate waiting for something he could stomach like his mother's

Danish Pudding. After supper, the entire family congregated in the living room for the weekly Friday night rosary. The group of five knelt around the small room, each with their favorite spot to lean. Mary Helen, the baby, lay on a blanket. During Lent, the family used the Sorrowful Mysteries of the Rosary. Alice made the sign of the Cross and started , "In the Name of the Father and of the Son and of the Holy Ghost." The group recited the Apostles Creed, 3 Hail Marys, then Alice soloed with, "The Agony of Jesus in the Garden—The 1st Sorrowful Mystery." This was followed by the Our Father, 10 Hail Marys, and Glory be to the Father . . .

The next leader was Paul who began, "The Scourging at the Pillar—The 2nd Sorrowful Mystery . . . Our Father who art in heaven . . . " Harry paid little attention as he droned responses to the Our Father and Hail Marys; they flowed without conscious thought. Instead, he remembered a year prior seeing how his father used to kneel leaning against his favorite chair. It almost brought a tear to Harry's eye as the memory made him winch. As they finished the fourth of five decades, his mother interrupted his day dreaming with, "Harry, wake up, it's your turn." Harry quickly returned to the present and began his decade, "The Crucifixion of our Lord—The 5th Sorrowful Mystery . . . Our Father who art in heaven, hallowed be thy name . . . "

The rosary took the family just over a half-hour. As the last Amen, pronouncedly louder than the rest, echoed through the house, the family quickly dispersed. Harry slipped into the kitchen for a glass of milk, and then went upstairs to find his brother Joe laying on the bed reading by candlelight. Harry interrupted his brother's reading with, "Joe, do you think dad died because we've been bad Catholics?"

Joe stopped reading and turned to Harry to answer, "No way. Harry, you must be the most serious teenager in St. Paul. Where did you get such a ridiculous idea?"

Harry answered, "Every week I go to confession on Saturday afternoon and say the same stuff. You know, 'Bless me Father for I have sinned. It's been one week since my last confession. I lied once. I had impure thoughts' . . . "

Joe cut Harry off, "That's enough Harry, I don't want to hear your confession. How does that have anything to do with Pa dying?"

Harry continued, "After Father Patton gives us our penance, we're suppose to reflect on our sins and try to improve. But every Saturday, there I am back in the confessional telling him the same bunch of sins. Doesn't the church say that Jesus died for our sins?"

Joe replied, "Yes, I guess so."

Harry resumed, "Well, there you have it. By simple logic, if our sins killed Jesus, why couldn't they have killed Pa?"

Joe had to stifle a laugh as he answered, "Pretty complicated reasoning for a punk. I think you've been listening too closely to those nuns over at St. Andrews. All that business about Jesus dying for our sins is to make us humble in life and continue supporting the church until we die. There's no way that your sins had anything to do with Pa dying. He died of pneumonia, plain and simple. Remember Mary Donnelly? Well she died of pneumonia just like Pa, and she didn't have any sinning kids, so you can see that your logic doesn't work." Joe returned to reading indicating that the conversation was over.

Harry stayed lost in thought for a moment, and then decided to return downstairs and listen to his sister Alice practice her piano.

One of the most interesting events during Holy Week for Harry was the singing of the Latin Hymn **Tantum Ergo** at the end of the Maundy Thursday service. Throughout the entire Lenten season, Sister Bernice would come to Harry's eighth grade classroom with her hymn books in hand to drill the boys and girls in this solemn song. With a conductor's wand in her right hand, she would rat-tap-tap the teacher's desk to get the students' undivided attention calling out, "Children, pay attention. You were a little off key yesterday. I'll give you the proper chord with my harmonica so you can get off on the right foot." She would next raise the tuning harmonica she carried in her left hand to her mouth, and blow the chord she desired. After identifying the chord, she would raise the wand and harmonica up above her head as she raise her eyebrows, and then drop her arms with the wand and harmonica to her waist indicating that the students were to begin singing. Her right hand, the wand, and eyebrows would never stop moving as she cajoled the singers to excellence. Harry had a hard time keeping from laughing as she gyrated in continuous motion leading the class, but knew enough to suppress the urge.

Holy Week started with Palm Sunday, but the days quickly moved to Maundy Thursday. Harry trudged through his paper route in just over two hours thinking about that evening's ceremony with his class' singing. When he arrived home, he glanced at the weather report: "SNOW". He didn't look forward to the evening delivery of the Dispatch. A quick breakfast and he headed off for school. When he arrived at St. Andrew's he headed for his desk right in front of his eighth grade teacher, **Sister Lordine**.

Harry and Joe Kane were assigned the first two desks so that the Good Sister could keep a very careful watch on their activities. Harry didn't know if he should be insulted or complimented on warranting such special treatment. Whatever the case, he frequently felt trapped in the little chair encircled by the desktop and Sister Lordine's probing eyes. He fidgeted at his desk locating his math book. His pencils, as usual, needed sharpening. His raised his hand and asked permission to leave his seat. Sister Lordine gently nodded her okay.

Harry sauntered over to the pencil sharpener and scanned the room as he pushed his pencils into the dilapidated device. The wall in front of the room held the ubiquitous crucifix. Below the crucifix were pictures of the twelve Apostles. Below the Apostles were pictures of Pope Benedict XV, Archbishop John Ireland, and a slew of Saints. To the right, near the classroom door, was a massive globe that Harry loved to spin as he exited the room at the end of the day. To the rear of the room were three oversized cloak closets. To the left were four massive windows, with a bookshelf running the length of the wall. The shelf held multiple copies of the catechism, three bibles, songbooks, and a series of reference books. As Harry looked outside, his mind wandered to springtime, despite the falling snow, as he waited the most important 15 minutes of the morning, namely recess. He finished sharpening his pencils, returned to his desk, and daydreamed as Sister Lordine droned on about fractions. When the bell rang at 10:00 AM sharp, it took Harry and his fellow classmates less than 60 seconds to put on their coats, mittens, and rubber boots and "hit the playground".

During the winter months, the favorite recess activity of the boys was playing pom-pom pullaway. The rules were simple. There were two end zones, or safety areas, approximately 50 yards apart. The game started with a one boy in the center. He was called the *'Poison Pawn'*. All the other boys were amassed in one safety zone. When the Poison Pawn called out "pom-pom pullaway", the boys in the safety zone had 15 seconds to run to the other safety zone without being tagged by the Poison Pawn. Anyone tagged, or not leaving the safety zone in the prescribed time, joined the Poison Pawn to tag other players. The game continued with the boys running back and forth between the safety zones until everyone was tagged. The first person tagged was the Poison Pawn for the next game. In the meantime, the girls were clustered in small cliques talking about the boys.

The Poison Pawn for the first game this Maundy Thursday was Tommy Halseth. Tommy was quite overweight, ergo very easy to tag at the start of any game. As a result, he was frequently the Poison Pawn, like today. As the boys grouped together in the west safety zone on the playground, however, Tommy did something unusual. He sat down and started playing with the snow that had fallen for the last two hours. George Scanlon was the first to notice something awry, and he called out, "Tommy, get up and let's get the game started."

Tommy didn't move, but he did answer, "Forget it George. I'm tired of always being the Poison Pawn. Get yourself another sucker." And with that comment he continued making a snow fort.

No one moved to take Tommy's place. Joe Kane, with mischief in his heart as usual, expressed an alternative, "Harry, let's help Tommy with his fort." Joe winked at Harry as he started for Tommy. With no pom-pom pullaway game in sight, Harry, George, and Clarence quickly joined Joe and headed for the center of the playground. Before recess ended, Joe and his crew had not only built a fort around Tommy, they had also managed to bury him up to his neck in the snow pack. Just as they finished the icy edifice, the bell rang signaling the end of recess.

The boys immediately darted for the building, leaving Tommy stuck in the snow fort. Harry noticed that Tommy had a desperate look on his face in his snow straightjacket as he called out, "Wait, don't leave me like this." Since Sister Lordine never tolerated anyone returning late from recess to the classroom, no one turned around to help Tommy and dare risk being tardy.

Once in the classroom, the boys and girls took off their coats, mittens, and boots, which they returned to the cloak closet, and returned to their seats. That is everyone except Tommy who was still buried in the snow. Sister Lordine glanced around the room and noticed the empty desk. In a menacing voice she asked, "Where's Tommy Halseth?"

No one was brave enough to answer. Harry, however, pointed out the window to the mound of snow that almost completely obscured Tommy. Sister Lordine took one look and cried out in panic, "Harry, George, Clarence, get out there and dig him out." The boys returned to the cloak closet, put on their winter coats, mittens, and boots for a second time, and headed for the playground. Within a minute, Tommy was extracted from the snow fort, soaking wet with a tear in one eye.

Harry, George, Clarence, and Tommy returned to the classroom. As Harry expected, the recess prank earned the entire class one of Sister Lordine's ritual "cleansings". Up and down the aisles she walked carrying a bucket of Holy Water, blessed by Father Patton, with a wand that Harry affectionately called the **Holy Stick**. Every step she dipped the wand into the holy water, and ceremoniously sprinkled it over the heads of the students as she repeated, "***Bless them Father, for they know not what they do.***" As Harry received his third splash of holy water, he thought to himself that they knew exactly what they were doing, namely having some fun in the snow. Even though Tommy Halseth was always crying, Harry decided that since he was in part to blame for Tommy's predicament, a mini-absolution from Sister Lordine might help his chances of reaching Heaven.

Sister Lordine quickly returned the class to business, "Children, time for your Religion lesson. Go over to the book shelf and get a **Baltimore Catechism**" Harry and the other students silently went to the window book shelf and grabbed a copy of the book as Harry wondered what the city of Baltimore had to do with a catechism. After they all resumed their seats, Sister continued, "Open your books to Chapter 2 and respond as shown . . . What should be the effect and fruit of true faith in the Christian?"

The students responded in unison, "Charity, or love, and good works."

The questions from Sister Lordine, and answers from the students continued, "What means do we have to know good works from bad?"

"God's commandments."

"What are the two divisions of the Ten Commandments?"

"Love of God, and love for our neighbor."

"If the whole law is contained in two commandments, why are they divided into ten?"

"In order to more clearly set forth our duties towards God, and towards our neighbor."

"What are the Ten Commandments?"

"1. I am the Lord thy God; thou shalt not have strange gods before me.

2. Thou shalt not take the name of the Lord thy God in vain.

3. Remember to keep holy the Sabbath Day.

4. Honor thy father and thy mother.

5. Thou shalt not kill.

6. Thou shalt not commit adultery

7. Thou shalt not steal.

8. Thou shalt not bear false witness against thy neighbor.

9. Thou shalt not covet thy neighbor's wife.

10. Thou shalt not covet thy neighbor's good."

Harry didn't have the slightest idea what adultery or covet meant, but figured that they must be adult sins and of little concern to him at his tender age. His biggest problems were commandments 2 and 4. Harry wondered whom to honor now that his father was dead, or if he was forever relieved of breaking that portion of the fourth commandment?

The Catechism lesson concluded with the students closing their books and answering a random sampling of the same questions from memory. Shortly thereafter, lunch began.

The rest of Harry's day was quite uneventful, until he returned to St. Andrew's Church for Maundy Thursday service that began at 5:00 PM. Harry figured that only the most solemn of religious services began at that late hour, so he knew that this Mass was one of the most special in the liturgical calendar. All the eighth grade students came in their school uniforms. The girls wore their white blouses with Peter Pan collars underneath navy blue jumpers with belts and a scalloped bodice. The boys wore gray wool pants, light blue shirts, and bright red vest sweaters. Since the students were an essential component of the service, they were assigned the first two pews on the left side of the central aisle.

Mass began in the traditional fashion with the introit, epistle, gospel, creed, and offertory. There was a significant deviation, however, when Father Patton washed the feet of one of the parishioners symbolizing Jesus washing the feet of the Apostles the night before he died. Fortunately, he only washed one man's feet and not twelve as Jesus had done during the original ceremony. Harry was glad he didn't have to take his shoes and socks off to be washed in front of the congregation. The remainder of the ceremony followed a typical Mass. At Holy Communion Harry, with all due solemnity, followed his classmates to the altar railing where they each received the 'Body of Christ' for the last time until Easter Sunday. Within minutes, Mass ended.

At the end of Maundy Thursday main service, the altar was completely cleared to emphasize the coming severity of the loss of Our Lord on Good Friday. To expedite the process, Father Patton led a Procession of the Blessed Sacrament to an alcove on the side of the church. As he solemnly set the Chalice with the Body of Christ in the side tabernacle, the students' hour of glory came. Sister Bernice came around in front of the students, conductor's wand and harmonica in hand. She very quietly blew into the harmonica and motioned the class to begin. Harry, along with his twenty classmates, gave an exquisite performance:

**Tantum ergo Sacramentum Veneremur cernui
Et antiquum documentum novo cedat ritui
Praestet fides supplementum Sensum defectui
Genitori, Genitoque Laus et jubilatio
Salus, honor, virtus quoque Sit et benedictio
Procedenti ab utroque Compar sit laudatio. A-men.**

Harry didn't have a clue what the words meant, but he figured that it probably was lauding Jesus for the courageous act of self-sacrifice that he was about to perform. Harry returned home with his mother. He noticed that she seemed to have a slight smile on her lips as they departed St. Andrews Church. Harry wondered if she could have actually picked his voice out of the chorus as they sung Tantum Ergo, but decided that his singing wasn't anything to rave about, so she must have heard good news from Mother Superior about Mary Helen's tuition.

Good Friday passed, as always, on a somber note. Holy Saturday started out for Harry with the morning paper delivery, a lazy morning, and a humble lunch. As the afternoon started, Harry decided to take a nap to marshal his energy for the long evening ceremony. The evening delivery of the Dispatch went without a hitch, and supper past uneventful. Finally, at 10:00 PM, Harry headed off for St. Andrew's Church and the evening vigil service. Along the way he stopped to pick up George Scanlon. Harry knocked on the Scanlon's front door and was greeted by George's father, Samuel who said, "Good evening, Harry. George is putting on his coat and boots. He'll be with you in a minute. Say a prayer for me tonight during the service." Harry noticed that Mr. Scanlon had a tumbler in his hand with some amber colored fluid and ice cubes. Since it was extremely common in Harry's neighborhood for the adults to "conclude Lent" on the evening of Holy Saturday, he knew that Mr. Scanlon must be drinking his favorite Scotch. Harry, however, felt obligated to refrain from eating candy, his Lenten abstinence, until Easter Sunday morning.

George came to the front door, and the boys headed for St. Andrew's. The two met Clarence in the sacristy where they put on their long black cassocks and short white surplices. Since Midnight Mass was to follow, the boys had to make preparations for a regular service as well as the Holy Saturday ceremony. Father Patton looked especially solemn as his layered the priestly garb. The boys first duties were passing out candles in the rear of the church as the congregation arrived. Mrs. Olsen tried to light her candle immediately with her cigarette lighter, but Clarence admonished her that she must wait until the signal from Father Patton. At 10:29, the boys returned to the sacristy.

Father Patton was putting on his final article of vestment, namely his purple cope, as the boys returned. Harry picked up the crucifix and Clarence a censer and vase with incense. George's hands were left unencumbered to be used very shortly for a special purpose. Father Patton turned off the overhead lights, and the foursome entered an almost pitch dark church. The first order of business was the **Blessing of the Light**. The group walked past the altar and sanctuary and headed down the center aisle of the church to the very rear. Upon arrival, Father Patton said the first of many special prayers in front of the **Paschal Candle**. Father turned to Clarence and carefully extracted, one at a time, five grains of incense from the vase that he inserted into the candle in the shape of cross. Each grain symbolized one of the five wounds Christ suffered. Finally the Paschal Candle was lit from a piece of flint. George then took the candle from its holder and led the group to the Gospel side of the sanctuary. Here he placed it into its permanent holder.

At this time, each member of the congregation walked up to the Paschal Candle and lit his or her own candle. Harry thought that the shadows and flickering light from the candles gave the entire church an almost surreal atmosphere. He couldn't imagine a more beautiful moment in the liturgical calendar. The next order of business was the **Four Prophecies**.

The group headed for the Epistle side of the sanctuary where Father Patton began, in Latin of course, the Genesis story of the creation of man to share God's life. As Father Patton was telling the story, Harry almost chuckled thinking how he kidded George's father that Adam and Eve left the Garden of Eden because there were no jobs. Harry explained to Samuel Scanlon how he had listened to Samuel tell of the beauties of Ireland, Clarence's dad tell of the beauties of Sicily and Mt. Etna, Knut Swenson tell of the beauties of Sweden, and finally Mr. Jorgenson the beautiful fjords of Norway. In each case, they, or their ancestors, had come to America looking for jobs. And so Harry concluded that the only reason Adam and Eve would ever leave Eden would be for a job, just like all his neighbors and their ancestors had left their personal Edens. Samuel rapped Harry on the head and told him to get along to school and listen more carefully to his bible lessons.

Father Patton concluded the first prophecy with a verse from a psalm and a response from the boys. The foursome next headed for the middle of the church. Here Father Patton recited the story of the Jews Exodus from Egypt. As Father Patton spoke, Harry couldn't help but think of his geography lessons where he wondered why it took Moses' people 40 years to find their way the pitifully short distance from Egypt to Israel and the Land of Plenty. This prophecy also concluded with a psalm and a response. The foursome next headed for the left rear of the church where the Father recited the story of the New Jerusalem. The final prophecy, the warning to remain pure and shun temptation, was recited in the left rear of the church. All told, the four prophecies had consumed more than forty minutes.

The final rite of the ceremony was the **Blessing of the Water**. The foursome headed for the Baptismal Font in the front of the church. In the practice sessions from Sister Bernice, Harry learned, for the first time, that there were several types of Holy Water. First there was **Blessed Water** used in the font in church which Harry always dutifully dipped his hand and crossed himself on entering the church. Second there was **Gregorian Water**, which is actually composed of wine, salf, and ashes, and only used in the consecration of a church. Finally there is **Baptismal Water** composed of olive oil, balm, and water, used, naturally, for baptisms. This final section of the ceremony included quite a bit of incense. Harry counted five separate times that Father Patton added incense to the censer, took the censer, and swung it in gentle arcs as he circled the Baptismal Font. Each time Harry would get a strong whiff of the aroma, and a stinging in his eyes. By the end of the fifth circumnavigation, Harry eyes were tearing so bad that Father Patton erroneously believed that he was deeply moved by the experience.

The end of the Blessing of the Water coincided with midnight and the beginning of Easter Mass. Harry noticed Samuel Scanlon and a score of other "night people" arriving just as the Mass started. Harry, George, and Clarence were quite tired by this time, but the excitement of the late hour kept their energy level high. Harry was very relieved that he had asked his brother Joe and neighbor Joe Miller to take the paper route Sunday morning.

After midnight Mass finished, Father Patton took Harry aside in the sacristy and asked, "Harry, why were you crying in the ceremony?"

Harry answered, "Too much incense, Father. Every time you waved the censer, the incense blew right into my eyes."

Father Patton continued, "Really, I thought maybe the spirit of Our Lord was moving you to become a priest?"

Harry was much too tired to think of a clever response, so he nodded his head from side-to-side, then quickly joined George and Clarence taking off his altar boy clothes. Harry headed straight home.

When Harry arrived home, he entered through the back door into the kitchen. He immediately found the candy bar he had hidden the day Lent began. He tore off the wrapping, stuffed the bar into his mouth, and headed for bed. As he lay down to sleep, pleasant thoughts of a huge early afternoon Easter feast of ham, scalloped potatoes, string beans, and Aunt Sarah's divine Angel food cake entered his mind. It would be interesting to see what Aunt Sarah and Uncle John's daughters, Eleanor and Elaine, would be wearing. For Harry, the arrival of these cousins, in their Easter regalia, bonnets and all, signaled the official end of Holy Week and Lent.

8

TROOP 92 SETS FIRE TO PRESBYTERIAN CHURCH

Spring finally arrived in Minnesota the last week in April. It was a beautiful Saturday morning as Harry set out for his paper route at 5 AM wearing only a light jacket. As usual, Putzer joined Harry on his route. The weather was perfect: 55 degrees, not a bit of wind, and the smell of blossoms in the air. He felt an unusual exhilaration as he whirled through the neighborhood delivering the morning newspapers. Not even the sight of Mrs. Moses's chow dampened his spirits. He finished his route in record time.

After delivering the last newspaper, Harry returned home and headed around to the back door. As he approached the back yard, he heard a series of hammer raps and some sawing. A quick listen identified the source of the noise to be the garage. Wondering what could be happening so early on a Saturday morning, he looked in through the garage door. There was his brother Joe with his friend Jim Lethert working away at two saw horses, cutting and hammering apple crates. Harry asked, "Joe, what's going on?"

Joe answered "We're building a canoe. The Boy Scouts just created a new merit badge for canoeing, and we want to be the first in our troop to get it".

Harry asked, "Good luck, do you want some help?"

Joe responded "Not yet, but thanks for the offer."

Harry smiled at his brother's initiative, then entered the kitchen through the back door. He tossed the last newspaper on the dining room table, and noticed his mother's **red ledger book** at the end of the table. The sight of the ledger gave him a sudden pain in the pit of his stomach, like someone had punched him. Sheila had been long gone to Mankato and the nunnery for over two months, but Harry had not stopped thinking about his father's funeral, his sister's exile to the nunnery, and family expenses. Harry listened, heard no sounds, and looked down at the ledger book on the table. Satisfied that no one was around, he quickly opened the book to one of the pages, and scanned the entries that his mother had entered into very neat columns:

January 1927, Expenses

Item	Amount
Groceries	21.26
Meat	4.38
Milk	10.00
Clothes	5.28
Shoes	7.05
Car Fare	3.20
Insurance	2.00
Medicine	1.05
Gas	4.61
Coal	13.75
Total	**73.57**

Okay, he thought, that doesn't seem so bad. Just under $74.00 for most of the essential family needs. He turned the page and noticed some more entries:

Received from Mrs. Raasch	$25.00
Newspaper December Collected	$68.45
Bill	$41.89
Profit	$26.56
Peter's music lesson for one week	$1.00
Alice's piano lesson for one week	50 cents

Finally he found two bills. The first bill was from Dr. Hugh Ritchie, their dentist on Dale and Como for $3.00 and the second bill was from Lake Shore Meat & Groceries, Nick Torok proprietor, 834 Como Boulevard, for $5.24. Harry rifled through a few more pages, but gave up trying to find the total family income. His mother had been specific with some details, but utterly lacking in other, more important, information. Since the family had lasted 3 months since his father's death without being taken to the poor house, he decided that somehow the McCools were going to survive without their primary breadwinner. Furthermore, he knew his mother was far too frugal to spend money on music lessons if she didn't have enough money for essentials. He even felt proud that he was bringing in more than $25 each and every month to help support the family.

With the financial load somewhat lessened, he ate a quick breakfast and headed out the back door to look for a ball game. Two steps out the door and his next door neighbor, the Swede Andy H. Johnson, stopped Harry to ask, "Where is Sheila? I haven't seen her for quite some time?"

"She doesn't live here anymore," replied Harry.

"Is she sick?" Andy wanted to know.

"No, she isn't sick."

"Has she run away from home?"

"No, they took her to Mankato."

"Who took her to Mankato?"

"The nuns from St. Andrew's came and took her right after my father's funeral."

"When is she coming back?" inquired Andy.

"Never."

"Never?" in disbelief asked Andy.

"She goes to high school and then college at the convent in Mankato, and after that she will be a nun."

After hearing this information, Andy told Harry "wait right here". He spun around and went back into his house to tell Esther, his wife, the news.

Esther came to the back door and continued the questioning of Harry. "What is this about Sheila?"

"She has gone to Mankato to become a nun," said Harry.

"Did Martha let her go?"

Harry said, "Sheila wanted to be a nun and my mother let her go."

Esther returned with, "Martha will miss Sheila's help with the wash and cleaning."

"It won't be with the cooking. I can tell you that," said Harry.

"Couldn't Sheila cook?" asked Andy.

Harry returned with, "All I have to say is that they better have good cooking nuns wherever she goes. I know that our meals are going to improve with her out of our kitchen."

"But Sheila has grown wonderful carrots and lettuce for so many years in your backyard. I can't believe that she never learned to cook. Who canned the vegetables?" inquired Esther.

"My mother canned them just like she used to do in Denmark", answered Harry.

"I wouldn't worry about her eating; all the nuns I've ever seen look pretty healthy to me," said Esther.

"What do you know about what the nuns look like beneath all those uniforms?" demanded Andy of his wife.

"Are there any Presbyterian nuns?" asked an interested Harry. After a second, however, Harry thought it best to change subjects. "Is Buddy ready for the Tenderfoot Initiation on Friday?"

"Buddy will be ready, I promise you," said Andy. And turning to Esther he said, "Right, Mother?"

At that moment, Mrs. Raasch, Martha's neighbor from the house out back, appeared as she always did whenever two or more neighbors talked together. "What's happened?" she asked Esther.

"Nothing you already don't know," said Andy. Mrs. Raasch was not a favorite of Andy's, but after discovering that she gave his mother money, he decided to cut her some slack.

Mrs. Raasch's death rattle voice whispered back to Andy, "You must excuse me, I want to talk to Esther alone."

"What can you tell Esther that I don't already know?"

"You'd be surprised," said Mrs. Raasch.

With that remark, Mrs. Raasch took Esther off to the side of the garage, out of Andy and Harry's hearing range, and said "Do you know, Esther, what has happened to Sheila?"

"Of course, everybody knows in the neighborhood," replied Esther (thinking now that I have finally been told).

"You don't know what *I know*," rattled Mrs. Raasch in her deep throaty whisper.

"And what do you know?" asked Esther.

"I know that in a Catholic family, one of the boys goes into the priesthood."

"What makes you think any of the three McCool boys will be a priest?"

"I didn't say which one, yet," and this Mrs. Raasch said with a knowing look in her eyes.

"It can't be Peter, the oldest, because he has to make money. Ditto for Joseph and Harry. Martha can't work with that little one year old baby, so she needs all three of her sons working," said Esther.

"What kind of job do you call riding a bike for the Western Union?" snarled Mrs. Raasch.

By this time in the conversation, Andy and Harry were off by themselves doing their own talking and trying to ignore the two nosey ladies.

"Five dollars a week is what Peter will make delivering telegrams, so I hear," said the whispering Mrs. Raasch.

"You know that $5.00 can buy a month of meat and bread for the whole family." And this came with finality from Esther who had just two children to feed.

"If Peter makes $5.00 a week, then Joseph will make just as much carrying papers to over 200 customers," added Mrs. Raasch to continue the analysis of the widow Martha's income. "So," continued Mrs. Raasch, "What will they do with Harry?"

"I thought that Harry was carrying the newspapers now. Do you have some inside information to the contrary?" asked Esther.

"No, but he is the next to go, believe me I know. Joseph will resume carrying the newspapers, and Harry will be sent off to the Seminary."

Esther wasn't sure that she liked Mrs. Raasch and her "inside" gossip news. "How do you know, and what do you know?" she asked her neighbor.

"Priests are always trying to get their Mass servers to become priests like them".

"How would you know that. You are not Catholic."

"Martha told me the whole story one day when Harry had to serve Mass for a funeral of my neighbor, Billy Carson. He died, as you know, from alcoholism."

"So Harry is the next to go?"

Mrs. Raasch corrected Esther, "I didn't say he was going for sure, I just said that Catholic form in a one parent family dictates that one of the boys go into the seminary."

Esther pondered all this new information for a second, and then walked away from Mrs. Raasch. Before entering the kitchen she stopped at her back door and turned to look at Andy and Harry. "Andy!" she yelled. "Come in the house. I want to talk to you." Esther then went inside. Andy gave Harry a slight nod like the boss is calling and walked quickly into his house with Esther.

Once he got into the kitchen she said, "Andrew, you know you have to work with our boy Buddy on the Boy Scout Initiation that comes Friday night, right?"

Andy changed the subject, "What was the latest scoop with gravel voice Raasch?"

"It's a secret and she swore me to tell no one . . . not even you."

"If it is a secret, why is she telling you?"

"She knows I can keep my mouth shut."

"She hasn't heard you yell around here."

Just then Buddy came into the room.

"Dad can you help me learn one of these Scout Laws?"

"I never was a Scout. We didn't have them in Sweden."

"I only have to learn one Law. Here's the book. See if I have it right."

"Before I ask you if you know your assignment, are the Boy Scout's officials aware of what you and Harry did when you tried to burn down the McCool's garage?" Andy was unrelenting in reminding Harry and Buddy of the incident. When Harry and

Buddy were five years old they started a fire in the McCool garage. It almost burned down a Model T. Ford and an invention that Harry's father and friend, Mr. Dodd, were building to replace gas as a motor fuel. "Aren't there requirements to become a Boy Scout, like no past criminal activity?" chuckled Andy.

"I didn't start the fire. Harry started it."

"Why did the both of you go and hide under the bed in the back room of our house if Harry was the one who started it?" asked Andy.

"I wanted to protect him because he helped me out the garage window where I was stuck."

"You were too fat to get out by yourself?" laughed Andy as he retold the story Buddy didn't want to hear about anymore.

"Harry saved my life. That's why I took and hid him away from the firemen."

"Remember what the fire chief said?" continued Andy. "He said if you two were any older he would have called the cops and have you taken to the police station."

"He didn't scare me and Harry when he mentioned the police station. He scared us when he said he would tell you, though" replied Buddy.

"I thought you ran because of the damage to the McCool's Model T Ford."

Buddy was quick to correct him, "That wasn't the main damage. The main damage was to an invention that Harry's father and his friend, Mr. Dodd, were working on in the garage . . . A CAR THAT WOULD RUN ON WATER AND NOT REQUIRE ANY GAS!"

"Is that the reason they had that big lathe in there?" asked Andy.

"Yes, but unfortunately Dodd died before they completed the project," said Buddy sadly.

"How would they heat the water to make it run the car?"

"Beats me dad, I am just a dumb kid."

Just then Harry knocked on the Johnson's back door and asked, "Is Buddy ready for Boy Scout Initiation?"

Andy answered "Esther tells me that the big Initiation will be held in our church, the Presbyterian one across the street from St. Andrews."

"That's right, this Friday night at 8: 00 P.M."

"I thought you Catholics couldn't go into a Protestant church."

"This is an exception approved by our Bishop."

"Why?

"Our Scout laws says . . . 'He (Scout) respects the belief of others'. I guess the Bishop is going along with that sentiment"

"That is pretty big of the Bishop. Does the Pope know this is going to happen?"

The conversation was interrupted with a sing-song call from Harry's mom of "H A R - R Y, time for lunch." Harry shrugged and then darted out the back door bringing the conversation to an abrupt end.

That evening as Harry went to bed, his mind returned to the ledger book and his father's funeral. Despite his earlier relief over the family finances, he couldn't get to sleep and his uneasiness about the future returned. He elbowed his brother Joseph awake and whispered "Joe, are you ever scared now that pa is dead?"

Joe turned over and muttered "No, go back to sleep."

"Why not", persisted Harry.

Joe realized that Harry wasn't going to be easily appeased so he continued "Ma is too tough to let anything happen to us. Harry, you're too young to understand that I'll miss pa, but a little part of me is relieved that pa is dead. He never laid a hand on you, but he sure whipped Peter enough, and my turn was just beginning. I can still feel my arm hurting from the time he yanked me in the house for breaking that garage window. So, no, I'm not scared."

Harry persisted "Has ma ever hit you or Peter?"

Joe answered "Never, and she never will. Besides, she spends most of her time worrying about us. She would never think of hurting any one of us. Although I think Alice could use a cuff on the head sometimes. She acts like some kind of princess around here."

Harry asked "Aren't you afraid that ma won't have enough

money to send us to school, and we'll only be able to get dead-end jobs the rest of our lives?"

Joe answered, "Harry, you need to lighten up and have more fun. You are not going to have to deliver newspapers the rest of your life. Take a look around and have some laughs. Forget about the money and school. Ma has it under control. You'll get a grownup job when you get into your twenties. We all die some day. The problem is to have the best time you can before it happens."

The reference to dying didn't sit too well with Harry, but he did understand his brother's drift, and said "Okay, Joe. I just wish I could be more like you and Pete. You guys are always laughing and making jokes. What's your secret?"

"Move fast and kiss all the girls you can" answered Joe with a laugh. And with that, the conversation ended. Harry laid awake another half hour mulling over Joe's advice, but the thought of waking up at 5 am to deliver the papers finally diverted his attention and put him to sleep.

The Boy Scouts have a very impressive initiation for a Tenderfoot. Before the Initiation, Harry sailed through all the requirements. He learned the motto, "Be Prepared." He perfected the special left handshake and the three-fingered salute. He knew the meaning of the badge and the uniform. He learned with no trouble the history of the United States Flag and the forms of respect that must be paid to it. He learned to tie and untie many useful knots. "The readiness was all." And like all new Tenderfeet, to all appearances he was Trustworthy, Loyal, Helpful, Friendly, Courteous, Kind, Obedient, Cheerful, Thrifty, Brave, Clean and Reverent.

He was all that until the Friday night of the Initiation. Harry's mother, Martha, had cleaned the uniform—a hand-me-down from a neighbor about the same size as Harry. Martha then told Harry to do those things you won't find in the Boy Scout Handbook, "Shine your shoes, comb your hair, brush your teeth."

Alice came home from her bookkeeping job just as Harry was about to leave. She couldn't help but notice his Scout Uniform and said, "Did you get a baseball bat when you bought that? Or did five men sell you that outfit?"

Harry hated his sister belittling his uniform. It was one of the reasons he was attracted to the Boy Scouts in the first place. His father always used to say "nothing makes a man more desirable to a woman than a sharp uniform, especially a uniform with medals". Now that Harry had the uniform, all he needed to do was earn some of the Boy Scouts merit badges to complete the look.

"That's an old Foreman and Clark joke Alice," replied Harry. "Don't tell me about the four men and just one Clark either."

Martha kept the conversation more serious by saying, "The uniform doesn't belong to him, Alice. He just borrowed it from a friend of yours, Gil Bratner."

In disbelief, Alice said, "Gil Bratner was never a Boy Scout. All he ever scouted for was girls." With that remark Alice left the room—her chin held high.

"We'll be at the Initiation, Harry. I can't answer for Alice," said Martha. Martha knew that Alice didn't care to see Boy Scouts when all her interests lay with the bookkeeper she worked for at the big bakery.

"I have to go a little early before the Initiation," Harry told his mother. "Father Patton wants me to bring a jug of Holy Water over to the basement of the church. It is one of the Bishop's stipulations for letting us go into a Presbyterian Church."

"Does the Father think there are some evil spirits running around there?" asked Martha.

"No. I don't think so. He also wants me to bring High Mass candles that he offered for use in reciting our Scout laws"

"Aren't Buddy Johnson and his parents members of that Presbyterian Church?"

"They sure are," replied Harry. "And Andy and Esther will be in the front row."

"What Scout law does Buddy have to give?" asked Martha.

"Thrifty is his assignment," replied Harry.

"And yours?"

"Mine is Reverence."

"What are the rest of the laws?" inquired Martha.

Good student that he was, Harry said the rest of them for his mother's admiration—"Trustworthy, Loyal, Helpful, Friendly,

Courteous, Kind, Obedient, Cheerful, Thrifty, Brave, Clean and Reverent." After finishing the Boy Scout Laws, Harry left for the ceremony.

The Initiation was to take place in the basement of the Como Warrendale Presbyterian church right across the street from Fr. Patton's rectory. Of course it was a mortal sin to go into a Presbyterian Church. But on Initiation night, an exemption was granted by the Bishop on two conditions, namely (1) High Mass candles were to be used by the Tenderfeet in the ceremony and (2) a jug of Holy Water would be nearby in case of fire. Harry wondered why Holy Water would be any better for putting out a fire than regular water, but a young Catholic boy never questions a senior member of the religious establishment.

The ceremony was most impressive. At least that is the way it was planned. Twelve little Tenderfeet each hold a candle. All the auditorium lights would be put out. Each candle would be lit. The first Tenderfoot would recite from memory why a Scout is Trustworthy. The second would tell why a Tenderfoot was Loyal. The third why he was Helpful and each subsequent Tenderfoot would recite his own little short message. The last Law—Reverence was Harry's.

In the rehearsals prior to the ceremony all went well. No candles were lit in rehearsals because they were too valuable to be squandered in practice sessions. No one knew just how long a High Mass candle would last for this ceremony, because none was tried. Even Harry, the good altar boy, only had experience in lighting the candles before Mass, but then putting them out immediately after Mass. He never actually saw a High Mass candle burn completely in one session.

Memory lapses on the part of the eleven Tenderfeet were never anticipated because all went so smoothly in the rehearsals. At 8:00 P.M. the Initiations began. Scoutmaster Yeno (also the eighth grade baseball coach) took his position in front of the Tenderfeet—dressed as he should be in full Scoutmaster regalia. Yeno loved the thrill of wearing the full uniform better than his filthy old baseball sweatshirt. From his broad brim hat to his hiking boots he beamed. He pulled his neckerchief smoothly around his neck and held it in place with his hand carved slider. "Wear your uniform proudly," he often reminded the Tenderfeet while he trained them.

Harry's mother, Martha, came to the Initiation with her neighbor, Mrs. Raasch. Martha gave Mrs. Raasch strict instructions about how to recite the Pledge of Allegiance to the Flag. She was not to say it as she said it once before—that is in Hungarian.

After the Pledge of Allegiance, the ceremony commenced. Yeno started with "Before we begin, I have one announcement. Troop 92 is to have an overnight on the St. Croix River in August. I'll let the scouts know ahead of time what they need to bring." Yeno finished by giving the Boy Scout salute to the audience. He smartly turned to his left, walked side stage, and switched the lights off. Each of the twelve scratched the floor with a match and lit the candle held high in shaking hands. Yeno suggested making a fire without matches as found in the Boy Scout Handbook, but when the pastor of the Presbyterian Church heard of the methods used to do his, he stopped it at once. He didn't want any flint or sparks starting a fire inside his church. Despite this precaution, his fear was to be soon justified.

Front row and center sat Andy Johnson and Esther, his wife. They waited expectantly for their son, Buddy, to recite his rendition of the Scout's Law. "A Scout is Thrifty." The first candidate, Robert Paulson, spoke out loudly in the darkness. His mother had cut his hair and slicked it down like the screen idol of the time, Ramon Navarro. His shoes shined in the darkness. His new uniform smelled like 99% Ivory soap. It was just too bad that the audience couldn't see or smell this output of her homework.

Master Paulson gave his Scout Law in one breath. "A Scout is Trustworthy. A Scout tells the truth. He keeps his promises. Honesty is a part of his code of conduct. People can always depend on him." Paulson had held the audience spellbound! His mother clapped. No one else followed her example.

Out of the darkness Yeno spoke, "No clapping until the ceremony is over please."

The next scout to recite was Joe Kane. His law was Obedience.

Yeno could not have selected a more inappropriate scout than Joe to recite this law. Joe was in perpetual trouble with his parents as the result of his antics. If there was trouble to be found, Joe was front and center. His latest prank was painting one of his neighbor's garage walls brown right after his neighbor had finished painting it blue. This earned Joe and his parents an embarrassing trip to the police station where Joe agreed to repaint the garage wall blue.

Joe had a silly smirk on his face as he recited "A Scout follows the rules of his family, school, and troop. He obeys the laws of his community and country. If he thinks these rules and laws are unfair, he tries to have them changed in an orderly manner rather than disobey them." As Joe finished, Harry wondered what law Joe was going to break next.

The next scout was Harry's buddy George Scanlon. His law was Bravery. George told Harry that he was the perfect scout for this law since he always stood "Brave" on the athletic field. Harry did have to admit that George's height certainly lent substance to his claim. George boomed out "A Scout can face danger even if he is afraid. He has courage to stand for what he thinks is right even if others laugh or threaten him." George would have a chance to show his Bravery much sooner than anyone expected.

Some of the boys' voices came through the darkness high and confident. Some came through low (whisper like) and steady. But all, except Master Paulson, came through slow. The slower the Tenderfeet spoke, the faster the candles burned. Too fast. By the time they reached the law, Cheerful, Harry's candle was down to an inch. Harry's friend Clarence Zacardi began his ordeal on the law Cheerful. Clarence forgot how to start the Law which was "A Scout looks for the bright side of life." Clarence began to cry.

One of the other scouts whispered "A Scout looks . . . " But he was quickly interrupted by Yeno's admonition "No help." Clarence cried louder. Finally, through the tears and the wailing, Clarence managed to remember enough to sob out why all Scouts should be Cheerful.

After the Law Cheerful came Thrifty. Buddy Johnson, Harry's neighborhood friend gave the Thrifty Law. "A Scout . . . ," quoted

Buddy. "A Scout works to pay his way to help others. He saves for the future. He protects and conserves natural resources. He carefully uses time and property."

Andy and Esther Johnson, in spite of Yeno's instructions, applauded. The next to the last Law, Clean, was up to Bobby Glazinski, the sloppiest boy in the Troop. He was a sloppy eater, a sloppy dresser and addicted to sniffles, besides. He sniffled before he began his recitation on "A Scout is Clean." Scoutmaster Yeno had anticipated trouble with Bobby, and was prepared for the inevitable, so he quickly tried to correct Bobby by whispering in a muffled tone, "Don't sniffle, Bobby."

The warning didn't help. Bobby sniffled louder to keep from sneezing. It didn't help, and he sneezed. The sneeze blew out his candle. "Light his candle," cried Yeno.

Harry reached over quickly and helped Bobby light his candle from his own candle. Bobby then told everyone why a Scout is clean. "A Scout keeps his body and mind fit and clean. He goes around with those who believe in living by those same ideals. He helps keep his home and community clean."

All the candles continued to burn bright and too fast. By the time they came to Harry (after he had helped Bobby), his candle was down to a half an inch and burning low. The candle burned steadily. No so with Harry's hand which now began to tremble with fear that the candle wouldn't last through his recitation. And he was right with that fear.

Harry began his law "A Scout is reverent toward God." To the horror of all, he screamed something definitely not in the Boy Scout Manual as the candle burned the final wax onto his fingers. Using his baseball skills, Harry threw the candle (still lit) as far as he could off to one side so it wouldn't hit the audience. It hit the base of the stage curtain setting it on fire.

"Fire," yelled Yeno. "Call the firemen."

"Where is the phone?" yelled Harry back to his leader.

"In the ladies room," volunteered the Presbyterian minister.

"What is it doing in the ladies bathroom?" boomed Yeno.

"By the ladies restroom, not in the restroom!" yelled the minister back to Yeno.

While this verbiage took place, Andy Johnson was already on the phone. Being a member of the congregation, he knew where the phone was and got to it. As the audience looked around in near darkness, Andy screamed to Esther, "Go stand in front of the stained glass window so the fireman won't come through that way." Too well he knew how fireman liked to use those axes to break in the easy way . . . that is right through the windows.

There was no need for the firemen. Yeno and the minister took charge. Yeno blew his umpire whistle that he always carried with him. It froze everyone in the church. He screamed in a controlled voice. "All of you now go into our buddy system. Take the hand of the person next to you. Each of our Tenderfeet will do the same. Now everyone march behind our Tenderfeet directly to the door."

It was the first time in the history of St. Paul that Protestants and Catholics walked hand in hand. While the majority of the audience and troop were being led to safety, there was the matter of the fire. It looked like the Bishop had been particularly prescient in requiring the jug of Holy Water. In fact, the only water near to douse the fire was the jug of Holy Water from Father Patton's church. The minister grabbed the jug before Yeno could reach it. "It's our water," cried Yeno to the minister.

The minister didn't quite understand how the ownership of the Holy Water had any pertinence to putting out the fire. "I don't care who owns the water," returned the minister. "It's my church that is burning."

Father Patton stepped in and said "Let him have it Yeno, it's an emergency." At father's orders, Yeno let the jug go reluctantly.

One problem came up unexpectedly. The minister with a mighty turn couldn't get the cap off. Then he cried to Andy, "Tell Esther to stand in front of the stained glass window by the front door. It is the most costly." He didn't need to bother; Esther was already stationed in front of the window thanks to her husband's foresight.

Father Patton took the jug away from the minister, opened with one quick turn, and handed it to Yeno. Meanwhile, the fire was being put out by the three "Brave" Musketeers Harry, George, and Joe Kane. They knew that a Scout was always prepared to

". . . face danger even if he is afraid". As a result, instead of rushing toward the exit with the other Tenderfeet, they headed right over to the fire, which they promptly stamped out. By the time Yeno came rushing in with the jug of water, the fire was just smoke.

At this time, the firemen arrived outside the church with their alarms wailing. They quickly looked around for the source of the fire, but only saw people milling around in the street. The fire chief was the first on the scene and he asked Andy, "Where is the fire, and why is that woman standing in front of the stained glass window with her arms spread out?"

"The fire is out, and that woman is my wife" replied Andy. "She is protecting the church window from your fire axes in case you thought it was the quickest entry into the church."

The chief laughed out loud and said, "People have very good imaginations. We have never once broken an expensive window to get at a fire. Who owns this church?"

Right at the same time as the chief's last remark, Father Patton and the Presbyterian minister came out the door. Father Patton was holding the Holy Water jug to his chest. "Minister Harry Huse is the minister of this church, chief," volunteered Andy.

The chief approached Father Patton thinking he was Huse, because of his collar. "How did this fire start, your honor?"

"I am not your honor, that gentlemen (pointing to Huse), however, is the minister."

Turning to Huse, the chief asked again, "How did this fire start?"

"It was started by the Boy Scouts."

"Did they purposely start this conflagration?"

"No, chief. It took place during their Initiation ceremony."

"You mean to tell me that part of a Boy Scout Initiation is to start a fire?"

Father Patton interrupted, "A candle burned one of the boy's fingers and in pain he accidentally threw the candle into the stage curtain. Three of the scouts stomped the little blaze out within minutes."

"Who put the fire out?" asked the chief. His question was ignored as the party's attention was diverted by the commotion around the main fire engine.

The sirens from the fire engines continued. Down from the fire engine came the rest of the crew tumbling through the crowd. Then through the crowd came Andy Johnson bellowing "You're too late. The fire is out." Dejected fireman (axes in hand) climbed back into the engine.

The fire chief turned from the minister and advanced to Andy, hoping for a better response. Angrily he demanded, "Was this a false alarm?"

"No sir. One of our new Tenderfeet Scouts accidentally lit the church's stage curtain on fire."

Still mad, the fire chief said, "Do you expect me to put in my report that Boy Scouts started this fire?"

"You can put in your report what you want to put in," returned Andy. "I'm just telling you what happened."

"I was a Boy Scout once. They're supposed to use two flints of steel to start a fire."

"This was done with a holy candle."

"I got a good hold on the Holy Water jug," interrupted Huse. "But the cap wouldn't come off. While I was doing this, the young boys stomped on the curtain to put out the fire. Father Patton took the jug away from me and got the cap off himself. He then poured all the Holy Water on the curtain, which was already smoldering thanks to the efforts of the boys."

"So this Holy Water didn't actually put out the fire?" asked the fire chief who hurriedly wrote this down in his report.

"It was a waste of Holy Water throwing it away in this fashion," concluded Father Patton. "I certainly didn't mean to spread our Holy Water here in this Protestant church. Only we Catholics are permitted to use it, in blessing ourselves for separate needs. Maybe it wasn't wasted though. Perhaps the holy water will entice some of the Presbyterian parishioners to come over to the true church."

The fire chief could see that the discussion was leading away from the fire, so he said "I don't need any more facts for my report." He closed his notebook and walked away sputtering to himself. As he came up to his hook and ladder engine, he found the 12 Tenderfeet surrounding it with eyes of wonder. "No ride today boys," sadly said the fire chief to the scouts, now officially called Tenderfeet.

Buddy Johnson, Andy Johnson's son, came forward and asked the chief, "Would you mind telling me the answers to some questions assigned to me by my eighth grade teacher, Joseph Hyde?"

"What course is that?" the chief wanted to know.

"He teaches current events, and I think this fire is an event he will want to know about."

"You were here, you can tell him just a much as I can tell you."

Buddy ignored the advice and continued "The following are fill in questions for my story. The first question . . . Why are fire engines painted red? The second question . . . How fast can a fire engine truck go? Third question . . . What is the decibel level on your fire engine's sirens when they are going full blast?"

The chief replied: "Put those questions in a letter to me and I will take them up with our Firemen's Board at our next meeting. I am sure we will need a committee to look into this—only because all fire engines are not red anymore. Some are now white. The color depends on what each chief likes best!"

"You have been a great help already Chief. Thank you," said Buddy Johnson, politely. As he walked away, however, he was shaking his head in confusion that the fire chief didn't know the answers to his simple questions immediately.

Yeno called out to the departing fire chief "If he gets all the right answers, he (when he reaches Eagle Scout) can have my job."

"I don't want to be a Scoutmaster, Mr. Yeno. I want to be a journalist. As you know a journalist searches for stories that the public should know about, and this fire is one of them," concluded Buddy.

Buddy's father, Andy, came over and said to the chief, "Is this boy bothering you with all his questions?"

"Frankly, yes," said the chief.

"Buddy," scolded Andy, "Go find your mother, we are going home now."

"Yes sir."

At this final response the firemen left. With the excitement over, the new tenderfeet and entourage called it a night and returned to their homes.

The next morning, Harry pulled one of the morning papers from the delivery bundle and read the headline

BOY SCOUT TROOP 92 SETS FIRE TO PRESBYTERIAN CHURCH

The complete news item appeared in the Metro section of the paper as follows: "Boy Scout Initiation for Tenderfeet last night ended in an unwanted fire. In the ceremony, each candidate held a lighted candle while reciting a Scout Oath. In the process of saying why a Scout is Reverent, candidate Harry McCool ignited his fingers and threw the candle into the stage curtain in the auditorium of the Warrendale Presbyterian Church. Scoutmaster Yeno picked up a jug of Holy Water nearby. Yeno couldn't get the cap off the jug and gave it to one of the guests at the ceremony, Father Patton. Father got the lid off the jug and poured the Holy Water on the curtain, dousing the fire immediately. No one has as yet explained to your reporter what Catholic Holy Water was doing in the Presbyterian Church. Mr. Yeno tells me that all the boys in the Initiation are now Tenderfoot Boy Scouts having withstood the test under fire."

Harry felt slighted that the news article failed to mention how he, George, and Joe stomping out the fire. Harry also suspected that the Holy Water mini episode was misreported. It planted a seed in Harry to always be careful about getting the full facts of any story from the newspaper, even his own St. Paul Pioneer Press.

Yeno's version of the fire was somewhat different than the local Newspaper. Yeno reported to the Boy Scout council, "It sounds like we wanted to start a fire. Harry McCool just threw the candle as far as he could after he burned his fingers. All the parents jammed the exits yelling to get out, until I restored order with the *buddy system*. When Andy Johnson made the phone call for the fire department the rest of the Tenderfeet class just stared at the fire and it was a good one for a very short while. No one was burnt, and no lives were lost. The only casualties were

Harry's hand and the pride of my boys. Father Patton blamed the Presbyterians for not making the church fireproof, and finished with saying the fire was just a prelude to the Hell they were going to anyway."

Harry never forgot the fire in the Presbyterian Church, thanks in part to the souvenir scar on his left hand, and he never did set foot inside a Presbyterian Church again. He was convinced that God, despite the dispensation from the Bishop, was sending a message loud and clear to Harry that a NON Catholic Church was completely off limits to a Catholic boy.

9

LINDY LANDS

Charles A. Lindbergh and Spirit of St. Louis. c. 1927.
Photo courtesy Morrison County Historical Society collections.

The headlines in the St. Paul Pioneer Press morning paper that Harry delivered May 22, 1927 read

Charles Lindbergh Flies Atlantic Alone

Nearly 100,000 Parisians rushed onto the tarmac of Le Bourget Airport to cheer a new international hero as the Spirit of St. Louis touched ground. When his Ryan NYP monoplane landed after a 3600-mile flight of more than 33 hours, not even the two companies of French soldiers could keep the crowd from engulfing Lindbergh and his plane. Born in Detroit and raised in Minnesota, Lindbergh didn't know what the fuss was all about, and he wasn't too sure that he liked it.

Very few of Harry's customers were awake at 6 A.M. to get the news. Harry himself was more interested in the sports headline that read: "Babe Ruth and Lou Gehrig all tied in home run derby." There was a fierce battle between Gehrig and Babe Ruth for the home run crown, and Harry wanted Lou Gehrig to upstage the mighty *Babe*. As of May 21st, they each had 9 home runs. Harry, being a true conservative Minnesotan, preferred the quiet, modest, Gehrig to the loud, flamboyant, Ruth.

The first customer that Harry found up and alive was Bob Merry who lived in a bungalow right across the street from the Floral Shop on Front Street. He was nibbling on an orange while waiting for Harry to bring his paper. Harry was afraid of Merry for good reason. He was known to be a bit peculiar while showing off unbelievable feats in his homeroom at Washington High School. One of his favorite tricks was swallowing live fish and frogs.

Merry got up from his front steps and went to his gate to meet Harry, thus saving Harry the trouble of folding and throwing his newspaper to the door. His good morning question surprised Harry. "Did Lindbergh win the race for the $25,000?" asked Merry.

"What $25,000?" asked Harry.

"Don't you read your own paper?" sarcastically came back Merry.

"I deliver the paper. No one says I have to read it," smiled

Harry. Of course Harry actually did read the newspaper, but rarely before returning home.

"Let me explain the $25,000 then," said Merry. "$25,000 was offered for the first nonstop flight from New York to Paris. I read this in your paper and I quote, 'Lindbergh took off from Roosevelt Field on Long Island at dawn yesterday overloaded with gasoline his plane sailed like a drunken seagull barely clearing the trees at the end of the runway'."

Harry felt that although Merry was an oddball for swallowing live fish and frogs, he evidently was no fool since he could remember details with a photographic memory. His quoting an article from the paper verbatim impressed Harry.

"Pardon me, Merry, I have to deliver another 178 more customers the news on Lindbergh." And with a curt good bye Harry left Merry.

After delivering 4 more papers to Merry's neighbors, Harry headed back to his starting point at the corner of Dale and Como Avenues. You may recall that Harry had to do some backtracking to cover his customers located on adjacent streets. Upon returning to Dale and Come Avenues, he put on a second sack of papers. (He normally needed two sacks to carry his 180 papers). No activity as yet could be found on Dale or Como other than Merry. Harry did, however, expect to see some lights on showing people looking for the **Special on Lindbergh.**

Just then a big streetcar came roaring up from Dale Street heading for Grand Avenue. The motorman waved at Harry with a friendly smile as usual. Streetcars were big business back in the twenties. In fact, the streetcars were so busy that each one contained not only a motorman but also a conductor. The conductor was in charge of keeping the trolley on the wires on which it ran. Any member of the Como Gang who never pulled a trolley off the wire and stopped the streetcar was 'chicken', as that was his or her entrance into the Como Gang. Harry smiled as he recalled his cousin Roberta inadvertently pulling the trolley off its tracks during the Winter Carnival.

Harry trudged up to the first customer on the hill and across the street from his paper delivery corner. The sixth house on the hill was a church that was never occupied and thus no delivery was ever made there. All were good paying accounts, German mostly, and the sixth customer was a man called Jensen, who was from Denmark. Harry found out too late that he should never have told Jensen that his mother's maiden name was also Jensen. Thereafter, each day Jensen would call Harry a 'son of an immigrant' and he would make *immigrant* sound like a swear word.

Just as expected, Jensen was up eager for the historic news of Lindy's feat. Jensen yelled down to Harry "How are you today, you son of an immigrant?"

Harry winced as Jensen said *immigrant*, but managed to return with, "I am O.K." Harry then walked away and headed for the rest of his customers. He already had enough of this Jensen guy and the sooner he got away from him, the better.

Harry passed by the empty church and moved east to Simon Street where more of his customers lived. Simon was the east end of Harry's route. No customers on this street were any trouble for Harry except for one guy named Moldenhauen, a smart, well dressed, Hungarian who chided Harry for his ragtime looks. He wouldn't be up for the news about the historic flight of Lindbergh. His only interests were in the latest movies starring Clara Bow, and when she would appear again in a Silent Movie Film. The problem with the Moldenhauens was that they took their own sweet time paying the bill. Far too often Harry would have to be back two and even three times to collect the monthly bill for papers. Harry couldn't believe that the monthly 35-cent fee was such a hardship for anyone.

He cared less when he threw the delivery to the Moldenhauen house on this historic day. Sometimes it landed in the bushes next to the steps, and sometimes on the lowest step. Harry wasn't revengeful, just irritated by the Moldenhauens. His next delivery after the Moldenhauen's house was the last apartment on Simon Street. From there, Harry returned back to Como Avenue.

He slipped behind the apartment house and came out at the biggest house on Como Avenue, the Gould Mansion. Gould was a seller of seed for cattle and grass. He was rich. He was especially rich when compared to his neighbors, who mainly worked for the railroads, the busiest industry of the 20's. But nobody was getting as rich as Hill the Empire builder, nor Weyerhauser, the lumber mogul. Harry would often stop at Gould's for a slight rest to admire the new Packard parked for all to see on Como Avenue. Harry liked Gould, not just because he gave him a $5 tip at Christmas, but also because he always smiled and regularly gave Harry a friendly "Good Morning!"

Mr. Gould was up early this morning waiting for the newspaper. Surprisingly, Gould's question was not about Lindbergh's flight when he asked, "What's the weather forecast, Harry?"

"You surprised me, Mr. Gould. I thought you would be interested in the news of the day," said Harry.

"And what news would that be, young man?"

Harry was quick to reply, "The nonstop flight of Charles Lindbergh from Long Island to Paris, completely alone!"

"I already heard the news on my radio, Harry. Right now I am more interested in the weather."

"Why?"

"I sell seed Harry. Rain helps my seed grow wherever it is planted. That's why I am always obsessively interested in the weather."

Harry thought he better look up the spelling of *obsessive* when he got home as he examined the weather report for Gould and quoted, "Partly cloudy, breezy and a little cooler. Does that help?"

"Not at all Harry, I am looking for, and hoping for, rain! I just planted seed in the Governor's front lawn and I want it to grow."

Harry was taken aback by the reference to the governor, and asked, "You work for Governor Christiansen?" with surprise showing in his voice.

"I have been one of his Republican buddies ever since I helped him defeat Floyd Olson for Governor in the last election," proudly boasted Mr. Gould.

But Harry couldn't spend any more time talking politics. Mainly, being a very young man, he didn't know much about the likes and dislikes of politicians, and even more importantly, he really didn't care. He was, however, impressed that Mr. Gould was on such intimate terms with the governor.

Gould's delivery was just two blocks away from Harry's last stop on Como Boulevard. After completing Como, he had to cross the Northern Pacific railroad tracks. Just over the tracks, Harry came to the Nightingale Food Store, and then reached his mother's favorite meat store, Toreks. By this time, Harry was just about out of the first sack of papers. He increased his delivery speed after being held up by Gould for a little longer than usual.

The next house on Harry's route was between the Northern Pacific railroad track and Jessamine Street, which was the last street before the tracks. The owner was Mr. Creek. Creek's house was high on a hill, far from the street by a good 20 yards. There were two open targets for Harry to avoid when he would stand in the street and toss the paper aimed at Creek's porch, namely the hollyhocks and the roof. On windy days the paper either landed on the roof or in the hollyhocks. It was not tough for Mr. Creek to dig a paper out of the hollyhocks, but a paper thrown on the roof usually ended up stuck in the gutter, impossible to reach without a ladder. This irritated Mr. Creek, and, after an irate call to the McCool's home, Harry always had to return with another paper.

When Harry delivered the afternoon paper, he was often times met by Sally Creek, the eight year-old daughter of the Creeks. She followed Harry until he reached the last customer, the Trainers on Front Street just off Como Place. Harry couldn't shake her, but she gave him company and that broke up the day for him when he made the last tour of his route about 5:30 P.M. But on this historic morning Sally must have still been asleep.

At 1023 Como, Harry met an early riser and baseball fan, Robert Sullivan. During the mild spring, summer, and fall months, Sullivan was up and caught the paper as Harry hurled it to him. Sullivan was a movie projectionist in a downtown theater, and with that connection, Harry and his brothers sometimes got into the movies free.

"There is great news coming to the movie business in a few months, even more exciting than Lindbergh's flight," said Sullivan. This interested Harry. He wondered what could be more exciting than flying solo over 3600 miles of water. Sullivan smiled as he continued with "I heard all about Lindbergh on my radio, but I am still interested in what the morning paper has to say about it."

It came to Harry at an early age that most people have many seemingly mundane things closer to their hearts than what was occurring in the outside world. He knew that Gould's first interest was in the weather and how it would affect his business. Sullivan, on the other hand, was interested in what was new in the movie business that might affect his future as a projectionist.

Harry politely asked, "What's new in the movies that you say is of great interest?"

"You know all about the silent movies that you see at my theater, don't you?" asked Sullivan.

"Yes, that I do," answered Harry.

"Soon you will hear what you now only see, can you believe that?"

"You mean the people in the movies will talk and you can hear them?"

"That is exactly what I mean," replied Sullivan.

"When can I see and hear the first one?" and Harry was anxious about his query.

"The first one will be a musical with Al Jolson called **'The Jazz Singer'**. It is suppose to reach downtown St. Paul later this summer."

"What's Jazz?" asked Harry.

"Only the newest, hip, American music happening," answered Sullivan.

"Never heard of it," replied Harry.

"Well, I'm not surprised. It's pretty big mostly in Chicago and New York, but it's coming here soon. Mark my words," said Sullivan.

Harry mulled over the thought of a movie with sound, and then asked, "What's going to happen to old Paul, the organist, if the movie has sound?"

"I guess he had better start looking for another job," laughed Sullivan.

"Maybe the sound will be a flop. Anyway, please let me know

when you have the first showing so I can tell my brothers and sisters. I'm sure that they'll want to come too."

"O.K.," agreed Sullivan. "Now tell me all about Lindbergh or should I just read about it in the newspaper?" inquired Sullivan.

"Sorry, I don't have any more time to chat. After you read the story, be certain that you tell your three daughters about it. I am guessing that they will be quizzed by their teachers in school tomorrow, since it's a very big current event" advised Harry to the father of three: Marion, Catherine, and Lillian. Harry was not a big conversationalist. In fact, just the opposite, a long conversation like he was having today bothered him, mainly because it was holding up his delivery to all his remaining accounts.

So, Harry hurried his last delivery on Front Street and went home. His mother was the only one up and she had just finished making his breakfast of cream of wheat, toast, and ovaltine. She asked about the paper, "Let me see what is in there about Charles Lindbergh." Dutifully Harry handed his mother the last paper in his sack and spun to the basement door, opened it and hung his sacks in the usual place, halfway down the cellar steps. "Any one up for the big news?" continued his mother.

"Three that you would know, Merry, Gould, and Sullivan."

"Not another soul?" she asked.

"Not a one."

"Were you surprised?" asked Martha.

"Yes, I thought a lot more customers would have been waiting for a report on Lindbergh's flight," responded Harry. "Gould mentioned that he heard it on the radio. Do you think that radios are going to replace the papers someday for giving the latest news?" Harry started worrying about a sudden drop in paying customers, followed by a drop in family income.

"I doubt it. Most people like to take their newspaper and read it cover to cover so they can enjoy the news" answered Martha. "Remember how your dad used to sit it his favorite chair for over an hour after dinner reading the Dispatch?"

"Yah, I guess your right Ma. No way people are going to stop reading their papers and listen to the radio all day," said a relieved Harry, now recovering the income lost 30 seconds earlier.

"I'll bet that someday soon Lindbergh will be in our town for a big parade down University Avenue. You know he comes from Little Falls, north of here, and I'm sure he will go up there too."

"How do you know all this stuff, Ma?" asked Harry.

"I keep up-to-date by reading your paper. That's how," replied the *Stubborn Dane*. Martha had picked this nickname up from her neighbor. They all knew she was a stubborn dame from Denmark, and so the name had stuck. Harry finished breakfast and headed off to Sunday mass.

Later that morning as Harry was deep in thought reading the newspaper, his mother came and interrupted him by asking "I have something important for you to do, Harry. Am I breaking up something critical?"

"Well, what I am doing is not important for you alone, but it is for the future of all of us."

Martha, his mother, smirked and replied, "You mean there is something more important in the world than putting up our screen windows to keep the mosquitoes out of our home this summer?"

Harry wasn't sure if his mother was making a joke, so he answered "The world outside Ma. Lindbergh is making news everywhere he goes. I thought Pete and Joe were going to do that job this afternoon?" Harry tried not to smile thinking about how his older brothers frequently buffaloed his mother by procrastinating their jobs with lame excuses.

Martha became impatient, "Harry, stop your nonsense about your brothers. Find Joe and Peter and put up those screens NOW. If you wait any longer, it'll be fall and we'll have cooked inside all summer without any breeze."

Harry realized that he wasn't going to win this battle and the heat of summer wasn't far off, so he put the paper down and went out to the garage to look for his brother Joe. As expected, Joe and his buddy Jim were working on the canoe. Harry interrupted them with "Joe, finish up. Ma says we have to put up the screens today."

Joe answered, "Okay. Give us 15 minutes and I'll be ready to help. If you haul all the screens out, I'll make you a new home plate for your games in the empty lot from some of the left over wood."

Harry responded, "It's a deal." Harry found his brother Peter and started bringing the screens out for their spring cleaning, prior to hanging them on the windows. True to his word, Joe showed up 15 minutes later to start the long ordeal of changing from winter storm windows to summer mesh windows. Harry dreamed of heroics like flying the Atlantic to keep his mind off the time consuming window exchange, which took the three boys the rest of Sunday.

The next day was Monday, and Harry delivered papers as usual. After finishing his breakfast, he put on his jacket and headed for the back door. "So long, Mother," and away he went to school just a half mile away as the crow flies. The shortest route would be via Como Boulevard, but he was forbidden to cross the Northern Pacific Railroad tracks at the end of Barrett Street, which ran into a dead end at Jessamine. Instead, his route to school was turn left on Orchard, go six blocks to Chatsworth and take a right, pass under the tracks going three blocks as Chatsworth rounds the corner and becomes Van Slyke, take an immediate sharp left onto Como Avenue as it went by the church, and there you came to the school.

School doors were open when Harry arrived, and Sister Mary Brennan was at the east door welcoming the half-awake children. "You didn't cross the railroad tracks, did you Harry?" asked the good nun.

"I came my usual way Sister, right down Orchard to Chatsworth and down Chatsworth until it turns into Argle and VanSlyke. And here I am right on time."

"Say no more, Harry. You don't have to go to confession to me on your route here."

"Our city fathers sure messed up the streets, or they had friends who they liked to name streets after," said Harry all too knowing the confusing labyrinth of his paper route.

Sister Mary Brennan was one of six teaching nuns from the nearby convent. They had almost five hundred students under their constant care and supervision. In July of 1910, Father Thomas A. Patton became pastor of St. Andrew's. Father Patton was a native of Ireland, and had 900 parishioners. In 1911 he reported to his superiors that, "there are no business or professional men in the parish except for one prize fighter." Harry later discovered that Father Patton was well qualified to be a prizefighter himself. Actually there was a prizefighter in the parish by the name of Mike Gibbons. Mike was related to the famous heavyweight Tom Gibbons who lasted 15 rounds against Jack Dempsey—then the world's heavyweight champion.

When Harry arrived at his eighth grade classroom, Sister Lordine appeared to be all excited about Lindbergh's flight. She asked Harry to give a full report on it at class that morning, which he reluctantly agreed to do. Harry got up in front of the class and read right out of the paper all about Lindbergh's flight and arrival in Paris. One of the smart girls in the class (in fact at that time all the girls were not only smarter than the boys, but also began to grow taller, or so it seemed to Harry) questioned Harry. "Tell me, Harry, just how Mr. Lindbergh is going to get himself and his plane back to the United States?" asked Catherine Elm, a sister to one of the Lay teachers.

"I don't know how he is going to get back," replied Harry.

Sister Mary Brennan interrupted Harry with a remark: "Look it up in your paper and tell us when you find out."

Harry mumbled "Yes, Sister", and returned to his desk.

After school let out for the summer, Harry closely watched the Ruth/Gehrig home run derby, but also (per his mother's advice) kept track of Lindbergh's activities after his landing in Paris. Here are some comments taken directly from the Pioneer Press:

> *Within hours after his landing, Lindbergh was acting just like in his barnstorming days doing spins, and rolls. The Spirit of St. Louis flew over hundreds of thousands of Parisians near the Arc de Triumphe and the Eiffel Tower. He left France in a field of glory and headed for Belgium. Seventy five thousand people met him at Brussels as well as King Albert. Every newspaper*

had a different sobriquet: 'Lucky Lindy', 'The Lone Eagle', 'Eagle of Liberty', 'The Monarch of the Air', 'The Flying Idol', 'The Bird of the Clouds', 'America's Son', 'Columbus of the Air', 'Eagle of Liberty', 'That Airplane Man'.

Harry continued his lookout for more on Lindbergh, and just what Lindbergh was going to do to get back to the U.S.A. After reading the paper for a week, Harry finally found just how the plane, the Spirit of St. Louis, would be brought back to the U.S.A. He called the initial inquirer, Catherine Elm, to tell her. She lived on Front Street and he had no trouble finding her phone number. "Hello Catherine this is Harry."

"Harry who?" she asked.

"Harry, the paper carrier from Sister Lordine's class."

"Our paper carrier's name is Louis, Louis Torok."

Harry ignored the slight and continued "I told Sister Lordine that I would find out just how Lindbergh would get his airplane back to America. Since school is out, I thought that I would call you since you seemed so interested."

"Now I remember you Harry, very bright and cute. Did you call me to take a ride with you on your bicycle around the lake?" hopefully asked Kitty.

"Of course not. I called to tell you just how Lindbergh will get the Spirit of St. Louis back to our country." Harry wondered how Kitty got the idea that he wanted to spend time with her on a bicycle ride.

Kitty was disappointed he was not calling to take her for a ride around Lake Como. Nonetheless, she continued on her social train of thought by whispering over the phone, "Did you hear the latest?"

"Latest what?" whispered back Harry, thinking that some dark deep secret was about to be revealed.

"George kissed Eleanor in the clothes' closet the last day of school."

Is that the big secret thought Harry, as he returned to a normal tone of voice and said "That's their problem, now getting back as to why I called."

"I thought you liked Eleanor. Aren't you jealous?"

"I am too busy carrying papers to be jealous," returned Harry. "Here, Kitty, is what happened with his return" and Harry read "President Calvin Coolidge ordered a warship—the U.S.S. cruiser Memphis to bring the Colonel and The Spirit of St. Louis back home. Under Lindbergh's supervision the plane was crated and delivered by Lindbergh to the U.S.S. Memphis. Before his return, Lindbergh was treated royally in Great Britain. After Lindbergh left Belgium, he flew to London. Expecting a few Britons, Lindbergh flew over the Tower of London while below was a crowd of one hundred thousand Englishmen. Lindbergh then met, upon landing, the Chancellor of the Exchequer, Winston Churchill. Churchill's comments were sent all over the world when he said of Lindbergh, 'He represents all that a man would say, all that a man should do, and all that a man should be'."

Kitty stopped Harry from reading any more about Lindbergh with: "Stop Harry, I get the picture. He is the hero of the day all over the world."

"You got that right, Kitty, but did you know that that there are a lot of other very interesting things in the newspaper."

"Like what?"

"The Piggly Wiggly on Grand Avenue was robbed yesterday," said Harry. "You know how the crook did it?"

Kitty was a very practical girl and asked, "Am I supposed to know?"

"No, the robber set an empty bag on the back counter. On the bag the clerk found a note that read, 'Hand over all your money or I'll shoot you'."

"Why are you telling me about this robbery?" asked Kitty.

"I just want to show you that I read my own paper," Harry returned crisply. "Something else I read that your mother and father might like to know."

"What is that?" she answered getting tired of hearing all the news.

"Calvin Coolidge has been told not to go to the Wild West show in Rapid City."

"Who told him that?"

"An organization called The American Humane Society."

"And who are they?"

"They're a group against cruelty to animals. The Wild West show has bulldogging of steers and bronco busting, and the Society claims that's being brutal to animals."

"Okay Harry, enough with the news. I suppose that you are going to read me the Obituaries, next?"

Harry thought this very clever of the young girl, but then realized that she was just being a smart aleck. He added one last item "One thing I forgot to mention, Kitty. Rapid City is where the President plans to go for his summer vacation."

After this comment, Kitty said goodbye, and hung up. Harry felt relieved when she hung up the phone. Talking to a girl was very strenuous, and Harry was near exhaustion from the short conversation. He made a mental note of asking his brother Joe for some tips on how to talk to a girl.

Ever since Merry made the comment about Harry not reading the paper he delivered, Harry vowed to read all that was fit to print. Whereas he had been skimming articles in the past, he now read some articles more than once. He made up his mind to get all the news he could find on Lindbergh's flight over the Atlantic. He knew from reading his paper that the receptions in Paris, Brussels, and London were minor compared to Lindbergh's reception in New York City. For future reference, Harry cut out many excerpts from the paper to be shown to his classmates when school restarted in the fall, two of which read:

On June 10, 1927, the cruiser Memphis passed through the Virginia capes with Lindbergh and the crated Spirit of St. Louis on it. A convoy of four destroyers, two Army blimps, and forty airplanes accompanied him. Lindbergh's comments were: 'I wonder if I really deserve all this?' The Memphis toured up the Potomac and Lindbergh's mother, Evangeline, met him for the first time since his solo performance across the Atlantic Ocean. Lindbergh and his mother were the guests for the night of Calvin Coolidge, who insisted on it. Coolidge gave Lindbergh the

Distinguished Flying Cross and promoted Lindbergh right there and then to Colonel in the United States Reserve Corps. (Side note: Ruth 18, Gehrig 14 home runs)

On June 13, Lindbergh flew over Baltimore, Wilmington, Philadelphia, and Trenton. Sometimes upside-down as thousands from below in the street and on rooftops waved to him. He landed on Mitchell field on Long Island, New York. Three hundred thousand people greeted Lindbergh at the Battery. New York City offices, schools, stock exchanges, and most of the national financial markets were closed for Lindbergh Day. As Lindbergh rode the mile up Broadway from the Battery to City Hall, four million people filled every inch on the sidewalk and every window along the way. The ticker tape and shredded paper was so thick that few could see Lindbergh or the skyline through the 'Snowstorm'. (Side note: Ruth 21, Gehrig 14 home runs)

Harry spent most of his time, however, playing baseball with his neighborhood friends, and between delivering the newspapers every morning and every evening (except for Sundays), he found his summer slipping away very fast indeed.

10

BALL GAME ON BARRETT STREET

Barrett Street is neither long nor wide. It is stuck between the Calvary Cemetery to the south and the Northern Pacific railroad tracks to the north. Its total distance is a scant 2½ blocks. In 1927 most of the homes on this block were modest two story structures built right around World War I. Barrett street had none of the Como Lake shoreline elite. What it had was mostly blue collar with a few white collar workers that included a policeman, a restaurant owner, a switchman who worked on the railroad, a painter, a teacher, and other good working people. 1023 Barrett stood in the middle of the 2nd block up from the cemetery nestled between a bungalow very much like itself and a shack that you'll here more about later.

Across the street from 1023 was an empty dirt lot full of weeds and rocks. This lot was Harry's **Yankee Stadium**. The kids used the flattest rocks in the lot for bases, and everything was 'in play'. With homes on both sides of the infield, the neighborhood kids felt like they were playing ball inside a tennis court with an open end towards center field. The backstop was the garage of two sisters named Lynch, who lived on Avon, which was a block east of Barrett Street. Home was a wooden plate made by Harry's brother Joe, set on the dirt lot 10 feet from the sisters' garage. Next to the Lynch's home on Avon Street was the residence of three girls whose father owned an Irish pub on Front Street, two blocks from the northwest corner of the Calvary cemetery. Left field was the home of Al Streibel who owned the parrot that squawked continuously from his cage on the Streibel back steps while the boys played baseball on the empty lot.

Barrett Street separated the infield from the outfield.

Across the street from Streibel were Harry's friendly neighbors Andy Johnson, his wife Esther and their two boys, Donald and Buddy. Andy was a tinner. He was ready to go fishing any time of the year. His target was always the same game fish: Walleye Pike, Pickerel, and Muskellunge. He never had to go far from St. Paul to find fish. One of his favorite haunts was White Bear Lake. Andy simply went east on Larpenteur for 3 miles, and then north on the new US Route 61 another 4 miles and he found himself on the shores of this beautiful lake in less than 20 minutes. Just before each outing his wife, Esther, could be heard shouting and carrying on something fierce. One would think he was headed for Canada over 500 miles away for a month's vacation to warrant such abuse. Besides fishing, his only other vice was shooting off his shotgun at midnight come New Year's Eve for the entire neighborhood to hear.

Unfortunately for the baseball kids, the left field foul line intersected Streibel's back porch. Streibel did not like kids, having none of his own. If your baseball hit Streibel's house, you had trouble. He usually came storming out his back door, flyswatter in hand. The swatter was an intimidation device. Streibel never actually hit any of the baseball gang with the feeble stick. A far more annoying problem than Streibels' fly swatter was his pet parrot. He kept his parrot on his back porch in a golden cage. Its favorite line was, "Polly want a cracker." Harry learned the value of constant baseball chatter like 'hey batter, batter . . . you hit like my sister' to drown out the parrot's irksome voice. Of course, batting like one of Harry's sisters was no compliment.

Left field for the baseball 'diamond' was Andy Johnson's front porch, and left center was Harry's front porch. If you hit a ball onto Harry's roof just above his bedroom, you were immediately awarded a home run. Harry's mom, Martha, liked to sit on the front porch in the summer and swing on the lazy hammock. She didn't mind the boys playing baseball across the street, nor did she mind the ball landing on top of her house; at least she knew where her boys were located. Since the front porch and upstairs bedrooms had soft mesh screens over the windows, there was little danger of hit balls breaking glass.

Baseball was Harry's first love, not only because he could play it all summer, but also because he played it very well. He had the best arm in the neighborhood, mainly from using his arm every morning and afternoon throwing papers to his customers, sometimes as far away as 90 feet. His batting eye was also excellent, due in part to his 20/15 vision. Unless it was raining, Harry would be game for an afternoon of baseball with his neighborhood pals all summer long.

One hundred and fifty feet from home plate in Dead Center field was a small shack (so dubbed by the neighborhood families). This poor excuse for a house was owned by a woman and her two daughters. The mother was Mrs. Horn, and the daughters were Margaret and Alice. They had no inside toilet facilities, only an outhouse that they said was their gem of American Architecture. Any ball hit from home plate 150 feet to and through the open door of this gem was automatically a home run, considered out of the park. In fact it was never retrieved by any of the boys nor returned by anyone for obvious reasons. To use a golf expression, the ball was considered "unplayable." The younger Horn girl was known as a boy chaser. She loved the boys, and since they were often playing baseball in the empty lot, it only seemed natural for her to spend as much time as possible playing too. She actually was quite good at playing ball. With most neighborhood games needing a girl or two to round out the lineup, Alice Horn, being the best girl player around, was a welcome addition to any team.

Right field belonged to a friendly man called Smiling Gil Bratner. Smiling Gil lived on the corner of Barrett and Hatch Street, or right field as the boys called it. He scorned the baseball games and the boys who played it. He was somewhat of a dandy, and rather loathsome of playing sports. His work was in the clothes industry, a salesman in Montgomery Ward's men's department to be exact. He specialized in men's suits that came with two pairs of pants. Gil looked out of place on Barrett Street with his fancy clothes. His strength was dancing, in which he was the only one in the whole neighborhood who could do the Charleston. In fact, on Saturday nights, Gil always went dancing at the Coliseum Ballroom, which was located, by the St. Paul Saints Minor League ballpark. It was easy for Gil to get there, he just took the Como Harriet street car to Dale Street and from there the Dale street car to University and from University the street car to Lexington Avenue.

The Coliseum Ballroom was the favorite spot for all the best dancers in the Como Lake area of St. Paul. Late on Saturday nights, when Gil returned home from the Coliseum, he would ask the Como Harriet motorman to turn up Barrett street so he would be closer to his home on Barrett Street. No amount of persuasion would work on the motorman. He would always leave Gil off at Chatsworth, the 'official' streetcar stop. Harry thought it rather odd that after exercising all night on the dance floor, Gil couldn't walk the short two blocks from the streetcar stop to his home. It was unfortunate that Gil didn't play ball because he had a good arm, that he proved every time he threw the ball back to the players who might have hit a home run off his front porch. His popularity reached its height the night he and Margaret Horn won the Marathon dance contest at the Coliseum. Gil bragged he could have gone on dancing for 30 more hours had not Margaret dropped to the floor in exhaustion.

Across the street from Gil, along the first base line, lived Jack Straub, a policeman. Straub's mother was a member of the altar and rotary society. Besides praying for her son (who lived the dangerous life of a policeman), she and her friends played their favorite game of cards, 500, every Wednesday. A ball game during the card game was not approved by the society. But there was nothing they could do about it because Harry's mother, Martha, played 500 with them. There was an enigma that surrounded the Straub house for Harry, and one day he asked his mother to solve the mystery. "Why is it, mom, that every Saturday afternoon as I go to carry papers a beautiful girl gets off the Como Harriet streetcar and goes to officer Straub's house? The next morning when I leave to carry my Sunday papers, the same woman leaves on the Como Harriet streetcar. This pattern repeats every Saturday and Sunday."

Martha told Harry, "It is none of my business nor yours, either."

Martha did not solve the mystery and Harry never dared ask her again. Still curious, one day he decided to ask Jack, "Hey neighbor, who is that women that visits you every weekend?"

Jack answered, "She is a cousin of mine from Mankato and visits us weekly." Jack completed his statement with, "You kids better watch out for cars when you play ball. One of these days if you don't watch out, someone will get run over." Harry should have paid closer head to this warning.

In the middle of July, Harry made big plans for the *baseball game of the summer*. It would be the Barrett Street Royals against the members of Boy Scout Troop 92. The game was to start at 11 am Wednesday the 20th of July. Harry would captain the Royals, the name he gave to his Barrett Street regulars, and his friend Joe Kane would captain Troop 92. The game was to be played on Harry's home field, namely the empty lot across the street from his home. One of the advantages of playing on the empty lot was that each team could manage the field without a shortstop or center fielder. Between the narrow dimensions of the field, and the tall elm tree that gobbled up most fly balls to center field, there was no reason to have two infielders by second base, nor three outfielders. In fact, the second baseman could handle most of the balls up the middle, many of which fell softly from the elm tree. All this meant that Harry could tell Kane he needed only seven players and all members of the team had to be legitimate Boy Scouts, or sisters of a Troop 92 scout. He knew Kane, on some occasions, brought in "ringers".

Kane called Harry on the phone the day before the game and gave him his lineup:

Captain and pitcher—Joe Kane
Catcher—Mike Redford
First base—Yeno
Second base—Clarence Zacardi
Third base—John Donahue

Kane then said, "That's all I have for sure now. The other players I will bring with me tomorrow."

The five announced players were legitimate members of Troop 92, but the two unknowns worried Harry, given Joe's penchant for ringers. Nevertheless, he decided to wait and see what Kane was up to when he brought his full squad.

Harry responded, "Sounds good, Joe. Don't forget to bring at least one bat for your team. I'll bring the ball." Harry used the term 'ball' euphemistically since the sphere he owned was completely black from all the tape used to preserve its shape, and had little resemblance to a fine new white baseball that was used by professionals. The reminder to bring a bat was necessary since Harry had no intention of letting the opposition use his bat (also tightly wrapped in black tape to extend its life).

Harry announced his team to Joe as follows:

Pitcher—Harry
Catcher—Harry's brother Joe
First base—Ed LaBarre
Second base—Gladys Miller
Third base—Joe Miller
Left field—Katy Thenes
Right field—Mary Thenes (Katy's twin sister)

Harry called this team his magnificent seven. He felt particularly clever in choosing the two Millers for the infield. They lived on the other side of Al Streibel. Harry knew from experience that since Al Steibel's home was so close to third base, his infielders had to be on good terms with the old grouch, or some sure outs could turn into base hits as they became distracted by his antics. It would be particularly important to calm Streibel down if anyone hit his house with a line drive that could shake up his fancy living room filled with Irish Waterford. Another reason for starting the Millers in the infield: Gladys was on good terms with Streibel's parrot. Her hobby was bird watching, and she loved to help Al fill the big 12-inch by 18 inch feeder every day. Streibel was likewise partial to Gladys and always called her "My little chickadee baby." Gladys, in return, could identify every bird that flew in and around Al's house, from Blue Jay's, Red Bellied Woodpeckers, Orioles, Cardinals, Doves, Black-capped Chickadees, Larks, Robins, Wrens, and Thrushes to Palliated Woodpeckers. Not only could Gladys identify the birds, but she could also spell them, for she won a contest at Como School as the best speller of all the students. Harry smiled as he envisioned the infield problems for Joe Kane's team.

Joe Miller and Gladys, his sister, were children of an immigrant, George Miller, originally from Greece. George left Greece in 1910, and, like many of his relatives, came over to America via a series of train and boat rides to open a restaurant. He located his business in downtown St. Paul on St. Peter Street amidst many Germans just a block away at the Assumption Catholic Church. George Miller's Café and bar did not have a good reputation, as St. Peter Street in the 20's was a hangout for vagrants and the lost souls from the Assumption Church. Streetlights were gas lamps in 1927, and many a time did Harry go accompany his neighborhood friend Joe Miller helping Joe's father light the lamps at night and put them out in the morning. Harry also helped Mrs. Miller to keep Joe and Gladys away from George's questionable patrons.

It was not easy for Harry to find a good, honest umpire for the game, but he did come up with one from an unexpected source: his sister Alice, who volunteered and Harry selected her without any questions from Kane. Kane liked his sister, especially those long strawberry blonde curls. He found no objection to her being chosen as the umpire. Harry felt that she might not know a ball from a strike but she would know what was right and what was wrong. There was no question that she was authoritative, and none of the neighborhood kids would dare give her any lip. At exactly eleven on July 20th the game started. Harry initially objected to Kane having Yeno, a man in his twenties and Boy Scout leader, on first base. Kane reasoned that a big target was needed for Troop 92's wild arms. Harry finally said O.K. because despite Yeno's age, he had seen Yeno try to catch a baseball before.

Alice took the head umpire stance behind Harry on the pitcher's mound and cried, "PLAY BALL!"

Kane had given Harry his batting order:

1. Sally Strong, doctor's daughter, right field
2. Betty Strong, her sister, left field
3. Clarence Zacardi, second base
4. Kane, pitcher and clean up hitter
5. Redford, catcher
6. Donahue, third base
7. Yeno, first base

The two added players, namely Sally and Betty Strong, were sisters of Troop 92 member Carl so Kane hadn't tried to bring in ringers. At least that's what Harry thought at first.

Per instructions beforehand, they had no shortstop or centerfielder because of the elm tree. The first hitter, Sally Strong, walked up to the plate and went into a crouch. Since Sally was only 4½ feet tall on her tiptoes, the strike zone looked like a shoebox when she bent over. It was most difficult for Harry to throw strikes to such a small target, and he threw her four balls for a walk. The second batter, Betty, same height and same crouch as her sister, was also walked on four pitches. Harry started to appreciate Joe Kane's strategy about his two unnamed players: short girls hard to get out. Clarence Zacardi was up third. Before he came to the plate he combed his beautiful dark black hair. He hit the first pitch into the Elm tree and before the ball came out of the tree the two girls scored. This left Zacardi standing on what he thought was second base with his hand on the tree. Harry came over and tagged him out. Clarence yelled, "I'm not out, I was holding onto the tree. Isn't that second base?"

"No," replied Harry. "Second base is that rock you should have been standing on, not just holding onto the tree."

"I refuse to be called out," he shouted.

Alice, the umpire, came over and shouted in Clarence's ear, "You're OUT. Leave the field."

"I'm not going to leave the field, I'm going to stay right here," challenged Clarence.

"You're WRONG, Clarence" declared Alice. The ring of authority of Alice's voice scared Clarence, and he left to go to the bench. Harry smiled as he watched Clarence's futile effort to win an argument with his big sister.

The next batter was a left-handed hitter, Kane, captain of the Troop 92 team. Kane went through the pattern set up by big league players who hitched up their belts, pulled their cap down over their eyes, and slammed the bat against the home plate. He was ready to hit a home run. Harry started Kane out with a high fastball that just missed Kane's chin. Kane just dug his shoes further into the dirt and went through his same motions as before. He hitched up his pants, pulled his cap down and slammed the plate with his bat. His extravagant preparation appeared to be fruitless when he swung at Harry's next offering and sent a high, lazy fly ball over Harry's head into the elm tree and second baseman Gladys Miller. Gladys got under the ball and was all set to catch it but it fell next to her just missing hitting her in the head. Harry yelled at her, "Didn't you see the ball?"

Gladys just said, "Yes, but just as the ball was coming down from the elm tree, I spotted a beautiful Blue Jay in the top branch."

While Harry and Gladys discussed the merits of her fielding, Kane was running all the bases and made home plate just as Gladys finished her alibi. Kane considered it a home run, which it was. "Nobody will believe that story, Gladys," grunted Harry.

"Mr. Streibel will love to hear that there are Blue Jays in the neighborhood looking for his feeder," persisted Gladys.

With Gladys still looking at the Blue Jay, Harry walked over and picked up the ball lying at her feet, and headed back for the pitching mound. The next batter up was Mike Redford. Mr. Nightingale, the grocer, affectionately called him the 'candy counter kid' because Mike loved eating candy bars that gave him a big stomach. Harry, still disgusted over the last play, threw a fast hard one on the inside of the plate. Mike couldn't get out of the way, and the pitch hit him right in the stomach. There was plenty of blubber, though, and it didn't hurt Mike one bit. He strolled down to first base munching on a candy bar that he pulled out of his pocket.

Next up was the Eagle Scout John Donahue. He blasted Harry's first pitch over the elm tree. It soared above the highest branches and landed on the roof of 1023 Barrett Street. Per game ruling, this was a home run. Donahue, like a pro, just trotted around the bases after Redford, making the score five to nothing. Yeno was next up. He swung late on Harry's first pitch and hit a screamer down the first base line into foul ball territory. The ball hit the Straub house broadside with a resounding 'Smack'. The four members of the Altar and Rosary society jumped from their 500 tables as if they were shot. Mrs. Straub was the first to come out the back door, cards still in hand. She spotted big Yeno waving his bat to get her attention. "Sorry," cried Yeno.

"What are you doing playing with these young boys and girls?" scolded Mrs. Straub.

"They asked me to fill in on this game," apologized Yeno. "Joe needed one more player."

"Don't you have a job?" probed Mrs. Straub.

"Right now all I do is fill in at the Workhouse helping the superintendent guard the prisoners who live there," Yeno replied.

"There must be a shortage of 30 day sentences or you should be over there now" hounded Mrs. Straub.

Yeno walked apologetically towards Mrs. Straub, who was now accompanied by the other 500 players, namely Harry's mother, Martha, Mrs. Zimmerman and Mrs. Madden. "Go easy on him," pleaded Martha to Mrs. Straub. "He is a wonderful Scoutmaster."

"O.K., Martha," agreed Mrs. Straub. She waved a threatening hand at Yeno. "Don't let this happen again."

"Yes, Ma'am," responded a downcast Yeno.

The sound of Yeno's liner smacking into the Straub home aroused a few spectators from nearby. The two Lynch girls, Mabel and Helen, came out to stand by their garage, which was a backstop for the field. They appeared to be gossiping to each other. Both taught German in the Washington High School off Rice Street. "Was the ball lost?" Mabel asked Harry's Brother Joe, the catcher.

"Guton tag Herr Joe," cried the older sister, Helen.

"I don't know yet. Yeno's having trouble with Mrs. Straub and her card players. You see my mother over there with them, Miss Lynch?"

Helen came back with German to Joe, "Gibt es noch etwas davon?"

Joe, in desperation, turned to Mabel for translation, "What did she call me?"

The other sister, Frau Mabel, said, "She just said, 'It is a very beautiful day.' No harm meant in that Joe?" These girls knew all the members of the McCool family by their first names. Joe had anticipated some remark not too kind as he had run ins with these two sisters before.

Helen continued in German, "Ich hatte gesprochen."

Joe to Frau Mabel: "Did she swear at me?"

Mabel responded, "All she said was that she has spoken."

Harry said to Joe, "Don't try to understand German. You will have to take their class in school to learn it. Those two girls are right out of Germany. Let's get on with the game."

The 500 card players went into Straub's house for more cards. The commotion was over for now. Yeno was still at bat. He popped up the next pitch to Ed LaBarre and was out. Harry promptly walked the Strong sisters again, but got Zacardi out on a soft-liner to Joe Miller, his third baseman. With three outs in the scorebook, the Barrett Street Royals came to bat.

Harry was the first batter for the team. Since the Royals were already behind by five runs, they needed base runners, not heroics. As a result, Harry forewent trying for the big home run, and tried to bunt his way on base. Unfortunately, a wily Kane smelled the ruse, and threw Harry out. The biggest surprise was Yeno catching the ball. Brother Joe was up next. He could see that Donahue was hugging the third base line, so he push a grounder between second and third that rolled to a stop in front of Betty Strong, the left fielder. While Betty talked with her sister, Joe made it all the way to third base, just beating the throw from Zacardi, who had retrieved the ball. Next up was Harry's first baseman Ed LaBarre.

LaBarre was part French and part Indian, his father French and his mother Ojibwa Indian. Ed's French ancestors came to St. Paul via Canada and the Hudson Bay trading company. Ed lived with his mother, two brothers, and a sister in a shack like the Horns on the corner of Victoria and Orchard. They used the same outdoor facilities as the Horns. Ed LaBarre was by far the best hitter on the Royals. Ed LaBarre hit the first pitch from Kane over Barrett Street and it headed right for the outhouse. Unfortunately, for no apparent reason, some member of the Horns or the LaBarres had left the front door open to the outhouse. In a wink of the eye, the ball disappeared from sight through the open door into the building. Joe and Ed scored easily as no one from Joe Kane's team wanted to get the ball. Harry called the game off right then and there. Even though his team was behind, Harry had a motive for finishing the contest early, and he didn't want any more trouble with Mrs. Straub.

Before the big game on Barrett Street, Harry had, as usual, delivered his papers in the morning with Putzer. The paper had plenty of news. Headlines in the St. Paul Pioneer Press read,

Bears vanish as Bulls Soar!!
Five Year Old Prince Made King of Rumani.
Babe Ruth, Lou Gehrig Play Saints Today!
Coolidge Pans for Gold in Mystic, S.D.
New Dodge Prices Drop from $1,000 to $875

Despite wanting to beat Joe Kane and his Troop 92 team, Harry wanted ever more to see the Babe and Lou Gehrig play baseball. The Babe and Yankees playing the Saints was a rare visit indeed, and he couldn't fathom missing the chance. The game was to be held in nearby Lexington Ballpark, so Harry didn't figure there would be any problem getting to the field. The only problem that remained was finding someone to deliver his afternoon papers. When the game was stopped for an "unplayable lie", Harry hurried right home to change into clothes for the game. After changing, he went over to the Straub's home and broke up the 500 game to ask his mother about delivering the afternoon papers for him. She had helped him before, especially on Sundays. Most important, she knew the route. Martha couldn't imagine stopping this boy of hers from seeing the Yankees. This might be the only time he would ever get to see the Babe and Lou Gehrig in his lifetime. She agreed to take his route, but told Harry "This is a one time deal. Don't expect me to do this again. It's your responsibility." His mother, Martha, saved the day!

Harry was elated. By this time, Joe Kane had returned home and found his dad eager to see the exhibition baseball game. Joe asked if he could bring Harry, and his dad obliged by calling and asking Harry if he wanted to see Babe Ruth with his son. If so, he would pick him up right after 1 P.M., and give him a ride with his son to Lexington Park in time for the game. Harry would be Kane's guest, "Be sure and bring your brother, Joe, to the game too," urged the father.

On this beautiful Wednesday in July Harry was excited, unfortunately too excited. When he heard Kane's car honking outside, he rushed right out the front porch full speed ahead. Without looking to the right or left as he ran out of his house, he plunged right into Gil Bratner's oncoming car, head first. The car rolled over him as he lay in the street. The fender of the car tore open Harry's left ear. Blood was all over his face. Gil jumped out of his car after stopping, and picked up Harry in his arms. The only noise was Harry's screaming. Gil said, "I didn't see him coming."

Kane, and his son Joe, without a second thought of calling anybody, took the bleeding boy away from Gil and laid him in the back seat of their car. Mr. Kane immediately drove Harry to the only doctor they knew existed in the neighborhood, Hugh Ritchie the dentist. Ritchie's office was on the second floor above the drug store on the Northwest corner of Dale and Como Avenues. Dr. Ritchie took one look at Harry and made a frantic call to Dr. Waas, a medical doctor who lived right by Como Lake. Waas was in Dr. Ritchie' s office within 10 minutes, one half hour after the accident. Dr. Waas checked for broken bones, and determined that, despite the blood, it was nothing serious. Dr. Waas and Dr. Ritchie had Harry all bandaged up and ready to go home in a matter of minutes.

When Kane took Harry home, he was greeted by the women from the 500 club including Harry's mother Martha, who as they put it, "Was worried sick over the accident." Martha felt relieved when Harry showed up with the Kanes sporting a bandage around his head, but not looking the worse for wear.

"Thank God!" she cried and took Harry and put him right on the bed in the porch. Gil Bratner himself had called the police and they arrived just as Martha was putting Harry on the porch. Gil and Joe's father gave the police report just the way they saw it. There was no need to arrest Gil for reckless driving as it was plain to all sides that Harry ran into the car, and Gil never saw him or could have stopped. Harry told his mother that Kane, his son, and Harry's brother Joe should go onto the game for a once in a lifetime appearance of seeing the great Babe Ruth and Lou Gehrig. Harry was doomed to sit while the great Ruth and Yankees played the St. Paul Saints. Eyewitnesses to the event would be his brother Joe and his friend Joe Kane. Harry just stayed at home on his bed on the porch and moped. His mother carried the papers and got Joe Miller from across the street to help her.

The next morning, Harry was so anxious to read the results of Ruth's visit to the Saints that he got up as usual to deliver his papers. He completely forgot about his injuries and headed right over to his paper pickup point. He grabbed the first paper and read the headline, "20,000 see Yankees defeat the Saints in exhibition 9 to 8." Another headline that baffled Harry was, "Bears Vanish as Many Stocks Soar." This headline interested Bob Marry whose father was a stockbroker. As his son put it, "My father is making a ton of money through the stock market, but I don't know why. But with his luck, it could go for nothing."

As Harry walked his route, he was hoping to talk to Mr. Kane or Joe about the game from the day before. Luckily, Mr. Kane was up and came to the door as Harry arrived with the newspaper. He greeted Harry with: "How are you feeling today? You had quite an escape from injury that could have been serious yesterday."

"I'm O.K. today, Mr. Kane. Thank you. Tell me what happened. I read that Ruth didn't hit any home runs yesterday?"

"My son, Joe, and your brother Joe, had to see the game from the centerfield. There were so many people at the game that they had to put the overruns into the area behind centerfield. We got pretty close to Lou Gehrig, but Ruth was on first base signing autographs most of the game from kids who ran to see him from the stands. I heard at the game that Gehrig leads Ruth in home runs right now by one. Ruth has 30 home runs and Gehrig has 31. We did see 'The Babe' hit 3 doubles, and would you believe we saw him pitch the last inning?"

Harry showed his knowledge of Ruth's career with his next statement: "Didn't he start out with Boston as a pitcher?"

"That's right," agreed Mr. Kane. "You sure know your baseball."

"Any commotion during the game?" asked Harry.

"We did have some excitement from our short stop, Leo Durocher, who questioned some of the balls and strikes from the umpire. He was almost thrown out of the game, but finally realized he had lost the argument and shut up. Harry, let me see what the paper says about the game," said Mr. Kane as he reached for the newspaper. Harry handed Mr. Kane his newspaper and Kane read the account of the game.

"Babe Ruth is known in the United States by more people than our President, Calvin Coolidge. Ruth is the most photographed man in the world, even more photographed than the Prince of Wales. Here is an interesting headline about the game," said Mr. Kane. "Ruth and Gehrig Find Pen Mightier than Bat to Thrill Boys. The story goes on: The pen was mightier than the bat at Lexington Park yesterday afternoon when the Yankees stopped to play the Saints. The Yankees were traveling from St. Louis to Cleveland on their way to another American League pennant for sure. Babe Ruth and Lou Gehrig, twin exponents of the home run art applied about a quart of ink autographing baseballs and scorecards for small boys. But neither managed to find the range of the distant right field fence, much to the disappointment of the largest throng Lexington Park ever held for a baseball game. Nearly 20,000 fans filled the grandstand and bleachers and cut down the playing area by forming a solid wall around the outfield. They witnessed about everything that a single baseball game can show in nine innings, and stayed to the finish despite rain in the closing acts."

Harry's brother, Joe, was waiting at the front door for Harry to get home from carrying papers that morning. "How's the head today? Are you bleeding?"

"Thanks for your interest, Joe. I am O.K. today."

"You're late getting home from your deliveries. Why?"

"I had a long talk with Mr. Kane about the Yankee game against the Saints yesterday," answered Harry.

"Well, don't be too disappointed. You didn't miss any home runs by either of the Yankee twins, Ruth and Gehrig. All they could hit were doubles. Ruth hit three doubles and Gehrig hit one double. The big hitting star," continued John, "was our third baseman, Foss. He went five for five against two Yankee pitchers, Pipgras and Miller. The Saints scored four runs in the eighth inning. That was the excitement of the game. In fact, a fan who sat next to the Yankee dugout during the game told me on the way out of the game that if it weren't for Ruth's pitching in the ninth inning, the Saints would have beaten the Yankees. I'll let you read what the paper's sports writer, Dick Cullum, says about the game and ninth inning."

Harry sat on the front porch and read all about the end of the game. Oscar Roetiger got the only hit off Ruth, a double in the ninth inning. Durocher, the Saints shortstop, got the attention of the fans when he questioned Umpire H. Johnson's knowledge of the strike zone. Ruth struck out Pilette to end the game. That ended Harry's analysis of the ballgame. Under Dr. Waas's orders, and starting to feel some after effects from the accident, Harry went upstairs to bed to recover from his run in with Gil Bratner's car. The next morning Harry noticed that Gehrig had hit two home runs in Cleveland and passed the Babe in the race, 35 to 34.

11

TROOP 92 GOES OVERNIGHT ON ST. CROIX RIVER

June weather in Minnesota is usually quite pleasant. The days are warm, but not too warm, and the evenings are mild and cool. The first week of July is usually the same. The end of July and month of August, however, are another story. The days are insufferably hot, and the nights rarely cool enough to permit good sleeping. The upstairs' bedrooms at Barrett Street, sans air conditioning or fan, only attenuated the problem. As summer of 1927 coasted into mid July, the predictable heat wave hit St. Paul. As if this wasn't enough suffering, the mosquitoes that bred nonstop in nearby Lake Como had taken up permanent residence in Harry's backyard. He couldn't even step outside in the evening without a score of the nasty little pests making a pincushion out of his arms. It was with great anticipation, then, that Harry looked forward to a Boy Scout overnight scheduled for mid August on the St. Croix River. He expected relief from the heat, if no respite from the bugs.

It had been almost four months since the fire fiasco in the basement of the Presbyterian Church during Troop 92's Initiation ceremony. Despite Harry's initial anxiety over the consequences, he had not been dismissed from the troop for starting the blaze. In fact, Harry's quick thinking in stomping out the stage curtains with George and Joe Kane elevated their stature among the fellow scouts. The Musketeers were mini celebrities amongst Troop 92, and the starting of the fire provided a continual source of ribbing from his friends.

The upcoming Boy Scout Overnight was on Harry's mind Saturday the 6th of August as he left home to pick up his papers at Dale and Como. Harry had almost completely recovered from his auto accident. A scar over his left ear would be the only permanent damage to his head. Following his usual route, he passed the Calvary cemetery and thought of his father who had died just 7 months earlier. Harry's most vivid memory about his father was the time James whipped his older brother Peter for smoking. It didn't stop his brother from smoking, but it sure stopped Harry from even thinking about smoking. Harry would grow to appreciate this little legacy from his father more in later years as several of his friends died from lung cancer.

Harry loaded his paper bags and delivered his first paper to the floral shop on Front Street. As was usual for Saturday morning, the shop was knee deep in arrangements that would be placed on the nearby graves of dearly departed loved ones. After delivering the paper to the floral shop, Harry walked back up to Como and Dale and started his half-mile trek down the road to the Northern Pacific Railroad Tracks crossing. His first customer on the Avenue was old lady Olson who was sitting on her front steps weeping. Harry could do nothing to stop the flow of tears from the old lady's eyes. But he had been through this ordeal in the past with Mrs. Olson. He stopped and asked her, "Why are you crying so much this early in the morning?"

"I always cry the first Saturday in August," sobbed Mrs. Olson.

"Why do you always cry the first Saturday in August Mrs. Olson?" asked Harry for the umpteenth time.

"It's for that fisherman I married in 1902 who died August 8th two years ago on a Saturday."

"How did he die?"

"He drowned while fishing in the St. Croix river," she replied.

Harry had heard the answer a dozen times before, but knew she never tired of talking about the old fogey. He humored her by asking, "Did he fall out of the boat?"

"Yes, he was caught in a storm, and the boat was a canoe. I always told him he should use a rowboat, but he insisted on using a canoe. Said that's the way the Dakota Indians fished, and by God they knew what they were doing . . . I'll bet they never fell out of their canoes and drown! Why didn't he listen to me? Now I'm all alone and miserable."

Harry never knew how to respond to her grief, so he simply nodded his head. He didn't want to tarry any longer with Mrs. Olson, though. Three of her cats had begun to cuddle up to Harry's sneakers, and Harry did not like cats. What bothered Harry even more was her parrot. The old lady had taught the bird to say, "Good bye, Harry." So Harry happily left Old Lady Olson with the cats meowing and the parrot chirping, "Good bye, Harry."

Before he reached the Northern Pacific tracks, he came to Yeno's house, his Scoutmaster. Harry never knew Yeno's last name. He was just that good old boy from Como Avenue. He was waiting at his door as Harry came around the corner. Yeno had good news, which he shouted to Harry, "Troop 92's overnight is going to be next Friday and Saturday, Harry. I need you to check with John Donahue on the canoes and sleeping bags."

"Great news, Yeno! I'll go by his home after I finish my route. By the way, my brother Joe has just finished his canoe for the trek. Joe and his friend Jim Lethert have already tested it on Como Lake."

"And it didn't sink?" asked an incredulous Yeno.

"Of course it didn't sink. He and his pal made the canoe right from instructions they found in the Boy Scout Manual. Joe said that the Boy Scout Manual is never wrong, and he had no fear that the canoe would work the first time he put it into water. In fact, he said that it was as smooth as silk in the Lake," boasted Harry.

"Good," smiled Yeno. "I'll need his canoe and a few more canoes to get Troop 92 across the St. Croix River from the Minnesota shoreline." Scoutmaster Yeno had planned this overnight with the boys for the past four months. It would be on the second Friday in August. All troop members would have to be alerted about the day and what to bring for the overnight.

Harry wasn't quite finished talking about Joe's canoe. He continued with the construction history of the craft. "My brother's canoe is made of pine wood furnished by Widmer Grocery store. The store got the wood from apple crates. It was not exactly made like the canoes the Ojibwa and Dakota Indians made, but the important thing was that it did float. He is looking forward to getting that new Boy Scout Canoeing Badge now that it is finished."

"Tell your brother good work. I'll look into that badge at the next scoutmasters meeting." As Yeno was answering, he wondered whether Joe's canoe would float on the currents of the St. Croix. The quiet shallow waters of Como Lake were a contrast to the deep running waters of the St. Croix. Yeno resolved to make sure that every scout had a life preserver before setting foot in any of the boats to be used for reaching the island in the middle of the river.

After getting Yeno's news about the overnight, Harry continued on his route. His next stop was Joe Kane's home, which was on Grotto Street near the Cemetery Superintendent's house. Joe lived with his parents and was a character and one half. You my recall his *Obedience* recital at the Boy Scout initiation. With the latest scout information from Yeno, Harry now had definite news about the overnight. A light was on at Kane's basement, which usually meant that Joe's father was up. Many times Harry had seen Joe's father taking his shower in the early morning hours. Since Mr. Kane didn't go to work early, the ritual always mystified Harry. Harry rang the back door bell. Joe's dad came to the door draped in a towel. "What in the hell are you waking up the family for at this hour?" he snarled.

"Where's Joe? I have an important message," Harry's voice trembled as he made this remark.

Mr. Kane looked over and behind Harry as he asked "Is he in trouble again? Is it in the newspapers? You're not with the cops are you?"

Harry glanced back wondering what Mr. Kane was looking for, as he answered "No, Mr. Kane, I'm not with the cops I'm here to tell him about our Boy Scout overnight trip."

Since Joe wasn't in trouble, Mr. Kane let out a sigh of relief and changed the subject with a question, "Has Ruth hit any more home runs?"

Harry handed Mr. Kane the newspaper with a remark, "See for yourself, Before yesterday's game, it was almost a dead heat between Gehrig and Ruth."

Just then, the wild kid of the Kane family, Joe, came to the door and asked, "What's up Harry? I see you got the old man up and roaring?" It appeared that young Joe had no fear of his father and thought it rather humorous that his dad was steamed up.

Harry replied "I just saw Yeno and he tells me that the overnight for us Boy Scouts will be on the St. Croix River next weekend."

"Ah," smiled Joe. "Very good. I still have some fireworks left over from the 4th. They'll sure put some life into that trip."

Great thought Harry, just what we need, another Troop 92 fire. After a brief Boy Scout salute, Harry left the *Obedient* Joe with his father's stern look portending more trouble ahead. His father, a truck driver for Waldorf Paper Co. took no nonsense from anyone, especially his own kid. Harry heard Joe's father swearing loudly at Joe for not showing his father respect. In fact, the language was nothing a young Boy Scout should hear. As Harry hurried off he could hear the familiar "Joe, if you think I'm going to let you get in some fool trouble with that Boy Scout Troop, you have another thing coming. I'll show you . . . "

Harry hurried off hoping to find more receptive ears for his good news about the overnight. He walked past the Front Tavern. Between the Tavern and the corner was a cemetery monument company. He gently tossed the paper to an open porch, then turned the corner and headed up Crowell Avenue. The first house to his right was the Zacardi's home. And here would be the worst scout in the troop, Clarence. Clarence could not even start a fire with two flint stones and some cotton. The home was a place of sorrow one year before when Clarence's brother dove into the YMCA swimming pool and hit his head on the cement floor of the pool, killing him instantly. Harry was certain that the Zacardis would move back to Mr. Zacardi's home in Zafferana on the eastern slope of Mt.Etna in Sicily after the tragedy. Many a time Harry listened to Clarence's dad, Angelo, pine for the homeland that he had been forced to leave in 1905 as a teenager to seek work in America. Harry could practically recite papa Zacardi's voyage to America:

> It was November 1905. I was 15 years old. There was no work, and no land for me to till. The sun was shining, and Mt. Etna was blowing off smoke across the Ionian Sea. I'll never forget the beauty of the sky, the water, and my homeland. My mother gave me one valise to pack my clothes and 1000 lira, all the money she had saved for my future. The boat ride across the Atlantic was horrible. Every morning I woke up, ate breakfast, and threw up over the side of the ship. All day long the ship rolled left, then right, then left, then right. I never want to go on the sea again as long as I live. When we got to New York, the skyline was incredible. The buildings, the people, the ships were everywhere. Ellis Island was a pit. So many people, so many languages, so much confusion that I'll never know how I got past the customs' official with my limited English: 'Hello, I am Angelo. Thank You'. Luckily my uncle Giovanni met me and got me a train ticket to Chicago. What a nightmare 10 months I spent in the stockyards there. All the bosses took advantage of my innocence. I wanted desperately to return to Italy, but once again fortune turned me elsewhere. My uncle Giovanni had a friend in St. Paul who needed railroad workers. The next week I took the train to St. Paul, started working immediately, met my wife, and had my boys. The rest is history.

In time, all wounds healed, and the Zacardis did not return to Italy. It did, however, take a good year for the family to overcome their grief. Harry wondered how long it would take before his family would heal from the death of his father.

Nobody was awake at the Zacardi's home, so Harry threw the paper up to the steps and hurried on the rest of his route. Harry was happy that the family was still asleep—especially the mother. She blamed Harry for any and all the trouble that her son, Clarence, got into. One Saturday morning, Harry, his brother Joe, and Clarence got into trouble with the police. The trio began the morning by taking the streetcar to downtown St. Paul. They paid their way into the Lyceum Movie House, which was showing "Rackety Rax" starring Victor McLaglan and Greta Nisson. Harry incidentally paid the way for all three. They climbed in the darkness to the balcony and seated themselves. Just as the movie started, the manager of the theater, Don Donahue, and two cops came up to the balcony. They stood in front of the three boys and the manager pointed his finger at the three of them as he said, "There they are! Officers take them in, especially the good-looking dark haired one. He is always sneaking in here."

The two cops took all three by the back of their necks and dragged them to the police station just a block away. Each of them was given a chance for a phone call. Harry showed the cops his torn up tickets, and seeing the stubs, they were excused. Nevertheless, Joe called home to explain just what they were doing in the police station. Of course, after being pressed by his mother, Clarence said that it was all Harry's fault. Harry got mad at Clarence not because he called his mother and fingered Harry. No, Harry was always in trouble with Mrs. Zacardi, nothing out of the ordinary there. Instead, Harry was mad that Clarence did not stick up for his good friend and share the blame. In fact Harry suspected that Clarence's mere presence with him and Joe got them into trouble because he was always sneaking into the downtown theaters.

When Harry and Joe got home, their mom relayed how an angry Mrs. Zacardi had called to blame Harry for the entire incident because her son would never sneak into anything, not even a cookie jar. Harry's mother, Martha, never did like Clarence with his slicked down hair and pleasant smile. She wasn't too keen on their Italian heritage either. She agreed passively with Mrs. Zacardi, but didn't take it any further. To Martha it was just a case of an overly protective mother trying to shift the blame.

After finishing his route, Harry quickly checked the home run derby: Ruth 35, Gehrig 37. He then headed over to Summit Ave., just west of Snelling, where Eagle Scout John Donahue lived. When Yeno was appointed Scoutmaster, the church committee named John Donahue as assistant. The committee knew that Yeno was new to Scouting, but John, as an Eagle Scout, knew it all.

Maybe even more important, Donahue's father was a local building contractor of considerable means. He would see to it that the troop would be well heeled with equipment on any camping trips. For the trip to the St. Croix, Yeno was hoping that Mr. Donahue would provide the canoes, tents, and a few sleeping bags. Harry knocked on the front door just before 9 A.M. The youngest of Donahue's eight children, a small redheaded boy, answered the knock by opening the door and saying, "Well?"

This definitive question stumped Harry for a moment. Meanwhile, the young boy gave what he thought was the Boy Scout salute. Actually, the scout salute was simple enough. Instructions from the Boy Scout manual read, *"Cover the nail of the little finger with your right thumb. Raise your right hand, palm forward with the three middle fingers upward. Next bring your hand smartly up to your head until your forefinger touches the edge of your right forehead and above your right eye."* It appeared from Harry's viewpoint that the boy put his right thumb under his nose and with the other four fingers, waved. Harry did not like that at all. The little brother of John's did not have the Boy Scout salute down pat at all. This was very disappointing for the brother of an Eagle Scout.

Harry tapped the boy not quite so gently on the top of his head and told him, "Go get your brother John, monster."

John appeared at once and said, "Did the brat give you his version of the Boy Scout salute?"

"Yah, but he's not very funny, John. Yeno sent me over to check on the equipment for the St. Croix overnight next Friday."

"O.K., Harry. Does the rest of the squad know?"

"So far I've only told Joe Kane, but I am sure the word will spread fast. Here is the patrol group as I understand it from Yeno: you, me, Joe Kane, Mike Redford, Peter Paulson, Clarence Zacardi, Buddy Johnson, George Scanlon, my brother Joe, and Bill Callahan; counting Yeno there will be eleven of us. You know, John, we have been talking about this overnight for months. I have dug up all the information I could find about the St. Croix. First of all, we have to be very careful on crossing to the island from the Minnesota shore. The St. Croix is very turbulent in this area. The river stretches over 154 miles down the border of Minnesota and Wisconsin. The rocky cliffs along the river were formed millions of years ago by glaciers. This wild and dangerous river joins the Mississippi River at Prescott, Wisconsin. Along the way are osprey, blue herons, deer, raccoons, beavers, and even black bear."

"I hope you realize Harry," interrupted John, "we will need tents on this overnight. The scout treasury doesn't have the money to buy all we need."

"I know, John. Can you talk to your father about this," said Harry. "He told me one time that he would pay us for what we need. 'Spare no expenses' he told me. Is he still good for that offer, John?"

"Of course, he will be good for whatever he promised," returned John.

"Well, we need three tents that can hold 4 people each, and 5 canoes. My brother Joe just finished building a canoe, so include that one in the count. And I need to check on sleeping bags" said Harry.

"Okay, I'll check with pa and make sure the canoes and tents are in order."

"If your dad can help with the tents and maybe 3 or 4 sleeping bags, then Yeno is going to send out a letter with the items that each scout must bring. Anything else each scout brings is up to his mother or father within reason. That's it for now, John. I better get on to another member who will be with us, Bill Callahan, over there on Fairmount Avenue."

Harry left Summit and headed over to the Callahan's home. Bill was up and just back from Mass where he was everyday. Harry greeted him with "Good morning, Bill. I have some good news for you."

Bill smiled, "You want me to carry papers for you on Sunday?"

"No," answered Harry. "Nothing like that at all. Remember the Boy Scout's overnight?"

"Yeh, I've been waiting all summer. When we go, Harry, be sure I get the responsibility of getting wood for the fire" pleaded Callahan.

This was a rather unusual request for responsibility on the overnight, thought Harry. "Well, I tell you Bill, all those assignments will be up to Yeno, the Scoutmaster. Tell him," advised

Harry. Bill's mood seemed to change as Harry told him to ask Yeno. "You don't seem too happy about this overnight, Bill. What is the matter?"

"I just want to be in charge of gathering wood for the fire. Is that so unusual?" Callahan questioned.

"Yes, ordinarily no one volunteers for gathering wood for the fire" suggested Harry. It had never occurred to Harry the reason behind Callahan's request for gathering wood was that he was afraid to sleep in the dark. That fact came out during the overnight. Harry left Callahan and decided that the spreading of the 'good news' wasn't so much fun after all. Let the rest of the troop find out for themselves he thought.

The next day, Yeno sent a letter to the parents of each scout that read:

> *Your boy is in for the adventure of a lifetime: an overnight on August 12th to Whispering Winds Island in the middle of the St. Croix River returning the 13th. We shall take care of him as if he was our own. The theme for the overnight is to be 'Leave No Footprints'. I will leave it to you to make sure he has the correct equipment along. This personal gear should include: first aid kit, toothbrush, comb and a case to hold the comb, pocket knife, lightweight water canteen, flashlight, book bag, insect repellant, and, most importantly, toilet paper. We also recommend he carry the Boy Scout Handbook, and hiking socks are optional as is candy and gum. Every Scout should prepare himself to become a useful citizen and give happiness to other people. Pick up time will be 9 am sharp at the Presbyterian Church on Como Avenue. Remember 'Be Prepared'.*

The Wednesday before the overnight, Yeno called a meeting of all the troop members destined for the night on the St. Croix. He reported: "I have already chosen the campsite. It will be on the Whispering Winds Island in the St. Croix River. It can only be reached by canoe. We can take the new US Highways 61 and 8 to get us to the river, but no motorized vehicles are allowed on the island. When you pitch your tent, make sure there are no overhanging tree limbs. Look for shade from the sun and protection from the wind. At night, damp air and insects tend to settle toward the valley. A campsite half way up a small hill may be breezier, drier, and have fewer mosquitoes. You should bring two gallons of water each for drinking and cooking. If you take water from the river, it must be purified before use. For firewood, look for dead twigs and fallen branches. Pitch your tent several hundred feet away from the St. Croix. Anything else, read the Boy Scout Handbook. Here are your assignments:

John Donahue	Drive and bring tents furnished by his father
Peter Paulson	Set up tents
Joe Kane	Get the food for the night meal and the morning breakfast
Mike Redford	Set up tents
Clarence Zacardi	Bring guitar and lead the campfire singing
Harry McCool	Store the bacon and eggs in a cool place for breakfast
Bill Callahan	Gather wood and build campfire
Joe McCool	Drive McCool Model T
George Scanlon	Buy potatoes, meat, eggs, toast, jam and jelly from the treasury of the Troop
Buddy Johnson	Set up tents
Yeno	Drive and supervise the whole undertaking

Yeno continued with "While I don't expect anyone to be swimming in the St. Croix, I am still going to put up a buddy system. At intervals of the day, I will blow my referee whistle and have each one of you tell me where your buddy is. Here is the buddy line-up: "Harry McCool and Scanlon, Kane and Zacardi, Redford and Callahan, Paulson and Johnson, Joe McCool and Donahue. Any objections will be of no use. This is the buddy system for the whole time we are in camp."

The Friday of the overnight arrived with the sun shining in the sky, and not a cloud in sight. Wind velocity was 5 mph and coming from the northwest, no problem. There were three cars with plenty of room for the scouts and their gear. The new US roues 61 and 8 proved very convenient for reaching the river in just over 2 hours. Canoes were no problem, John Donahue's father had his trucking department get four canoes plus Joe's canoe and set them down on the Minnesota side of the St. Croix River. All the scouts had to do was show up with their gear, get in the canoe and glide across the river to the campsite. Two boys to a canoe, and Yeno had his own canoe and led the way across. All the boys had life jackets, as prescribed by the manual and all is well that ends well, and this much of the trip did end well as all six scouts and their leader, Yeno, got to the other side without drowning. Much to Yeno's surprise, Joe McCool's canoe made the crossing without a hitch.

Food was aplenty, and it was carried in Yeno's canoe. Kane and Scanlon brought enough food, candy and eggs, etc., to cause Yeno's canoe to overflow. There would be no hunger strike on this patrol. The perishable goods they gave to Harry.

After arriving on shore, the boys dragged their canoes away from the river and started to unload the gear. Yeno and Donahue headed off to pick a campsite. A short trip up a nearby hill produced just the spot: a flat grassy knoll with a splendid view of the river.

Yeno drove a stake into the ground to make the center of the site, and then returned to the shoreline to give more instructions. First order of business was the campfire. "Bill," Yeno called to Callahan.

"Yes, sir," cried Bill as he dropped his backpack down and saluted Yeno.

"Do you have an axe in that backpack?" Yeno asked.

"Yes, sir," replied Bill.

"Bill, do you know the safety rules in handling an axe?"

"I sure do, Mr. Yeno. I learned them all from the Boy Scout Handbook."

"Why don't you just run off the safety rules in using an axe, Bill, before you get started."

Bill began "American pioneers used the axe to cut trails through the wilderness. Because of its size and the way it is used, the axe can be more dangerous than other wood tools. Remove the sheath only when you are ready to use the axe correctly. Always use sturdy leather boots when you are chopping with an axe. Leather will not stop a blade from hitting your foot, but leather may limit the extent of your injury. You will notice, Mr. Yeno, that I am wearing leather boots."

Yeno said, "Good start, Bill. You must have plenty of room in which to swing the axe. Check your clearance by holding your axe by the head. Slowly swing the handle at arm's length all around you and over your head. While cutting be sure that other people are at least 10 feet away. I cannot emphasize this tip enough; never carry an axe on your shoulder. Place a sheath over the axe blade whenever it is not in use. Carry the axe with one hand, the blade turned away from you. If you stumble, toss the axe away from you as you fall. Now you can gather the wood and build the campfire. I must go see if Peter, Mike, and Buddy know how to put up the tents."

While this was happening, Harry began to dig his deep hole for overnight storage. He put the bacon and meat on the bottom of the trench, and the eggs on top where they could not be broken. Or so he thought.

As Yeno turned his attention away from Bill, he didn't notice that Bill had a tube mailer with him that could hold a set of golf clubs. He wasn't to learn until later that the carton contained a machete, ordinarily used to cut and clear the underbrush in the Latin American Countries.

By this time the tent trio of Redford, Paulson, and Johnson had hauled the tents up the hill to the selected campsite and begun the set up. Yeno caught up with Mike and Peter, but couldn't see Buddy anywhere. Peter was standing near what looked like a half up tent. Yeno asked him, "I am looking for Buddy. Where is he?"

Peter answered, "Right now he is in the middle of that tent to your right."

"This is a perfect time to test our buddy system" Yeno said. He took his whistle from around his neck and blew it loud and often. In that moment the erect middle part of the tent collapsed.

Peter anxiously cried to Yeno, "Buddy was holding up the tent while we put in the stakes. When he heard the buddy whistle, he must have dropped the pole he was holding, thus collapsing the top of the tent."

Yeno could not believe what he saw. "You mean he was holding the tent up while you were staking it?"

"That was the idea. It was Buddy's idea to hold the tent, not mine."

"We better get him out from under that canvas before he suffocates," an alarmed Yeno cried.

The boys tugged open the tent and Buddy came out gasping air from under the canvas. He even smiled. "I heard the buddy whistle and dropped everything," gasped Buddy.

"It must have been a frightful experience," offered Yeno.

Meanwhile the other four pairs of buddies heard the whistle and came running, Harry with George, Joe with Clarence, Bill with Mike Redford, and Joe McCool with John. Each pair raised their hands to show they had found each other and with the show of hands Yeno said, "No alarm boys. I was just testing my buddy system."

"Why does Buddy look so pale?" asked Donahue; the Eagle Scout knew trouble when he saw it.

Peter offered an explanation, "Buddy read the instructions and came to the conclusion that it would be easier to put the tent up from the inside and then we could put stakes in where they belong."

"I am happy he didn't suffocate," added Yeno. "What do we do now?"

John Donahue took over. "Leave the tent erection to Harry and me. Stand aside you three," (motioning to Mike, Buddy, and Peter).

As John and Harry went to work, Yeno asked, "Who made the decision on what tent we should all use?"

"My father did," answered John. "He wanted all of us to be comfortable."

Harry interrupted and said: "John, we had better teach Mike, Peter, and Buddy how to get the other tents readied for the rest of us."

"That sounds like the right thing to do," smiled Yeno, rubbing his two hands together in glee. Yeno took a moment of the squad's time and said, "Here is something to think about as you go about your assignments today. We need a name for this squad. Here are some suggestions: Alligator, antelope, bat, beaver, bear, bison, bobcat, cobra, dragon, eagle, flaming arrow, fox, frog, frontiersman, hawk, Indian, liberty bell, lightning, moose, owl, panther, pheasant, pine tree, raccoon, ram, rattlesnake, raven, roadrunner, scorpion, shark, stag, tiger, Viking, wolf, and lastly a wolverine. Underline the names you think we should call our patrol and turn them in at the campsite tonight. Meanwhile Bill, you and George get started on finding a site for tonight's campfire. O.K.?"

"Yes, sir," replied Bill and George in unison.

Yeno then handed the two an excerpt right out of the Boy Scout Handbook that read, "For a safe fire, select a spot on gravel, sand or bare soil, away from trees or bushes, dry grasses and anything else that might burn. Look overhead for branches that sparks could ignite. Clear site of boulders that may be blackened by smoke or large tree roots that might be harmed by too much heat. Clean the fire site down to bare soil. Make a circle about 10 feet across. Rake away pine needles, leaves, twigs, and anything else that might catch fire. Keep a pot of water close to the fire site for emergency use."

By two o'clock the tents, campsite, and campfire circle were complete. The time had arrived for exploring the island. Yeno gave the assignment: "Boys, as part of earning your Camping Merit Badge, I want you to hike for one and one half miles. Upon returning to camp, the troop is to make a Map of the island. Mike and Bill, you go north. Harry and George, you go east. Pete and Buddy, you go south. Joe and Clarence, you go west. While you boys hike, Joe McCool and John are going down to the river to help Joe finish the Canoeing Merit Badge requirements. Remember boys, stay with your buddy and **Leave No Footprints**

Mike Redford and Bill Callahan, armed with his machete unbeknownst to Yeno, set out to the north. A short time after they started, Bill asked Mike "Do you have a compass?"

Mike responded "No. Why would we need one? The St. Croix runs north and south, right?"

"Right. How does that help?"

"Here is the plan," plotted Mike. "We go straight north for 45 minutes, and then turn around and head straight back south to camp."

"Sounds good to me," agreed Bill. And off they went, Bill leading the way with his machete. As they chopped their way through thick brush and long grass with Callahan's machete, they could hear the mighty St. Croix rolling nearby. One would think no compass would be needed with such an obvious landmark so close by. Bill had total confidence in Mike's plan for returning to camp.

While Joe and Bill were going north, Harry and George went east. Since the island had a narrow east-west dimension in comparison to its north-south dimension, they reached the river within minutes. Harry asked George "Do you want to go north or south?"

"Neither" answered George. "Yeno said go east, and that's exactly what we've done. No need to keep walking and get ourselves all tired out. Here, have a candy bar I brought along just in case we got hungry."

As Harry and George sat down next to the bank of the river to eat candy bars, they watched as Joe McCool and John Donahue carried Joe's canoe down to the river. Within seconds they were in the water and paddling north, upstream. When Joe and John were about 2 miles upstream, Joe jumped out of the canoe. Harry stood up and pointed as he yelled "George, quick get help. Joe's going to drown."

George, being no lifeguard, needed no encouragement. He jumped up and ran for the camp. Meanwhile, Harry watched in alarm as the current was carrying Joe. Not wanting any part of the river, he looked around and spotted a long tree branch that lay on the ground nearby. He picked up one end, dragged it to the river's edge, and timed tossing the other end into the river just as Joe floated by. Unfortunately, Joe wasn't looking for help. Part of his requirement for gaining the Canoeing Merit Badge was to jump out of, then climb back into a canoe. The tree branch hit Joe in the back of the head, temporarily stunning him. Luckily, Joe had his life vest on and was in no danger of drowning. Harry, not privy to the assignment, watched in horror as Joe floated further from shore. Just then Yeno arrived and asked, "What's going on Harry?"

"It's my brother Joe. He fell out of the canoe and when I tried to save him I knocked him out. He's going die."

By this time, Joe had regained his bearings. John had been tracking alongside Joe waiting for him to climb back into the canoe. Within a minute of Yeno's arrival on the scene, Joe had accomplished this feat, and the two boys navigated the canoe back to shore. Joe was furious and he shouted at Harry "What were you doing? Trying to kill me?"

"No Joe, honest. I thought you fell out of the canoe and were going to drown. I was trying to save your life by pulling you out of the river with that branch."

The pathetic look at Harry's face told Joe that he was suffering worse for the incident than Joe himself. He let his brother off the hook with "Well, little brother, your intentions were good, but next time call out to me before your throw anything in my direction." Harry forced a weak smile and headed back for camp.

Returning to Mike Redford and Bill Callahan, the first part of the trip to the north worked out just fine. After all, there were headed away from camp, and any direction was the right direction. After hacking and trudging for ½ an hour, they decided that it was time to return. They looked for the river, but were too far from the shoreline to see any water. Bill started to lose confidence in Mike's plan and asked, "Mike, I can't see the river, how do we know which way is south?"

Mike looked just as puzzled as Bill, but seemed to have alternatives, which he described as follows: "Don't worry Bill. If it gets dark, we simply look for the North Star. It's over the bear in the North Pole. Since we started out north, we head in the opposite direction from the star. However, sunset is quite a ways off, so we'll have to use the *watch method*."

Mike proceeded to hold his watch flat. He then placed a short twig upright against the edge of the watch at the point of the hour hand. The objective was to line up the hour hand with the sun and thereby deduce which direction was south. Both Mike and

Bill knew this method but were too deep in the brush to get much of a shadow from the obstructed sunlight. Mike tried the system anyway, but he dropped his watch into the deep thicket. Gone was a watch given to him by his father. Mike and Bill shrugged, and then Bill said, "Mike, look at the path through the trees. All we have to do is retrace our steps using the chopped grass and branches as our guide. How easy can it get."

Mike laughed and said, "You're right, just like Hansel and Gretel. Lets get going. I'll bet Yeno has blown that whistle three times since we left."

When they arrived, Yeno saw them coming and made this observation: "Did you two run into a bobcat on your trek?"

Bill and Mike's faces showed scratches as though they had a fight with an alley cat. "No," answered Mike, "we just cut down a few overhead branches on our way to our destination with Bill's machete."

Yeno came back with, "Machete, eh. What happened to Leave No Footprints?" When neither Mike nor Bill dared answer, Yeno promptly walked over and took Bill's machete. With a disgusted look, Yeno finished with "wash up and get ready for your meal."

"Yes, Sir," replied both Bill and Mike, and each gave Yeno the Boy Scout Salute.

Yeno wondered what could go wrong next as the boys returned to camp. He started looking forward to a nice supper, and some lazy songs around the campfire. Much to the pleasant surprise of the patrol, Yeno decided to do the cooking. Harry knew how Yeno liked to eat, and was not about to trust the cooking to some, young, inexperienced scout. He even brought his own cooking stove.

So while the exhausted boys lay down for a nap after their hiking ordeals, Yeno prepared the meal. With Yeno cooking, the squad could not have received a better meal had they been back home. Hamburgers, corn, boiled potatoes, carrots, and of all things, spaghetti on the side. The only bad news for the sweet tooth scouts was that there was no dessert. As soon as the meal was done, clean up began with Donahue in charge, and the Eagle Scout knew how to clean up.

It was awhile before Bill Callahan got the campsite fire going. But to the wonderment of all, he did get it started. He refused help because he wanted to show his fellow scouts that he could put two sticks together and start a fire. There on the shores of the St. Croix began the night events of Troop 92. Yeno announced that the squad name chosen was *Flaming Arrow*. The moniker would soon be an apt omen for the evening. Clarence and his guitar started it with the good old stand by song, "Home on the Range." He followed it, as the whole squad joined in, with "Sweet Sue" and "My Darling Clementine." As the fire started to die down, Yeno called it bedtime, and the boys headed for their tents.

Everyone was pretty tired from the long day, and went straight to sleep. Everyone, that is, except for Joe Kane. He had waited all day for the 'midnight hour'. As the campfire reduced to ashes, he quietly pulled his fireworks from his knapsack and inched out of the tent. He looked around at the other tents and noticed Bill Callahan putting more wood on the fire. He waited for several minutes after Bill finished stoking the fire and Bill returned to his tent. Joe then decided that the time was ripe. Just perfect, he thought. He headed for the edge of the clearing away from where they had pitched their tents. He didn't want to light the firecrackers and cherry bombs one at a time. No, Yeno would be out in a flash at the first sound and would stop all the fun. Instead, he had a master plan to display a firecracker extravaganza nonpareil. He brought a twisted piece of string dosed in gasoline three feet long with the firework wicks wrapped at 3-inch intervals around the string. His plan was to simply light one end of the string and 'run for cover'. With all in readiness, he lit the string and ran behind the nearest tree. Within seconds the first firecracker exploded.

As expected, Yeno was out of his tent in a flash toting Bill Callahan's machete looking for the source of trouble. He immediately spotted the exploding fireworks and headed straight for the action. Unfortunately, Harry's hole for the breakfast eggs was directly in Yeno's path. In the dark, he never gave a second thought to the hole, and much to his surprise, plunged head first into the abyss and crushed the two dozen eggs all over his chest. As he fell, the machete flew through the air striking the tree that Joe Kane was hiding behind. Joe crouched down lower as the other scouts crawled out of their tents and ducked behind the nearest trees. Just then one of the cherry bombs shot into some brush and started a mini fire. Clarence panicked and ran for the river. One problem, he didn't know how to swim. Harry and George found their water canteens and quickly dosed the fire. Within seconds the fireworks had all exploded and the episode was over.

Yeno climbed out of the hole and immediately blew his whistle. The buddies formed up in front of him. A quick count showed that Joe Kane and Clarence Zacardi were missing. Yeno sent the scouts out in the four compass directions with instructions to call out if they found the missing duo. Peter and Buddy found Joe hiding behind a tree within a minute. Meanwhile, Joe McCool and John Donahue had headed for the river and found Clarence, soaking wet, tangled in some bushes along shore. They extracted Clarence from the branches, and hauled him ashore none the worse for wear.

Yeno called the group together and announced "Boys, good work putting out the fire. Joe, John, thanks for rescuing Clarence. I guess we know who's to blame for this mess." The entire troop glared at Joe Kane. "I want you all to get back to bed for the next fours hours. We are going to break camp at 5 am and head home. I don't want any more accidents or surprises. Your parents trusted me with your well being and I'll be dammed if I am going to let them down."

Yeno found the machete buried in the tree where Joe was hiding, returned to his tent, and thanked his lucky stars that no one had gotten hurt in the fireworks fiasco. He didn't get another minute of sleep that night, however, thinking about what a disaster the overnight had been. His high hopes of 'Leaving No Footprints' had ended up in a trail across the island of broken brush and branches from a machete, the campsite nearly burned down, and two scouts almost drowned. For the next four hours he couldn't keep his mind from worrying what might happen next. Good to his word, Yeno, at 5 am in the morning, broke camp and

Troop 92 headed home. Several of the parents found their sons on the front steps of their homes that Saturday morning fast asleep.

Troop 92 had one more meeting wherein Yeno announced his resignation. With no one willing to brave the antics of Troop 92, the group disbanded. Thus ended Harry's career as a Boy Scout.

12

LINDY COMES HOME

After Mayor Hodgson (left) had introduced Colonel Lindbergh at the St. Paul airport, The Lone Eagle made his first public address in Minnesota and stepped down to be photographed with the Twin Cities mayors. Mayor Leach of Minneapolis (right) accompanied Colonel Lindbergh from the Wold-Chamberlain field to the major events in St. Paul. Courtesy of the St. Paul Pioneer Press.

On August 23, 1927, three months after the historic transatlantic flight, Harry's newspaper, the St. Paul Pioneer Press, greeted Colonel Lindbergh with the headline "The Blonde Viking of the air is home to Minnesota today." He landed at the St. Paul Airport, and before he reached the Lowry Hotel, an estimated 300,000 people greeted him." The local people of influence planned an elaborate parade for Colonel Lindbergh. Harry took particular note about the Lindbergh travel path through the two cities shown in the paper. After the Colonel stored his Spirit of St. Louis at the World Chamberlain airport hanger, he was to go through Minneapolis and then through St. Paul down University Avenue. Harry turned to the sports page and checked the home run race: Ruth 40, Gehrig 39. Looked like it might go down to the wire.

The summer of 1927 was the time when Harry began to have feelings about girls. He never really had much time for them, given not only his twice a day paper deliveries, but also his interest in baseball. That summer, however, he started to look at the neighborhood girls in a different light. He was even known to say hello to a girl or two on his afternoon paper deliveries, that is if they were outside as his passed. There was one girl in particular that Harry took a shining to, namely Eileen Monroe.

Harry had no idea how to talk to a girl, let alone ask her to witness Lindbergh's parade. He did, however, have two very worldly older brothers, namely Peter and Joe. Peter was almost twenty, over 6 feet tall, with sandy brown hair. Something about him made the local girls swoon. Harry had even seen Peter come out of Sally Bruckner's home on more than one occasion as he delivered the morning newspapers. Harry didn't have any idea what Peter was up to, but since Sally was quite the neighborhood looker, he figured that his big brother must really know women. It was with great confidence in his brother Peter's taste for good woman, that Harry caught up with Peter that Tuesday morning before Peter went to work and asked, "Peter, I need some advice".

"Well, squirt, what do you want to know?"

Harry hated Peter calling him squirt, but he needed some help from his big brother, so he bit his tongue and answered, "I was wondering how to ask a girl to go see Lindbergh's parade today."

Peter forced down a laugh and answered, "It's simple, look her straight in the eye and say 'hey doll face, let's go see Lucky Lindy'."

"Your kidding, do you really call a girl 'doll face'?"

Peter replied, "Of course, they love it. Take it from me. A woman never tires from being admired."

Harry continued, "What do I do if she says 'yes'?"

"Play it cool, and don't babble like you always do around here. Women love the strong silent type. Your too small to carry off the strong part, but at least you can keep quiet."

Harry decided that he wasn't ready for any more *advice* from Peter, so he shook his head in bewilderment and left his brother to finish shaving. That left brother Joe as his best hope. Despite being less than 2 years older than Harry, Joe was already a full 8 inches taller than Harry, and his head of jet-black hair seemed like a magnet to the neighborhood girls. With high hopes for some useful direction, Harry went out to the garage where Joe was usually to be found tinkering on something and asked, "Joe, how do I make a good impression with a girl?"

Joe responded, "Are you going to ask that Genevieve girl out?"

"No, Joe, I told you I only went over there that one time to help Sheila win the musher race. Besides, what makes you think I'm going to ask any girl out?"

"Don't be a putz, Harry. Of course you are going to ask some girl out or you never would have come to talk to me. I'll bet Peter has already brushed you off."

Harry winced at his brother's insight but continued, "I don't know how you figured I already talked to Peter but your right. Besides, I'm not sure I want his type of advice. Are you going to help me or not?"

Joe softened to his little brother's plight and answered, "Harry, I've already told you to just be yourself and have fun with life. There is no right nor wrong way to deal with a girl. They're all different and ain't that wonderful. Lighten up on the dos and don'ts of dating, and see if she likes you the way your are. If that doesn't work, look for another girl, they're plenty around our neighborhood alone." Harry decided that big brother advice wasn't all it was cracked up to be, and he thanked Joe. He went back inside the house no more enlightened about girls than before these two brotherly conversations. Maybe it will just come to me when I see her, her thought.

Harry reentered his home through the back door where he was confronted by his mother who said, "Harry, it's time to make some more root beer. Let's go downstairs."

One of Harry's responsibilities in the home was checking on the root beer as it fermented. He also occasionally helped his mother make the stuff. The process wasn't too complicated:

- Step 1: Get some water and add some yeast.
- Step 2: Combine root beer extract and sugar.
- Step 3: Add water with yeast to extract and sugar. Mix.
- Step 4: Pour into serving bottles and cap tightly.
- Step 5: Wait and watch for a couple of weeks.
- Step 6: After carbonation is complete, refrigerate for enjoying at your leisure.

Step5 was Harry's responsibility. Martha figured that since Harry had to go into the basement twice daily to get his paper route bags, this was the perfect opportunity to check on the fermentation process. If he forgot to check the bottles daily, there was the risk that the bottles could explode. When this happened, and it did happen, Martha would glare at Harry and send him into the basement to clean up the mess. Harry decided that he developed an unnatural fear of basements based on this job. He was convinced that one day he would go to check on the root beer, and one of the bottles would explode in his face forever scarring him for life. Fortunately, this dire prediction never occurred.

Martha and Harry went through the motions of preparing the root beer in less than 30 minutes. Mission accomplished, Harry asked, "Anything else, mom?"

Martha answered, "Nope, that's it. You can go outside and play with your friends."

Harry needed no further encouragement. He was out the back door in a minute looking for some of his neighborhood gang to play ball. Several friends were across the street playing catch, so he grabbed his glove and joined in for the rest of the morning.

When Harry finished his lunch on this August day, he brushed off his uncertainty about talking to a girl, and worked up the courage to phone Eileen Monroe. She had been pestering him about going for a bike ride around Como Lake for several weeks. A bicycle ride around the lake was considered quite romantic by the girls in the area, although the boys didn't share the gushy sentiment. He dialed her quickly and almost screamed on the phone, "Eileen here is our chance to go on a bike ride to view an important event."

Eileen returned with: "What important event is that, Harry?"

"Well you've been after me all summer long to take a bicycle ride with you. Now here is your chance. Jump on your bike quick and come over to my house. We'll ride over to the corner of University Avenue and Dale Street where Colonel Lindbergh will go by in the big parade."

"Wonderful. I will be over in a flash."

Harry's mother could not help but hear Harry's plans. "Be careful over on University. It is the busiest street in the city, and all those Tin Lizzies will be all over the place trying to get a look at Lindbergh."

"Don't worry Ma, our bikes can out run those cars. They have to catch you first before they can run you over," replied Harry rather cocky like for someone who had been hit by a car three weeks earlier. He then went through the kitchen to pick up his paper route bags.

Eileen was at Harry's home within 10 minutes, a veritable flash just as she promised. Her home was only a half-mile away, seeing as she lived in the big house right on the shore of Como Lake. Harry and Putzer were outside waiting for her arrival. "O.K. Eileen? Good timing. Let's go," cried Harry.

"Is your dog coming along?" asked a disappointed sounding Eileen.

"Yes, Putzer comes everywhere with me now that Sheila has

gone off to the convent," replied Harry. "Don't worry, he doesn't bite anyone."

"What are those bags around your neck?" continued Eileen.

"I explain later," answered Harry.

The trip to University and Dale began by going to the end of Barrett Street, taking a left onto Front Street, followed by a short one half mile to Dale Street. Next came a right turn onto Dale Street aimed south for University another two thirds mile away. Eileen beat Harry to Dale Street by 100 yards. Harry was no gentleman and did not let her get there first; she was just a faster cyclist. What Harry did not know at the time was that Eileen was a tap dancer and ballet student. The workouts for these professions kept her feet always on the move, and she was in excellent condition. After she waited for him at Dale Street, Harry raced past her intent on beating her to University Avenue.

Eileen cried out as Harry went ahead of her going down hill past Minnehaha, "Keep moving Harry, Lindbergh must be on his way, and I don't want to miss him."

It was Harry's idea to see Lindbergh, and he had no intention of letting her see the Flying Ace first. As Harry arrived at University Avenue, he noticed that the St. Agnes grade school children (all in uniform) had taken all the best sightseeing space on the corners of Dale and University. Their colorful uniforms made a wonderful spectacle. Harry, Eileen, and Putzer needed to go west on University Avenue one half block before they could find an open spot. The two kids sat on their bikes just below a two-story red brick building, while Putzer sniffed everyone and everything in the vicinity. Harry did not know at the time that they were located in front of the Hammer Department Store.

While waiting for Lindbergh's parade to arrive, Harry overheard two women in front of him talking. One said to the other: "I hear that Lindbergh attended the University of Wisconsin–Madison."

The other woman asked, "How do you know that?"

"I'll tell you why I know," returned the first lady. "My cousin attended that school and was in the same course as Lindbergh. Rumor at the time was that he flunked engineering."

"I never heard of such a thing," responded lady number two.

"He, my cousin, tells me that Lindbergh was always racing around the campus in a motorcycle, scaring everybody in sight."

"You had better check your source of information. Is that cousin of yours reliable? Lindbergh is a national hero, and there are always people trying to shoot down the current king of attention. I think they call it jealousy"

"Look," cried the first lady, a woman well over six feet in high heels, "here he comes now!"

Just then Lindbergh went by waving to the crowds from his Packard car. As Harry and Eileen were straining for a look, a whole pail of water came down on their heads. Harry looked up just in time to see two girls laughing as they ducked back into the house. Since it was a typically warm summer day, the water didn't feel too bad, and they dried off very quickly.

A man standing next to the two ladies said in a voice for all to hear, "If that young man is so dumb, how come he built an airplane by himself, did all the testing of it, and was the first to fly it out there in San Diego, not to mention across country and the Atlantic Ocean?"

The two ladies slumped away after this interruption. The last word the gabby one was heard to say as Lindbergh motored by was "Isn't he cute?"

Lindbergh went by in a flash. Harry and Eileen couldn't have seen him for more than 10 seconds. Nonetheless, Harry felt like the trip was a total success. He got a glimpse of a true American hero. How ironic, Harry thought, that Lindbergh was now the most recognizable and respected person in the world after flying across the Atlantic completely alone.

As Harry and Eileen prepared to go home they heard a score of comments about Lindbergh like: "I'll bet he is sick of all this commotion."

"Why, he's just a boy?"

"Look. He's smiling, isn't he adorable?"

"Isn't he a dear? He looks so solemn."

Ignoring all these remarks, Harry said to Eileen: "Let's go home Eileen. I have to carry the afternoon St. Paul Dispatch."

"I hope the next time you call me you have enough time for a proper bike ride around Como Lake," protested Eileen.

As they mounted their bikes to start back, Harry responded with, "Let me explain why I have to leave. You see Eileen, I carry the Pioneer Press in the morning, and the St. Paul Dispatch in the afternoon. It's just past 3 o'clock now, and I want to be at my pickup point no later than 3:30. It takes me almost two hours to cover my route. If I don't deliver all my papers by 5:30, my customers get irritable. And guess what? Irritable customers are terrible tippers at Christmas time."

"What about Sunday, like Sunday afternoon around the Lake?" Eileen was not too concerned about how often Harry delivered his papers, just when he was free to take the scenic (and romantic) route around beautiful Como Lake. Harry acted as if he hadn't heard the question and rode off.

Ten minutes later, Harry and Eileen were back to the six-sided intersection of Como, Dale, and Front, namely Harry's newspaper pickup point. Harry had been mute for the ride back, but now responded to Eileen's last question, "We'll talk later about Como Lake. Good bye, Eileen, Putzer and I have to deliver the papers." As Harry dismounted his bike and started to load his paper bag, Eileen departed and continued down Como Avenue to go to her beautiful home on the west side of the lake.

Harry considered Eileen very cute and personable, but not worth a steady diet of bicycle riding. As a matter of fact, he didn't like her asking him to go for a ride around Como Lake. Harry loved his independence, and the thought of anyone, not to mention a girl, scheduling his time made him absolutely panic stricken. Between his paper route and his freedom, he decided that spending time with a girl, even one as cute as Eileen, was just not in his immediate future. Harry wondered when he would see the attraction to girls that seemed so prevalent in his older brothers, but the ride with Eileen to see Colonel Lindbergh was the last bicycle ride Harry would take with any girl for some time to come.

13

STARS AND STRIPES FOREVER

One of the great traditions in Minnesota is the State Fair that occurs around Labor Day every year. The fair started in 1864 and evolved from a modest show that highlighted agriculture into a resplendent extravaganza that maintained its agricultural roots but added entertainment, fireworks, thrill rides, and the bizarre "freak show". For Harry and his friends George Scanlon and Joe Kane, it marked the end of summer with school lurking just around the corner.

The Minnesota State Fair Grounds was less than two miles due west of Harry's home on Barrett Street. The cost to get in? 50 cents, or 75 cents if you wanted to attend the grandstand shows. That kind of money could buy a lot of bread and ice cream. Harry, George, and Joe never even considered paying to get in. After all, the Fair had a mere 7-foot fence (although the top had three lines of barbed wire). For these three youths, seven feet was nothing; but one had to be careful to get over the barbed wire. It had to be done with caution. A more significant danger than the barb wire topped fence was the horsemen that "rode the lines" looking for freeloaders like Harry and his pals. Besides the fear of being trampled by the horse, the security guards were a most unfriendly bunch if they caught a lad sneaking into the fair.

Harry began Saturday the 3rd of September as he began every day: delivering the newspapers. A quick look at the Sports page told him that Ruth had 44 home runs, while Gehrig had 43. With fun and the freak show in mind, Harry set off with Joe for George's home on Kilburn Street, a scant six blocks away. When they arrived, George's dad, Samuel, greeted them. Whereas Harry learned practically nothing from his father Edward about his Irish heritage, he learned more than he could remember from Samuel Scanlon. Of course Harry's dad was born in Mankato whereas George's dad was born in Belfast, Ireland.

George's parents, Samuel and Shannon, had married in Ireland in 1910 and almost immediately set out for America. On the boat, with no real destination in mind, Samuel made friends with a fellow passenger. The new acquaintance convinced Samuel to forgo the big cities like New York and Chicago, and head for the friendlier Twin Cities of Minneapolis and St. Paul. Samuel took the advice, and found himself in the Como Lake area.

Samuel was a big, gregarious Irishman that had a smile for everybody. He made friends quickly, and within seven years worked his way through the St. Paul Public Works department to become head of Parks and Recreation. Harry's pal George was born in 1914. The one fly in this ointment was George's mother. Shannon began pining for Ireland and her hometown of Belfast almost immediately after the ship departed England for America. She pestered Samuel over the years to return to her beloved land, but Samuel insisted that they give America a fair chance. Fate intervened with the onset of World War I, and Shannon held her tongue from the start of the war until the cessation of conflict. With the resumption of peace in 1919, however, she resumed her crusade. Samuel finally relented and sent her, along with George back to Ireland one cold day in February of 1920.

Shannon hadn't bothered to inform Samuel that she was pregnant, and that one of the reasons for her wanting to return to Ireland was to have her mother nearby at the birth of her second child. She got her wish and gave birth to her daughter, Winifred, in August of 1920. Ironically, by this time Shannon realized that Belfast was no longer home. Like many an Irish expatriate who had returned home, she turned around and headed back to America for keeps. Samuel concluded that sending Shannon to Ireland was the best investment he ever made!

Samuel was holding what looked like a walking stick as he greeted Harry this fine Saturday morning with a big, "Hello Harry, where to today?"

Harry responded, "George, Joe, and I are off to the Minnesota State Fair. Want to come along?"

Samuel answered, "No I have to polish my Shillelagh."

Harry looked quizzical and asked, "What's a Shillelagh?"

Samuel laughed and said, "What kind of an Irishman are you, Harry? Don't you know anything about your ancestor's country? I suppose your going to tell me that you don't know leprechauns, shamrocks, or the blarney stone either?"

Harry felt offended, so he responded, "Yes, I know about the little green men, the luck of the Irish, and kissing some dumb rock, but I never heard of a Shillelagh. Remember, I am part Danish and Scottish as well as being part Irish."

Samuel decided that Harry needed some more Irish education so he began, "Let me tell you some more about your heritage. Ireland's troubles really started with that crazy queen Mary when she began colonizing our land with her Protestant English cronies in the 16th century. Isn't that a hoot. Catholic queen, protestant subjects. Her stepsister Elizabeth might have eased the problem if it weren't for that rebellious Shane O'Neill. Harry you must know something about the AOH?"

Harry interjected, "Yes, they carried my dad's coffin at his funeral."

Samuel resumed, "No, I mean their history. You know they began in the 16th century to help protect the clergy from those English Protestants?"

Harry answered, "Not really, I though they were just a bunch a friendly Irishmen that loved to drink and tell stories about the old country."

Samuel decided to fast forward the story and said, "Not exactly, but let's move to our times. That English/Irish, Catholic/Protestant conflict is still with us today, and may never end. Right now one of the real forces in Ireland is Sinn Fein. They started in 1905, and have vowed to make Ireland 'self-reliant, and self-supporting'. They had some success when they got the Proclamation of the Republic endorsed in 1919, but now the country is split into two parts . . . Now we finally get to my Shillelagh."

"When I lived in Belfast, the Protestants formed a group called the 'Oranges'. We Catholics were the 'Greens'. There is no loved lost between these two groups, and a smart man carries protection. Voila, in comes the Shillelagh, named for a small village in Ireland. How would you like to be hit by this club?" Samuel raised the big stick over his head and pretended to strike a phantom Orange.

"No thanks," answered Harry.

Samuel resumed, "I should think not. Well my Shillelagh is made of blackthorn and I keep it polished to remind myself of where I came from. It wouldn't hurt you to read up a little on your Irish heritage, Harry. Maybe this short history lesson will motivate you to get better educated?"

Harry answered, "Yes, Mr. Scanlon," but was thinking more about how relieved he was that the Minnesota State Fair horsemen didn't have Shillelaghs than he was thinking about his Irish heritage. He finished with, "Can you call George now?"

Samuel smiled and said, "Yes, Harry." He turned back inside and yelled, "George . . . , Harry and a buddy are looking for you." He then turned back and said to Harry and Joe, "I'm sure he'll be down in a minute. Have fun at the fair." With that last comment, Mr. Scanlon went back inside whistling and polishing his Shillelagh. George appeared almost instantly and the three boys headed off for the fair.

Harry's mother, Martha, objected to him going to the Fair with Joe and George, but she knew they would want to go sometime and those two were as dependable as anyone else was. His only assignment in going was to promise his mother that he would go to the women's building and see if his cousin, Rosemary had won any ribbons for her baked bread. This Harry promised to do.

The sun was shining, the sky was blue and after a two-mile

walk, they came to the outskirts of the Fair. Big posters were everywhere. They read:

>Minnesota State Fair is Here!
>Enormous Fair Displays
>Auto Races!
>Equestrian Races
>Horses and Cattle Everywhere!
>Hot Dogs—Fast Horses—Burgeoning Commerce—
>Pretty Girls on the Midway!
>A Wilderness for New Immigrants, the Minnesota Dream!
>Best of All!! In Person, **John Phillip Sousa** and
>His 69 Piece Band!

Joe had a good idea on how to get over the fence and get by the horsemen riding saddle to keep culprits from sneaking in. He explained his scheme slowly to Harry and George: "Here is the plan. As you know from past history, the horseman we call Dan Patch, rides between Como Avenue and Midway Parkway. I will go down to the Como entrance and you two go to the Midway Parkway entrance. I will draw Dan Patch's attention as I try to get over the fence on Como. This will distract Dan Patch and he will head for me. As he does, you two jump the fence at Midway Parkway. Got it?"

In unison Harry and George said, "Got it."

Harry had a question: "Where shall we meet after we get in?"

"I see in the paper," replied George, "that the real Dan Patch is on exhibit in his own tent near the Grandstand. Meet us there, Joe." And the fearsome trio went to work. Harry and George went to the Midway Park entrance, while Joe stationed himself at the Como entrance. Within seconds one of the horseman spotted a suspicious looking Joe. As the horseman approached, Joe climbed halfway up the fence, but jumped back down and pointed up Snelling Avenue at his pals Harry and George as they jumped quickly over the fence into the Fairground and disappeared into a nearby building. And, as the horseman went in vain for Harry and George, Joe leaped the fence and barbed wire in record time and headed for the Dan Patch exhibit.

One problem arose when Harry and George climbed the fence. Harry deftly leapt off the barbed wire one second before George, while George got his pants caught in the barbed wire. As they regrouped at the Dan Patch exhibit, George showed Harry and Joe the tear in the bottom of his pants. The great horse, Dan Patch, never as much as gave a snort to the three boys as they looked at this magnificent specimen who still held all the trotting records in the world.

For all the Fair visitors there was, next to this magnificent animal, his track record on a poster:

> *You fair goers are extremely lucky to witness, live, in person, a foal of* **Dan Patch**, *the Equine King of All Harness Horse Creation, the worlds Greatest Champion of all Champions—his sensational winning of all his races against the highest class race horses of his time . . . the Fastest Harness Horse the World has ever seen! The Fastest Pacer and trotter of all time.*

"That sure is a big horse," said George. "Where does he come from?"

Harry replied, "I read that Dan Patch comes from Savage, Minnesota. The town Savage is named after M.W. Savage, a rich man who runs a business called International Stock Food Co."

George was amazed at Harry's knowledge. "Did you make that stuff up that you just told me?"

"Of course not," responded Harry. "I only know what I read in my newspaper."

Joe laughed and interrupted with, "George, that isn't the *real* Dan Patch. Look at the poster. It says 'foal of Dan Patch'. That means it's just a child from Dan Patch. My dad loves to follow the horse races, and he said that the real Dan Patch died almost 10 years ago. You're so gullible, you believed it was the real Dan Patch because Harry said so. It's time you realized that he doesn't know everything!"

Harry didn't like being corrected, but as he looked closer at the poster he noticed that Joe was indeed correct. The sign did say 'foal of'. The realization by the boys that they weren't seeing the REAL Dan Patch dampened their interest in the exhibit. They

DAN PATCH FACTS

The Patch, driven by Myron E. McHenry, his first professional trainer and driver. McHenry was given much credit for making the horse into a champion.

- BRED/FOALED — 1895–1896, OXFORD INDIANA (April 29, 1890)
- SIRE: Joe Patchen
- DAM: Zelica
- [a] DESCRIPTION: color — mahogany with a small white star on the forehead
  - weight — 1165 pounds
  - height — 16 hands
  - girth — 73½ inches
  - shoulder measure — 73½ inches
- OWNERS: Dan Messner (1896–1901)
  - M. E. Sturgis (1901–1903)
  - M. W. Savage (1903–1916)
  - (Mr. Savage purchased Dan Patch for $60,000—the highest ever paid for a pacer.)
  - (A "pacer" is defined as a horse with a gait in which the legs on the same side move together)
- RECORD: paced a one mile track in 1 minute, 55 seconds at the Minnesota State Fair in September, 1906.
- RETIRED: 1909 to the 700 acre International Stock Food Farm in Savage, MN.
- DIED: July 11, 1916 (Mr. Savage died the next day.)
- BURIED: secretly on the Savage farm.

Courtesy, Scott County Library, Savage Branch

sauntered out of Dan Patch's tent and appeared puzzled as to what their next move would be, since there was so much to see.

"I have no idea what to do," offered Harry. "Let's first decide what we don't want to see. Over there a block away from here is the women's building. See what it says on the door: quilts, sheets, dresses, and aprons. I say no way for us to be caught in there. Agree?"

Joe and George agreed, "No way."

George came in with his not-to-see suggestions: "I don't want to see cows and pigs, and I will tell you why. I don't like milk and I don't like ham and from cows and pigs come milk and ham!"

Harry commented: "What do you eat to live on if you don't drink milk and eat ham sandwiches?"

George answered, "I eat hot dogs and peanut butter sandwiches."

"O.K.," returned Harry, wondering what George thought hot dogs came from. "Joe, what don't you want to see?"

Joe smiled, "I agree with George. Need I say more?"

In harmony Harry and George replied, "No."

"I have one more I must not see," said Joe. "I don't want to see any artistic paintings or stuff I don't understand in the first place."

Harry changed the tone from not-to-see to want-to-see by mentioning something completely new to the Fair, "Let's go see the airplane exhibits. The paper said that it features the seaplane 'The Spirit of San Diego' which is a replica of the Lindbergh 'Spirit of St. Louis.'" Joe and George agreed this place was a must to see.

George had his own ideas for what to see at the Fair. "We have to go to the Midway, there are lots of games we can play down there."

Harry wasn't so sure about going into the Midway because of the many Gypsies. "Before we do anything, let me tell you two about the Gypsies that congregate in the Midway," interrupted Harry. "Most people live in the same country that they are born in, not so with gypsies. They are always on the move. Most people believe the gypsies roam the countryside in search of new places to beg for food, clothing, and money so they don't have to work.

Gypsies have lived in Europe as outsiders for hundreds of years. Most gypsies are nomads because they are unable to find a place where natives will allow them to settle. The gypsies' main occupations appear to be fortune telling and begging. It appears that the gypsies at this Fair are all nomads who bear no allegiance to any country. When we do go to the Midway, keep on the lookout for this bunch!"

"As long as we are down on the Midway, let's see the Freak Show, O.K.?" asked Joe.

Together, Harry and George replied, "O.K. with us."

"I haven't discovered yet how we will get into the grandstand to see the auto races," mused Joe.

"Let us cross that bridge when we get to it," offered Harry.

The first challenge the three boys ran into as they left the Dan Patch tent was a haggard woman standing next to a scale for taking a person's weight. She spotted the threesome and called out as she beckoned them to come over, "Take a chance boys . . . let me guess your weight. If I am not correct you will earn the prize of your selection." Next to her on a table was an assortment of animals from bears to lions to monkeys. George figured there was nothing to lose so he walked over and stood in front of the scale. "Don't get on the scale until I guess your weight," she said. The old lady felt his muscles and tapped him on the head. She made the remark, "You look about 155 lbs."

"If you say so," replied George, knowing he was just around 150 lbs. soaking wet.

The lady advised George of the rules, "If I am within 3 lbs. you lose. Understand?"

"Find out what you lose, George," cautioned Harry, the smart one of the three.

George, however, ignored the advice. The woman guessed, "I'm going to say 150 lbs. You can get on the scale now."

George stepped onto the oversized scale and the needle settled on 150 lbs. The gypsy looking woman cried out in excitement, "I win young man. You lose, I guessed your weight."

"I lose what?" asked a surprised George.

"A quarter of money," answered the woman

A stubborn George replied, "I don't have a quarter. I didn't know the rules of the game. I thought it was for nothing." From behind the tent by the scale came three gypsies right out of Europe. They didn't like George's looks. And he knew it right away. The three boys took one look at the scraggly looking characters and got lost in two seconds in the crowd. The quickest escape route took them towards Machinery Hill.

Machinery Hill was not on the boy's list of 'must see', but they were looking for safety. On the way they passed the fish, game and forestry exhibit. As they passed it, they caught sight of a large Brown bear at the entrance. It was stuffed, however, and so the boys ignored its ferocious countenance and headed inside to continue their escape from the gypsies. All kinds of fish were swimming in the tanks: pike, minnows, muskellunge, bass, and sunfish. A fisherman's paradise if there ever was one. They also found fur-bearing animals; a taxidermist had done his job well for they sure looked real. As the boys exited the rear of the building, they glanced in all directions. With no gypsies in sight, they continued their route.

When the boys arrived at Machinery Hill, George climbed aboard a huge green *John Deere Tractor* and pretended that he was running it. One of the machinery exhibitors came up to George who was atop the tractor and asked, "Do you know why we are here at the fair young man?"

George mistook the question as he answered, "I am here to see the Midway with its freak shows," as he smiled.

"Frivolous waste of time young man. I will tell you why we are here," said the exhibitor. And he proceeded to do so: "The Minnesota State Fair shows farmers and other visitors new ideas in farming. Farmers are using new machinery to increase their output: raise better grain, better fruit and stock. Remember this kid, when the farmers are successful and prosperous, the business in the country is correspondingly good. The Midway has nothing on the great equipment shown here," he finished with a proud smile. After this lecture the machinery expert said, "Now get off that tractor kid, and let that man standing in line try it." George needed no more prodding and he jumped off the tractor.

The Old Como Gang Long Gone

"Let's keep going George, we're not welcome here," said Harry.

The boys looked around for the gypsies, spotted no one, and turned their route towards the Midway. On the way to the Midway, the boys passed the Penny Arcade. "Let's take a look at what's here guys," Harry suggested.

"O.K.," they both said in unison.

The sign *Penny Arcade* was true to its name. This area was reserved for movie projectors that showed an odd assortment of short films for one penny. Harry noticed that boys from down on the farm occupied almost all the machines. Despite having little money to spare, the boys did drop a penny in one projector. The film showed bikini-topped, grass skirt clad, women doing a Hula dance in black and white, and it ran for only three minutes. Each boy saw it for one minute apiece. Harry felt it was a waste of money. He had read all about freak shows and was in a hurry to see what freaks were on display this year.

In the past (or so he read in his paper), freaks were a big attraction at fairs. Past Minnesota State Fairs had included the fat lady, the India rubber man, the armless wonder, Joey the dog-faced boy, pairs of Siamese twins, troupes of midgets who often posed with giants or willowy girls and the like, the poor fellow with the hair and whiskers of a lion, and the mechanical man. There were also such interesting people as sword-swallowers, fire-eaters, contortionists, and folks with tattoos. There had been gimmicks like the tallest man in the world marries a midget, and the world's largest fat lady marries the slimmest man in the world, six feet tall at 105 lbs. There were world record holders like Chang, the Chinese Giant, nine feet tall, with arms that measured six feet, Pasqual Pimon the two headed Mexican weeping wonder who gave a galley of onlookers a tearful weeping, and the man with the largest mouth in the world who proved it by swallowing his whole fist.

The freak show once had an "Upside-Down Dancer" who did the jig standing on his hands, a Burmese juggler who never touched with his hands the things he juggled, and Lulelataska the snake charmer. Always popular were performers who ingested broken glass, ping pong balls, and bugs. Most famous was Teh

Hu, an ostrich who swallowed poison beans, cork, cottons, or wool. Then came the Great Waldo, who swallowed tennis balls and large lemons, regurgitating both of them. Harry came to the conclusion that the Fair attracted a lot of country folk who were more interested in freaks than tractors because they saw plenty of farm equipment, and little of the wonders of the world.

On the second floor of the grandstand the boys found what they thought was a real freak. They noticed a staircase that receded upward in the shape of a pyramid. At the top of the staircase was a man's head, a good-looking guy with a mustache and bright shining teeth. The illusion appeared that a man's head sat on top of a pyramid of horizontal lines. Not one of the boys thought this to be true, and Joe tried to prove it was a gimmick. He got hold of a piece of paper and threw it at the lines. The paper stuck between the lines telling the boys the man actually was standing inside a series of steps to make it appear that he had no body. The smiling mustached man's face turned grim when he saw the paper on the steps and he snarled out of the corner of his mouth at Joe, "Go home, kid. I think I hear your mother calling you."

At the sound of his voice, a guard appeared and took Joe by the arm forcibly, pointed him at the nearest exit sign, and ushered him away from the bodiless wonder. Harry and George dutifully followed their pal in trouble, and resumed their travels to the midway. Harry recalled once seeing a poster advertising the Siamese Twins, Daisy and Violet. They had been joined at birth and could not be separated; they were a big attraction all over the country. But that was not to be for when the boys walked over to Midway, no mention was made of the twins on exhibit.

Instead, as they arrived at the heart of the Midway, they came to a hustler in a little booth in front of what appeared to be a Bearded Lady. The barker was very impressive with his pitch: "All for the magnificent sum of one dime—two nickels, ten coppers, one tenth of a dollar, the price of a shave or a haircut; the greatest, most astounding aggregation of marvels and monstrosities gathered together in one edifice . . . Hear ye! Hear ye! Gathered from the ends of the earth, from the wilds of darkest Africa, the miasmic jungles of Brazil, the mystic headwaters of the Yan-tse-Kiang, the cannibal isle of the Antipodes, the frosty slopes of the Himalayas and the barren steppes of the Caucasus. Sparing no expense, every town, every village, every hamlet, every nook and cranny of the globe has been searched with a fine-tooth comb to provide this feast for the eye and mind. A refined exhibition for cultured ladies and gentlemen . . . No waiting . . . No delays . . . Step up ladies and gentlemen and avoid the rush. Tickets are now selling in the doorway." And the backdrop to this astounding bargain was a huge picture of the Bearded Lady!

Harry splurged for George and Joe as he paid the 30-cents admission to see the Bearded Lady. The lady was seated on a rocking chair on a pedestal high above all the attendees. She welcomed questions from the audience. The first question came from Harry, "How long is your beard?"

She replied in what Harry took to be a Midwestern accent, "My beard is two feet long."

"How long have you had this beard?" continued Harry with his questions.

"As long as I have been in this country," replied the Bearded Lady.

"When did you learn to speak English?" asked a brave Joe.

The bearded lady avoided the question with a question of her own, "Any other questions?"

Harry then said, "You talk just like my Aunt Mag from Mankato, Minnesota."

"Does she have a beard?" sassed back the Bearded Lady.

"Not the last time I saw her," said Harry. "The man on the barker announced to all of us that they looked all over the globe for you. Just how did they find you?" asked Harry. Just then the barker appeared on the scene and approached the three boys.

"Where are you smart kids from, anyway?"

"We are from right here in St. Paul, over by Como Lake," said Scanlon. "And we don't think this lady is from where you said she was from, like Brazil?"

"Come over and see me in the corner boys, I want to talk to you."

When they got to a corner away from the rest of the paid audience, Harry demanded, "We want our money back; you tricked us with your spiel."

"Look here punks, if you three just quietly leave I won't call the officer in charge of the Midway."

Joe came back with, "For thirty cents we'll leave in peace, sir."

"No way will I give you your money back. I never did tell you exactly where this poor old bearded lady came from."

"Let us go over to her now and ask her just where she comes from," demanded Harry.

"Oh no you don't," snarled the barker. "Here," he said, digging into his pockets and coming out with thirty cents, "now leave."

Happily the boys left, they had made their point, and got back their precious money. As they left, Joe turned around and took one last shot at the barker, "Tell the poor old lady she needs a shave." He then turned to Harry and George and said, "Let's hurry up and get to the band concert by John Phillip Sousa. It's the main attraction, and no way can they fake John Phillip Sousa."

In unison, Harry and George agreed. "Lead on, Joe." It took the boys almost 30 minutes to make their way from the Midway to the Grandstand. Along the way they bought some hot dogs and milk. As they arrived, they realized that, since they had sneaked into the fair grounds, they certainly didn't have any Grandstand tickets. George, however, came up with the solution. While sitting atop the tractor, he noticed that from Machinery Hill, there was an unobstructed view of the Grandstand. Since they didn't have the 75 cents needed to pay for tickets, they followed George to the 'free grandstands'.

It was one thing to have a band at the Fair, but it was quite another thing to have John Phillip Sousa in the flesh. The boys were not disappointed for in him they saw the real man. This was no Midway sideshow. Harry did a lot of homework to find out as much as he could about the great John Phillip Sousa. So the two boys, George and Joe, listened as Harry told them all he knew about Sousa. "First of all, the great maestro likes baseball as the greatest game in the world. He once boxed with Bob Fitzsimmons, 1899 heavy weight champion of the world. He has played golf with Bobby Jones, but never told his score as he thought that it wasn't proper to boast. In fact," continued Harry, "our local private country club, Somerset, invited him to play their course while he was attending the Fair show."

Harry even looked into the number of musicians in the Sousa band, and came up with the number 69 pieces of which the following were the real facts: "Six flutes, two oboes, twenty four clarinets, two bassoons, seven saxophones, six cornets, six trumpets, four French horns, two Euphonium Baritones, six Tubas, three percussion, and one harp. This," concluded Harry, "makes sixty nine musical instruments; a houseful of players if I ever saw one." Neither George nor Joe took notes on this count of players.

Before World War II put a more business-like face on American aviation, stunt flying was one of the most popular forms of daytime entertainment at the state fair. Fireworks and a potpourri of vaudeville and circus acts highlighted the evenings. Major upheaval came in 1927, however, with the coming of John Phillip Sousa, the first real "name act" at the Minnesota State Fair. The "Worlds Famous Bandmaster" had been on the road for over 35 years, and had never played a circus or state fair. With advance publicity he came with a newly composed "Minnesota March." He wanted to present it to the University of Minnesota. But they turned him down telling him it was too commercialized for the University. Nonetheless, he played it at the State Fair and it became a sensation in Minnesota.

The boys settled down on Machinery Hill and for 90 minutes watched the John Phillip Sousa Band play in the afternoon heat. For their finale, they played *'Stars and Stripes Forever'*. For the first time in their lives, Harry, George, and Joe heard this blood stirring American Masterpiece. As Sousa directed the musicians in his patented white gloves, a new pair at every concert, the boys stood, stomped their feet, and cheered as loud as their lungs would permit. Hearing the world-famous John Phillip Sousa band was a most fortunate, once-in-a-lifetime, experience for the boys. They saw all this from the top of Machinery Hill for free, so there was no need for them to "crash the gate", their original plan.

As the band finished its last number, Harry, George, and Joe were confused what to do next. They were afraid they would miss something when there was so much to do and see. Jugglers were everywhere, juggling mostly what appeared to be bowling pins—in fact, a few jugglers passed between them what looked like light swords, pretty risky, thought Harry. After the big grandstand show, the boys headed for home via the Midway. A sixteen-foot high canvas that was covered with what appeared to be the signs of the Zodiac fascinated Harry. Harry went by the gypsy-looking lady holding fort in front of the canvas. She peered at Harry as he read the canvas as follows:

Capricorn: the goat Dec 22 to Jan 20, half goat half fish;
Aquarius: water bearer Jan 21 to Feb 18, friendly, kind and caring;
Pisces: the fish Feb 19 to March 20, sensitive dreamer poet;
Aries: the ram March 21 to April 20 fiery, outgoing, most enthusiastic;
Taurus: the bull April 21 to May 21 most beautiful to all signs, romantic;
Gemini: the twins May 22 to June 21 fast thinker, quick witted, easily swayed;
Cancer: the crab June 22 to July 22 hard and crusty, cool, reserved;
Leo: the lion July 23 to August 21 natural leader, fiercely proud;
Virgo: the virgin August 22 to Sept 22 modest and hard working;
Libra: the scales Sept 23 to Oct 23 very sociable, warm-hearted;
Scorpio: the scorpion Oct 24 to Nov 22 private, deep thinking;
Sagittarius: the archer Nov 23 to Dec 21 boundless energy, loves challenge.

After Harry appeared to finish reading all about the Zodiac, the gypsy lady asked him: "Have you located yourself up there, young man?"

Harry ignored the query and asked, "I have a question about all this. Do you have time before your next performance to answer me?"

"I can give you five minutes, no charge young man. I like your looks," smiled the gypsy looking lady.

"I carry papers, morning and evening, to almost 200 people. I have one customer who waits anxiously every morning for the ***reading*** by columnist Jacqueline Bigar. Her column begins with the forecast under Aries and ends with Pisces. She waits, according to her husband, every morning until her husband brings her Bigar's thought for the day. Her name is Mrs. Salmon, and, per her husband, she was born on the 14th of February, St. Valentine's Day, or according to your chart there she is an Aquarius, or water bearer."

While Harry was talking to this gypsy, George and Joe stood off to one side minding their own business. George said to Joe, "What is Harry doing with those people that run this big canvas with those funny names on them?"

Joe returned with, "I don't know, but it bores me. Let's go for a ride on the merry-go-round. Harry will never miss us."

"O.K.," replied George, and off they went and jumped on the Merry Go Round.

Meanwhile Harry was getting into trouble. He talked too long, for the gypsy's partner came over and demanded, "What are you doing here?"

"I'm just learning all about astrology from your partner here."

"She talks to nobody unless I collect money first." Turning to the gypsy girl, he demanded: "No more talking with potential customers, Adeline, until I get paid."

"Yes, oh wonderful one."

At that moment, John Phillip Sousa's band, having finished their afternoon Grandstand Performance, came marching by, playing the "Stars and Stripes Forever." Almost all the people in the Fairgrounds came running to see the great leader—everyone, that is, but the gypsies, who as you know bear allegiance to no country, let alone America. Harry was happy for the interruption from the gypsy interrogation. After Sousa passed, he spotted Joe and George getting off the merry-go-round. He quickly joined them as they headed back to the Midway.

Last on the boys' list as a must-do was the Cannon Ball Roller Coaster. With 30 cents still left in their possession, they had just enough for one ride each on the famous Roller Coaster. They bunched into the first car, and screamed as the car plummeted up and down the metal tracks. When they exited the ride, they felt a sigh of relief that the car hadn't launched into space on one of the hair pin turns.

At the end of the Midway, they found the dancing Hula girls from Hawaii. The barker was shouting to all that could hear. "Come one, come all. See the most beautiful girls in all the world as they do their native dance, the hula! Step right up for only a dime they will take you back to the main dances from their native land, Hawaii." Harry, George, and Joe stepped up real close to see these girls. To a ukulele—playing accompaniment, they began a hula in their grass skirts to the enjoyment of all the onlookers.

One of the girls cried out: "Harry, how are you?"

Harry looked at the Hula girl and cried, "Is that you, Edna?"

He recognized Edna Schwartz from Avon Street on his paper route. She was a skater who had won many medals in the ice racing contests at Como Lake. "When can I see you?" smiled Harry.

"Next time you bring us the paper," was her curt reply as she performed the hula-hula into the tent for the show.

"Too bad we can't get in boys," Harry mentioned to George and Joe. "We are out of money."

Joe replied, "With no money we might as well go home."

Sadly, Harry and George agreed. So this woeful threesome walked to the Como exit and left the Fairgrounds. On their way home, Joe asked Harry, "Do you believe that Zodiac stuff? I see you were taken up with those gypsies."

"There might be something to what they say," Harry returned. "I have an aunt who reads what they call Tarot cards, fortune telling cards in case you didn't know."

"Tell me more, oh wonderful one," sarcastically Joe taunted Harry.

"My aunt May, who is part French and part Ojibwa Indian,

predicted my future as a paper boy for another ten years. Here is a true story of her predictions: one night her son, David came to stay overnight at our house on Barrett Street. In the middle of the night our phone rang, I answered. It was my Aunt May on the phone. She wanted to talk to her son, David; it was urgent. I went up the steps (he was sleeping in our back room with my other brothers) and I got him out of bed. I told my cousin David, 'Get moving! Your mother is on the phone in a condition.' David got up and fell down the steps, breaking his right arm. He got on the phone, and in her rattlesnake voice, my Aunt May told David, 'Don't go near the steps, my tarot cards tell me that you will get hurt.' There you have it. The cards foretold his fate."

Joe just thought it was a dumb story, and he didn't buy that fortune telling stuff. At the end of his tale, Harry changed the subject and asked the two boys, "What did you like the most about the Fair?"

George answered, "The Hula Girls. I saw one who lives on Victoria St. who did that Hula."

Joe had a different response, "Those Hula skirts remind me of what happens at our house on Saturday nights. Our family has a Columbia portable wind up Phonograph. On it we play records my father gets at the local record shop. Almost every Saturday night my father has me play some records on this portable. For instance, last Saturday, my mother dressed up in a Hula skirt and my dad asked me to play some records. He announced the ones he wanted me to play. I began with the record, 'The Girl on the Police Gazette' by Abe Layman and the Californians. Next I played John McCormick singing 'A Little Bit of Heaven Fell from the Sky One Day" and after that—the last one to play was "Hula Hula Hands" by the Hawaiian Minstrels. As the record was playing the last song, my mother did the Hula just as good as Edna Schwartz. And she danced off to her room for the night, followed by my father. I was then done with my assignment and that is where I would leave you with what I know about the hula. Amazing story, right Harry, right George?"

Both in unison replied, "Right Joe, amazing!"

The next morning, Harry read more about John Phillip Sousa: A self-made millionaire, Sousa was invited to several rounds of golf in the Twin Cities. He was made a Blackfoot Indian Chief, looked over all the new model automobiles at the show rooms on University Avenue, visited the cow barns at the fair, and was photographed with a cow. He even visited the Midway where he found one of his contemporaries, the leader of the Midget Band. He ordered hamburgers by the dozen, and knew his way with people, and seemed like a movie star to those who saw him. Harry never forgot hearing, live and in person, the Stars and Stripes Forever played by the master, John Phillip Sousa and his Band.

14

HALLOWEEN ON BARRETT STREET

Madden's outhouse

Halloween started as all days for Harry, namely delivering the morning Pioneer Press. The paper route weather was tolerable: Cloudy and 45 degrees, not bad for Minnesota at the end of October. September had been most eventful for sports fans. The Babe had gone on a tear in September and ended the season with 60 home runs, while Lou Gehrig only managed to reach 47. The Yankees had annihilated the Pittsburgh Pirates 4 games to none in the World Series. For Harry, it had been the start and end of his football career.

Harry "tried out" for the Como Junior Football Squad. Trying out meant simply showing up at the Como field on the second Saturday in September. Pop Warner and organized peewee football with fancy uniforms, shoulder pads, helmets, and spikes were still years away. Selecting the backfield was simple enough—straws were drawn to pick the more desirable positions of quarterback, fullback, and halfbacks. Whoever lost the draw played the line.

Harry's Italian buddy, Clarence, never won a draw. Unfortunately, he wasn't fast enough to play end, big enough to play tackle, nor could he block well enough to play guard. Hence, Clarence played center. Clarence really didn't like football and he moaned and cried a lot on the field. Back in the 1920s everyone was playing the single wing formation where the four backfield players lined up several yards behind the center. As a result, the center had to flip the ball through his legs and sail it air born to a back. As center, Clarence sometimes launched the football way over the quarterback's head. This never seemed to bother Clarence nearly as much as putting his head down below his shoulders to center the ball. The reason: it messed up his beautiful curly black hair.

The first game for the Como Junior Squad started out inauspiciously. After the first play, Clarence came back into the huddle and combed his hair—moaning about his locks the whole time.

"Why are you crying, Clarence?" Harry asked.

"Because my hair is messed up," cried Clarence.

"If you want to play football, Clarence, you're gonna mess up your hair," admonished Harry.

"I don't want to play football," continued Clarence.

Harry, befuddled, asked, "Then why are you're here?"

"Because my father wants me to be a man and play sports," answered Clarence as he stroked his hair ending with a two-finger set on his waves.

Harry gave him a sympathetic look and said, "Did your father ever play football?"

"No."

"Why not?"

"They don't play football in Sicily." Clarence said this while holding back a flood of tears.

"Well just get in there and center the ball the best you can Clarence." And with that, Harry took the little guy by his shoulder and set him down in the middle of the huddle. Three plays later, Clarence renewed his stifled sniffling. It was apparent that someone had smacked him in the nose—for it was bleeding. But he just kept playing until Harry ran to the sideline to talk to coach Yeno. Yes, the same Yeno who had just recently quit as leader of the Boy Scouts had found another way to occupy his time, namely coaching football.

"Coach", said Harry. "Sorry about that last fumble".

Coach Yeno never accepted any sorry stuff and said, "What happened?"

"The ball slipped when it was centered . . . "

"Slipped?" Yeno scowled and snorted. He was obviously in no mood to accept this as a reason for fumbling.

"Yeh, Coach," explained Harry. "The ball is too slippery to handle."

"Slippery", roared Yeno. "From what? It isn't raining."

"Clarence's blood is all over the pigskin."

"Is Clarence bleeding? I can't see anything behind all that hair."

"Well no one else is bleeding!" This time Harry became a little aggravated with Yeno.

"Maybe I better pull him out," mused Yeno. He then turned to the bench to see his choices to play center. Clarence's replacement at center, Louie, was up in a tree eating popcorn. The only other available substitute was Fragile Bones Joe Kalinski, the one Polack in Harry's neighborhood. "Kalinski?" shouted Yeno.

Fragile Bones answered, "Yes, Coach?"

"Kalinski, get in there and take Clarence's place as center."

"Yes Sir." With that Fragile Bones Joe jumped up from the bench and ran out onto the field. He took two steps from the bench on the field, and immediately stumbled over the first down chain breaking his right wrist. Yeno rushed over to Fragile Bones, and determined that a trip to the hospital was in order. He coaxed Popcorn Louie out of the tree and sent him in to take Clarence's place. From there, things got worst. By the end of their first game, the team was too banged up to continue. Harry's season and career in football had begun and finished in his very first game.

Halloween eve, or literally the evening before All Hallows, is meant by the Catholic Church to be a religious vigil of preparation that occurs before the very important All Saints' Day on November 1st. On Barrett Street, however, it had an altogether different meaning, namely mischief and mayhem. This Halloween, though, was to be a grand demonstration in how the plans of three young lads can seriously BACKFIRE.

Francis Madden, who lived on Barrett Street in the block between Orchard and the railroad tracks, was the top player in the Drama that was to take place. Harry's mother, Martha, called Madden the "bum of Barrett Street." She had good reason for giving him this moniker. He looked like a bum. His pants appeared that he slept in them, his hair was never cut. His shoes needed repair, and his shirts never saw a washing machine in real life. But worse of all, he smoked everything from a corncob pipe to Chesterfield cigarettes and cigars. His butts from the cigarettes alone paved Barrett Street.

On the eve of Halloween, Francis took Joe Kane aside while Joe was playing touch football with the Barrett Street regulars (namely Harry, George Scanlon, Joe Miller, Ed LaBarre, and Harry's brother Joe) in front of Madden's home. He guided Joe to his front porch, sat him down on his swing, and said, "Now Joe, I got plans for you tonight."

"Why me?" Asked Joe.

"Someone in your group is picking up cigarette butts. And the only reason is that someone wants to smoke, right Joe?"

"I am not talkin," returned Joe, suspicious of where Madden was heading with the conversation.

"I got a problem that you and your pals can solve. You know my neighbor Mrs. W. Wilson, is a new widow this year. Last year you dumped a sewer cover on her front porch, then you soaped all of her windows. This was done while Mr. Wilson was still alive. He tried to catch you in the act., but you got away. This widow has taken a liking to me. She was left a poor woman. So I found her a job as a waitress at Miller's Café and she, in return, has me over for dinner every Sunday. Now, to my point, Joe. I don't want you to pull any pranks on her. And in return, I am giving you," (he digs into his poor pockets) "three corncob pipes for you and your pals. You won't have to smoke those butts from the street. Here is a bag of Bull Durum," as he handed Joe the pipes and tobacco.

Joe took the pipes and tobacco and shook Madden's hand. He then said, "Thank you Francis. We won't touch her property. In fact, me and my buddies are making plans for tonight in ten minutes. Thanks for the smokes. Goodbye."

Joe rejoined Harry and George in the street and all three headed for their meeting place in the cemetery. To get in the mood for Halloween, Harry, George and Joe met under the Hammer monument. This "tombstone" was 36 feet tall and stood just inside the gate on Front Avenue, across the street from the Front Tavern. Here in the seclusion of the cemetery, the boys planned their night of fun oblivious to a real Halloween celebration going on to the northwest in Anoka, the HALLOWEEN CAPITAL OF THE WORLD. Even Harry's newspaper made no mention of Anoka and its unique halloed eve.

In 1920, Anoka civic leaders suggested the idea of a giant celebration with an evening parade of thousands of children. The children and adults were costumed (as witches with brooms plus bats and tramps, others with owls, even white elephants). And after these costumed characters paraded along Main Street, many people would distribute popcorn, candy and peanuts for all. A huge bonfire ended the celebration.

Joe, Harry and George, however, had some altogether different ideas on how to celebrate Halloween. As the three huddled under the Hammer monument, Joe was the first to speak. "Before we start our plans, let me tell you what Madden asked us to do. He wants us to stay away from the Widow Wilson's house. She likes him and trusts him, and to guarantee that we don't mess up her property, he gave us these three corncob pipes. Here is yours Harry, and here is yours George, fair enough?" George took his corncob pipe, but Harry hesitated. Joe continued, "What's wrong, Harry? Don't you want the pipe?"

Harry slowly answered, "My dad doesn't want me smoking."

"Isn't your dad dead?" asked Joe.

"Well yes, but I don't know?"

"Just take the pipe and think about it," finished Joe.

Harry, however, still looked dejected as he said: "I don't mind leaving Widow Wilson in peace, but these pipes kind of obligate us to overlook pranks on Madden himself. It's so much fun to overturn his outhouse. But if he's off limits, what about Gil Bratner?" The three schemers sat beneath one of the largest monuments in the cemetery and Harry began with something they wouldn't do. "One move we are not going to make this year is to scare the Zacardis' family."

Joe jumped in with, "why not?" This prank had been his favorite.

"Joe" returned Harry: "It is out of the question and I will tell you why. Last year you scared Clarence Zacardi's sister so bad she didn't go to school the next day. You were the fright of the night. You looked spooky in that white sheet over your head and dark glasses over your eyes. You didn't fool Mrs. Zacardi because she called your mother the next day and made things hard for you. Clarence's mother didn't get any laughs when you knocked on her door and her little girl answered. You told her you just came from the cemetery," (which was just ½ block away) "that you were from the dead, and were out walking for the night.

Joe laughed "I sure scared her didn't I? Here mouth hung open, and her eyes almost popped out of her head."

Harry replied, "No way that's going to happen this Halloween. Mrs. Zacardi even called my mother, and she gave me a tongue lashing. My mom hates to talk to Mrs. Zacardi on any subject, let alone one of our pranks. She thought it was a terrible thing for you to do with a white sheet wrapped around your head and a mask over your eyes She told me in no uncertain terms that there would be no scaring of little girls this Halloween."

George Scanlon, listening to all this broke in with his own thoughts and laughed when he said "I thought Joe looked pretty good in that white sheet and mask, he hasn't looked that good in years."

"Enough of this," Joe broke in and replied, "It was harmless. I was the only one who was really scared that night when I told my father where I got the white sheet."

Harry continued, "George you might not know pugilist Tolstoy is guard tonight for the women in the area. He's suppose to stop all pranksters of any kind from wandering into his territory."

"What is his territory?" asked Joe.

"My guess is from the cemetery to the railroad track," said Harry.

"What does that leave open?" asked George.

"He'll think that no one has the nerve to storm his house. So Joe, I'm suggesting that you put the sewer cover on his front porch."

"No problem," bragged Joe.

George came in with, "that sewer cover is 100 lbs., Joe. Do you need help in getting it off the street?"

"I don't need any help. The sewer is right in front of the Tolstoy's house, so all I have to do is take it from the street to his porch and that's a piece of cake."

George said, "While Joe is doing the sewer cover thing, I'll soap up Gil Bratner's house and car and let the air out of the tires on his Model T."

Harry interjected, "My plan is to lure Old Lady Moses' chow

into the cemetery and tie it to the back of this tombstone," as he pointed at the rear of the Hammer mausoleum.

"Let's meet back here at 7 PM," continued Harry. "We'll go over the plan one more time, and then split up. Afterwards, we meet to smoke our corncob pipes in Madden's outhouse at 8 PM sharp. Let's check our watches and be at the cemetery by seven." Harry still wasn't sure about the smoke, but figured he had enough time to sort out his ambivalence.

"Right," said Joe and George in unison, and they all gave each other the Boy Scout Salute.

It wasn't appropriate to give the Boy Scout Salute, as they certainly were not out to do good deeds, thought Harry. George looked concerned when he said, "How will I know when it's eight sharp?"

"Look at your watch, how else:" sneered Joe.

"I don't have a watch," said George with a slight sob.

"Ask somebody," suggested Harry.

Joe laughed, "that is some advice, you can do better than that Harry." With that, the boys broke up for the afternoon intent on reconvening at the cemetery as the night began.

After leaving Joe and George, Harry rounded the corner of his house and passed his neighbor Andy Johnson. Harry found Andy sitting on his rear steps with a shotgun in his lap. The shotgun was the same one that Andy used every New Year's eve to start off each year with a big bang. This obviously was not the reason he had it in his lap now. "Hello Harry," cried Andy, "are you and your buddies going to stay out of trouble tonight?"

Harry replied, "Of course, we're just going to hang out at the cemetery and look for ghosts. Tell me, Mr. Johnson, what are you doing with the shotgun on your lap?"

"You may not remember that last year someone turned over my outhouse. No one from the Como Gang admitted it, but a few stalwarts remember seeing three boys from Frog Town in this area."

"I remember, Mr. Johnson. No one from our vicinity would dare do such a dastardly act," said Harry, smirking under his breath: "at least not while you were looking".

"In case a few of that scourge on humanity show up they will receive a blast from me," threatened Mr. Johnson.

"I sure wouldn't like to be on the end of one of those blasts from your shotgun," smiled Harry. "Where are your two boys tonight, out scaring the citizens?"

"I have plans for them. They will be around later in the evening," answered Mr. Johnson with a glint of mischief in his eyes.

A couple of hours later, Harry set out to deliver the Dispatch. As he neared the home of Pug Barron, the pugilist, his mind returned to a morning one month earlier when Jack Dempsey fought Gene Tunney. The two rabid fight fans on his route, Pug Barron and Lee Tolstoy, were up waiting for the full debuts of how Dempsey lost on a long count. Pug Barron knew that Tunney would win once he got up from the floor after the controversial long count. Before he opened the morning paper he told Harry, "I knew Tunney was too fast for Dempsey. Tunney had a lightning left jab and a fierce right cross which stunned Dempsey throughout the fight."

Harry stopped Pug from going over the whole fight, "how do you know so much about jabs and right crosses?"

Pug smiled, "I know because that's how I eliminated my opponent when I was the Golden Globe Champ in my youth." Pug had evidently listened to the whole fight on the radio from Chicago. It was reported that over 100,000 witnessed the boxing event of the year.

Lee Tolstoy, the other pugilist on Harry's route, lived at the end of Barrett Street. He was up as early as Pug that morning, but for another reason. He was about to keep on his usual training schedule by running through the cemetery in his underwear, quite a sight for the young girls in the area. He was finishing his early morning workout when Harry had arrived a month earlier. Even though Harry was standing right next to him, Lee yelled out "I object to giving the title back to Tunney. He didn't deserve it after taking that long count. The referee's must have fixed the fight." Lee knew a little about fixing fights because that is how he got started on his way.

But the memory of the Tunney, Dempsey fight was gone from

Harry's mind when he spied Tolstoy sitting on his front steps as Harry arrived with the evening Dispatch. Tolstoy admonished him with this warning, "No funny stuff tonight Harry from you or your pals. I'm on duty for any dirty tricks you might be up to."

Harry feigned a look of hurt as he replied, "You think we would fool around doing tricks with you on duty right here on Barrett Street?"

Harry had done his research on Halloween, and Tolstoy didn't scare him. Nor did the committee of women on Barrett Street and the nearby Victoria Street scare him. These women were resolved to stop the mischief of pranksters running around turning outhouses and pulling trolley cars off the tracks. To that end, the committee had "hired" Tolstoy (a known tough guy) to do the patrolling duties. Tolstoy figured that a warning to Harry might reduce the incidents. But what could one guy do against a dozen sneaky culprits that knew the neighborhood like the back of their hands? The answer was: Not much. Had the police hired Tolstoy it might have been a different story. Harry already had one too many run-ins with the St. Paul police, and if they were around he would definitely keep a low profile. But Harry had no fear of Tolstoy reporting the tricks by pranksters to the women's committee.

Harry had established the area where he, George and Joe would confine their acts of folly for the evening; Barrett Street from the railroad tracks to the cemetery would be the north-south bounds. Grotto to Kilburn would be the east-west bounds. The old Indian cemetery was George's territory. No gravestones were in this cemetery, just Indian lore.

One area definitely out of bounds would be the corral that once kept Mr. Auston's cattle. The cattle were long gone after last year's Halloween. All 10 of Mr. Auston's cattle were let loose by vandals from what was called the Frog Town gang. It was a serious blow to Mr. Austin, as after the incident he committed suicide. No one knew why, he was such a quiet man, but all his friends and neighbors surmised that the cattle were his best friends and when he lost all 10 of them he had nothing left to live for. The cattle let loose eventually roamed down the railroad tracks where they were caught and slaughtered by the local meat packing company.

Harry was having second thoughts about his alliance with Madden. Madden didn't have too good a reputation in the neighborhood for honesty and good living. Harry began to think that this arrangement bought by corncob pipes was an alliance with the devil himself. He knew his mother, Martha, had no use for Madden. If Madden had heard of the Ten Commandments he missed hearing several of them, like honoring your father and mother. The Lord's name he used quite often in front of the children, but never in church. Thou shalt not covet they neighbors goods missed Madden completely, considering that when harvest came he gathered his neighbors' tomatoes, corn and carrots. Martha had seen Madden many times discard cigarette butts on the street opposite her house. Litter was his middle name, not Leo as written as his birth certificate.

When Harry arrived home from his paper route, he noticed that Andy Johnson was missing from his post. Andy Johnson did have other plans for his two boys, Donald and Christopher or Buddy as Harry called him. At that moment, Esther, Andy's wife was dressing the two boys in very scary costumes. Donald was an owl and Christopher was supposed to be a flying bat. Donald was an owl because he could sound like an owl. So his father said, "Donald, my boy, you make a wonderful owl, you moan and wail every time your mother asks you to make your bed or sweep the floor. You're like a ghost the way you make it sound so eerie. A owl doesn't sound as good as you."

So that settled the costume issue for Donald, and like it or not Donald sounded like an owl. So his mother made a costume that made him look like an owl. Donald tried to get the last word in by saying, "I can't be an owl, I can't turn my head completely around."

"Neither can an owl," smiled the know-it-all Andy.

Christopher was to be a flying bat. Bats are the only flying mammals. Bats eat fruit and flowers and a few kinds catch frogs and fish. The vampire bat lives on blood and living animals. But most bats eat insects, which makes them helpful to human beings. In many parts of the world, people believe that the souls of the dead take the form of bats and fly about at night. They especially like flying about in cemeteries like the one that Andy Johnson's boys intended to occupy while scaring away the pranksters from Frog Town. So just at twilight on Halloween, Andy Johnson took his owl (Donald) and his flying bat (Christopher) down to Front Street, which they promptly crossed to enter Calvary Cemetery.

Andy instructed his boys as follows, "I want you to hide behind those two stone entrances until I bring the Frog Town boys down for a little scare they'll never forget. I'll be pushing them with my shotgun to the entrance and yell to them 'get in there boys and don't ever come back.' As they get near to you, I will yell 'Go Ghosts'. That's your signal Donald to shout as loud as you can and you Christopher to run after the boys flapping your wings. Got that?"

In unison the boys replied, "Yes Father."

With those final instructions Andy went back to his post on his front steps with his shotgun. As he sat waiting for trouble, Martha came out the back door and asked, "Who are you expecting to dump your outhouse tonight, Andy, Mr. Atlas?"

"Just the Frog Town boys Martha. They'll wish they never came back here."

"Be careful, Andy, with that gun you might kill somebody," warned Martha. After that bit of advice, Martha went back into her house and left Andy sitting on guard duty.

Halloween pranks didn't scared Martha much. She was always too busy worrying about her boys. But she did know about Halloween mishaps, like the one that happened the year before to her next door neighbor Margaret Horn. Margaret Horn had read up on what apples had to do with Halloween. She had read a legend that Apples main use on Halloween was not to protect against evil, but to tell fortunes for the coming years. Its special powers lay in predicting who a girl's husband would be. One old-time ritual called for a girl to go alone into her room at midnight, sit down in front of her mirror, and cut an apple in nine slices. As she ate the slices, she looked into the mirror. If the spell worked correctly, her destined husband's face would take form in the mirror, and he would take the last slice.

What happed to little Margaret was not so good. She followed the ritual up to eating the first slice. When no face appeared in her mirror, she decided to coax destiny along by setting the remaining slices out on her porch. Unfortunately, instead of Prince Charming appearing to eat a slice and become her future husband, Francis Madden arrived to take the first slice. The bum happened to be out walking that midnight on Halloween. She would never marry that human skeleton in a million years, so the entire plan was a bust. She related the whole story to Martha the next day.

Another use of apples at Halloween was for bobbing. You had to have a big mouth to win. Apples were put in a glass jar full of water. The trick was to grab an apple with your teeth only. The girl with the biggest mouth was usually the winner. When the event took place in front of Martha's house, the winner was Margaret Horn's sister Alice. Her reputation as the biggest mouth was not only for the size of her mouth but for all the gossip she spread around.

As seven o'clock arrived, Harry set out for his meeting with George and Joe. The pugilist, Tolstoy, was already on duty. For the occasion he had put on his bright fighting shorts and was quite a sight. Just as the threesome approached their rendezvous point within the cemetery, a man and small dog went running by. Joe recognized the dog and said, "Look Harry, there goes Mrs. Auston's Pekinese. Was that Tolstoy in his shorts?" No one answered, but the trio laughed in unison. They returned to reviewing their plans, and then set out for their evening of pranks.

On his way to drop the sewer cover on Tolstoy's front porch Joe ran into a frantic Mrs. Auston, who cried to Joe. "Have you seen my dog? He ran away from home."

Joe curbed her anxiety with "Yes I did see him a couple of minutes ago. He was chasing someone down Front Street."

"Was he chasing a man in underwear?" asked Mrs. Auston.

"I didn't get a good look at the man. He was going by too fast in the dark of the night"

Mrs. Auston said, "I looked out of my windows to see what tricks you boys were up to and I saw this man in his underwear standing by the railroad tracks. My fearless dog, Henrietta, growled and I knew she would take off after this prankster, so I turned her loose on this guy, and off went the two of them. I called for my dog to come back, but evidently she was still interested in scaring this pajama clad man and that is the last I saw of the two of them," said a whimpering Mrs. Auston.

"You go home now Mrs. Auston, and I will see what I can do for you. You know this is a good night to stay home and protect your property."

"You are right, Joe. Bring my sweetheart home when you find her," and Mrs. Auston left to go home.

Joe turned away from Mrs. Auston and dodged through several backyards scouting out the activity in front of Tolstoy's home from several angles. His final stop was behind the Miller's old Packard parked in the driveway alongside their home. From this excellent vantage point, Joe waited for the cars to pass by, then went to the middle of the street and picked up the sewer cover with a groan and grunt. Turned out that George was correct, and the cover was VERY heavy. Joe finally rocked it off its hole just as a very tired looking Pekinese dog came up the street and nudged him. As Joe turned to look at the interruption, he noticed Tolstoy coming up the street. Joe quickly reset the sewer cover, picked up the dog, and took off through the Miller's back yard.

Joe crossed the street and wove his way through several more backyards arriving at Mrs. Auston's home with her little dog. A relieved Mrs. Auston offered Joe some freshly backed cookies, which put Joe several minutes behind on his timeline.

While Joe was busy with the sewer cover and dog, George was trying to let the air out of Gil Bratner's tires. Unfortunately, George's intense concentration on the left rear tire prevented him from seeing Gil come out of his home and get into his car. Before George realized what was happening, Gil put his car into gear and blasted off down the street. George had such a death grip on the tire value stem, that it was almost a second before he realized that his arm was being torn away from his body by the moving car. Instinct took over, however, and he relaxed his grip before getting seriously injured. The incident left George so shaken, that he headed over to the McCool's home.

It was 7:45 when Martha heard a knock on her front door. She really didn't know what to expect. But she was pleasantly surprised to find Harry's friend George standing there all smiles. "Excuse me Mrs. McCool, but can you tell me what time it is?" he asked.

"It's 7:45," answered Martha. "Why do you want to know?"

"I have to meet Harry at eight."

"Where is he now? I told him to be sure to be home by 8:15."

"I can't tell you exactly where he is right now. All I know is that he wanted me to meet him on the corner of Orchard and Barrett Street at 8:00 P.M."

"WELL," returned Martha. "Tell him I want him home by 8:15 P.M."

George Scanlon said good bye and left Martha, standing a little bewildered by George's request. His family certainly must have enough money to give their child a watch she thought.

In general, most of Barrett Street only feared pranksters on Halloween. There was one exception, however, namely the lady on the corner of Orchard and Barrett Street. She was a lovely woman who worried about everything. Her paranoia reached its zenith on Halloween. Hearing a loud and sudden noise did not disturb her, but she did fear the sudden appearance of a bat overhead. Fear warns us that danger is approaching and one problem with the woman in question, one Mrs. Solomon, is that she had a most vivid imagination. Her house, as far as she knew, wasn't haunted. But every Halloween, as night began to fall, Mrs. Solomon would arrive at Martha's and share her fears. "I see Martha," she would cry, "the bats are out again. It is that time of the year." Martha looked around but could never see any bats. She knew that you can't defend yourself against what you can't see, so she felt great empathy for Mrs. Solomon. Just last year one such invisible someone had overturned Mrs. Solomon's outhouse and she was sure that the invisible would happen again. The invisible was the work of demons that she couldn't see.

In Mrs. Solomon's case, the invisible someone was Francis Madden at work. Martha became acquainted with Mrs. Solomon over the years by listening to her many superstitions. Mrs. Solomon superstitions over the years could fill a book, like a) she knew that 13 was an unlucky number, b) if a candle turns blue, there is a ghost in the house, c) knocking on wood keeps bad luck from spoiling your plans, d) when fleas bite more than usual, it is a sign that rain is coming and lastly e) a wife can keep her husband from running away by burying a live horned toad in a jar under her house. So Mrs. Solomon kept Martha going with her troubles, fears and superstitions. Martha had her own fears this night. Where are Harry and Joe, and what are they up to this Halloween?

At that moment, Harry was busy luring Old Lady Moses' chow towards the cemetery. Harry chuckled to himself as his plan was going perfectly. The little chow was running after Harry with all its might, but Harry had no trouble staying ahead of the short-legged creature. They crossed an almost deserted Front Avenue just as a booming shotgun went off. Harry laughed out loud thinking of the poor Frog Town boys in Andy Johnson's clutches.

Back at the Johnson's home, three boys stood paralyzed in Andy's front yard. "OK boys start heading for your last resting place," said Andy. And the foursome headed down Barrett Street for the cemetery. The three Frog Town boys started to weep. As the threesome came up to the cemetery entrance at Victoria, Andy gave his prearranged signal and called out "Go Ghosts." Right on cue, Donald jumped out and started his very loud WHOOOOOOOOOOOOOOO and in the same moment Christopher appeared in the middle of the entrance and started flapping his bat wings and screeching at the same time as Donald's WHOOOO. As a final measure for instilling fear in the pranksters, Andy blasted his shotgun into the air one more time. Nothing more needed to be said. The three Frog Town boys took off down Front Street as fast as their legs allowed them. Last seen by Andy, they had turned right on Dale Street and headed home for

The Old Como Gang Long Gone

Minnehaha Avenue. The last ha ha on them. Andy never again had his outhouse overturned.

By this time, Harry had a perfect vantage point to watch the "spooking" incident in the cemetery. Unfortunately, the last shotgun blast had distracted him from his true purpose of snaring the chow. Just as Harry was recovering from laughing at the frightened Frog Town Boys, the little chow had finally caught Harry and nipped him on his heel. Harry swung around to grab the little mutt, but the chow backed off, then turned tail and headed for home. Harry had lost his opportunity for humbling his menace.

Meanwhile Joe Kane had left Mrs. Auston and was on his assignment on lower Barrett Street just before it reached the railroad tracks. His duties were to soap the windows on every house before he reached his destiny, Madden's outhouse for the big smoke. Unfortunately, he forgot that one of the houses was occupied by the local pugilist, Pug Barron. Pug stepped out of the bushes by his front door just as Joe started to soap the front window. He never got any further as Pug tapped him on the shoulder with this comment, "Looking for a fight, Joe?"

A startled Joe stuttered, "Not with you, Pug."

"Do me a favor will you Joe, just put that soap in your mouth and start chewing or else?" Pug had gone into a John L. Sullivan stance as he made this threat. Pug was too good for Joe and Joe knew it, so he obligingly started to chew the soap. Joe quickly moved away from Pug's threatening look and headed for Madden's outhouse. As soon as he was out of Pug's sight, he spit the soap out in disgust.

When Joe arrived at Maddens's, Harry and George were already in the outhouse, and so was Francis. All had their corncob pipes in their mouths. Harry still hadn't lit his tobacco. Madden helped Joe load his pipe with Bull Durum, and Francis, George, and Joe started puffing. Smoke soon filled the small outhouse. Some of the smoke filtered through the cracks in the outhouse and soon the place looked like a small chimney. Nobody in the outhouse dreamed that the smoke would attract attention. But nobody figured that Madden's next door neighbor, the widow

Wilson, was still up protecting her house from pranksters. She became alarmed and called the fire department.

The fearless firemen arrived soon, as the fire station was a scant one mile down Front Street. The fire hydrant nearest was right on the corner of Barrett Street and Como Place. The smokers were coughing so much from the smoke that they didn't hear the fire engine come up. They knew it had arrived when the water came through the door at punishing speed. Harry, George, Joe and Madden came running out of the outhouse and were further drenched with water from a very strong fire hose. That ended their corncob pipe smoking, and ended all other activity on Barrett Street that night. Harry didn't even try to explain to his mother how his clothes became soaked with water that night.

Halloween evening had been a complete bust for the fearsome threesome. All their major plans had BACKFIRED. George hadn't let any air out of Gil Bratner's car tires. Joe hadn't dumped the sewer cover on Tolstoy's steps. Harry hadn't managed to ensnare Old Lady Moses' chow. To boot, George almost lost his arm, Joe had to eat soap, and Harry had a nasty dog bite on his ankle. The neighbors were somewhat awe struck by the fact that practically nothing eerie or prankish had occurred in the neighborhood. Most were certain that Francis Madden was to blame, and they all silently accused him for what happened to those three "nice boys". For years to come, those three nice boys had great difficulty explaining to their mothers just what they were doing in a very small outhouse on October 31st, 1927. Harry never did smoke, nor did he partake in Halloween pranks from that year forward.

15

CHRISTMAS ON BARRETT STREET

The Christmas Season for a Catholic starts the first week in Advent. For Harry and the McCools, that was December 3rd, 1927. The weather didn't look good. A headline in the newspaper bore the ominous tidings: "34 BELOW HITS HIBBING . . . ST. PAUL MINUS 10 BELOW." If you could call it good news, Harry still had his paper route: Pioneer Press at 5:00 in the morning, the St. Paul Dispatch at 3:00 PM in the afternoon, and one delivery on Sunday. Older sister Alicia was still working as was older brother Paul. Since none of the McCool jobs was particularly well paying, it was fortunate that the cost of food was low. Eggs $.49 a dozen, Oranges $.48 a dozen, Grapefruit $.07 each, Pillsbury Pancakes (large package) $.37, and, most important of all, Christmas candy $.95 for a 5 lb. box. The inexpensive cost of candy meant that Harry could eat sweets with abandon, a habit that he still has today.

    The first festive occasion of the McCool Christmas season was usually Sheila's birthday on December 5th. Nothing much out of the ordinary ever happened on most birthdays at the McCools. The usual candles were lit and, if lucky, Martha would bake a cake. But the one birthday that stood out in Harry's mind was Sheila's. Every year his sister would take off her shoes and leave them on the doorstep for the night. Sure enough, every December 6th, someone (Martha of course) would fill the two shoes with a couple of apples and oranges. Martha, after constant questions from Harry explained to him all about St. Nicholas. "Here is the story behind St. Nicholas, which I took right out of the Catholic Encyclopedia:"

> *The feast of St. Nicholas is a children's festival that comes on December 6th. The Saint was a bishop who lived in Asia Minor during the 4th century. He was an especially popular patron saint of children during the Middle Ages. The festival is observed primarily in Europe. In some countries, children fill their shoes with straw and carrots. St. Nicholas comes on the night of December 5th, known as St. Nicholas' Eve. In the morning, the children, if good, find the straw and carrots replaced by small toys and cookies. But if the children had been naughty, they receive a whipping rod to remind them that someone was watching their behavior.*

Despite being envious of the special treatment that Sheila received on her birthday, Harry was silently happy that there were no customs around his birthday that punished bad behavior.

"As you know, Harry" said Martha. "Your sister, Sheila, won't be taking off her shoes this year, for she is in Mankato at the nunnery. But at least you can say a prayer for her on the night of her birthday."

"I will, Mother," said Harry. "Since we're talking about the original Santa Claus, St. Nicholas, you want to know who I think is our Santa Claus?"

"Go on," pleaded Martha.

"It's your friend Lucy from Duluth who sends us the gift box at Christmas."

"That is the name of a friend of mine from Duluth," replied Martha. "It's odd that you should remember her name. She will no doubt send us her Christmas package again this year."

"How did you meet her?" asked Harry, always inquisitive.

"I haven't. The social worker who calls on us here is from Denmark. Lucy knows this social worker and heard that someone from Denmark was living in Minnesota. She discovered our address and wrote me a letter. I told her how many children I have. Right away she started remembering us at Christmas."

"You've never met her?" asked an incredulous Harry.

"No" said Martha, "Never."

"Is she Catholic?" Asked Harry.

"Why do you ask that?"

"She sounds religious to me, that's why," replied Harry.

"I really don't know," said Martha.

"I sure like those little toys she sends each Christmas. It's more than any of your relatives send." And Harry seemed hurt at this oversight.

"If you are interested in Catholics, then you should know that you have the most Catholic aunt in the world, your Aunt Rose from Mendota. That rosary you get each year at Christmas from her is blessed by our archbishop."

"I use it occasionally on real cold mornings, I tell you. It makes the route go easier walking the early morning in sub-zero weather thinking about a prayer."

"Do you still start each morning at school with a prayer?" asked Martha.

"Yes and that isn't the only religion we get to start the day. Our pastor Father Patton comes in often with a quiz from the day's gospel."

"Here is a card that my friend in Duluth sent me for reading when things don't go too well." And Martha read from the card the following:

"God grant me the **Serenity** to accept the things I cannot change, the **Courage** to change the things I can, and the **Wisdom** to know the difference."

"Keep this card Harry, you may need it in your passage through life," said Martha.

Harry did keep the card throughout his life. Turned out to be the best advice that Harry ever received from his mother.

The second week of Advent, Harry was greeted at school with,. "I think that I shall never see a poem as lovely as a tree," so began

Harry's teacher at the start of the day's studies. "Does anyone know who said that?" asked Sister Bernard. Harry raised his hand. "Yes Harry" surprised like, asked the nun.

"That's a poem written by a man named Joyce Kilmer. It sounds like a girl's name, but it isn't. He (Joyce) was born on December 5th. The same day as my sister Sheila who as you know is now up in your nunnery in Mankato. Sheila learned that poem "Tree" because she found out about Kilmar's birth looking at an Almanac, and every year on her birthday she would recite the poem at our supper table."

"Thank you Harry, I am quite impressed," smiled sister.

Just then the school doors opened and in walked Father Patton, unannounced. The pastor, as usual, was stopping in for his test on the Bible and other religious subjects. He called it "wake up" time. "Today" began Father Patton, "we'll talked about Jonah. Now I'll read to you about Jonah, found in today's gospel." So he began today's reading:

"This is the word of the Lord that came to Jonah. The Lord said to Jonah, 'set out to the great city of Niveveh and preach against their wickedness which has come before me.' But Jonah made ready to flee to Tarshish away from the Lord. Instead of going to Niveveh, as instructed, he went down to Joppa and found a ship to Tarshish, paid the fare, and went aboard to journey to Tarshish, away from the Lord. The Lord however, hurled a violent wind upon the sea, and in the furious tempest, the sea was at the point of breaking up the ship. To lighten the ship for themselves, the mariners became frightened and threw its cargo into the sea. Jonah, however, knew the reason for the tempest and asked to be thrown overboard. The sailors obliged and Jonah was thrown overboard. The sea's raging immediately abated. In great fear of the Lord, the men offered sacrifice and made vows to the Lord. The Lord then made a great fish that swallowed Jonah. Jonah remained in the belly of the fish for three days and three nights. Then the Lord commanded the whale to spew Jonah upon the shore. This is the word of the Lord."

Right after reading this, Father Patton asked the pupils, "what would you have done in the whale for three days and three nights?"

Joe Kane was quick to answer "I would take my radio to listen to the news."

Mike (candyman) Redford come out with "I would take a three day supply of food."

Father looked upward with a shrug of despair, but the next answer pleased Father Patton. It was Gladys that suggested, "I would take my rosary and pray to the Blessed Mother to get me out of this whale and take me home to Barrett Street."

"Excellent, young lady," smiled Father, "and what's your name?"

"Gladys Miller. I'm Joe's sister. You know Joe, he's one of your altar boy servers."

"I am proud of you Gladys for suggesting prayer as the answer in a time of great need." Father Patton went to the door to leave. But as he opened the door he turned and said to Michael and Joe. "Boys think about your answers again, and consider what Gladys said." That concluded Father Patton's Bible message of the day.

Harry didn't know that his next door neighbor, Mrs. Johnson was originally an Irish girl by the name of Esther O'Neil. Her husband, Andy Johnson was considered quite the guy to talk an Irish girl into being his bride. An Irish girl? To marry a Swede? A Lutheran Swede besides?

Esther would read the obituaries every morning, looking for anyone of Irish decent from St. Andrew's parish. The third week in Advent she found one by the name of Kathleen Callahan. That morning Esther called Martha. "Any Irish funerals today or this week, Martha," she asked.

"Yes" replied Martha. "We have a funeral tomorrow for a girl named Kathleen Callahan"

"May I go with you to the funeral?" asked Esther.

"Certainly you may," said Martha. "We'll walk to church at 9:30 AM for the mass is to begin at 10:00 AM.

It seemed that Esther's husband Andy, didn't mind her going to a funeral but she never knew just why. So the next day at 9:30

AM, off went the two women to church. Martha knew that Esther went more for the singing than the mourning the passing of an Irish girl. She went to hear George Scanlan sing a few Irish songs. The Notre Dame choir director, Sister Agnes, had chosen George Scanlon for his singing not only because he could sing like John McCornick, but because he looked like Ramon Navarro.

The funeral went as usual. The eulogy given by Father Patton was what he always gave right out of the Book of Ecclesiastes.

> For everything there is a season and
> A time for every matter under heaven.
> A time to be born, and a time to die.
> A time to plant, and a time to sow.
> A time to weep, and a time to laugh.
> A time to mourn, and a time to dance.
> A time to tear, and a time to sew.
> A time to keep silence, and a time to speak.

When Father Patton finished this reading he turned to George Scanlon. "As a last request from Kathleen Callahan, we find she wanted to hear the best known song ever written in Ireland. It is called 'A Little Bit of Heaven.' Our favorite singer, George Scanlon, will now sing it for us." So smiling George stepped up to the lectern and sang.

> **Have you ever heard the story how**
> **Ireland got its name?**
> I'll tell you, so you'll understand from
> whense old Ireland came.
> No wonder that we're proud of that
> dear land across the sea,
> For here's the way me dear old mother
> told the tale to me.
> Sure, a little bit of Heaven fell from
> out the sky one day.
> And it nestled on the ocean in a spot so
> Far away;
> And when the Angels found it,

Shure it looked so sweet and fair,
They said, "Suppose we leave it,
For it looks so peaceful there."
So they sprinkled it with stardust just
to make the shamrocks grow;
'Tis the only place you'll find them no
matter where you go;
Then they dotted it with silver
To make its lakes so grand,
And when they had it finished, shure
they called it Ireland.
'Tis a dear old land of fairies and of
wond'rous wishing wells'
And nowhere else on God's green earth
have they such lakes and dells!
No wonder that the Angels loved its
shamrock-bordered shore,
'Tis a little bit of Heaven and I love
it more and more

All through the singing of "A Little Bit of Heaven," Martha could hear Mrs. Johnson weeping and sniffling. It appeared she was enjoying the ceremony, although she had never heard of Kathleen Callahan before. Rather odd, thought Martha, Mrs. Johnson felt so dearly for old Ireland, never having been near it in her lifetime. But the song "A Little Bit of Heaven" was just the beginning of Esther's weeping. The servers prepared the incense that the priest used near the casket, and the mass was over, but not the singing. George Scanlon next sang "I'll Take You Home Again, Kathleen."

I'll take you home again, Kathleen,
Across the ocean wild and wide,
To where your heart has ever been,
Since first you were my bonnie bride.
The roses all have left your cheek,
I've watched them fade away and die;
Your voice is sad whene'er you speak,

And tears be'dim your loving eyes.
Oh! I will take you back again,
To where your heart will feel no pain,
And when the fields are fresh and green.
I'll take you to your home again, Kathleen.

The pallbearers moved the casket slowly out of the church, as George sang this song. Esther wept profusely as did everybody else in the church.

Harry, Joe Kane, George Scanlon, Clarence Zooks, Michael Redford, Joe Miller and Gladys Miller loved to play hockey during the winter. The only problem was waiting for the ice to form on the lake. They agreed to meet after Kathleen Callahan's funeral, on the southern shore of Como Lake. All had decided that the time had come to clear the snow off the lake and begin to play hockey. Harry, Joe Kane and Clarence carried their skates to the edge of the lake near a large sewer (in the summer, the sewer brought water to the lake). Each took off his or her shoes and put on his or her skates, leaving their shoes by the sewer entrance.

Joe and Gladys brought the shovels to clear the snow off the lake (about to be ice rink). In twenty minutes the rink was cleared and ready for the first practice game of the year. Michael Redford's snow shoes were the goal post on one end. Joe Miller's shoes were the goal post on the other end. The only protection from a flying puck was the shin pads put on by all the participants. Shin guards were copies of the Saturday Evening Post Magazine, fastened to the shin with rubber bands taken from used tires.

Harry's skates were too large making it impossible for him to hold the blades steady. In fact, when skating, Harry's ankles were mostly what he skated on. The two best skaters were Joe Kane and George Scanlon. That was mainly because their parents had the money to buy them skates that fit. The puck was an empty aluminum can of carnation milk. There was no such thing as a referee to toss in the puck to start the game. It was always the party who brought the milk can who got the puck first.

Today's 'puck' was brought by Joe Kane, who played with Clarence and Redford. Harry's skated with George Scanlon, Joe Miller, Gladys Miller and whatever other Como kids showed up. Like football, Clarence skated only because his father said he should to be a man. The game went as usual, with Joe Kane scoring two goals and George scoring three, but then something happened that changed the game around. In came a kid from the western edge of Como. He skated onto the 'hockey rink', took the puck away from Clarence, and proceeded to skate around everybody including the two stars, George and Joe. This newcomer controlled the carnation can like it belonged to him. In fact, he had such control that he didn't let anybody else play. They soon found out his name was Galligan, and he had a brother named John.

Just as this stranger took over the ice, two policemen came up to the edge of the rink with a few pairs of shoes in their hands. "Any of you gentlemen missing these shoes?" asked the First cop, with a sinister look in his eyes.

Harry came up to the cop, looked at the shoes and said "I believe you have my pair of shoes in your hands, officer."

"What about the other two pairs, anyone see their shoes in my hand?" asked the cop. Joe Kane and Clarence step forward and reluctantly identified their shoes.

"Well" continued the officer, "I'll tell you where you can get them back."

"Please do," said the threesome.

"Just come with us over to the station and we will discuss it further. The rest of you consider yourselves lucky. Go on home and wait till the ice cover is deeper." The three boys followed the two officers to their squad car, and unsmiling got into the back seat. It was just a short ride to the station, located near the bridge that went over Lexington next to the streetcar stop (the Como Harriet Line Car). Each boy was given a phone call home. After the phone calls, the two officers gave the boys their shoes back and told them, "we'll give you a ride home and the explanation of why you were skating on the thin ice is up to you."

All three joined in saying "thank you" for the offer of the ride home.

Harry's explanation to Martha was "the sign that says thin ice was blown away, so we missed it. The officers knew that, so that's why they gave us a ride home and didn't put us in jail."

Fortunately for Harry, Martha was in a good mood when the cops brought him home. She had just received a letter from a woman in St. Andrew's parish who had a daughter in the Good Council Academy in Mankato. This woman wrote to Martha the following:

"I know what you'll be going through this Christmas with your daughter not home. My daughter, Mary Kay, is in Mankato in her fourth year as an aspirant to be a nun. When she left (and before) I dug out all the information I could find on the Notre Dame nuns. It was a most interesting discovery. The Notre Dame nuns are strictly a teaching order. Here is what they say:

> *As sisters we carry on the values and spirit of our pioneer heritage. We are committed to education that helps a person develop their gifts toward creating a better world. We have sunk our abundant deep roots into Minnesota soil and have poured Forth our energy in the form of education, Helping others to reach their full potential.*

"I thought," the letter continued, "this inspiring and exciting for any girl to have as an object in life. Not only do the nuns teach in the schools but they do cleaning, decorating and painting. They teach the altar boy servers their duties, and take care of the church and the sanctuary. They provide leadership for many activities like 40 Hours, First Communion, and, in some cases, even coach the baseball teams."

So ended the letter to Martha.

After this letter from the woman of St. Andrew's church, Martha's spirits improved. She had some misgivings sending Sheila to Mankato and the nunnery, so it was nice to read the positive charter for the Notre Dame order. With her psyche thus improved, she began preparations for the Christmas festivities, what little festivities that the McCools planned.

The first Christmas preparation for Martha was baking cookies. As she rolled the dough, her thoughts went to her daughter who would soon learn to teach what all the Notre Dame nuns taught, namely reading, writing, arithmetic and religion. Her daughter would be located in a school in Mankato that started in 1858. While Sheila didn't realize it at the time, she would be near the area where her father, Edward, was brought up. His family lived on Front Street in downtown Mankato. Over the years, Sheila would find herself attending the high school on Good Council grounds with one of her cousins.

Included in the letter from the fellow parishioner was the constitution of the school of the Sisters of Notre Dame, "Education means enabling persons to reach the fullness of their potential as individuals created in God's image, and assisting them to direct their gifts towards building the earth." The Notre Dame nuns were not alone in Minnesota. There were The Sisters of St. Joseph and St. Benedict in Crookston, Sisters of St. Benedicts in Duluth, Franciscan Sisters in Little Falls, Sister of St. Benedicts in St. Joseph, Sister of St. Joseph in St. Paul, and Sisters of St. Francis in Rochester. Martha put aside all this information and began to think of Christmas.

Most homes at Christmas meant the big three of shopping, decorating and cooking. The big three for Martha and her family, on the other hand, were with them all year long, namely food, clothing and shelter. Gifts at Christmas were a luxury. The only member of the family to get outside gifts was Harry, and those were from a few good customers who gave him a dollar on Christmas Eve for bringing them the paper on time for 365 days of the year. Out of 179 customers, Harry accumulated a grand total of $18.00 the Christmas of 1927. This he spent on a Christmas tree, decorations and candles to put on the tree, all being indeed a luxury.

A ton of coal arrived a week before Christmas, as usual. It was poured down a cellar window into what was called the coal bin. The coal bin was located in the real dark corner of the basement near the furnace. The coal served for another use besides heat, it was also used to fill a gallon pail used to hold Christmas tree in place.

Martha was only 16 years old when she came to America. But she kept memories of Christmas in Denmark in her head. One of her Danish memories was that the man of the house would get a necktie and a box of cigars. Her mother, Lena (short for Sorline), always received a few aprons for work in the kitchen. The big event as Martha remembered was Christmas Eve. Work everywhere in Denmark ceased at noon, and at 5:00 PM church bells started to ring out. After church she remembered the whole family went home for the Christmas Eve dinner. Once (and only once) a year they had a goose along with rice porridge, red cabbage and small potatoes. The desert was Danish pudding. She couldn't remember what gifts she had received for Christmas (so she knew they weren't much).

From Nick Torek the butcher, Martha decided to get a chicken and forgot about the nostalgic idea of a goose. Martha felt that the most she could do to duplicate her youthful days of Christmas in Denmark was to have Danish pudding for desert. While thinking about the meal for Christmas day, Martha (a convert to Catholicism) thought of confession and Communion and the mass of Christmas. As a Lutheran she had trouble going to confession, although she found it relieved her of many problems. Going to confession and stating the problems to the priest somehow relieved her of the anxiety affiliated with the problem. She couldn't explain it, just knew that it worked.

Armed with positive personal thoughts about the benefit of confession, she hounded her children to go to confession before Christmas. All agreed to go except Harry. He saw no need to tell anybody what he thought he had done wrong. Besides, hadn't God already let him down with the death of his father less than one-year prior? "I'm not going to Father Patton for confession. He'll recognize my voice."

"Don't worry about that, Harry. He'll never tell what you tell him."

"How do I know that he'll keep it a secret?"

"He's taken vows never to divulge what he hears in the confessional. That's why you can tell him anything you think is a sin," said Martha.

"As a convert, how did you ever get around to going to confession?" asked Harry.

"Here's my secret, Harry. The first time I went to confession, I had just become a Catholic, and still spoke mainly Danish. So I went to the confessional and told all my sins in Danish."

"What did the priest say to that?" asked an astounded Harry.

"He blessed me and said go now and sin no more of those Danish sins you've been committing."

"But I can't speak Danish?" replied Harry.

"Tell him the same things you have been telling him since you first confession," answered Martha.

"Okay, mom, I'll go to confession, but I still don't trust Father Patton."

"Harry, do you ever think about the people on your paper route?"

"Yes, sometimes. As you know, mother, I see the poor ones, that's most of my customers, and the rich ones, of whom there are very few."

Martha asked, "and who are the poor?"

"I talk of being poor as not having a new car and a nanny for their kids. The best poor man I know is Mr. Zooks. He (after a quarrel with his wife) pays me right on time every month. But if you don't need to work anymore you're wealthy. Each Sunday the whole Zooks family goes to church together and all go to communion. Mr. Zooks is a streetcar motorman, and doesn't expect to get as rich as Mr. Gould, the big seed man on Como Avenue. Mr. Gould I catch reading the New York Times, which he gets every day through the mail. He concentrates intensely on the paper with a deep furor on his forehead and appears to be reading the stock market sheet. Wealth to Gould is that he doesn't have to work anymore."

"If you get so wealthy you don't have to work anymore?" asked Martha

"Yes" answered Harry. "Mr. Gould told me one day that his next move was to buy a new car. He called it the latest model, and you won't believe it, but it can go 70 miles an hour and it has a rumble seat. He told me he is busy reading the stock market results for the day. He wants me to sell the New York Times but I have enough to do with the St. Paul paper morning and night."

Harry changed the subject. "I was given a copy of the New York Times by Mr. Gould. He said to me, 'Harry take this paper and read the Christmas message from the President of the United States, Mr. Calvin Coolidge.' I did read the message and it came in handy for school. My teacher, Sister Bernard, asked us pupils to work up a message for Christmas and for the New Year."

"What was your message for Christmas, Harry?" Asked Martha.

"I took our President's message:

December 1927
To the American People:
Christmas is not a time or a season,
but a state of mind. To cherish
peace and goodwill, to be plenteous
in mercy is to have the real spirit
of Christmas. If we think on
these things, there will be born to
us a savior and over us will shine a
star sending its gleam of
hope to the world.
Signed Calvin Coolidge"

"That's a wonderful message from the President of the United States for Christmas. I didn't see it in our paper," said Martha. "What was your message for the New Year?"

"Everyday at school we say the Pledge of Allegiance after our opening pray. My Boy Scout Manuel has an interpretation for the Pledge, which I quote:

I pledge allegiance	- - -	I promise to be true
to the Flag	- - -	to the symbol of our country
of the United States of America	- - -	a country made up of 48 states and several territories each with certain rights of it own

and to the Republic	- - -	a country where the people elect representatives from among themselves to make law for them
For which it stands	- - -	the flag represents the country
One Nation under God	- - -	a country whose people are free to believe in God
indivisible,	- - -	the country cannot be split into parts
with liberty and justice	- - -	with freedom and fairness
for all.	- - -	for every person in the country."

"Very nice, Harry" said Martha.

Sister Bernard congratulated Harry for his two choices for Christmas and the New Year. "I don't need bother anyone else," said Sister to the rest of the class. Joe Kane raised his hand just then. "Yes Joseph, you have something to add?"

"I have one suggestion for the New Year, Sister, if I may say it."

"You heard it is a free country, so go ahead Joe"

"I am combining Christmas and the New Year with my idea," smiled Joe.

"Let me hear it," replied Sister.

"I intend to give my friend Robert Galinski a box of Kleenex for Christmas and I suggest he use it all year to stop his constant sniffling." The idea was not well received by Galinski, but the girls all giggled happily approving the idea.

Sister rolled her eyes in consternation over what to do with Joe Kane, but simply dismissed the class for the year and sent them all home relieved for the holiday break.

Christmas to most families means a get together with uncles, aunts, cousins, grandparents, brothers and sisters with an occasional trip to see close friends. Whereas Harry had more cousins that he could count, relatives on his mother's side were far away in Utah (not to mention his California cousins), and relatives on his father's side were mostly in Mankato. The only relatives near to Harry were Uncle John and Aunt Sarah McCool who lived with their two daughters, Eleanor and Elaine, on Sherborne Avenue near Lexington ballpark. The mother, Sarah, was known mostly in the family circle as the best cook on the face of the earth for her angel food cake. The two daughters, according to their mother, were not only the smartest but also the prettiest girls on Sherborne Avenue, if not all of St. Paul.

For Christmas day, Martha invited Uncle John, Aunt Sarah, and their girls to an afternoon feast. Aunt Sarah always brought a wonderful bean casserole as well as her angel food cake. Prior to the meal, the children decorated the Christmas tree that Harry bought. Given Harry's past experience with fire, he played a rather passive role in the construction of the tree. He had to admit, though, that when it was finished, it presented a glorious and inspiring sight. For the remainder of his life, Christmas always reminded him of his two cousins, Eleanor and Elaine, confidently lighting the candles on the McCool Christmas tree.

On New Year's Eve Harry, Joe Kane and Clarence Zarcardi were given permission to go to a movie downtown St. Paul. They picked the movie, Gorilla. During the showing of the movie, Clarence lost Harry and Joe at the height of excitement in the movie, when the gorilla was taking a girl into the jungle. Harry and Joe heard a scream from Clarence who was scared the way you should be at such a movie. On the way home on the Como Harriet streetcar, Clarence begged Harry to walk him to his door, which Harry did. That ended the last episode of the year for three members of the Como Gang.

After arriving home from the movie, Harry waited up for the coming of the New Year. He took the time to reflect back on all that had happened. His father died, his sister Sheila went to the nunnery. His brother Paul got a job delivering telegrams for Western Union. But most important of all, the remaining members of his family were still together at 1023 Barrett Street. These thoughts put a smile on Harry's face just as a loud "KA – BOOM" exploded from his neighbor Andy Johnson's shotgun.

1927 had finally ended. The thoughts of what 1928 and the future would bring to the McCools put Harry to sleep.

EPILOGUE

Starting in 1928, Harry spent three years at the public high school, Washington High, in St. Paul. He then entered St. Thomas College on the west side of the city where he majored in History. Harry continued to carry newspapers until the day he graduated from college. On graduation day from St. Thomas College, Harry quit his paper route, much to the chagrin of his mother, who wanted him to keep the income from the route. Harry's love of talking induced him to get into plays in college, where he was considered some kind of matinee idol by the girls from St. Catherine's College.

Harry's mother, Martha, became the secretary of the AOH a few years later, and if Harry didn't know better, he might have thought she was born in Ireland instead of Denmark. Harry's older brothers were drafted at the start of World War II, while he remained home to support his mother and younger sister on a financial deferment. All three of the boys married in the 1940s, as did his oldest sister, Alice. His youngest sister Helen did go to St. Andrews grade school for eight years at the cost of $1 per year as promised by Father Patton. After college, she 'went west' where she met and married an Italian, and settled in Montana. Sister Sheila is a nun till this day.

The McCools survived not only the loss of their father, James Edward, in 1927, but managed to live through the stock market crash of 1929, and the depression that gripped the nation through much of the 1930s. Many years after 1927, Harry met and dated the older Hammer sister who dumped water on him and Eileen as they watched Lucky Lindy go by in parade. That relationship, however, is another story!

The Seed Man, Gould, did not fair so well in the late 1920s. True, he was declared a Millionaire by the New York Times in early 1928, but his stocks went into the dumpster in 1929, and he ended up having to go to work for the Pioneer Press in the meteorology department.

George Scanlon, the 'Brave' One, became an insurance salesman, Clarence Zacardi, the 'Cheerful' football player, became an artist, Joe Kane, the 'Obedient' prankster, became a lawyer.

Harry had a series of careers that spanned teaching, the FBI, selling novelties, and selling sunglasses before finding his true calling as an author. Harry never did become a priest.

ACKNOWLEDGEMENTS

The authors would like to thank the Minnesota Historical Society for all their help in researching Minnesota in 1927. Special thanks also go to the Andrea McCall and Suzanne McCall for all their positive contributions to the development of this script, and to Brian McCall and Betsy Peters for their painstaking working typing the manuscript.

Also Minnesota Transportation Museum, Inc., Scott County Library Systems, Boy Scout Handbook, Mary Sweeney for art and photographs, Pioneer Press, State Fair Museum director, and Vince Nonnemacher Sr. for his editing help!

ABOUT THE AUTHOR

Leo T. McCall graduated from the University of St. Thomas in St. Paul, MN. Currently he is employed as an advertising salesman for the Perlich Co. in St. Paul and District Manager of the Universal Photonics Company out of Hicksville, New York.

With a B.A. in English he started his career as an English teacher in a local St. Paul High School. Most of his career has been spent in business as a credit manager, sales manager, and advertising specialist. His career is as varied as the speech he gave while acting Jacques in "As You Like It" by Shakespeare, to whit "All the world's a stage . . . each man plays many parts."

Books: "Business is Baloney"
       "Murder in the Arboretum"

Michael J. McCall grew up in St. Paul, Minnesota. He attended St. Thomas Academy and the University of Minnesota where he graduated with a degree in Aeronautical Engineering. The lure of sunshine and aerospace then took him to Southern California where he began working at TRW designing and writing computer software. He currently works for Raytheon Systems and lives with his wife Suzanne in Torrance, California. They have two adult daughters.

  Michael's interests run from beach volleyball to golf to yoga, with an occasional foray into the literary arena. He enjoys writing about his travels, and "fine tuning" his father's lively prose. With retirement on the horizon, he plans on more golf, travel, reading and some writing to occupy his time.

NORMANDALE COMMUNITY COLLEGE
LIBRARY
9700 FRANCE AVENUE SOUTH
BLOOMINGTON, MN 55431-4399